MIDNI...

AT

MAIDENSTONE

HALL

MIDNIGHT
AT
MAIDENSTONE
HALL

ALISON CLARE

For Quinn and Mina

Praise for Midnight at Maidenstone Hall

"Alison Clare has written a brilliant novel of suspense and disorientation in which identities are obscured and nothing is as it seems. I couldn't put it down."—Elizabeth McKenzie, author of *The Dog of the North*

Chapter One

Marsden insisted on being greeted by his Christian name. His new Christian name. Even after days of practice, speaking this name repeatedly, the sound of his acquired alias stuck thick and heavy on his dry tongue. After going by one name for twenty-six years, it startled him still the strangeness of so suddenly becoming someone else, of so abruptly becoming Marsden Fisher. He had thought it would be easy, sloughing off his old life and embracing a brand new identity. Still, as he stood on the platform of Everingham station, introducing himself to a stranger, Marsden had to remind himself actively of whom he had become. He stuttered this new name when Lord Scarborough's chauffeur, Badeley, met him. The chauffeur greeted him only with a limp handshake before taking possession of Marsden's two heavy cases. Marsden kept a third piece of luggage, his violin case, clutched beneath his arm when he followed Badeley to Lord Scarborough's aging Rolls-Royce.

The rain fell in a steady drizzle as Badeley sped through country lanes with the confidence of a Yorkshire local, born and raised, fearing nothing for the safety of his passenger. Marsden huddled against the worn leather upholstery, bracing himself with shaking hands as the car shuddered and jerked, and he prayed that he hadn't survived four years of war only to die in a flaming automobile wreck. The spring of 1919 was the most miserable he could remember, the rain-soaked hills of Yorkshire muddy, the roads slick and dangerous. With dark skies embracing every corner of the horizon, summer showed no sign of approach in the north of England.

Marsden watched Badeley closely with tired eyes, exhausted from his

1

journey but not so weary he failed to notice the chauffeur's handsome confidence. The two men were close in age. Marsden was taller than Badeley and much darker. Badeley's blonde hair was short and stylish compared to Marsden's slightly wild chestnut mop. Marsden wondered if Badeley had left England during the war and decided he had not. He was too polished. Too unblemished. Too whole. Marsden imagined what it would be like to lean forward and reach through the window between the cab and the rear passenger seat, allowing himself the forbidden pleasure of running a thumb along the line of smooth skin between Badeley's collar and neat, shining hair. His shoulders rolled forward as he lifted one tentative hand, his arm almost lurching, tugged by an invisible thread, but stopped himself when the sleeve of his jacket receded to reveal the glint of a cufflink. Seeing his father's initials etched into the flat square of gold filled him with hot shame at the idea of touching Badeley. He snatched his arm back, tucking both hands into his coat pockets, and averted his gaze from the chauffeur's soft skin. Marsden already knew he and Badeley were not likely to become close friends. Mrs. Bradshaw, the proprietor of the employment agency that had placed Marsden with the Falconer family, had warned him that tutors were always set apart from the other household staff at Maidenstone Hall: eating separately, sleeping separately. But then, the previous tutors had been women, so perhaps things would be different for him. Marsden Fisher was something entirely new to the household.

Maidenstone Hall appeared suddenly through the wet haze, becoming visible as the car pulled onto the gravel road leading directly up to the estate. Marsden leaned forward in his seat, unexpectedly caught in awe at the vast home of the Falconers, or Lord and Lady Scarborough, as their official status dictated. The Hall was even larger than he had anticipated, the three towering levels climbing upward in cream limestone blocks. The windows were tall and numerous, an extravagant display of glass he was unused to seeing. The front door, dark green and standing well above the height of an average man, exuded a sense of mystery that made Marsden eager to see behind it.

The beauty of the Hall at once contrasted wildly with the shocking appearance of the east wing of the building. As the Rolls Royce swung toward the top of the drive, Marsden could finally see that the two upper stories of the Hall on this side had been almost completely gutted, the limestone blackened by smoke. The windows were primarily covered by canvas sheets and hastily erected wood planks to keep out the elements. Marsden pressed his face against the car window, mesmerized by the horrific sight. His dream of Maidenstone Hall, as magnificently opulent and a reflection of its wealthy owner, was rudely shaken.

Badeley parked the car, not directly in front of the Hall but by the servants' entrance at the rear of the west wing. Marsden climbed out of the car and ran through the rain to assist the chauffeur in removing his bags from the rear storage compartment. Badeley held the door to the servants' entrance hall open, and Marsden brushed past him in a wet flurry. A slender woman with ashen hair poked her head around a corner of the hallway, a thick wooden spoon in one hand, the folds of her aging face pinched together.

"You're dripping all over the floor, Badeley!" she said, waving the spoon. "Who do you think will have to clean that up?"

Badeley dropped Marsden's bags by the door with a careless thump. "Marsden, this is Mrs. Huston, our cook and general busybody. Mrs. H, this is Marsden Fisher. He's the new tutor."

Mrs. Huston lowered the spoon, her anger dissipating in the wake of intense curiosity. She swept a long section of loose grey hair away from her face, wide eyes surveying Marsden from head to toe. "They must be scraping the bottom of the barrel, then."

Marsden tried not to take offense. Hanging his coat by Badeley's on a rack beside the door, he ran a hand through the dense, wet mat of his hair. "What makes you think I'm the bottom of the barrel?"

The old woman shrugged. "You're the first man they've sent, you know. Lady Alice has never had a male tutor."

"I do know," he assured her. "The woman at the agency made it perfectly clear to me." Indeed Mrs. Bradshaw had been entirely bewildered when Marsden had entered her office, the advisement for the position at Maidenstone Hall in *The Sunday Express* clutched in his hand. She had

3

been reluctant to accept his application, but Marsden had insisted he be considered for the post. Short of any other applicants, Mrs. Bradshaw had quickly relented.

"She warned you then?" Mrs. Huston asked.

Marsden was taken aback. "Warned me? What about?"

Badeley and Mrs. Huston shared a narrow, knowing look when he sauntered past her, making his way into the warmth of her kitchen. Marsden followed without summons, drawn toward the smell of soup bubbling on the stove. Mrs. Huston's kitchen was sizable, designed quite clearly for feeding a large family and a barrage of guests.

Badeley sat down at the kitchen table, dropping onto a stool with an inelegant huff. "How long did Mary last, Mrs. H?"

"Nine days," said Mrs. Huston as she returned to her soup. "Poor love."

"And Charlotte?"

"A whole month, bless her. She did try."

"A whole month?" Badeley sighed. "It seemed much less than that. I fancied her, lovely Charlotte."

"We all knew that. Unfortunately, lovely Charlotte didn't fancy you all that much."

Badeley pouted. "What about little Laura Templeton? She fancied me!"

"Aye," Mrs. Huston agreed with a roll of her eyes, "and despite her aching heart, she bore the challenge of her charge for a grand total of seventeen days. I was sure she'd be the last they'd hire."

"So you see, Mr. Fisher—Marsden," Badeley held up a hand in apology when Marsden opened his mouth to object to the formality of his surname. "You are the latest of a long string of tutors hired to oversee the daily tedium that is the life of poor Lady Alice."

"Twelve in two years, I believe," said Marsden. "The situation has been explained to me."

Badeley smiled at Marsden with tight lips. "I seriously doubt that, my friend. But then you'll find out soon enough for yourself."

"Is she really that bad?" Marsden was beginning to imagine a monster child—a tenacious young lady on the cusp of womanhood, as uncontrollable as a wild animal.

Mrs. Huston answered with a genuine tone of affection: "Lady Alice? Oh no, she's an angel, if ever you did meet one. Sweet, well-natured—shy, to be sure, but such a clever young lady. I'm sure you'll like her very much indeed. All of the tutors have."

"So, Alice is not the problem?"

Mrs. Huston turned to the stove, presenting her back to him. "No, pet," she said over one bony shoulder. "She's not the one who's the problem."

Marsden opened his mouth again to question Mrs. Huston further when a shrill voice behind him made him jump.

"He's here, then? Why did nobody say?"

A petite woman of no more than thirty, dressed entirely in dour black, cut a striking figure in the doorway. Her pale hair, so blonde it was almost white, had been scraped back into a tight bun, and her neat, tiny hands hooked firmly upon her hips. Despite her diminutive size, Marsden was immediately intimated by her scowl. He caught the displeased twitch of her lips as she surveyed himself and Badeley seated at the table.

Badeley was quick to admonish her with a lazy smirk. "Hush yourself, Nancy. He just arrived a moment ago. Let the poor sod warm himself before he's dragged away to be examined."

"Her Ladyship was expecting him before luncheon. She'll be wanting to see him immediately."

"This is Nancy," said Badeley for Marsden's benefit. "She's lady's maid to the countess."

"Well?" she demanded. "Is he ready?"

Marsden remembered his luggage by the door and hesitated. "Perhaps I should put my things away first. My bags—"

"Badeley will take care of them," Nancy said, sneering in Badeley's direction.

Marsden did not like this suggestion. The idea of leaving his luggage alone with strangers made him nervous, but he knew that insisting on keeping his bags with him would arouse suspicion, and he shook his head to dispel the idea of Badeley and Mrs. Huston rifling through his bags while he was out of the room.

He took one last gulp of hot soup and stood to face Nancy. "I'd better not keep her Ladyship waiting."

Chapter Two

Marsden followed Nancy at a reserved distance. He loomed over her by over a foot at least, and yet, despite her petite stature, she moved at a pace so rapid he often skipped and ran to keep up with her. She guided him up the stairs from the basement service hall, leaving him to trail behind. As they crossed the large salon, he stared up in wonder at the towering ceilings and wide marble staircase, their size and luxury startling. A series of tall gilded mirrors framed the dark blue walls of the salon, their reflections creating the illusion of an even grander room. Marsden caught sight of his own image, flicking past him repeatedly, and grimaced at his unkempt appearance, shoving both hands quickly through his hair to tame the damp locks.

They passed through the imposing mahogany doors of the library, where the lofting ceiling met colossal bookcases lined with hundreds of leather-bound tomes. A grand piano stood in one corner of the room, its lacquered chestnut wood glittering in the light emanating from the fireplace. The ornate Oriental rugs matched the deep red of the velvet curtains draped across the expansive windows, drawn tight together despite the daylight hour. The room was gloomy in the dim light of the fire, and just a handful of dull electric lamps, and the smoke of the fire hung as a faint haze not drawn entirely up the flue. The gentle hum of a gramophone playing softly in the corner of the room, almost too quietly to hear the music clearly, vibrated in the thick closeness of the air.

Nancy stopped Marsden directly before an oversized maroon armchair where the lady of the house sat waiting. For reasons he could not quite explain himself, he had been expecting a dowdy countess, dusty after years of pacing the halls of an isolated country estate. Lady Scarborough, however, was still young, perhaps forty-five years of age. Her amber hair was swept back into an elaborate arrangement of soft curls, exposing the long line of her pale neck. The vibrant blue of her silk dress shone in stark contrast to the dark red furniture and draping of the old-fashioned library. The delicate bodice, embroidered with intricate gold flowers, featured two elegant panels of fabric crossed over the countess's chest. Although the thread still sparkled in the light of the fire, the pattern was visibly worn with age, and several fine strands had broken loose from the weave. Marsden was no expert in women's fashion, but he suspected the dress had been fashionable many seasons ago. Despite the aging wear of Lady Scarborough's outfit, Marsden suddenly felt all the more shabby, keenly aware of the threadbare sleeves of his damp jacket and badly scuffed shoes. But for his gold cufflinks, his sole possession of any actual worth, Marsden felt like a street urchin in front of this glamorous woman. He caught himself fiddling with the cufflinks as she stared at him and forced his hands by his sides in a sort of clumsy military stance.

Lady Scarborough did not stand to meet him but greeted him with a gracious nod and extended a delicate hand for Marsden to take in his own. He wasn't sure if he was supposed to shake or kiss her thin white hand, and so did neither, simply gripping her fingers for just a moment before letting go.

"Mr. Fisher," she said. "I'm so pleased you've come. Won't you take a seat?"

"Please, call me Marsden," he said, and this time, the name rolled comfortably off his tongue.

Lady Scarborough smiled, albeit wanly, her eyelashes fluttering. "I'm glad. We referred to all the other tutors by their Christian names, and I must admit it is my preference. Nancy, you may go."

Marsden had not realized that Nancy was still hovering, standing in the doorway. Upon being dismissed, she dipped her head and closed the library's double doors when she departed.

"She's an odd duck, isn't she?" said Lady Scarborough. "But she is a good worker and doesn't gossip, which is the virtue I require most from the servants in this household, Marsden. It's a small staff: Nancy, Mrs. Huston, our cook, and Badeley, whom you've met. We have a part-time housemaid, and Lord Scarborough's valet, Linton, also acts as Butler."

Knowing nothing of country estates, Marsden wasn't sure if this was a small staff but nodded as though he was sure of himself.

"My daughter, Alice," she continued, "will be your only concern while you are in this house."

"I understand, my lady."

Lady Scarborough's glassy eyes narrowed, her white face an impassable mask. What she honestly thought of him, Marsden could only guess.

"Can I offer you a drink, Marsden? Whiskey, perhaps? Or brandy?"

Marsden wondered if she was testing his sobriety, but cold to the bone as he was after the journey to Maidenstone, he quickly decided he did not care. "Brandy, please, my lady."

Lady Scarborough stood, exposing the full brilliance of her silk dress, lavishly embroidered, cutting straight down over her hips and hanging just above her ankles. Marsden pictured her in a London nightclub. She would fit right in. He noticed her slow gait as if she was taking special care to place one foot directly in front of the other. The velvet of her matching blue shoes scuffed together as her heels aligned from step to step. Her fingertips danced over a large arrangement of glass bottles on a nearby trolley before finally selecting one and pouring a generous quantity of brandy into two tumblers. Marsden nodded his thanks when she passed him a glass.

"I'm so glad you could take the position at such short notice," she said.

"Mrs. Bradshaw did mention that it was somewhat of an emergency," said Marsden.

Lady Scarborough's lashes dramatically fluttered as she returned to her seat. "Mrs. Bradshaw. What a bore that woman is. She honestly refused to send us any further candidates after the incident with poor Laura."

"Laura was the previous tutor, I understand?"

She stared into her glass, bringing the rim closer to her face, searching inside for something invisible. "Hmmm. She had a little accident. Nothing serious to mention, really, but I'm afraid I couldn't convince her to stay. Mrs. Bradshaw became distinctly less helpful after Laura ran away. Mind you, she managed to rustle up enough courage to continue the search when I suggested I take my business elsewhere. And here you are."

"I can assure you," said Marsden, "that I cannot be easily frightened away."

The countess smirked, reclining against the thick arm of the chair. "My dear boy, I can tell just by looking at you that you're not the kind of young man who can be scared off. The beard is not just laziness on your part, I can see. Particularly nasty scar, is it?"

Marsden leaned back into his chair. His fingers itched to cover the scar across his cheek, the line of it trailing from the top of his chin almost to the corner of his left eye. Some days, it still felt raw beneath the shelter of his beard, as if the piercing slice of a dirty bayonet lingered on his skin.

"Others had it worse, my lady. At least I made it out of the war alive."

Lady Scarborough raised the glass again to her lips, tipping its contents into her mouth in a rush. She swallowed heavily. "Our son, Simon, also served. He's gone now."

Marsden bit at his cheek. He purposely schooled his features at the utterance of Simon's name, desperate to hide any twitch, any sign of recognition. The resulting tightness in his chest forced him to hold his breath. He had not been expecting to participate in any discussion about Simon Falconer so soon after entering the house, and the last thing he wanted was to raise suspicion in his new employer. Although the name was more familiar to him than his new moniker, Marsden did not want anyone at Maidenstone Hall to know it. But Lady Scarborough failed to notice the hitch in his breath. Her mouth fell open as if to speak, but she muttered only to herself, excluding Marsden from her thoughts.

"I'm very sorry for your loss, my lady," he said.

"Yes," she said, jaw tight. "Quite."

"Were you able to bring him home?"

Lady Scarborough's only response was a sharp, cursory shake of her head. They sat silently for some time, the countess staring into nothingness over the rim of her empty glass. Marsden hoped that if he waited long enough, she would say something more about Simon, but the countess pressed her lips together, her nostrils flaring with every sharp intake of breath. Her bejeweled fingers clenched around the crystal tumbler, and her eyes were unnaturally wide when she returned her gaze to Marsden.

"The thing is, Marsden, that Alice is not well. She is almost twenty but certainly cannot be introduced into society, and she will most likely never marry."

Surprised by the segue in conversation, Marsden tried not to gape at Lady Scarborough. "I'm—well, I'm sorry to hear that. What exactly is her condition?"

"Oh, you needn't worry about that. She's not contagious. But she is certainly very fragile and has suffered particularly of late." Her eyes darted toward the closed doors, and she lowered her voice to say, "She is so much happier—calmer—when she has something to occupy her mind. With your arrival, I hope we shall all return to some sort of normalcy."

Lady Scarborough stood again, returning in a slightly meandering path to the liquor trolley, where she refilled her glass. She turned with the decanter still in hand. "Top up, Marsden?"

Marsden held up his glass. "I have plenty, thank you."

"Suit yourself. Alice loves to read. Novels, that is, and too much if you ask me. She has never truly applied herself to her history studies or French. Mrs. Bradshaw claimed that you speak both French and Spanish."

"Yes, my lady, I do."

"Very accomplished. Did you learn at school?"

Marsden nodded, although it was barely the truth. He had spent hours of his childhood studying French, Spanish, Italian, and Russian at his father's insistence long after the school day had ended. The old man had himself spoken to Marsden in German, a fact he could hardly divulge in the current post-war climate. Again, the thought of his father made his fingers twitch, and he noticed himself reaching reflexively for a gold cufflink.

Lady Scarborough did not notice Marsden's malaise. "And you play the violin, also?"

"Tolerably well, yes."

"Excellent. The doctor suggested Alice should keep her hands busy." She smiled in a brilliant display of perfectly straight teeth. "Very well, I should let you settle in. I'm sure you must be tired after your long journey." She pulled on the heavy rope that would ring a bell downstairs in the service hall.

Marsden was disappointed to be dismissed. He was overflowing with questions and wondered if Lady Scarborough had consumed enough brandy to loosen her tongue further should he stay with her and pry further.

"I was hoping to see more of the house, my lady," he said. "Get my bearings."

"Of course. That is an excellent idea."

"And will I be expected to start work with Lady Alice this afternoon?"

Lady Scarborough raised one slender eyebrow. "Yes, indeed. It is certainly far better that you meet her today."

Before Marsden could ask her what she meant, the library doors opened, and a tall, older man stepped into the room, one arm tucked behind his back. Dressed in a stiff black livery, he stood over six feet tall, casting a long shadow across the polished wooden floor.

"Ah, Linton," said Lady Scarborough. "This is Marsden Fisher, the new tutor. Will you please show him to his room? Marsden, Linton here will give you that tour of the house you hoped for."

Linton bowed his silver head. "Yes, my lady."

"And then find wherever it is Alice is hiding today. Introduce Marsden to her, will you?"

"As you wish, my lady."

The butler stepped to one side of the door, gesturing for Marsden to show himself out of the room. As soon as he was clear of the library doors, they were swiftly closed behind him, shutting Lady Scarborough alone once more inside her smoky mausoleum.

"Your bags have already been taken to your room," said Linton. "If you'll follow me, Mr. Fisher?"

"Please, call me Marsden."

Linton cast a weary glance down the length of his beak-like nose upon Marsden. "The ground floor consists of the library, his Lordship's study, the smoking room, and the conservatory to the east. To the west is the dining room, drawing room, and the Pink room."

"What exactly is a Pink room?"

"It is simply the Pink room, Mr. Fisher. But it is of no consequence to you. You will not need to familiarize yourself with any rooms on the ground floor but the conservatory and perhaps the library."

They climbed the wide marble staircase to the second level of the house. At the top, Linton guided Marsden to the beginning of a long, narrow hallway. "This," he said, "is the west wing. These are the family rooms."

Marsden lingered at the entrance to the west wing, hoping to see into its depths, but Linton turned him abruptly away. On the opposite side of the landing, a long draping swathe of antique white linen hung across the entrance to another hallway. The temporary curtain had been hastily erected at an uneven angle and nailed into the ceiling. Linton pulled back the cloth to expose the hallway entrance behind it. A charred door had been propped up between the walls, barring any entry to the rooms behind it. The lingering smell of smoke hung in the air, and a flurry of black dust fell from the curtain when Linton hoisted it away from the ruined doorway. Marsden stepped back, shocked by the stench of burnt decay.

"This is the east wing," said Linton, a tightness in his voice. "This part of the house is condemned and therefore completely out of bounds. For your safety."

"I saw a little of the damage from the outside when I arrived," said Marsden. "What happened?"

"There was a fire."

"As I can see. When did it happen?"

"Over two years ago. The blaze occurred during the war, so His Lordship couldn't commit to reconstruction." Linton dropped the curtain. "The staff accommodation is in the attic. You will always move between the attic and the lower floors via the staff stairway."

Linton exposed the staircase concealed behind a door at the entrance to the west wing. Marsden felt claustrophobic as he followed the butler up the steep, narrow stairs to the servants' quarters. At the top, Linton opened a door into a long hallway painted moss green, the once vibrant color now fading.

"This," said Linton, pointing to the second doorway to the right, "will be your room. The previous tutors had a room next to Lady Alice in the west wing, but I'm sure you can understand why this is more appropriate."

Marsden had been sure he would be largely ambivalent about his accommodation, but he was pleased by his room upon opening the door. It was small, but his alone, with enough space to fit a single bed, cupboard, and a long desk. The light filtering into the room through a single dirty window was bleak. Still, the safety and quiet of his little corner at Maidenstone Hall was a far cry from the filthy conditions he had endured during the war or even the hovel of a cheap boarding house room he had been sharing in Kings Cross since his discharge, his roommates coming and going quickly at the height of the Spanish Influenza.

His bags were stacked neatly beside the door, the violin case leaning against them. Marsden swallowed his sigh of relief at seeing his luggage— all his possessions in the world—safe in his presence once more.

"I will leave you to change, Mr. Fisher," said Linton, casting a pronounced eye of disdain along the length of Marsden's outfit. "I shall return shortly to escort you downstairs to the conservatory."

"Why the conservatory?" Marsden asked.

"I believe that is where Lady Alice is...hiding."

Chapter Three

When Linton had closed the door, Marsden relished a moment of privacy for himself. He peeled off his damp clothes, hanging them over a chair by the desk. Marsden had brought so few items of clothing and so many books that it took little time to unpack his apparel into the small cupboard. He dressed simply, donning a grey wool suit and a black tie. Despite the layers of fresh clothes, Marsden shivered at the chill in the room, so distinct after the warmth of the kitchen and library.

With his bags empty and stored above the cupboard, Marsden placed the violin case on his narrow bed. He sat to remove the violin and lifted the bottom layer of the case to expose a thin, hidden compartment beneath. Marsden checked the contents carefully, overwhelmed by worry that someone could have rifled through his belongings while Lady Scarborough interviewed him. However, the contents were undisturbed; his most personal letters and photographs were to be seen by no one by himself. He selected one of the photographs and held it close to his chest. Two smiling young men shone in the bright light of the bulb hanging above his head. Marsden barely recognized himself, clean-shaven and so much younger. Beside him, Simon Falconer stared out of the picture, alive and well. Marsden knew he paled in comparison to Simon, who was so tall, handsome, and immaculate in full lieutenant's regalia. The sepia portrait could not truly reflect Simon's beauty, the golden shine of his blonde hair, the sparkle of his green eyes. His glorious grin, twisted around the tip of a fresh cigarette, winked at Marsden from the crinkled photograph. He turned the picture in his fingers to read the spindly black ink trailing across the stained backing.

You know you've got the brand of kisses
That I'd die for

A fist rapped against the door. Marsden hurried to return the photograph to its hiding place and replaced the lid of the secret compartment. He put the violin back into the case and slid it under the bed. Marsden stood just as Linton opened the door.

"Lady Alice is waiting for you in the conservatory, Mr. Fisher."

Linton led Marsden back down the servants' stairway to the ground floor, the exit opening into the salon beside the main staircase. The dark gloom of the house evaporated as Linton strode ahead toward the conservatory, a glass-paneled room almost bursting with indoor plants. Delicately folded along a wide red chaise lounge was a thin teenage girl. Upon their arrival, she looked up from her book. Embossed upon its spine: *The Body Snatcher*.

"Lady Alice," said Linton. "May I introduce Mr. Marsden Fisher?"

Marsden's heart painfully contracted when he met Alice's gaze. Her green eyes were the mirror image of Simon's. She shared his delicate features and high cheekbones. But for the vibrant red of her hair, she could have been her brother's twin, and the familiarity of her gaze stole his breath.

Alice was equally affected by Marsden's arrival, her shy smile wavering and her long fingers twitching as she tucked a stray wisp of red hair behind one ear. Her cheeks flushed when she took his hand, and she could not maintain his gaze. "Mr. Fisher, I'm very pleased to meet you. You're just in time for tea."

"Please, Lady Alice, call me Marsden." Her fingertips were small and icy in Marsden's large hand, but he was reluctant to release his hold. The very sight of her had frozen him almost entirely in place.

"It's just Alice," she said, exhaling in a rush. "Nobody calls me Lady Alice to my face but Linton. Isn't that right, Linton?"

Linton hinged at the waist. "As I should, my lady."

"You may leave us, Linton. I can pour the tea myself."

The tilt of his head suggested Lion did not like the prospect of leaving Alice alone with Marsden at all, but the butler exited without a word, and

16

both hands clasped behind his back.

"Linton's a stiff old thing," said Alice when he was gone, "but he's been with our family my whole life, and we do rather rely on him. Won't you join me?"

Marsden sat at the small garden table while Alice tended to the teapot and two cups already laid out before his arrival. She had, he realized, been patiently waiting for him. Marsden examined her more closely as she leaned over the tray to take up the pot. Despite Lady Scarborough's insistence that her daughter was unwell, Alice did not appear sickly. In fact, he considered her to be incredibly pretty. Like her mother, she was ghostly pale, but her cheeks and eyes shone in the soft light of the conservatory. She shared Simon's refined looks but not his boisterous energy. As she poured the tea, Alice glanced repeatedly in his direction, eager to look at him but too nervous to hold his eye.

"Is it true you play the violin?" Alice asked when she passed a cup rattling in its saucer to Marsden.

"Yes, I do."

"I'm glad. None of my other tutors have been particularly interested in music. I've missed playing with someone."

Marsden took the tea gratefully, leaving the saucer in his lap and wrapping both hands around the warm cup. The conservatory had no heat, and the large glass panels did nothing to absorb the cold. Alice held a plate of sliced fruit cake before him. Although his stomach churned with hunger, Marsden took only one slice and rested it on the saucer.

"I understand," he said, "that you'd also like to improve your French?"

"Mother certainly seems to think it's important, but I don't see why it matters."

"You don't want to travel to France? Or Switzerland?"

Alice gave a sad shrug. "I would love to travel. But I won't."

Marsden noticed the movement of her hands when she stroked the length of her left wrist. A long, ugly scar crept along the white expanse of her exposed skin. It was thick and pink, raised high and perfectly straight. Marsden had seen such precise scars before and guessed immediately how the injury had occurred. Perhaps feeling his gaze upon her wrist, Alice quickly tucked her forearm along her green tea dress.

"When shall we start classes, Alice?" he asked.

Alice sipped at her tea, her right hand trembling when she lifted the cup to her lips. "I won't be here tomorrow but will return on Saturday. Perhaps we could enjoy a violin lesson then if you wouldn't mind."

"Whatever you wish."

"Thank you, Marsden," she said and stood. She wiped her hands vigorously over the soft fabric of her bodice as if ridding them of sweat. "I will see you on Saturday morning."

Marsden opened his mouth to speak but could not think of anything to say quickly enough as she hurried from the room. He twisted in his seat to see her disappear into the hall's darkness. With a bewildered sigh, Marsden tried to imagine how he had upset her and cursed himself for staring so blatantly at the scar on her wrist. Her appearance had thrown him—her striking resemblance to Simon—and he let his guard down.

Alone and unsure what to do with himself, Marsden finally helped himself to the slice of cake on his saucer, taking a hefty bite. He wondered if Alice would be the only family member absent from the house tomorrow. If he were not required to work, there would be plenty of time and opportunity to discover every corner of Maidenstone Hall. Free of obligation for a whole day at least, he could begin his search for the truth about Simon Falconer—whether he was still alive or truly dead.

Chapter Four

"I hope you slept well, Mr. Fisher?" Linton asked when Marsden joined the rest of the staff for breakfast.

"Tolerably well," said Marsden.

The truth was Marsden had barely slept at all. Awake in his cold bed for hours, his mind ran ragged. For half the night, he had been overwhelmed with thoughts of Simon. And with every memory of Simon, he could not help but recall his introduction to Alice, particularly her striking resemblance to her brother. The memory of her shy yet piercing stare made Marsden blush. Perhaps it had been too long since another human being had stirred any emotion inside him, or maybe it was his longing for Simon, but Marsden couldn't deny she had piqued his interest. However, she would not be present to distract him come morning, and with Alice absent and the day to himself, Marsden had spent much of the night imagining in which part of the house he would begin his search for Simon. He would explore every room at Maidenstone Hall if he had to, for any sign that Simon had been there recently.

As Marsden sat down with his colleagues, Linton presided over the top of the long table in the servants' dining room, with Badeley and Nancy framing him. A dark-haired girl Marsden had yet to meet was seated at the opposite end, slightly apart from the rest of the staff. When he caught her staring openly at him, she quickly averted her eyes.

"Hello," Marsden said and leaned toward the girl. "I'm Marsden, the new tutor."

The girl's smile, surrounded by pronounced freckles, was shy. "My name is Holly, sir."

Mrs. Huston bustled around the table, serving hot porridge, leaving the other staff to help themselves to bread and strawberry jam. Including himself, just six souls now sat together enjoying Mrs. Huston's cooking, but Marsden imagined at least twenty servants having once occupied the large dining room.

Marsden was just lifting a piece of buttered bread to his mouth when Linton rose, facing the doorway. The others followed his example, and Marsden rushed to his feet before he had even turned to see who had entered the room. His breath caught, and he almost choked on his mouthful when he saw Alice standing before them. One leather-clad hand resting on her slim waist, she wore a riding habit, except that she was not wearing a skirt but tight-fitting beige trousers. In her other hand, she held a riding crop and was tapping the tip in a jolting rhythm against her thigh.

"Don't let me interrupt," she said, bright and airy. "I just wanted some jam, Mrs. Huston."

Mrs. Huston wiped her hands on her apron while studying the floor with great interest. "I sent a jar up to you, my lady. Surely you've not finished it all?"

"Of course not, silly goose, but you sent up apricot, and you know how I detest apricot. I'd hate to go riding without having any breakfast."

Mrs. Huston snatched at the large jar of strawberry jam on the table. "I'm sorry, my lady. I have some strawberry preserves here."

"Thank you, Mrs. Huston." The young mistress laid the crop upon the table and leaned over Badeley's shoulder, taking a piece of bread from the table and slathering it with jam directly in front of the chauffeur's face. When she lifted the morsel to her mouth, her sharp eyes fell upon Marsden. Again, the familiarity of her stare unnerved him, his stomach clenching.

"And who is this?" she asked.

Confused by her lack of familiarity, Marsden did not think to introduce himself again. Rather, he wondered if she was joking with him. When he did not respond, one slim red eyebrow rose upon her brow.

"This is Marsden Fisher, my lady," said Linton. "Mr. Fisher, this is Lady

Beatrice."

Marsden couldn't stop himself from gawking. "You're not—"

"Requiring your services?" Her grin was sly. "No, Mr. Fisher. Unlike my sister, I have no interest in any further schooling." She took a large bite of bread and jam, exaggerating her chewing.

"Is there anything else you require, my lady?" Linton asked.

Marsden noticed that Linton, too, was uneasy around Beatrice. His hands were clenched into tight fists and pressed against the sharp seam of his trousers.

"No, thank you, Linton," said Beatrice around her mouthful. She paused to wipe at a droplet of jam along the corner seam of her mouth with a delicate thumb. "I know how you despise horses."

Linton grimaced. "Indeed."

Beatrice's eyes widened, alight with mischief. "Now I come to think of it, perhaps the new tutor could be useful to me after all. I'd hate to go riding alone. Perhaps you can accompany me, Mr. Fish?"

Marsden caught himself staring again, his mouth hanging open, and snapped his teeth together. He could not believe that the girl standing before him was not Alice, the same shy young woman to whom he had only yesterday been introduced. Her broad smile indicated a daring, cunning Marsden had not witnessed in Alice, but otherwise, Beatrice was completely identical, and he was not confident he could tell them apart if tested. Unsure of himself, Marsden glanced at Mrs. Huston, only to find the cook leaning heavily against the table, a bony hand clutching at the thin gold chain around her neck. Linton was also purposely avoiding his gaze. Nancy fixed her eyes on her breakfast plate while Badeley found something particularly interesting resting upon his shoulder. Only Holly stared unabashedly at Beatrice, a minute sneer tugging at one corner of her lips.

"It's raining," said Marsden finally. He nodded toward the fogged windows of the staff dining room, where a steady drizzle beat against the glass.

Beatrice stalked around the table, brushing unnervingly close to his left shoulder. When she passed him, a strong odor of perfume surrounded Marsden. It was a heavy, luxurious scent that he didn't recognize.

"So it is," she agreed with mock surprise, voice pitching unnaturally high as she peered through the window at the grey drizzle. "But just barely. I think I shall go out all the same. What do you say, Fish?"

"It's Fisher, my lady. Marsden Fisher."

"So you won't join me?" She turned to face him, her grin fading into a pout. "I'll be ever so lonely."

The curve of her lips was so familiar, so like Simon, that Marsden found his tongue suddenly tied tight. He tried and failed not to stutter. "I—I'm no horseman, my lady."

Beatrice's eyes narrowed when she leaned closer, whispering: "I think you're a terrible liar, Fish. But I'll forgive you. Perhaps you can make it up to me by saddling my horse, at least?"

Beatrice held his gaze so effectively in a vice that Marsden could not look away. He hesitated at the prospect of spending time alone with her but then imagined the questions he could ask her about Simon. At last, he said, "Of course, my lady."

Beatrice's cheeks lifted. "Excellent. Get your coat and follow me."

She dropped the last of her breakfast onto Badeley's plate and strode out of the room with a cracking slap of the riding crop against the door frame. When the echo of her riding boots had disappeared down the hall, the staff subsided into their seats and returned to their meal without another word, conspicuously avoiding eye contact.

"Nobody told me there were two," said Marsden, addressing the group. "Mrs. Bradshaw only told me about Alice. I didn't realize she was a twin."

Linton and Nancy busied themselves with their porridge. Badeley loosened the collar of his shirt, looking distinctly flushed. Holly glared at the doorway through which Beatrice had just disappeared, a sour expression on her round face.

"I'm not surprised the agency didn't tell you," she said.

Almost speaking over the maid, Mrs. Huston hurriedly said, "Alice is the only one you need to think about. Try to remember that, Marsden." She still clutched at her gold chain but released it to expose a small cross at its base.

22

"Well," said Marsden, "I had better make myself useful."

No one wished him farewell as he left the table to fetch his coat and follow Beatrice.

Chapter Five

The stable, a dilapidated wooden building a short walk downhill from the west wing, was quiet and gloomy when Marsden stepped inside. Beatrice stood at the end of one row of stalls, brushing out a blanket. She gave Marsden only a cursory glance as he entered the stable.

"Are you going to help?" she called.

Marsden lingered where he was, close to the entrance, watching her from afar as Beatrice prepared a saddle. He was still struggling to comprehend the reality of Alice having a twin, a sister so wildly different in personality and yet almost identical in appearance. He couldn't imagine why Mrs. Bradshaw had failed to tell him about Beatrice. Marsden had questioned Simon repeatedly about his family and his life in England. *My father is a bore, and my mother is a simpering leach,* he had told Marsden. *I don't know why you're so interested; you won't be meeting them.* Never had Simon mentioned his sisters. He had thought he knew Simon Falconer so well. Perhaps he had understood far less than he thought.

When Marsden did not move, caught up in his thoughts, Beatrice misread his silence. She tilted her head to stare at him, her hair tumbling loosely over one shoulder. "Afraid of me already, Fish?"

Marsden willed himself to step closer. "Should I be?"

"Everyone else is."

"Where is your sister today?" he asked.

"Is that why you've come out here?" she said, rolling her eyes. "To talk about my sister? Everything is always about Alice, you know. Alice, Alice, Alice…"

24

"I was just curious." Marsden caught the defensive tone in his voice and wondered at her nervous effect on him. Unlike the timid gentleness of Alice's nature, Beatrice was an intimidating wildfire, yet he couldn't turn away from her. Every move she made demanded attention.

"My sister and I are not on the best terms," she explained, scrubbing dirt off the saddle. "Our lives are completely separate."

"I thought twins were usually inseparable."

Beatrice fixed him with a cold stare. "Do you have any brothers or sisters, Fish?"

"I had a brother, my lady. He died young."

Her expression darkened, and her jaw became slack. "My brother is dead, too. Did Mummy tell you?" At his nod, she scoffed. "Of course. She tells everyone, you know. Her brave son, the war hero."

Marsden took a deep breath, unsure of his next question—uncertain that she would deem any query worthy of a response. "Where did he die?"

Beatrice brushed at the saddle with renewed aggression. Marsden began to fear his prodding had silenced her when she threw the brush down on the ground.

"I couldn't say," she replied. "Mummy only told me that he was dead. Help me with this saddle, won't you?"

Marsden hurried to obey, collecting the saddle and following Beatrice into the stall where a beautiful black mare stood with its nose in a trough. Beatrice flung the blanket over the mare's back and followed it with the saddle, hoisting it out of Marsden's arms and carefully placing it.

Marsden bent to fasten the saddle under the horse's belly and asked, "So your brother died in battle? Was he in France?" When he stood upright again, he was keenly aware of her staring at him with narrow eyes.

"I thought you were no horseman." She gestured to the saddle. "You did quite a good job there."

"I was a private, my lady, during the war. I was often asked to assist with the officers' horses."

"Is that why you're so interested in my brother? As a fellow army man?"

Marsden willed his face to become blank to avoid betraying any emotion.

"I'm just very sorry for your loss, my lady."

"Well, I suppose somebody should be. Are you coming riding or not?"

"I really don't ride."

Beatrice smirked. The mischievous twinkle that had faded upon mention of her brother returned to her eyes. "I still think you're a terrible liar, Fish. Pass me that bridle."

Marsden collected a bridle from the stable wall and handed it to Beatrice. She fitted it quickly and pushed past him, leading the mare out of the stable. He followed her outside. The steady drizzle of rain had ceased only to be replaced by an emerging layer of fog, creeping thickly up toward the Hall. There was almost no wind, but the white vapor was moving fast, inching through the trees that met the lake at the bottom of the hill.

Beatrice coughed suggestively, and Marsden remembered himself, rushing to take her heel between his palms to help her into the saddle. She did not look back when she called over her shoulder: "Enjoy your time with my sister, won't you? I'm sure it will be exceedingly dull."

Beatrice kicked at the mare's side, and the horse reared up, carrying her away from Marsden. He watched her ride until she had disappeared into the thick fog. Marsden walked down the hill a little to sight her, but the encroaching cloud had eaten her completely. It slunk toward the lake now, biting its edge. The water was still as the fog rolled over it, swallowing the lake from view.

Marsden started walking back toward the house and wondered how far he could get before the fog engulfed him. The air was still and damp, fragrant with the scent of wet grass. He inhaled deeply and considered taking full advantage of the reprieve from the rain and walking further across the estate, but he worried about getting lost in the fog, and, despite the foolishness of the notion, he admitted openly to himself that he did not wish to run into Beatrice again. At least not while she was on horseback and he was on foot. He bristled at the memory of her offhand dismal of her brother's death in response to his genuine expression of sorrow. *I suppose somebody should be.* Beatrice was, he decided, completely heartless.

Chapter Six

When Marsden returned to the servants' entrance, he discovered Mrs. Huston hunched over a mop in the hallway.

"Mind my clean floor," she said. "Everything all right?"

Her voice crackled with tension, and Marsden immediately knew she meant his interaction with Beatrice. "Yes, thank you, Mr. Huston. Lady Beatrice has dismissed me."

Mrs. Huston's shoulders sank. "Thank heavens for that. I was sure she would bully you into riding with her."

"I wanted to come in from the cold. I am rather desperate for a hot cup of tea."

"It's not tea time yet, and I'll be damned if I'm going to make it for you now."

"I'll make some for you if you like," he offered.

Mrs. Huston relaxed visibly, her wrinkled cheeks lifting with a smile, and directed him to the kitchen pantry. He filled the kettle, and while the water boiled over the stove, he located a teapot and two plain white cups and saucers.

"Where is everyone?" Marsden asked when Mrs. Huston brought the mop into the kitchen.

"Badeley drove his Lordship to the station. Linton is polishing his Lordship's shoes, and Nancy is with her Ladyship in the library. Holly has gone home."

"So early?"

"She only works half-time, so she's always finished before luncheon."

The water was boiling in the kettle, and Marsden occupied himself with warming the pot and then scooping in a large spoonful of leaves. Mrs. Huston sat at the kitchen table, and Marsden placed a cup before her.

"This is a magnificent estate," he said in conversation. "It's a shame about the fire damage. Is the east wing not at all inhabitable?"

Mrs. Huston shook her head. "Nobody could last a day in that mess. The Hall is a shadow of what it once was since the fire. What with the war and Master Simon's death, I'm afraid it will never be the same again."

Marsden understood her only too well. Since Simon had been reported dead, Marsden's life had been thrown completely off kilter, never returning to its center. Hoping to keep the conversation dedicated to Simon, he prodded further. "When was he killed? Before the fire?"

"Oh yes. Almost three years ago. The fire happened a little less than a year later. We were all hoping that the damage to the east wing would have been repaired by now."

"So, why hasn't it?"

"I couldn't say. I'd have thought Lord Scarborough hadn't lacked money since he sold off most of the estate, but he doesn't seem keen to spend it on the Hall."

Marsden paused in surprise, teacup at his lips. "He sold off the estate? You mean the land?"

"Aye. Most of it. The farms and all the land around them. He sold almost everything that was once attached to the house the moment the war was over. With his only son and heir gone, I suppose His Lordship couldn't see the need to keep it all." Mrs. Huston paused to drink the last of her tea, draining the cup quickly. "I'd better get back to work. What are you going to do with yourself today?"

"I thought I'd get to know the house better," said Marsden. "Perhaps do some reading. There is quite a spectacular collection in the library. Do you think that's permitted?"

"Just be sure not to disturb Lady Scarborough. The library is her territory, so be quiet as you go."

Marsden left Mrs. Huston to her duties in the kitchen and climbed the servants' stairs to the salon, intent upon investigating the rooms on the ground floor. Although Linton had suggested there was no need for Marsden to be familiar with most rooms on this floor, he had not explicitly forbidden access to any part of it. Marsden intended to take advantage of the quiet house and snoop around while the opportunity presented itself.

He discovered the dining room and attached drawing room directly beside the entrance hall. Despite their grandeur and lavish decoration, they were relatively uninteresting and dismally dark, the heavy velvet curtains drawn. Marsden inspected them only briefly, opening cigarette boxes and peering inside ornamental vases. The rooms were frigid and surprisingly dusty. Marsden ran a finger along the filthy mantle of the drawing room's empty fireplace and promptly sneezed when he examined his blackened finger. Next door, he located what he could only assume was the Pink room. It was indeed pink, the walls painted a pale rose color, but it was bleakly dull in the darkened room, the curtains here also drawn against the daylight. Dust sheets covered the furnishings. Marsden quickly lifted each linen covering, but anything of value had been removed; the shelves were bare, the tables empty of trinkets and decoration. For his trouble, he was left only with a furious need to sneeze again with all the grime he had disturbed.

Marsden made his way back across the black and white tiles of the salon to the dark hallway leading toward the conservatory. He opened the first door to his left and discovered it was the rear entrance to the library. Marsden peered into the room to see the narrow feet and calves of Lady Scarborough hanging from the armchair beside the fire. In a chair opposite, Nancy sat with her legs crossed and her nose buried in a book. When she didn't notice him, Marsden closed the door and turned to another on the opposite side of the hall.

After discovering his mistress in the previous room, Marsden turned the handle with more discretion. He opened the door just enough to see another man standing directly before him. Harrold Falconer, Lord Scarborough, turned immediately and was surprised to see Marsden peering into the study.

Marsden, too, jumped at the sight of the earl, shocked at having been caught in his snooping. "My apologies, sir," he said. "I didn't mean to disturb you."

Lord Scarborough was a lean man but broad across the shoulders. His short black hair had faded into streaks of grey around his ears, with fine lines of white also peppered through his sculpted mustache. He held a smoking pipe and lifted it to his lips, taking a long drag before saying, "It's Mr. Fisher, isn't it?"

Marsden's hand remained fixed upon the door handle. "Yes, sir. I'm so sorry for barging in on you. I was looking for the library."

"Well, you're here now. Come in properly."

The small study was dark and smoky, the curtains drawn across the windows. A wide mahogany desk was positioned on one side of the fireplace. On the other side, a long mirror faced the desk. The earl sat behind the desk and sucked again on his pipe, turning his face to stare at his reflection in the mirror as he exhaled the smoke in a long, delicate stream.

Without raising his eyes to Marsden, he said, "Mrs. Bradshaw claimed you were a soldier, Mr. Fisher. Which battalion?"

"Please, sir, call me Marsden. And yes, I was. In the eighteenth, sir."

"I can tell." Lord Scarborough made a show of abandoning his reflection to inspect Marsden, eyes raking him from head to toe as if judging the younger man's character solely by sight. Marsden was keenly aware that he had not been invited to sit and stood rigid before Lord Scarborough with fingers twitching by his sides. He had the distinct feeling of being on parade.

"We're expecting a lot from you, young man," the earl continued. "Alice hasn't had a tutor for months, but my wife assured me it would be worth our while to employ you. I was against the idea, I must admit, after what happened with the last girl. But perhaps you'll have the magic touch."

It was, Marsden thought, a strange thing to say. Assuming that the earl meant to compliment him in some peculiar fashion, Marsden said, "I'll certainly do my best, sir."

"I'd expect no less from an infantryman. Face the Huns, did you?"

"Yes, sir. Were you in the field, sir?"

Lord Scarborough's chest expanded. "No, I was in London this time around. At the war office, I was working with General Murray. I did my bit in the field against the Boers, of course. I served with Kitchener, you know."

Marsden did his best to appear impressed, peeling back his cheeks and lifting his brow with mechanical precision. He guessed that Lord Scarborough was perhaps fifty, still younger than many battalion commanding officers he had encountered during the recent war. It must be an incredible privilege of being an earl, Marsden thought, to decide whether or not you would lower yourself into muddy trenches with the other men of your nation. Destroying farms and imprisoning civilians was the kind of warfare Lord Scarborough was accustomed to. The sodden battlefields of France would no doubt have been a terrible shock to him after the dry plains of South Africa.

"We should talk more about it," said Lord Scarborough. His dark eyes lit up as the thought occurred to him; "You should join us for dinner."

Marsden's heart leaped into his throat at the thought of the opportunity the earl presented. "Dinner with the family? Is that usual?"

"Not particularly, no." Lord Scarborough's smile was suspiciously vulgar. "But then, your predecessors were simpering nitwits, so I never felt the urge to converse with them. Besides, I'm sure you'll provide much better conversation than the women."

"I would be delighted to join you, sir, but—" Marsden waved his hands down the length of his dull brown suit, old-fashioned and overly worn. "I'm afraid I have nothing suitable to wear to dinner."

Lord Scarborough's brows knitted as though he agreed Marsden's attire was a severe impediment. "I doubt you'd fit into any of my suits. How tall are you?"

"Six feet, sir."

"A hair shorter than my son, but perhaps something of his will do. I'll have Linton arrange something for you."

He made the suggestion so casually that Marsden balked in shock. "Sir, I didn't mean to suggest—"

"Don't be silly. There's no point in being sentimental about these things."

Lord Scarborough waved a casual hand in the air and returned his attention to the documents on his desk. Marsden lingered, unsure if he had been dismissed. When the earl looked up, it was not at Marsden, hovering before in the doorway, but again at his reflection. He brushed his fingertips at the fine edge of his mustache and said, "I'll see you at seven o'clock on the dot, Marsden."

Marsden showed himself out of the study and closed the door. Having already been caught prying into corners of the house where he was not invited, his bravado at searching the rest of the rooms waned, but a thrill of excitement raced along Marsden's spine at the thought of being invited into the family's inner circle. He had not expected such immediate access to their private lives. Although he had not found any sign of Simon having been in the house, he was sure he could use Lord Scarborough's invitation to his advantage. Maidenstone Hall was the last place he knew Simon to have been seen alive. Marsden now wondered if Lord Scarborough would admit it.

Chapter Seven

An hour before dinner, Linton knocked on Marsden's door.

"I understand," Linton said, "that you have been invited to dine with the family."

Judging by the deep lines between the butler's eyes, Marsden suspected this news had greatly unsettled Linton, and Marsden couldn't help but enjoy the satisfaction he felt at the older man's discomfort.

"Indeed I have, Mr. Linton."

Linton gestured down the hallway of the servants' quarters. "I will show you to Viscount Simon's rooms."

Marsden's heart fluttered as he followed Linton downstairs to the west wing, so overwhelmed was he with a sudden and morbid sense of panic. He feared how he would react when surrounded by the remnants of Simon's life. He feared he was heading toward a tomb—or a trap. Most of all, he was desperately afraid that he would lose control of his emotions and give himself away. He had been so careful to hide the evidence of his relationship with Simon, the letters and photographs concealed in the base of his violin case, his every response to Simon's name carefully controlled. If he began to weep the moment he was immersed in Simon's former life at the Hall, it would all be for nothing.

Simon's bedroom was already well-lit when Linton showed Marsden inside, the lamps giving the room a warm glow. Marsden momentarily allowed himself to imagine that perhaps Simon was alive and residing at Maidenstone Hall, sleeping every night in the very room. The room was free of the musty smell an abandoned space often has, and it was cleaned regularly; unlike the unused rooms on the ground floor, there wasn't a trace of dust to be seen, and the windows were spotless. The bed was perfectly made with crisp corners and plump pillows. The only clue the room had long been uninhabited was the empty fireplace, the grate devoid of ash and charred wood. It was ghoulish to Marsden. A terrible, aching itch raced along his neck as if he were aware of someone watching him from a dark, hidden corner.

Marsden's attention was drawn to the neat dressing table, almost bare but for a handful of combs and a frame featuring a photograph of the young Viscount himself. He allowed himself the guilty pleasure of staring at the picture of Simon. It was, he realized, the only portrait he had seen in the house. It was a surprising realization that no other family images were displayed throughout the Hall but for this sole portrait of Simon.

Distracted by the photograph, Marsden was startled when Linton cleared his throat.

"If you will follow me into the dressing room, Mr. Fisher."

Linton guided Marsden through a door at the opposite end of the bedroom. The dressing room was beautifully maintained, pristinely neat, and clean. Linton had already taken three dinner suits from the large wardrobe and hung them for Marsden's inspection. The butler stepped behind him, grasping the shoulders of Marsden's jacket and guiding it down his arms.

Marsden closed his eyes as Linton guided his arms into a pristine jacket and imagined Simon wearing the same suit. He shrugged, sinking deeper into the fine wool, dropping his chin to sniff at the lapel. Marsden had to breathe in deeper, dragging the faint scent into his heaving lungs, but it was there: the faintest hint of cigarette smoke. He let the smell permeate his senses, the distinct smell of sunburnt Turkish tobacco—Simon's favorite, gold-tipped Murattis.

"How does it feel?" Linton asked.

Marsden forced a shaky smile. "This will do very well. Thank you, Linton."

Linton eyed the over-long sleeves. "The sleeves are a little—"

"It will do. It is only one dinner."

"And the trousers? Would you—"

"They'll fit, I'm sure."

Linton passed the trousers to Marsden. "I still think you should try them on to ensure they will be comfortable, Mr. Fisher. I will give you some privacy."

Linton left Marsden alone in the dressing room, closing the door behind him. Marsden clutched the trousers to his chest and sank onto a chair. He pressed a fist against his thundering heart, feeling overheated in the thick jacket. Running his hands over the sleeves, wondering when Simon had last worn this suit, Marsden suddenly found breathing difficult. He couldn't believe he had expected Simon to be in this house, waiting for him. Marsden had imagined the scene over and over, walking through the main door of Maidenstone to find Simon alive, infinitely proud of himself for having duped the entire world into thinking him dead.

But Marsden had been sorely mistaken. Despite their cleanliness, there was no sign of anyone, let alone Simon, having recently occupied these rooms. The morbid time capsule of Simon's former bedroom was nauseating, and Marsden felt childish for being so disturbed.

There was a solid knock against the door, and Marsden sprang to his feet, throwing off Simon's jacket. He ran a trembling hand over his face, swiping away a fine layer of nervous sweat. The door opened again just as he folded the suit jacket and trousers over one arm.

"They fit," Marsden assured Linton before he could speak. Clutching at the suit, Marsden scurried past the butler back through the bedroom. When Linton escorted Marsden out of the family wing, Marsden paid close attention to the route from the family's quarters back to the servants' staircase. He hung just behind Linton, memorizing the length of the hallway and the paintings directly outside each doorway, including an ugly still-life depicting a vase of tulips opposite the door to Simon's bedroom. Marsden wondered which closed entrances hid Alice and Beatrice's rooms but did not ask Linton. Marsden anticipated that he would come to discover every corner of the house soon enough.

Chapter Eight

Marsden was sure to enter the dining room at precisely seven o'clock and was preceded only by Lord Scarborough. The earl was standing behind his chair at the head of the table, staring down at the pocket watch cradled in his hand. Only his eyes lifted to recognize Marsden's arrival.

"Well," said Lord Scarborough, "you at least have a decent sense of time, Marsden." He tucked the watch into his waistcoat pocket and gestured to the seat at his left. "Come along then. You'll sit beside me. The ladies are late as usual."

As soon as he had spoken, Lady Scarborough teetered into the room. The black satin she wore was more appropriate in a London ballroom than a dusty dining room in the middle of the countryside. Her smile faded when she noticed Marsden standing beside Lord Scarborough, her eyes roaming over the borrowed suit. Standing beside him, she traced her fingers down the jacket's left shoulder seam.

She said, "I see you found something that fits. Although Simon was a little taller, I think. It really does suit you, Marsden."

"Where is the girl?" Lord Scarborough asked, tapping the back of the chair before him.

"I'm here." Beatrice sashayed into the room, shining hair waving loose over her shoulders. The red velvet of her dress, matching so closely to the color of her hair, sparkled as she sauntered to the table. She placed her hands on her hips and gave a suggestive shimmy, the beaded hemline of the skirt shaking and reflecting the light. "Do you like my new dress?"

"Your hair, dear," said Lady Scarborough. "Nancy would have helped you with it."

Beatrice gave a careless shrug. "I don't know why you worry about it, Mummy. It's not as though there's anyone here I have to impress."

Beatrice winked at Marsden and took her place on the other side of her father, sinking into the chair with a loud sigh. Marsden pulled back the chair beside him for Lady Scarborough. She gave him a tired smile as she melted into the chair, the lines around her eyes crinkling deeply.

"You spend too much on dresses, my darling," she said without looking at Beatrice. A wilting smile was Beatrice's only response, preferring instead to examine the perfect curve of her fingernails in the sparkling light of the chandelier.

With both ladies seated, Lord Scarborough and Marsden took their places. A floorboard creaked, and Marsden looked over his shoulder to the door, expecting Alice, but instead, Linton appeared, carrying a soup terrine. As if he'd been waiting outside the dining room door to hear the scrape of the chairs as the family sat down at the table, Linton immediately commenced the dinner service in complete silence. Starting with Lady Scarborough, he circled the table, allowing each diner to ladle soup into the bowl already placed before them.

The soup course proceeded in stilted variations of tepid conversation and silence. Lord Scarborough complained about his journey to York earlier in the day, the train overcrowded, and the first-class carriage stuffy. Lady Scarborough made every appearance of paying close attention but said little. Marsden noticed the deliberate way she clutched at her wine glass. Beatrice stirred her spoon around the bowl in listless circles, consuming little of the thick broth. Marsden almost tipped a spoonful of soup down his shirt front when something hard smacked against his shin. He tried to make the movement casual when he leaned back enough to look down and see one black slipper beside the chair. A matching shoe slapped against his legs a moment later, and Marsden glanced up to see Beatrice staring at him with a smile so minute it moved only one corner of her mouth.

"Did you enjoy your ride today, my lady?" Marsden asked, conceding to offer Beatrice the attention she craved.

"I did," she said. "It's such a shame it was my last opportunity."

Lord Scarborough scowled at Beatrice. "None of that, please."

"Daddy's selling the last of our horses," she explained, ignoring her father's foul expression. "They're being collected tomorrow. Today's ride was somewhat of last hoorah, if you will."

"They've become an extravagance," said Lord Scarborough. "You're the only one who rides, and I'll be damned if I'll keep paying for the stable's upkeep."

"If Alice bothered to get in the saddle occasionally, I'm sure you would keep them."

Lord Scarborough snorted and shook his head, resembling an irritated stallion himself. When irritated, Marsden remembered, Simon had often done the same thing, imitating a wild, furious beast when the worst of his temper rose to the surface and simmered, desperate to be released. Simon had not resembled his father particularly, but in the flick of his chin and the lengthening of his jaw, Marsden could see so many of Simon's mannerisms reflected in Lord Scarborough. In looks, however, Simon had taken after Lady Scarborough, just as Beatrice and Alice had.

At the recurring thought of Alice, he wondered again why she was not at the dinner table with the rest of the family. Marsden turned to Lady Scarborough: "Speaking of Lady Alice, will she not join us for dinner?"

"Alice is not here," said Beatrice. She over-accentuated her speech, virtually spitting her sister's name through tight teeth.

"Alice will be back tomorrow," said Lady Scarborough. "She is so looking forward to her lessons."

"And I, as well, my lady," said Marsden. "I must say it's impressive that a young lady her age is still intent on continuing her education."

Lord Scarborough lifted his napkin to his mouth, coughing into the linen. "Mr. Fisher, did my wife not explain that you would only tutor Alice every other day?"

"Every other day, sir?" Marsden looked from the earl to the countess, but neither spoke. He risked a glance at Beatrice, only to find her smile devious.

"Have you decided upon a story for him?" she asked her parents.

"Please don't," said Lady Scarborough, her tone pleading. "Can't we enjoy a pleasant evening for once?" She reached for her glass and gulped at the white wine served in anticipation of the fish course.

"Alice is very unwell," said Lord Scarborough. "She seeks treatments regularly at a hospital in York. She is there almost every other day."

"She *is* gone every other day," said Beatrice.

Lord Scarborough ignored her. Silence followed as the family dedicated themselves to Mrs. Huston's second dish of baked trout. The fire blazed at the end of the room, and Marsden was increasingly aware of the thick wool of his borrowed suit. He was sweating inside the jacket's heavy confines and couldn't resist pulling the shirt collar away from his neck.

Lady Scarborough noticed his discomfort. "Are you all right, Marsden? I hope the jacket is not too tight."

Marsden couldn't be sure if she was genuinely concerned for his comfort or if she feared he would damage her son's wardrobe. He desperately wished to throw etiquette aside and remove the jacket but instead said, "I'm quite all right. Perhaps I'm still getting used to wearing civilian clothes again."

Lord Scarborough's back stiffened, mustache dancing on his top lip. "There is no greater pride than wearing the uniform of your country on the battlefield. Isn't that right, Marsden? That's what I always told Simon."

"Where exactly did your son serve, sir?"

"The Somme," said Lady Scarborough, reaching again for her wine glass only to find it empty. She gestured to Linton, who in turn cast his gaze upon Lord Scarborough, looking for instruction. When the earl failed to notice the unvoiced question, Linton relented and refilled her glass.

"St. Quentin?" Marsden probed.

Lady Scarborough looked questioningly at her husband. He, too, hesitated but finally answered, "He was at the first engagement. Almost three years ago."

"He must have been with the Territorial Force?"

Lord Scarborough cleared his throat. "No, he was regular army. He signed up in '15."

"Did you volunteer too, Fish?" Beatrice asked.

"I did, my lady."

"Why?"

Marsden choked on a mouthful of wine. He wiped at his mouth with the back of a hand and said, "I beg your pardon, my lady?"

"Why did you volunteer?" Beatrice said to clarify.

"Well, I—"

"It's just that it seems to me that signing up for death and devastation is a rather silly thing to do."

Marsden set his jaw. "It was my duty, my lady."

Beatrice's smile was no longer jovial. "My brother was keen to go too, you know. He was particularly drawn to violence."

Lady Scarborough cradled her forehead against one hand. Her whole arm trembled with the weight. "Must you?" she said.

"Must you always take his side? Dear, precious Simon—"

Lord Scarborough slammed a fist beside his plate, making the table tremble. Lady Scarborough's wine glass tipped over, and she let out a cry.

"That's enough," he said, snarling, teeth bared at his daughter.

Beatrice folded her knife and fork over her barely-eaten meal. "Very well, Daddy. I'm sure we've presented enough of a show to poor old Fish for one night."

The color on Lord Scarborough's face rose in varying shades of pink, his lips moving without words as Beatrice rose and stalked barefoot out of the room. Lady Scarborough half peeled out of her chair as though she would chase after Beatrice but sank almost immediately back down again when her husband cleared his throat with an angry growl. She took another large gulp of wine, elbows slumping against the table. Marsden didn't know where to look.

Lord Scarborough cast his napkin aside with a vicious slap of the linen against the table. "I apologize, Marsden," he said, "but I'm afraid I've lost my appetite. If you'll excuse me." When he stood, his chair tipped out from under him and landed on the floor with a thud. He stepped over it with an ungainly stride when he left the room.

Lady Scarborough placed a light hand on Marsden's wrist, and he was mortified to see tears swelling along her lower lashes.

"Marsden, I'm terribly sorry about this. Linton, could you tell Mrs. Huston that the staff may finish the rest of the dinner? I've had quite enough to eat."

"Shall I ask Nancy to join you, my lady?" Linton asked.

"No, no. Take Marsden with you, will you? No doubt he's still hungry."

She heaved herself out of her chair when Linton drew it back from beneath her and stood wobbling for a moment, a heavy gulp visible along the length of her pale throat. Marsden jumped hastily to his feet and wished Lady Scarborough a good night as she stumbled out of the room. He began to wonder if this was what Simon had hoped to keep from him. No matter how earnest his begging, Simon had refused to invite Marsden to visit Maidenstone Hall with him. Marsden had thought the denial cruel and became convinced Simon was ashamed of him. Now, reeling from the disastrous evening with the gruff Earl of Scarborough, his drunk wife, and troublesome daughter, Marsden imagined that it was the Falconer family of whom Simon had honestly been embarrassed. Even with her apparent illness, Alice had been the only family member who had not exhibited disgraceful behavior since Marsden's arrival.

Without a word, Linton took the fish plate in hand, and Marsden understood his only recourse was to follow the butler's example and collected up a barely touched plate of green beans. They took the dishes downstairs to the kitchen, where Mrs. Huston was busy preparing a rack of lamb upon yet another gleaming silver platter. Her face fell when she noticed Marsden and Linton standing in the doorway.

"Not again," she said, throwing down a handful of rosemary sprigs.

Marsden left Mrs. Huston to her cursing and headed into the servants' dining room, where Badeley and Nancy were smoking cigarettes and playing cards.

Badeley immediately laughed. "Another family dinner comes to an unhappy conclusion, I presume?"

"Happen often, does it?" Marsden asked. He placed the dish of beans on the table and sat down opposite Badeley.

"Fairly often. At least you got to escape early. Was it horrible?"

"Dinner was certainly…enlightening. Beatrice seemed particularly intent on upsetting her parents."

"She absolutely delights in it," said Badeley.

Nancy clicked her tongue. "Keep your voice down. One of these days, she'll hear you."

"I'm not afraid of Beatrice."

"That's because she's never tried to set your hair on fire."

Two glasses of wine with the family had loosed Marsden's caution, and he couldn't hold back a snort of laughter, but his amusement was cut short by the severe scowl that crossed Nancy's brow.

"Wait," he said, grin fading, "you're not serious, are you?"

Badeley heaved a sympathetic sigh. "Poor, Laura."

"That's why she left? The previous tutor?"

"Did no one tell you?" asked Nancy.

"No. All Lady Scarborough would say was that there was an accident." Of course, Marsden realized, she had been reluctant to say any more—if indeed it had not been an accident.

Mrs. Huston appeared in the doorway with the platter of lamb. "No smoking in here! We're about to eat!"

Badeley's eyes rolled to the ceiling but diligently stubbed out his cigarette in an empty teacup, exhaling the last of the ashy smoke from pursed lips. Nancy followed his example, and as the thin white vapors curled toward the ceiling, Marsden's nose wrinkled at the foul smell.

"Those aren't Murattis, are they?" he asked.

Badeley's annoyed grimace exploded into a surprised laugh. "Murattis? Who do you think we are? Greek bloody royalty?"

"We roll our own," said Nancy. "It's much cheaper. I didn't know you smoked."

"I don't, I just.." Marsden held his tongue. Just hours before, he had been accosted by the distinct scent of Simon's favored brand of Turkish cigarettes wafting up from the lapels of his dinner jacket. But he had been overwhelmed at the time with memories of Simon. Healthy, vibrant Simon, alive and smiling around the golden tip of his favorite cigarette.

If they had been interested in his answer, the others quickly forgot he had been speaking as the remainder of their supper arrived. Nancy's hand-rolled cigarettes were hurried off the table as Linton appeared with a platter of sausages and bland steamed cabbage, the supper Mrs. Huston had been intended for the downstairs dining room. Marsden waited until the rest of the staff had helped themselves to their meal before he attempted to direct the conversation. The horrendous attempt at a family dinner was the obvious place to strike hot.

"What is the reason for their dislike of each other?" he asked. "Beatrice and her father."

"I think it's fair to say that Beatrice does not really like anyone," said Nancy.

Marsden thought she might be right. In his short acquaintance with Beatrice, she had spoken ill of every member of her family and shown little respect to the staff.

"You know," he said, "when Beatrice walked into the kitchen this morning, I was sure she was Alice. They're completely identical. How on earth do you tell them apart?"

"They're very different personalities," said Nancy and took an aggressive bite of sausage.

"It was exceptionally confusing when they were children," said Linton. "Lady Scarborough insisted they dress exactly the same. It amused her."

"Have you been with the family that long?" Marsden asked.

Badeley pointed his fork in Linton's direction. "Linton's been here forever. Been with his Lordship since the crucifixion, he has."

"And you, Badeley? How long have you been with the family?"

"Since just before the war. Started as a footman."

"And you were a bore even then, Badeley," said Nancy.

Badeley's smile was sour. "I get paid more now, though, don't I, Nancy?"

They glared at each other across the table, and Marsden felt the need to clear his throat, to force the tension to dissipate.

"And what happened to everyone else?" he asked. "There must have been a much larger staff in the house at one point."

Almost as one, the staff cast their gaze down the empty length of the table at which they huddled on one end.

"Many men who worked on this estate signed up to serve their country," said Mrs. Huston, "just as you did, Marsden."

"And the rest?"

"Most were dismissed when much of the house was shut up during the war," said Nancy. "Master Simon had just died. The earl and countess were in mourning."

"Is that why there are no portraits of the family?"

"Portraits?" Nancy asked.

"I just thought it was unusual to have no family pictures in the house. The only one I've seen is of the Viscount in his bedroom. Were the rest put away when the house was shut up?"

Nancy did not blink. "I wouldn't know. Perhaps the housemaids from that time packed them away, but those girls are long gone."

"So, you were the only ones kept on? They didn't take back any of the old staff?"

"I became cook during the war," said Mrs. Huston, "but the only staff hired since have been the tutors and Holly."

Marsden thought again of the dusty, cold rooms and abandoned east wing. The Falconers were surely in need of a larger contingent of servants. "But it's strange, isn't it? They're content with so few staff in a house this large?"

"Strange," said Badeley, "but true. Still, I've got a job, so I can't complain."

"No," said Linton, glaring at Badeley down the length of his nose. "You can't."

44

Chapter Nine

As he waited for the house to fall into the silence of the night, Marsden made a mental note of the series of strange facts and blatant lies he had heard since his arrival at Maidenstone Hall; the unexpected appearance of Beatrice and her loathing of Simon, Alice's self-harm and her mysterious treatments at the hospital in York; the peculiar dismissal of the household staff during the war. But most confronting was the talk of the war and Simon's death. He tried to guess why the Falconers were so determined to convince him that Simon had been at the Somme when they had not even agreed upon a story about where he had served and died. Simon had been AWOL for three months when the first engagement at the Somme had commenced. The family was lying, and Marsden intended to prove it. There was little doubt in his mind that the evidence was somewhere to be found in Maidenstone Hall. It was, after all, where Simon had written his last letter to Marsden.

He pulled it out of the violin case now, leafing through the bundle of letters until he found the evidence of Simon's arrival at Maidenstone. The paper was heavily creased and thinning, softened by Marsden's clumsy hands.

My dear T, it read: *Have you forgiven me yet? If it's any consolation, life at Maidenstone is beastly. Have not yet discussed an escape plan with the old man as we agreed. How I wish now that I had brought you with me for entertainment.*

If only, thought Marsden, he had been with Simon. None of this charade would have been necessary. But they had not traveled together. Marsden had stayed in Edinburgh for the remainder of their leave, wasting away the money Simon had left with him. He had remained alone, nursing the aching throb of a continuous hangover, righteous in his fury and entirely sure he would see Simon again. But no one ever saw Simon again, apart from the Falconers.

He wished now that he had bid Simon farewell with kind words. He had been so angry after the display Simon had put on with the mistress of their boarding house, flirting and touching, all to make Marsden jealous. It would have been challenging enough if she had been interested in returning Simon's flirtations. But she had not, and that only made things worse.

Marsden gritted his teeth as a fierce itch rubbed the inner walls of his nose, desperate to break free. He brought his elbow against his mouth and allowed the sneeze to erupt against the rough tweed of his jacket. The moisture that nagged at the corners of his eyes again brought forth memories of cigarette smoke, the way it occasionally made his eyes and throat burn when it came in contact with his face. He was sure he could smell it now, seeping from under the gap beneath his bedroom door, filling the small space with the scent of Turkish cigarettes. He wondered how close Badeley's room was to his and if perhaps the chauffeur was awake and smoking within the personal comfort of his bed. But the rich scent that circled his head was not that of the cheap tobacco Nancy and Badeley had been smoking before dinner. It was the aroma of the expensive Turkish cigarettes so favored by Simon. The smell always lingered on every inch of Simon's long body, in his hair, on the tips of his smooth fingers, but especially on the soft corners of his lips.

Marsden crossed his legs and shook his head to shift the memories. He checked his watch. It was just before midnight, and no footsteps had sounded outside his door for some time. Although the entire house was fitted with electric lights, he had found a handful of half-burned candles in the desk drawer and lit one now. Hopeful that the last of his colleagues had gone to bed, he removed his shoes, ready to creep through the sleeping house. When he reached for the switch to turn off this light hanging from the ceiling, the bulb flickered and made a strange buzzing sound. The light flared suddenly, the filament crackling and flashing momentarily before resting. Marsden thought it peculiar, but when the bulb did not spark again, he thought nothing of it and flicked the switch.

The lights in the hallway of the servants' quarters were already dark. Marsden closed the door behind him and crept down the hall. The floor beneath his feet creaked and groaned under his weight, and Marsden winced with every step. His head swiveled repeatedly to check over his shoulder, ensuring he was alone. All about him was silent but for his own heavy tread and hot breath. The doorway to the staircase threatened to reveal him when Marsden opened it, squeaking so loudly that he was sure it would wake one of the staff. He hurriedly closed it behind him and descended toward the second floor, holding the candle before him with a trembling grip. Marsden was halfway down the stairs when the faint sound of glass smashing startled him. He stood hunched in the stairwell, clutching at the candle, holding his breath. The sound resonated again from a floor below him, the distinct high-pitched rattle of glass breaking. Again and again, the crashing tinkle of breaking glass echoed in the dark. When the sound ceased at last, Marsden waited, ears straining, remaining rigidly still with his free hand braced against the cold wall of the stairwell, but the house was suddenly silent. There was no sign of anyone emerging from the staff rooms, but someone was moving about downstairs, Marsden was sure, the hurried scuffle of footfall echoing on the floor below him.

He began to lose his nerve, edging backward, raising himself one step in retreat. A violent chill raced along the length of his spine. The candlelight flickered as if caught by a breeze, making his shadow dance on the close walls. Then, a bracing gust of cold wind swept suddenly up the stairs, lifting the hair on the back of his neck in a sharp prickle. He had reversed another two steps when a woman's scream resonated around him as surely as if she had been in the stairwell beside him. Marsden leaped in fright and dropped the candle. It extinguished immediately, and he cursed under his breath. Hands resting on opposite walls, Marsden fumbled for purchase of his surroundings, stooping to search for the candle. He misjudged the height of the steps and slipped, feet landing awkwardly and forcing him to twist and catch himself before he fell down the stairs. For a desperate moment, Marsden did not know which way was up or down in the dark.

The awful scream came again, louder this time and longer. Marsden abandoned the candle and scrambled up the stairs, half on hands and knees. He came close to slamming the crown of his head into the door at the top of the stairwell as he lumbered about in the black, hands flailing before him for purchase. The screams continued intermittently even as Marsden finally found the door handle and burst into the servants' hallway. The closed doors of the other staff bedrooms did not open, nor did he hear any sign of them rising at the sound of the tortured screeching that continued to resonate from downstairs. No one was running to help.

Frightened and panting, Marsden dragged his hand along the wall until he found the second doorway and let himself into the safety of his room. Even with the door closed, he could hear the woman's tortured shrieking, the piercing cries resounding as though she was on the very edge of death—or perhaps not from this world at all. He pressed his hands tightly over his ears but couldn't block the sound completely.

Finally, the screaming ceased. Marsden leaned against the door, gasping for breath. He was ashamed of his fear, but the horrible cries had made his heart pound in panic, and when he switched on the light, he finally felt his terror begin to ease.

Marsden left the light on when he all but leaped into his bed. The silence continued, and his labored breath was now the only sound in his ears. The house was utterly still.

Marsden checked his watch once more. It was just after midnight.

Chapter Ten

In the musty room of a dilapidated inn, Simon shoved him against the closed door, firm hands dragging Marsden's shirt down his arms. The first kiss they had been able to enjoy in days was indelicate and desperate. The pungent scent of Simon's cologne surrounded them. Marsden sighed into the kiss and melted against Simon's roving hands as they unbuttoned his trousers and slid into the confines of his drawers. *You can't stay angry*, Simon whispered against his ear when Marsden hissed in pleasure. *I know you'll forgive me.*

Marsden woke with a start, jolting under the covers, and was momentarily confused by his surroundings. He surveyed his tiny bedroom in the early light of day and finally remembered where he was. Sprawling back against the bed, he tried to hold onto the dream, but it was already gone, the last lingering sensations of Simon's touch disappearing in the wake of full consciousness. The disappointment, a deep and cavernous drop of his stomach, was devastating.

Marsden grasped at the memory from which the dream had arisen. He and Simon had argued many times while on leave, a culmination of moments where they had fought and came back together in a violent passion. If Marsden had known it would be the last days they'd have together, perhaps he wouldn't have been so quick to be jealous—of Lord and Lady Falconer, for the time they stole with Simon; of the other men in the regiment, for their admiration and fawning desperation to impress Simon; and of the pretty girls who smiled and simpered when Simon paused to wink at them. None of them knew Simon Falconer the way Marsden did. And as for the boarding house mistress, in the light of day, it was easier to remind himself that it had all been a misunderstanding, that he had overreacted to Simon's playful advances, that Simon had only been trying to make him jealous.

Marsden rose and dressed with little care. Few of his clothes fit him properly anyway. He had lost significant weight in the days since the war, his trousers and vests hanging loose, but the cost of new garments had been beyond him. So many times, Marsden had considered selling his cufflinks. The solid gold would fetch him enough to move out of the London boarding house at least, but they were all that he had left of his father. Not to mention that they had become a part of his daily routine, the mundane act of threading them through his shirt sleeves, the comforting distraction they afforded his fingertips when he was agitated or nervous. He refused to linger on their significance any more than this, whether he kept them out of sentimentality or a masochistic, cutting reminder that banished sons inherit nothing.

Marsden at least took the time to ensure his tie was neat but only bothered with a lazy sweep of a comb through his hair. It flopped and bounced before his eyes no matter how he pushed and pulled at the strands, which were perhaps a little overgrown. His beard was overly long, too. Marsden imagined what he had looked like before the war: face smooth and wiry hair cut close to his skull. The boy he remembered himself to be was long gone. He could no more return to his life before the war than he could return to a cold and empty existence in London now that the country was again at peace. Not without Simon. Without Simon, he had nothing and no one.

He checked his watch and realized he had five minutes to go downstairs to the conservatory by eight o'clock. Retrieving the violin case from beneath his bed, Marsden opened its stiff latches and removed the violin to reveal the hidden compartment. Sleep had eluded him after his failed attempt to search the house. The terrible screaming had not continued, but Marsden left the light on all night, staying awake for hours in his cold room, reading and rereading his letters from Simon. When he had finally succumbed to fitful dreams, he left them on the desk, close at hand to his bedside. Now, Marsden allowed himself a moment of melancholy, briefly tracing the delicate features of Simon's face in a photograph before returning them to their hiding place. He knew better than to leave them lying around in his room where anyone might find them should they come snooping.

Marsden replaced the violin and closed the case. Checking his appearance one more time in the mirror, he tried to tame his hair with a last sweep of his hand and then went downstairs, taking the violin with him.

The conservatory was brutally cold when Marsden entered. Alice was waiting for him, curled on the chaise lounge with a green blanket wrapped around her legs. She was wearing a long-sleeved, pale blue dress, and in the white light of the conservatory, Marsden could clearly see the frayed edges of her sleeves. Her amber hair was arranged high and neat upon her head. A book rested against her bent knees, and she almost dropped it when he cleared his throat to announce his presence. Alice's eyes lit up when she met his gaze, a gentle blush lifting her cheeks.

The edge of a smile colored her voice when she asked, "We can play today?"

Marsden placed the violin on the table and sat opposite her, vigorously rubbing his hands. "Later, I think, when we're a little warmer. What are you reading?"

"*Jane Eyre.* Have you read it?"

"A long time ago. What do you think of it?"

"I don't particularly like Jane very much. And I feel sorry for Mr. Rochester's wife. But I've read it a dozen times all the same."

"I can see you like to read."

Marsden nodded toward a tall stack of books piled on an end table beside her. The collection wasn't entirely what Marsden would have expected a young woman of high breeding to enjoy; *The Canterville Ghost, At the End of the Passage, The Turn of the Screw.* He wondered if they had first belonged to Simon. He had loved ghost stories. They were not to Marsden's taste at all. One volume sat alone beside a half-empty cup of tea on the end table. Marsden picked up Robert Dale Owen's *Footfalls on the Boundary of Another World* and flipped through the pages.

"Are these books all yours?" he asked. Ghost stories were one thing. Spiritualist drivel from America was another thing entirely, and he was surprised that the Falconers allowed their daughter to indulge in such sensationalist writing.

"There's little else for me to enjoy around here," said Alice.

"At least you go away often. How was York?"

A fine crease folded between her eyebrows. "York?"

"Your father mentioned that you receive treatment in York every other day."

"I prefer not to talk about that." Alice placed *Jane Eyre* beyond her feet. "I heard about last night."

"Do you mean the screaming?"

Her spine stiffened. "I was talking about dinner."

"Oh, I see. I suppose Beatrice told you it was not a particularly happy event?"

Alice's laugh was mirthless. "I gather that Beatrice thoroughly enjoyed the evening."

"I get the impression," said Marsden, recalling the slap of Beatrice's shoes against his shins under the table, "that your sister quite enjoys causing trouble."

When Alice's shoulders reflexively curled, her whole body shrinking before him, Marsden thought he had been too bold in his criticism, but she held his eye when she spoke:

"Beatrice is an expert in trouble. She excels in it."

"Is that why I haven't been employed as her tutor also? Would she disturb our lessons?"

"Beatrice has no interest in learning," Alice assured him. "She wants to ride her horse, bully the staff, and terrorize our parents. She wants to escape and never come back."

"Will she?"

"Will she what?"

Marsden opened his hands before her as though the answer could be found between them. "Escape?"

Alice hesitated, fiddling with the frayed sleeve of her dress. "Not on her horse, she won't. It was taken away this morning. Can we play some music now, please?" She didn't wait for him to answer, standing and collecting his violin from the table. "We'll go to the library. I keep my violin there."

Marsden forced down a surge of panic when she collected up his case and stormed toward the library. He imagined it falling open, the violin and the rest of the contents tumbling out, and the staccato beat of his heart became violently loud in his ears. Marsden hurried after her, hands itching to reach out and snatch back the violin, and could only relax when she placed the case on the piano. He closed the rear door of the library behind him while Alice fetched her violin from a bare shelf.

"I like Vivaldi," she said, offering him a sheet music booklet.

Marsden leafed through the pages but could barely see their contents in the dim lighting of the library. The fire raged, and a pair of ornate lamps by each doorway offered a weak orange glow, but his eyes strained to read.

"There's nowhere near enough light in here," he said. "I'm going to open the curtains."

"No," said Alice, taking a jolting step toward him. "Mother likes to keep them shut."

Marsden didn't hear the panic in her voice and strode undeterred toward the windows. "We can close them again when we're done playing."

He flung the velvet curtains apart with such force that a thick layer of dust exploded into the air around his face, making him cough. Marsden pushed each panel separately to the very edge of the window, allowing the light to flood into the library. Despite the grey morning, the air was clear, and he could see for miles over the estate from the Hall's position atop the hill. The black water of the lake winked at him as the drab clouds parted briefly enough for shards of sunlight to bounce upon its opaque surface.

"Why does your mother like to keep the curtains shut?" Marsden asked. "There's a terrific view of the lake from here. It must be beautiful in the summer."

When he turned to face her, Alice had retreated into the shadows, the toes of her slippers just behind the corridor of light streaming through the curtains. Her grip on the neck of her violin was so fierce that Marsden thought it might break between her fingers.

"It's so much colder when they're open," she said.

Marsden returned his attention to the sheet music, leafing through the pages. "Come along. Let's start with the D Major. *Largo.*"

Alice kept her gaze fixed on the floor as she pulled a music stand away from a corner nook of shelving and placed it at an angle that allowed her to keep her back to the windows. Marsden set out the sheet music for her, and she took a few moments to prepare, rotating the fine tuners. Alice placed the rest under her chin and glanced up at Marsden, looking for instruction. He nodded, and she began to play. Her eyes remained focused on the music, brows furrowed in concentration as she wielded the bow back and forward across the strings in smooth, measured strokes. He let her play through the short movement but stopped her with a raised hand before she could move on to the next.

"Your bowing is atrocious," he said. "It's in three-four. You can't just rake the bow back and forth."

Alice stared at her feet, a soft blush rising on her cheeks. "It's been a long time since I've had a lesson."

Marsden opened his violin case and fished out a pencil. He began drawing open boxes above the notes on the sheet music, humming to himself. "Wherever I've put this symbol," he said, still drawing, "that's where you down-bow. Understand?"

Alice gave him a look of muted frustration, brows pinching, but began to play again, occasionally hesitating to rearrange the bow and follow his penciled directions.

"You're not used to being corrected, are you?" he asked as she continued to play. He didn't mean to be cruel, but he could see the streak of contempt in her face at being forced to study rather than simply play for enjoyment. "Who did you learn with?"

"Martin Baranski," she answered, jaw tight. "He was Polish. He'd catch the train from York every Saturday to teach us."

"You and Beatrice?"

"Simon and me." Alice finished the moment again and looked up at Marsden expectantly.

"Better," he admitted. "Was Simon as good as you?"

"No, but he loved the lessons. He was very attached to Martin. Shall I play something else?"

At the mention of Simon's relationship with the former violin teacher, Marsden's imagination ran wild, and a wave of jealousy gnawed at the back of his throat, forcing him to cough. "No, the same again. Let's perfect the bowing. I'll play with you."

Marsden retrieved his violin and quickly tuned the instrument. He could sense her impatience, the soft tap of one slipper nagging against the floor, but Alice lifted her violin again in preparation. Marsden could, at last, see something of Beatrice's temperament in Alice's expression. She held herself in a manner completely different from her sister—rigid, spine straight, displaying nothing of Beatrice's free spirit—but now he recognized that the girls shared the same scowl. Her determined expression of impatience remained as she worked through the movement again, with Marsden playing alongside her.

Before Marsden and Alice could finish the movement for the third time, an angry yell resonated from outside the room. Alice's bow faltered mid-stroke, her narrow chin lifting from the violin. Lord Scarborough's muffled shouts could still be heard even though the rear door of the library was closed. Alice let her bow drop to hang loosely between her fingers, the horse hair bouncing against the skirt of her dress.

Alice and Marsden stared at the library door as the earl lost his temper in ever-rising tones. Finally, the door swung open. Lord Scarborough stormed into the library with a stack of papers clenched in his fist, the sheets saturated with black ink.

The earl glared at Alice, the handful of papers held high for her to see. Alice's white face remained passive as she stared back. Eventually, Alice turned her back on her father and lifted the violin to her chin. She started to play again, and Lord Scarborough threw the ruined papers in the air. He was shaking, angry beyond expression, and said nothing when he stalked back into the hallway, the floorboards shaking under his thunderous footfall. Marsden stood, mesmerized by the flurry of paper as it floated momentarily and then scattered across the floor. Alice played on with steely eyes.

When she had completed the movement again, Alice lowered the violin and placed the bow on the stand before her. "Can we do something else now, please?"

Marsden pointed at the papers. "What was all that about?"

Alice gave a sharp shake of her head and packed away the violin. "Perhaps we can discuss *Jane Eyre* now? We may as well go back to the conservatory and do some reading. It's almost time for tea." When Marsden put his violin away in its case and collected it off the piano, Alice stopped him with a gentle hand on his elbow. "You can leave that here, you know."

A wave of warmth surged under his jacket where she touched him, and Marsden quickly drew away to bundle the case under his arm. "Thank you, but I prefer to keep my instrument with me."

Alice strode to the rear door of the library, stepping right on top of Lord Scarborough's ruined papers. His case in hand, Marsden followed her, pausing to peek at the documents. At the top of one half-blackened page, he read "Bill of Sale." Following Alice into the hallway, Marsden saw that the door to Lord Scarborough's study was wide open. She continued toward the conservatory, but Marsden poked his head into the study and was shocked by the chaos he found there; papers were strewn across the floor, the chairs upturned, and black ink spilled across the surface of the earl's desk. The mirror, so carefully placed to present the earl's reflection at all times, was not simply broken but smashed to pieces; the glass littered across the wood floor.

The heavy footsteps of someone running on the floor above him forced Marsden's chin up, staring at the ceiling. A door slammed, and Lord Scarborough's outraged tones could be heard again. Marsden couldn't make out what was being said, but the earl's rant continued overhead. There was no response, but Marsden was sure he could safely guess the recipient of Lord Scarborough's ire. Beatrice.

Chapter Eleven

"Did anyone else hear the screaming last night?" Marsden asked when Mrs. Huston placed a bowl of soup before him. The small core of servants was seated for lunch; Marsden was framed by Badeley and Linton, with Nancy sitting directly across from him.

"I didn't hear anything," said Nancy, keeping her eyes on her meal.

"Me neither," said Badeley.

Linton said, "Perhaps you had a nightmare."

Marsden shook his head. "No, I was definitely awake. No one else heard it?"

"Well," said Badeley, "I certainly heard Lord Scarborough's explosion this morning, that's for sure!" Linton cleared his throat, and Badeley dropped his spoon, raising both hands in surrender. "We all heard it, Linton! He wasn't exactly quiet about it."

"He stormed into my lesson with Lady Alice and threw a stack of papers onto the floor. I saw the state of his study."

"That was—" Linton paused, his head tilting like a watchful bird. "It was certainly unfortunate."

"Was it Beatrice who did the damage, do you think?" Marsden asked.

Mrs. Huston sat down next to Nancy. "Why would you think that?"

"I heard Lord Scarborough storm upstairs to accost someone, and I assumed it was Beatrice. I haven't seen her today, so I wondered if she'd been banished to her room or something like that."

"Well, it certainly wasn't Alice," said Mrs. Huston. "She would never cause such a mess."

Nancy's lips curled into a pouting scowl. "And wasn't it a pretty mess for me to clean up?"

"Do you have any complaints about your station, Nancy?" Linton asked, the bite of a warning clear in his question.

Nancy kept her eyes lowered. "I certainly preferred my station when we had housemaids on the premises for more than a few hours a day. Mind you, if His Lordship is going to sell the house, I might not have to worry about my position for much longer, will I? What's to say they'd keep any of us on?"

Mrs. Huston clutched at Nancy's sleeve. "You don't think His Lordship will go through with it, do you?"

"And why wouldn't he? He sold off the rest of the estate. His son is dead, and the title with him. I'm sure Lady Scarborough will be pleased to settle in London."

"Why is the title dead?" Marsden asked. "Does Lord Scarborough have no other family to inherit the title?"

"None. It will dissolve upon his death."

"But Alice and Beatrice will inherit the estate regardless, will they not?"

"I'm not sure how much there will be left to inherit." Nancy dabbed a napkin at the corner of her mouth but failed to hide her sneer. "And how were your lessons with Lady Alice this morning?"

"She seems to be a very accomplished young lady," said Marsden. "Truly, I'm surprised she still requires a tutor at her age. I gather that His Lordship was against hiring another."

"Alice still enjoys having lessons," said Mrs. Huston. "It can be a lonely life out here in the countryside. Her Ladyship understands that."

"So it was Alice I heard screaming last night?"

"I still suggest it was a nightmare, Mr. Fisher," said Linton. "Or perhaps just the house creaking in the night."

Marsden scoffed. "The house creaking?"

"Never underestimate the stories a house this age could tell you, Mr. Fisher."

Mrs. Huston shuddered. "Oh, don't, Mr. Linton. You know I can't bear talk like that. I can barely sleep some nights as it is."

"Mrs. H thinks the house is haunted," said Badeley with a smirk.

"It's alright, Mrs. Huston. I know exactly what you mean," said Marsden, recalling the terrible screaming and his dream of Simon. "I can't sleep either."

Marsden spent much of the afternoon's French lesson with Alice, watching the way her delicate fingers plucked at the pages of Dumas' *Les Mille et Un Fantômes.* Although she stammered on the odd word, her pronunciation was excellent, and again, Marsden wondered why she was so desperate for a tutor. He suspected the long line of women who had come before him were supposed to have been companions to a lonely young woman rather than legitimate teachers. Marsden wasn't sure if this was the role he was supposed to fill, but at least the pretense of Alice needing a tutor had given him access to the house. His heart had virtually leaped out of his mouth when he saw the advertisement for a position at Maidenstone Hall. He didn't usually believe in fate or even God, but on that particular occasion, sitting at the breakfast table of his boarding house with the newspaper in hand, he was willing to wonder at some sort of divine intervention in bringing him to Simon's family home.

As Alice turned a page, her sleeve rode up just enough for Marsden to see the thick scar raised from the white skin of her wrist. The sight of such a vicious wound made his stomach twist in sympathy, and his fingers itched to touch his own deep scar. Two years later, the memory of the bayonet meeting his cheek was still agonizingly fresh. He knew full well the savage agony of flesh knitting itself back together. He was still staring when he realized she was speaking to him, her green eyes wide as she waited for a response.

"I beg your pardon?" he said.

"I said, do you think much about the war?"

Marsden felt wholly exposed, as though she had reached inside his brain and picked out the thoughts at the forefront of his mind. "What makes you ask?"

"When my brother came home on leave, he often had that same expression you're wearing now. Like he was a million miles away."

Marsden's breath caught at the sudden admission. He jumped at the information. "Your brother came home during the war?"

Alice chewed on her lower lip. "For just a few days. He was on leave."

"Did he talk much about the war?"

"Mostly, he complained about it. But sometimes, I thought he might have liked it, in some sense, the way he bragged about how brave he was for serving. Did you?"

"Like it? No. Absolutely not."

Alice stared him directly in the eye, her face tilting to catch a lie in his eyes. "But?"

"But what?"

"I suppose you made some friends, at least."

Marsden thought of Simon in the trenches with him in Verdun, of an unexploded mortar shell landing by his feet and Simon appearing out of nowhere, lifting him and seemingly carrying him through the air away from the radius of the blast. When he opened his eyes, the dust settling around them, it was to see Simon Falconer grinning at him in victory. The moment had solidified their bond: made a god of Simon to Marsden. It was far more than friendship forged between them.

"Yes," he said at last. "Yes, I did."

Alice's expression hardened. "I envy you. I don't have any friends. Not anymore."

"I gather you and your sister are not friends?"

"We were friends a long time ago when we were children. Now we can't even be in the same room together." She stared wistfully down at the cover of her book, the thin skin of her hands drawn tight across her knuckles. "I think that I've had enough for the day."

"As you wish." Marsden prepared to leave. "Until tomorrow, my lady."

"No. I won't be here tomorrow."

"Ah, of course. You'll be in York?"

She did not respond and turned away, quietly staring into space when

CHAPTER ELEVEN

Marsden left her alone in the conservatory.

Chapter Twelve

Marsden guessed that it was just before midnight when the lightbulb above his bed began to crackle and was amused to discover her was correct when he checked his watch. Annoyed by the flashing buzz of the filament, he quickly lit a candle and turned off the light switch before the flaring bulb could truly irritate his eyes. He put on his dressing gown and socks, ready to creep out into the hallway. He had waited patiently for the last hour for the final sounds of the other staff settling into their rooms for the night and was now ready to recommence his search of the house.

This time, no screams disturbed him as he descended the staircase to the west wing unhindered. In the darkness, Marsden crept slowly, counting the doors, looking for the tulip painting hanging across from Simon's rooms. When he found it, he pressed his ear against the door and found only silence. He snuck into the room with only the light of the candle illuminating the space before him.

Marsden closed the door and turned first to the dresser. When he opened the top drawer, the shining surface of a silver cigarette case immediately caught his eye. Marsden recognized the case at once and snatched it up. His racing heart calmed when he slid it into his dressing gown pocket as if it was a tonic to his fear of being caught in Simon's rooms uninvited.

He investigated the rest of the dresser, opening and closing each drawer. They were littered with various, sundry items: hair combs, handkerchiefs, and a collection of expensive cufflinks. Nothing truly caught Marsden's attention until he found a package tucked into the back corner of the bottom drawer. He snatched at it, almost tearing the fine paper wrapping when he pulled it away to reveal a collection of photographs. Sitting on the bed, he sifted through the pictures, stiff, formal portraits of the Falconer family; Lord and Lady Scarborough, standing side by side, but not touching; Alice and Beatrice as children, no older than ten years, seated together in matching white pinafores. Even as children, he could not distinguish one from the other. They sat like porcelain dolls, identical in every way.

Marsden felt vindicated. He had guessed there must be family portraits hidden somewhere in the house, but now that he had found them, he couldn't imagine why such a prominent family had not displayed them proudly throughout the house. He didn't believe Nancy's suggestion that they had been packed away by housemaids and forgotten, not when they had been so deliberately concealed in Simon's bedroom.

Very few of the portraits were recent, at least to Marsden's eyes. There were no portraits of the twins as teenagers. Then, Marsden came across another picture of Simon. Like the others, it was a formal studio portrait of the young viscount in his army uniform. Simon's chin was lifted, a stiff sense of pride exuding from his broad stance. The picture left Marsden feeling cold, knowing as he did how Simon would later come to resent the uniform. He returned the photograph and re-wrapped the package before returning it to its hiding place inside the dresser.

The rest of Simon's bedroom was pristine but soulless, with no sign of a recent visit by its past occupant—except for the cigarette case. Simon had definitely brought it with him when he visited on leave. Marsden performed a last perfunctory sweep of the bedroom and dressing room—rummaging through the cupboards and checking under the bed—but there was no other sign of Simon's presence. The cigarette case was the only clue. He couldn't help but be disappointed. Marsden had been sure he would find more, perhaps Simon's uniform or other belongings he had brought home to Maidenstone, but nothing was helpful.

Marsden had placed his hand on the doorknob, ready to leave, when a creak sounded outside the bedroom door. He blew out the candle and held his breath, waiting for someone to enter the bedroom, but there was only silence in the long seconds that followed. Marsden cursed himself for being so nervous. Then he cursed again for having blown out the candle. The memory of becoming lost in the dark confines of the stairwell the night before returned to the forefront of his mind, and his stomach turned with the niggling return of panic.

Blind in the dark, Marsden fumbled for the door handle and let himself out of the room. He felt his way through the darkness to the main landing, where at least the faint light of the half-hidden moon shining through the windows above the main staircase illuminated the area enough that he could find the door to the servants' stairway. Marsden took his time, creeping up the stairs and dragging a hand along the servants' quarters hallway wall to feel for his bedroom door. He slipped inside and fumbled for the light switch.

In the safety of his room, Marsden drew out the cigarette case and opened it. There were four gold-tipped cigarettes inside. He held up the case to the light to read the inscription.

You know you've got the brand of kisses that I'd die for.
Always yours, T.

Marsden snapped the case shut and held the cold silver against his forehead. It soothed the sudden flush of heat that had raced along his spine and into his face. He had found the case in a pawn shop near their boarding house in Edinburgh, and the purchase had cost him a small fortune. Simon had barely seemed touched by the gift when Marsden had presented it to him, smiling as though the gesture wasn't worth the effort, and yet, Simon took the cigarette case with him when he traveled to England only days later. *Just a few compulsory days with the family, old chap,* Simon had promised before they parted ways. *With any luck, my father can get us out of the bloody mess.* When they parted, hidden away in the confines of their room at the Edinburgh boarding house, Simon had kissed Marsden briefly, abruptly. Marsden wanted to clutch at him, to hold his lover closer, just a little longer, but he was still so angry. So jealous. When Marsden did not return the kiss,

Simon only smirked and patted his cheek a little too hard. *I'll be good,* he said. *I promise.*

Marsden fumbled under the bed for his violin case, dragging it onto the mattress. He removed the violin and hid the cigarette case in the false bottom. Marsden could finally breathe easily when he slid the case back under the bed and found that he was suddenly and completely exhausted. Eyes drooping, he didn't even bother to undress again before climbing into bed. The adrenaline that had flooded his veins while searching Simon's room faded, but the thrill of finding the cigarette case still ignited a flame in his rib cage. Marsden tried remembering the last time his heart had thudded so hard in his chest. Not since the war. Not since the last time he had held Simon and cared about anything at all.

Chapter Thirteen

Marsden woke late. When he finally made his way down to the service hall, he discovered Mrs. Huston alone in the kitchen, scrubbing at a large saucepan in the sink.

"You're too late for porridge," she said without looking up from her task, "but there's plenty of toast and boiled eggs left over."

Marsden thanked her and set about heating the kettle to make tea. Badeley appeared in the doorway just as the water began to boil. He was dressed to go out, coat and hat already donned, gloves in hand.

"I wish I could sleep as late as you do, Marsden," he said. "We're about to leave for church. You coming along?"

"Is everyone going?" Marsden asked.

He desperately hoped that he would not be required to attend the service. He was tired after his late-night adventures and liked the prospect of being left alone in the house. It would be an excellent opportunity to search the corners of the house he had yet to access without being disturbed.

"The earl and countess don't care whether or not we go with them. Linton and Mrs. Huston usually go like clockwork. Nancy goes if she doesn't have too much work to do."

"And you?

"I go sometimes. Some of the girls in the village are distracting enough to get me through the service."

"I won't go then if you don't mind," said Marsden. "I'd rather rest a little if I'm not going to be needed."

Badeley scoffed. "You won't be needed. Lady Alice is not in residence today. I'll find you later, and we can have a drink."

Badeley retreated, and Marsden wondered at the strange way the chauffeur had over-articulated the words *in residence.* Mrs. Huston took off her apron and bade him a good morning, setting off to worship with the rest of the household. Marsden sat down at the kitchen table to enjoy his breakfast in peace, relishing the temporary quiet.

The brief spell of tranquility evaporated when Beatrice stomped into the kitchen, heels slapping against the slate floor. At least, he assumed it was Beatrice. Her hair hung loose over her shoulders, and she held a heavy red coat in one arm. Her grin when Marsden hoisted himself to his feet was feral.

"Fish!" she said. "I was hoping to find you."

"Can I help you, my lady?" he asked, even though he feared her answer. He did not want to be of help to her at all today.

"I'm going to walk down into the village. Will you accompany me?" She held up a hand before he could answer. "Don't say no. I will not take no for an answer today."

Even as his heart sank, something about Beatrice's giddy smile made the corner of Marsden's mouth twitch. The right-hand corner of her lips lifted slightly higher, just as Simon's had done when he grinned. Beatrice was in a good mood, and he reasoned that a long walk would allow them to speak again without her mother and father present. Beatrice was a woman who spoke her mind, and she did not hold back on the topic of Simon.

"Of course, my lady," he said.

"Good man," said Beatrice, beaming at him. "Have you finished your breakfast? Good. Get your coat."

Marsden abandoned the last of his meal and hurried to fetch his coat. Beatrice met him at the servants' entrance, and as he passed her to open the door, the same intense scent of the perfume he'd detected on their first meeting filled the air around her.

"my lady," he said as he dragged on his coat, fumbling with the buttons in his haste, "your perfume. Do you mind me asking after the scent?"

Beatrice's giggle was wicked as she turned to look at him over her shoulder.

"Have you been smelling me, Fish?" She snickered when he attempted a denial and said, "It's Lily of the Valley. Do you like it?"

She didn't wait for his answer but danced ahead into the brisk morning air. They circled the west wing and walked together down the length of the drive.

"Isn't this wonderful?" said Beatrice. "I love spring days like this."

It was indeed a beautiful morning. The air was bitterly cold, but the sun was already shining. A bank of grey clouds loomed in the far distance, but for now, at least, the weather was fine. Marsden turned his face toward the sunlight and noticed the way it made Beatrice's hair glitter.

"It certainly is nice to be out in pleasant weather," he agreed.

"Much better to be out in nature than stuck in a stuffy church, don't you think?"

"I don't have anything against church, my lady."

She laughed at him, white teeth exposed and glinting. She reminded him of a hyena he had once seen at the London Zoo, smiling but dangerous.

"How very diplomatic of you, Fish. We'll go that way." She pointed to a rough path that led away from the main road that would take them into the village. Instead, her choice of rugged path would lead them alongside the forest.

"I thought you wanted to go into the village, my lady?"

Beatrice laughed again. "Don't worry, Fish, your virtue is safe with me. We'll only be alone a short while. I want to visit some friends before we go into the village."

The forest to the north of the estate was beautiful—thick with old growth and fragrant with the scent of Scots pine—and Marsden enjoyed the calm of the nature around him, even as Beatrice chatted away. Marsden wondered how often she had someone to talk to. Beatrice spoke energetically about the changing season, the wildflowers bursting forth in the forest in the last days of spring. A trilling bird song chimed in the distance, and she delighted in recognizing the call as that of a nightingale. Her enthusiasm for the allure of the natural world was infectious, and Marsden, too, began to look more closely at the landscape, admiring the grand height of the oak and sycamore trees.

"Do you walk daily, my lady?" he asked when she took a breath.

"That's not possible," she said and bent at the waist to pluck a long blade of grass and twist it around her fingers. "But I do like to get out when I can. The land is so beautiful here."

"It's a pity your father has sold so much of the estate. I gather he didn't see the need to maintain the land when your brother died."

"My father likes to put painful things out of sight. Including me."

"Is that why you like to avoid everyone?" he asked. When Beatrice pulled a face, scrunching her nose, he explained, "I didn't see you at all yesterday. Were you outdoors?"

Beatrice did not try to conceal her delighted smirk. "Did you miss me, Fish?"

Marsden resisted the urge to deny her, although he feared encouraging her flirting.

"I just thought there must be a lot of hiding places in a big house like Maidenstone. Dark corners where you might not be easily found if you did not wish to be." Dark corners in which Simon could have hidden if he did not wish to return to duty. Shadows in which he could be hiding even now.

"Not so many as you'd think," said Beatrice. "I assure you, I was floating around somewhere."

"And your sister," he said, coaxing. "Is she floating around somewhere today?"

Beatrice came to an abrupt halt. Marsden's knees ached as he stopped just ahead of her, jolting at the sudden break in movement.

"What is that supposed to mean?" she asked, her tone dark and eyes narrowing.

"I was just wondering what kind of treatment she could receive every other day. Does she really go to York?"

It was a point that had made no sense to Marsden upon learning of Alice's regular disappearances. He knew very little of medicine, but he imagined several possible treatments that could be administered at such a distinct interval. Injections, he had pondered, or perhaps electric shock treatment.

Or maybe, she was not receiving treatment at all but meeting someone.

"Goodness," said Beatrice, "how on earth would I know? I'm not Alice's keeper."

Marsden shrugged. "It just seems odd—"

"Let's not talk about Alice anymore, Fish. You'll ruin my mood."

Beatrice stormed on ahead, and Marsden hurried after her. They veered off the path, following a low stone wall bordering farmland.

"Your friends live here?" he asked, surprised. A dilapidated cottage stood just beyond the wall. Two men were crouched on one side of the roof, repairing the tiles.

"The roof's coming along, then?" Beatrice shouted when they were close enough.

Startled, one man lost his footing and slid a few feet down the new tiles. Both men stared down at Beatrice with matching expressions of wary surprise. They had the same prominent nose protruding from their ruddy faces. One was much older, and Marsden guessed they were father and son.

"Lady Alice," said the elder of the two men, "we weren't expecting you."

Beatrice lifted one hand above her head and waved merrily, unconcerned that she had been mistaken for Alice. The older man hurried to the ladder propped against the side of the house while keeping one eye fixed on Beatrice.

"This is my friend, Marsden Fisher," said Beatrice when he joined them. "Marsden, this is Mr. Carlisle."

Carlisle wiped a dirty hand against his trousers before offering it to Marsden. "Any friend of Lady Alice is welcome, sir. For what do we owe this pleasure, my lady?"

Marsden wondered why she didn't correct him and even considered doing so himself, but Beatrice silenced him with a hand on his forearm.

"I was hoping your wife has made some of her delicious scones this morning, Carlisle. Could we come in for a visit?"

Carlisle's face and neck flushed red; his hesitation was painfully awkward. He shuffled his feet and stared back at the front door with a twitch, lifting his left cheek. If Beatrice noticed his discomfort, she didn't let on, continuing to shine her brilliant smile upon him. At last, Carlisle nodded and ushered them into the house.

Mrs. Carlisle was in the kitchen when they entered. Her hair was streaked with rough patches of grey, but she was at least ten years younger than her husband. Portly and pink, she was the ideal farmer's wife.

"Lady Alice," she said and bobbed into an awkward curtsy. "How nice to see you."

Beatrice gave her a knowing grin. "Is little Grace here, Mrs. Carlisle? I thought it might be nice for Marsden to meet her."

Mrs. Carlisle nodded her head at Marsden. "Good morning, sir. Grace is in the garden with Lucy, my lady."

Beatrice clapped her hands together. "Wonderful. Come on, Fish."

Marsden tried to follow her but almost walked straight into her back when Beatrice stopped and turned to say, "Oh, and if you have any scones, Mrs. Carlisle?"

"I'm sorry, my lady," said Mrs. Carlisle, stammering, "not this morning. But I made some apple cake yesterday if you'd like to try some?"

"Oh, lovely! I'm sure Marsden would love some, too."

Beatrice opened the door and ran into the garden, leaving Marsden behind. He shared an embarrassed smile with Mrs. Carlisle, hoping to convey every possible apology for their intrusion. The fuchsia in the older woman's cheeks only deepened before she turned quickly away, and Marsden followed Beatrice outside.

The Carlisle's garden was simple but pretty: a large patch of lawn edged by neat hedges of lavender. A clothesline took up a small portion of the grassed area, but the rest was wide open for a little girl's play, sitting upon a large red tartan blanket with another woman who matched Mrs. Carlisle in looks. Her daughter, Marsden guessed.

"Lucy!" said Beatrice when she rushed over to the blanket. "We've come to visit!"

Unlike her parents, Lucy did not scramble to fawn over Beatrice—instead, she scowled openly, her mouth twisting downward in clear disgust. Lucy smoothed back her dark hair but did not attempt to stand.

71

"my lady," said Lucy, "we weren't expecting you today."

"So I've been told." Beatrice knelt upon the blanket next to the little girl, stroking the child's short blonde curls. "Hello, my darling. Did you miss me, Grace?"

Grace was a petite toddler, her wide green eyes staring at Beatrice with calm recognition. She held up the wooden toy in her hand toward Beatrice. "My duck," she said.

Beatrice patted Grace's rosy cheek. "Yes, darling. Aren't you clever?"

Marsden stood back, astonished by this new incarnation of Beatrice. The child had an incredibly calming effect on her. Although she wore her usual savage grin, it was the first time he had seen Beatrice smile in genuine joy, her normal pulsing energy subdued almost to the point of serenity.

She raised her free hand to shield her eyes from the sun and shared that smile with Marsden. "Say hello to Grace, won't you, Fish? Gracie, this is my friend Marsden."

As he knelt before her, his hands resting on one knee, Marsden marveled at the clarity of her green eyes. Everything about her—delicate eyebrows, rosebud mouth, and high cheekbones—were astoundingly familiar. His stomach tightened uncomfortably. The little girl reminded him of Simon so much that he found himself staring unabashedly at her long, pretty face. Time froze about him, and Marsden held his breath.

Grace considered him with equal fascination, reaching toward Marsden's face.

"She likes your beard," said Lucy. "She's always trying to get her hands on the face of any man with a beard when we go into the village."

Grace smacked a hand against Marsden's cheek. She giggled and stroked his beard with clumsy fingers. When she brushed against his scar, he tensed and fought the urge to push her hand away. Grace was at once small and fragile but also incredibly intimidating.

"Hello, Grace," he said at last. "What big eyes you have."

Beatrice laughed, and Grace, now at an age when children laugh just because an adult does, joined in giggling. She leaned into Beatrice's arms, eager to be held. Over the girl's head, Beatrice gave Marsden a mysterious smile. Lucy sat back on her heels, her brow tight. One hand hovered just above her lap as if waiting to catch Grace should the need arise—or perhaps to snatch her back.

Mrs. Carlisle appeared with a heavy tray, a cracked teapot, and a set of stacked blue cups rattling as she tottered across the uneven grass.

"How wonderful," said Beatrice when Mrs. Carlisle placed the tray on the blanket. "A picnic. You love picnics, don't you, Gracie?"

Grace was already reaching for the cake, and Lucy smacked her hand with a warning look demanding patience. Marsden saw the fire in Beatrice's eyes as she took up the girl's hand, bringing the little fingers to her lips for a healing kiss.

"Grace and I will share a piece of cake," Beatrice said and helped herself to a slice.

When Lucy turned an exasperated expression of dismay toward her mother, Marsden considered the young woman's dark hair, eyes, and complexion and compared her features to Grace's fair curls and pale skin. Grace was an anomaly, alien to the Carlisle family. There was also no ring on Lucy's hand.

"Do you live here with your parents, Miss Carlisle?" he asked, still openly examining Grace, judging the familiar color of her eyes.

"Yes, sir," she said. "My brother and his wife live in the village, but I still live at the farm."

"So Grace is not your daughter?"

The line of Lucy's lips elongated across her face, and she spoke through gritted teeth as she admitted, "Grace is adopted."

"How old is she? Three?"

"Two."

Marsden inhaled, an intake of breath ready to interrogate Lucy further, but Mrs. Carlisle interceded, hoisting a teacup in front of his face before he could speak.

"I haven't seen you in town, sir," said Mrs. Carlisle, virtually breathless in her haste to change the topic of conversation. "Are you just visiting the hall?"

"I just took a position at Maidenstone Hall. I've been hired..." Marsden's words died. He had meant to say he had been employed as tutor to Alice, but as far as he could tell, Beatrice was happy to let the Carlisle's believe she was Alice. Fearful of ruining the game and bearing her subsequent anger, Marsden didn't dare give Beatrice away.

"He's the new tutor," Beatrice answered for him. "Mummy's still obsessed with me learning French, you know."

"Really?" said Lucy. "I thought perhaps you were courting."

A hot blush of embarrassment swept Marsden's cheeks, but Beatrice only cackled.

"Come now, Lucy, courting would hardly be appropriate. I haven't even been presented at court." She leaned toward Marsden and said conspiratorially, "The Carlisles are as bad as my parents, always hoping that I'll get married and move away and have a dozen babies."

One soft curve of her cupid box lips curled upward, revealing a hint of her teeth, and Marsden recognized the darkness in her joke. Lucy, too, noticed the shift in Beatrice's tone and shuffled closer to Grace. As if in retaliation, Beatrice urged Grace to sit on her lap and fed a piece of cake into the little girl's mouth.

Pain blossomed in Marsden's jaw, and he realized his teeth were grinding together, matching the ticking rhythm of a nagging suspicion rising and pulsing behind his eyes. Side by side, Grace and Beatrice sitting together, the possibility of a family resemblance became all the more apparent. Marsden was confident he could guess where Grace had come from. If she was a little more than two years old, she could have been conceived the spring that Simon had visited Maidenstone Hall on leave. She could easily be Simon's daughter. Watching Beatrice fawn over Grace, playing the doting aunt, the thought—the very idea of such a betrayal—made Marsden want to vomit. He clamped a hand over his mouth and then forced a fake cough to excuse the jolting movement of his arm.

A dark veil of clouds passed over the farm, the cottage garden losing sunlight and the picnic overshadowed by encroaching darkness. None of the women noticed Marsden's discomfort as they stared at the grey sky all at once.

"I think it might rain," said Mrs. Carlisle.

Lucy immediately began to collect the tea cups and plates. "We should take Grace inside. I suppose you'll be wanting to walk back before you get caught in the rain, my lady?"

Marsden worried that Beatrice would make a fuss, but instead, she nodded and kissed Grace on the head.

"We don't want to get wet, do we sweetheart?" She relinquished her hold on Grace and accepted Marsden's hand when he offered it to help her stand.

Lucy hefted the tea tray onto one hip and took Grace's hand firmly with the other.

"Take care that Lady Alice gets home safely," Mrs. Carlisle said to Marsden. He caught and held her gaze. "Of course."

Ignoring Lucy's cold disdain, Beatrice crouched to kiss Grace one last time. "Goodbye, dear girl. Thank you for the cake, Mrs. Carlisle. Don't trouble yourself to see us out. Marsden and I will go through the side gate. And we'll visit again soon."

When Beatrice turned away, Lucy's nostrils flared, and she drew Grace closer to her side. Marsden bowed his head in a quick nod to the Carlisle women and then dashed after her as Beatrice disappeared around the side of the house.

Chapter Fourteen

"Who is Grace?" Marsden asked Beatrice as they walked back to the main road. "Where does she come from?"

"They say she's the daughter of a family friend," said Beatrice. "She's a sweet little thing, isn't she? I feel sorry for her, being raised by that trollop of a farmer's daughter, but what can one do?"

A terrible fear began to formulate in Marsden's brain, his striding pace stuttering at Beatrice's side as a thought occurred to him. Beatrice had wanted Marsden to meet Grace. She had wanted him to see the little girl and recognize the family resemblance. The idea that Beatrice had already seen through him—had already guessed the reason for his keen interest in Simon and decided to taunt him with Grace's existence—reignited the same nausea that had struck him dumb in the Carlisles' garden.

"Why did you bring me here?" he asked. "Why did you want me to meet Grace?"

"You make it sound as though I had an ulterior motive," she pouted. "I wanted to see the Carlisles, and you accompanied me. That's the whole of it."

"You seem very fond of the girl, that's all. How did you meet her? Did you already know the family?"

"You ask an awful lot of questions, Fish. Has anyone ever told you?"

Beatrice picked up her pace, ensuring that he faced her back. She was striding ahead so quickly now her red curls bounced energetically with every step. Already fearful that he had aroused too much suspicion in Beatrice, Marsden fell silent, sure that the topic of conversation was now closed.

They continued without conversation, Marsden with his hands stuffed into his pockets, shoulders hunched against the cold wind, Beatrice drawing the lapels of her red coat higher around her face. He kept his eyes on the ground, distracted by the now obsessive concern over Grace's parentage. With his gaze lowered, the village appeared out of nowhere, the skirting houses emerging from behind a cluster of sycamore trees. Every house was a varying shade of white with simple matching cottage gardens. The muddy roads were well worn, and Marsden took Beatrice's elbow in hand lest she slip. She slowed enough to allow him to guide her around the worst of the muddy puddles.

"Where are we going?" he asked when they arrived at the village's main street.

"To church, of course," Beatrice replied.

Marsden assumed that the morning's service was over, the busy high street milling again with people going about their business, hitching their skirts above the mud and tipping their hats against the cold breeze. As he and Beatrice made their way down the street, the locals gazed upon Marsden longer than he would have liked. They appeared shocked, then hesitant, pausing to gawk. They parted, making a clear birth of them both. Their stares rankled Marsden's nerves, but Beatrice did not pay any attention to the astonished stares.

They walked not into the church but to the graveyard west of the old stone building. The cemetery was well cared for, the gravestones clean and tended to regularly, layered with flowers or tidy ornaments. Beatrice moved confidently through the shaded graves, her red coat sweeping through the long grass with a pleasant swish. As Marsden trailed behind her, a clap of thunder sounded in the distance. The dark clouds above them grew closer, descending upon the village and absorbing the light. Marsden shivered when a cold wind rushed against his back.

Beatrice stopped at the far end of the graveyard, where the stones were much and grander before a tall marble slab ornately decorated and more than a little ostentatious. Marsden stood behind her, staring over her slim shoulder. His stomach dropped. Simon Falconer's grave was immaculately kept; the grass was trimmed, and fresh flowers were arranged beautifully in a vase to the right of the gravestone. Marsden had been holding his breath, and the exhale escaped him in a startled rush. The stone was still relatively new, polished, and clean. He stepped backward, putting himself apart from the depth of the grave he imagined below. A dark shadow crept behind his eyes, and for a moment, he worried he might faint. This, Marsden thought, could not be how his search for Simon ended.

Beatrice spoke without turning to face him as though she could read his mind: "Of course, he's not down there. Daddy felt it desperately important to have some official marker of his death. The war hero needed a memorial, as it were."

Marsden gulped, his mouth dry. "Where is he actually buried?"

"Daddy tells people that Simon's body couldn't be retrieved. They couldn't bring everyone home, you know." The glance she gave him over her shoulder was pitying. "Of course, you know that. The stone is just for show, but I'm glad of it. I sometimes like to come here and remind myself that he is truly dead and gone. I sleep much better when I do."

"How can you be so heartless?" Marsden asked quickly, before he could censor his thoughts, and was embarrassed by the tremor in his voice. "Didn't you love him?"

She turned to face him front on. "Why do you care?"

Marsden gulped in the face of her piercing stare, the lies he had weaved becoming jumbled on the tip of his tongue. He was almost convinced at that moment she had him trapped. "I just think," he said, "it unkind to speak ill of the dead."

Beatrice held his gaze, green eyes fixed and regarding him with such deep intent that Marsden was sure she could read his discomfort. Lightening flashed across the church spire. Another clap of thunder sounded closer, virtually shaking the ground beneath them, and within seconds, a light shower of rain began to fall.

Beatrice raised one hand over her forehead to shield her eyes from the rain. "I think that's our cue to head home."

Marsden did not follow her straight away when she retreated. He stooped to read the finely engraved epitaph on Simon's tombstone.

Simon Harrold Falconer
Beloved son and brother
1894—1916

It was, to Marsden, a terrible dream from which he longed to be released. He reached a shaking hand toward the stone, fingers aching to touch the engraving. If he felt it, perhaps it would be real to him. Or, maybe he would wake up from the nightmare in which he found himself trapped.

A car horn blared behind him, and Marsden jumped at the sound. At the cemetery gate, Badeley had parked the Rolls-Royce and was leaning out of the open window, waving. Marsden followed Beatrice back through the rows of gravestones toward the road where she was already at the car, standing idly in the rain and talking with Badeley. He was speaking to her with apparent urgency, eyes wide. Badeley passed her a folded piece of paper, and Beatrice, in turn, pushed a coin into his outstretched hand. Marsden joined them just in time to see her sliding the paper into her coat pocket.

"We've been summoned back to the dungeon," she said. "Hurry up then; we're getting wet."

Marsden held the door open for her. When she climbed into the back of the car, he caught Badeley's narrow eyes and understood that trouble was afoot.

"Is Daddy very angry?" Beatrice asked as the car sped toward Maidenstone Hall. The rain was now pouring in a heavy stream, and she raised her voice to be heard by Badeley in the front cab.

"Yes, my lady," said Badeley.

Beatrice smiled and sank back into her seat to stare out at the green scenery racing past the passenger window. "Good," she said.

Back at the Hall, Linton waited for Beatrice at the front door with a large black umbrella over his head.

"I suppose I had better go and face the music," she said, placing a hand on Marsden's knee. "Thank you for coming with me today, Fish."

Her fingertips slid up his thigh, and a fierce blush traveled up Marsden's neck, sliding beneath the dense protection of his beard. He turned quickly to hide his reaction to the unexpected touch as she climbed out of the car. Beatrice hurried inside, Linton close on her heels.

Badeley parked the car in the garage and said, "Lord Scarborough was livid when we returned home from church to find Beatrice gone." He kept his voice low even though no one was nearby to hear them. "No doubt he'll want to have a word with you."

"Is she not allowed to leave the house?" Marsden asked. "She's a grown woman."

"It's not that she went out. It's where she went that's the problem."

When they entered the Hall through the servants' entrance, Lady Scarborough was sitting at the dining table, a cup of tea and a plate of biscuits before her. Marsden thought to sneak past the servants' dining room but froze in the doorway as he saw Mr. Carlisle seated beside Lady Scarborough, grey cap cradled in his lap. The countess's eyes were glassy when she spotted him standing in the doorway and she beckoned to him with a sad smile.

"Marsden," she said, "I was hoping to speak with you. Will you join me in the library?"

Mrs. Huston stood in the corner of the dining room, hands clenched around the skirt of her apron. The cook's face was long with strain when she stepped closer to Lady Scarborough.

"Why don't you stay, my lady?" she suggested. "It's much warmer down here. There's no fire in the library this morning."

Lady Scarborough swayed a little in her chair. "No, thank you Mrs. Huston. I would very much like to go up to the library. Marsden will come with me."

She rose slowly, leaning on the table. Marsden stepped forward to offer his elbow.

He said, "If you don't mind me saying so, you seem a little weary today, my lady. Won't you lean on me?"

Lady Scarborough took his arm, her weight heavy upon Marsden when she faced Carlisle. "Thank you so much for coming to see us, Mr. Carlisle. I'm so grateful you brought this matter to my attention."

Carlisle stooped his head and shoulders, a sloppy but official gesture of humility. The farmer clutched the cap to his chest, wringing at the grey tweed.

"My goodness, Marsden," Lady Scarborough said, clutching at his elbow as he guided her toward the stairs in a cautious shuffle, "you are quite damp."

Marsden helped her up the steps, carrying much of her weight as she leaned heavily against him. The walk across the vast salon was tedious, the countess deliberately placing each step in a peculiar wedding march. At the entrance to the library, Marsden held the door open, and she tottered ahead of him, heading straight for her usual armchair by the empty fireplace. With a tired sigh, she gestured toward the seat opposite, beckoning Marsden closer. The intermittent shouts of Lord Scarborough could be clearly heard despite the thick walls of the library.

"They're in the study," Lady Scarborough explained when Marsden sat down. "I'm afraid he's very angry with her today. Yet again."

"my lady," said Marsden, "if I had been aware that she was not permitted to leave the house—"

"I know. I know; it's hardly your fault." Lady Scarborough sank deeper into the armchair, casting a wistful glance toward the liquor trolley only a few feet away. "It's the Carlisles, you see. They're not our tenants anymore. My daughter does not understand the importance of this point. She thinks she can just waltz onto their property whenever she likes."

"The Carlisles were very generous, my lady. I think Beatrice is very fond of the little girl they have taken in."

"You saw the girl?" Lady Scarborough sat a little straighter in her chair. When Marsden nodded, her face softened with a wistful smile. "I hear she's a pretty little thing. Is she pretty?"

Marsden remembered Grace's exquisite green eyes—the same vibrant color as Lady Scarborough's. Of Simon's eyes. "Very pretty," he agreed. "Very sweet, too."

"I almost wish I had joined you. I would so like to see her." Lady Scarborough's smile faded, and she collapsed back into the armchair. "Marsden, you must promise me you won't let her talk you into accompanying her to that place again. My daughter is not welcome there."

"I'll do as you wish," said Marsden. "But I suspect she will return as soon as she can. Do you know why the girl so besots her? Did she perhaps know Grace's parents?"

Lady Scarborough's nostrils flared. "Of course not. What on earth would give you such a ridiculous idea?"

Marsden didn't dare admit that the notion arose from the suspicion that Grace was Lady Scarborough's own grandchild. "I've just had an extraordinary day, my lady. I couldn't say why Beatrice wanted me to go with her to the Carlisles. And then, when we were there, they seemed to think she was Alice. She didn't correct them, and I thought—"

"A game," Lady Scarborough insisted. "It's just a little game she plays. As for why she dragged you along, I suspect it was in the hope that she wouldn't get in trouble if you went with her."

A loud crash sounded from the study, and both jolted in their seats. A door slammed, followed by more shouts from Lord Scarborough.

"She was quite wrong on that account," Lady Scarborough continued. "I must ask you, Marsden, to promise you will not encourage my daughter's poor behavior. I'm afraid my husband could not countenance such another mistake on your part. We would certainly hate to lose you when Alice is very much enjoying her lessons. Do you understand?"

Marsden understood only too clearly. The idea of being banished from Maidenstone Hall so soon filled him with panic. He needed more time. "Of course, my lady. I promise you."

"Thank you, Marsden. You may go now."

Lady Scarborough rubbed at her arms, and Marsden wondered how she could bear to remain in the library without the fire ablaze.

"Shall I ask Mrs. Huston to light the fire for you, my lady?" he asked.

Her head rolled lazily against the back of the armchair, a movement so loose that Marsden thought it would tumble off her shoulders if possible.

"No, Marsden," she said. "Thank you. I am quite content."

Content. The word was heavy in her mouth, forcefully punctuated. As Marsden left her alone in the cold library, he suspected that Lady Scarborough was a woman who would never be content ever again.

Chapter Fifteen

At luncheon, Mrs. Huston asked Marsden to take a plate of sandwiches to Badeley in the garage. He had not yet been inside the dilapidated wooden building that housed Lord Scarborough's car. He was surprised to discover that it was little more than a poorly converted barn with little inside but a workbench for Badeley's tools and a small potbelly stove in the corner. He found the chauffeur polishing the car, and Badeley groaned with delight when he saw his lunch in Marsden's hands.

"I was just about to go in," he said, wiping his filthy hands on a cloth. You saved me the trouble."

They sat together on two old crates in the corner of the garage. A small stove had been installed in one corner, and the two young men huddled around it as they ate lunch.

"Were you in trouble with His Lordship when we got back?" Badeley asked.

Marsden swallowed a large mouthful of roast beef sandwich. "He didn't even ask to see me, but Lady Scarborough made it clear I wasn't to follow Beatrice on any further adventures."

"Aye, she gets away from them now and then. But then I'm sent to find her, and I usually always track her down in the same place."

"The cemetery?"

Badeley hummed in agreement. "The cemetery. Sometimes the Carlisle farm, if they let her in, but more often than not, she'll be at the bloody cemetery."

"I was under the impression," said Marsden, "that she didn't mourn her brother's death all that much. I thought perhaps she hated him."

"That's a bit of an understatement," said Badeley. "It's no secret that both girls hated him from a young age."

"But why? Do you know?"

"Simon was a hard young man. His lordship is certainly not an easy fellow, that's for sure, but his son…" He paused, and Marsden leaned closer. Badeley shook his head and offered a reluctant smile. "Well, he's gone now."

Lured into the intimacy of their secret conversation, Marsden asked, "Why did you dislike him? Is it because you and Lady Beatrice are friends?"

Badeley snorted. "We're servants. We're not friends with the family, believe me."

"Then why are you passing her notes?"

"You're a spy then, are you?"

"Not at all, but I saw you at the cemetery."

"Sometimes I do things for her," said Badeley with a shrug. "Send telegraphs, or get her little bits and pieces."

"Why all the secrecy? What is she hiding?"

Or whom, Marsden thought. He liked to imagine her secret had to do with Simon, just as he had envisaged Alice's mysterious time away from the house was connected to her brother.

"You might not have noticed," said Badeley, "but His Lordship isn't too fond of his daughter. He keeps her on a tight reign. If he saw her giving letters or messages to Linton, he'd want to read them. Lady Scarborough tries to keep the peace between them, but she's not so useful these days in that respect."

"Is it just the drink?" Marsden asked. "Or is it something else that affects the countess so much?"

"If anyone could say they understand her Ladyship's—" Badeley hesitated in his choice of words: "—her Ladyship's habits, it would be Nancy. But her lips are sealed when it comes to the poor old soak, so I wouldn't question her if I were you."

Marsden had not given Nancy's strange relationship with Lady Scarborough much thought. She was very efficient, but he certainly never got the impression that Nancy was particularly fond of the countess. He wondered how such a stiff and sour maid had survived the dramatic culling of staff during the war when so many others were sent away.

"Why weren't the rest of the staff brought back after the war?" he asked. "Was it really because the family was in mourning?"

Badeley leaned back to eye Marsden with obvious suspicion. "You ask a lot of questions, you know that?"

Marsden shrank back and admitted, "You're not the first person to say so today."

"Trust me, do your work, enjoy your time off, and stop asking so many bloody questions. With any luck, you'll last a few weeks at least."

Thinking of Lady Scarborough's thinly veiled threat of dismissal, Marsden asked, "Unlike the other tutors before me?"

Badeley took a large bite of a sandwich and tried to speak with his mouth full: "Fortunately, you're not like the other tutors."

"No," said Marsden, thinking of his secret collection of letters and photographs hidden upstairs in the violin case. "I'm not."

When Marsden returned to the house, everyone was trapped indoors thanks to the rain, and he knew he'd have little chance to creep into the family rooms. He hoped to avoid the family for the rest of the day, but the moment he stepped out of the servants' stairwell and onto the landing of the attic floor, it was to see Beatrice standing outside his bedroom door. She was still dressed as she had been on their walk into the village, wrapped in the red woolen coat, although her feet were now bare. Her face was mostly in shadow in the dim light of the hallway. Fear twisted deep in Marsden's gut at the thought that she had been inside his bedroom.

"Is there something you need, my lady?" Marsden asked.

When she stepped out of the shadows, her face was red and streaked with the dried salt of her tears. "I just wanted to make sure that you were still here."

Having come so close to losing his position, Marsden felt little sympathy for Beatrice in her distress. "I wasn't dismissed if that's what you feared, although it was a near thing. I gather your father was particularly unhappy with you."

Beatrice snickered. "In case you hadn't noticed, Fish, my father is very fond of yelling."

Marsden side-stepped her until his back was against the bedroom door, barring her from his private space. Immediately, he realized he had made a mistake as she moved closer, shuffling toward him until he was pressed against the door. A sense of claustrophobia made his stomach clench. Beatrice fixed her gaze upon him so intently that he felt the skin around his scar begin to itch under scrutiny.

"You will be here, won't you, Fish?" she asked, tilting her chin to stare up at him with watery eyes. "If I need you? I know they hired you to keep Alice happy, but I hope I can count on you, too?"

Her face was mere inches away from his, and for a moment, Marsden thought she might try to kiss him. Perhaps, he thought, it wouldn't be so bad to surrender to her embrace, wrap his arms around her thin shoulders, and feel her weight against his chest. It had been so long since he had been held that Marsden was sure he had forgotten the comfort such a simple action could afford. He could close his eyes and imagine he was holding Simon once more. He could pretend that he was loved. If anything, perhaps she would soften toward him and be more prone to divulge her secrets. Maybe she would tell him all he wanted to know if he showed a little affection toward her. But the cloying scent of Lily of the Valley made him light-headed, and he drew his hands behind his back, hoping she would step away.

"You can trust me, my lady," he said. "You can tell me anything."

"Good," she said. "I'm glad."

Marsden didn't see her hand move until it was up against his cheek, the gentle brush of her fingers against his scar making him shiver. Beatrice stroked the length of his beard just once, and then she was gone. In the blink of an eye, she had disappeared down the stairs, and Marsden was left sagging against the door of his room. He rushed inside and slammed the door behind him, fetching the chair and shoving it under the handle. Marsden pulled out the violin case and removed the instrument. A rush of relief escaped his breath when he discovered his photographs and letters still safely hidden away.

The brief temptation to hold Beatrice close and take comfort from her embrace had shaken him. Now Marsden was eager to remind himself why he was at Maidenstone Hall and to whom he was most loyal. He held one picture aloft, stroking the sepia features and soft curls of Simon's blonde hair. The photograph could not convey the jade-green eyes, but it was not difficult for Marsden to recall them. He had seen the same color earlier that day; in the eyes of little Grace Carlisle, he had seen the same color earlier that day.

Marsden threw the photograph on the floor and crashed onto his bed, turning his back against his lover's face and all the shameful secrets he and Simon had been forced to keep.

Chapter Sixteen

arsden did not go down to supper. Badeley knocked on his door after the staff had eaten, but Marsden feigned a pounding head, and the chauffeur left him alone. So Marsden remained in his room well after the movements and noises of the house had settled down for the night, wrapped in a pile of blankets, trying to stay warm as the night grew colder. He sat on the bed, rereading old letters and confused over the day's events. The cruelty shown toward Simon made his blood boil. Badeley had called Simon hard. Alice had thought her brother liked the war. Beatrice claimed that he was drawn to violence. At the time, he had dismissed Beatrice's slander in the wake of her transparent dislike for Simon, but now, the memory of an incident with a private named Thwaites roared into Marsden's mind.

It wasn't the first time handsome Lieutenant Falconer had provoked the disapproval of his battalion. Still, Marsden recalled the hatred invoked among the other men as particularly vitriolic when Simon had disciplined the young solder Thwaites for foolish behavior. Marsden dug his letters out of the violin case and leafed through them, looking for Simon's correspondence after the incident. He had been away for a disciplinary hearing due to the episode with Thwaites, and Marsden feared that Simon might not return.

Never fear, wrote Simon, nonchalant in his bravado as ever, *there won't be any disciplinary action against me. They know who I am, who my father is, and what would happen if they tried to court-martial me. Some old fogey colonel said I should be charged with attempted murder. Can you believe it? All because I was trying to protect my men.*

Marsden put the letter away. He had long recovered from his furious bout of jealousy and was now again holding the photograph of Simon he had thrown down upon the floor in his anger. He put aside the memory of Private Thwaites and kissed Simon's face. It was true Simon had been abrasive, impatient, and demanding at times, but Marsden had seen these qualities as a display of strength. In Simon, Marsden had found someone in whose hands he could surrender his completely fragile and lonely life. By Simon's side, he felt safe, protected, and wanted for the first time in years. For the first time since his father had seen the basest truth of Marsden's desires and rejected him. Simon was his only family.

Marsden took out another photograph, a much older, more fragile portrait, and held it in the palm of his hand. The paper was fraying at the edges and torn at one corner. He had carried it with him through the war, a choice he now thought careless when considering that it was the only portrait in his possession of his parents together. He wondered what they would think of him now, his lonely life of misery and deceit. He had barely known his mother, but he was sure his father would think Marsden deserved every ounce of his despair.

Above him, the light bulb buzzed and flickered, throwing shadows across the photograph. He looked up at the bulb expectantly, waiting for the usual flare of electricity to subside as it had previously. He wondered for the first time if the electricity had been poorly installed in the staff quarters.

Barely moments later, the sound of screaming echoed up through the floorboards. Marsden sat up straight. He jumped to his feet as the screams sounded again. Alice. She was having one of her nightmarish screaming fits. This time, he knew there was nothing to fear. Marsden stood and hovered by the door, one hand on the handle, waiting for the wailing to subside. But it didn't.

The screams continued until they were joined by a second, deep voice. Marsden was sure it was Linton calling for help. Footsteps thundered down the hallway, and a pounding knock rapped against Marsden's door. He wrenched his robe and dragged the chair from the door handle. Rushing into the hallway, he saw Nancy racing toward the stairs. He called to her, and she paused at the top of the illuminated staircase, cutting a dark shadow in the electric light behind her.

"Hurry up!" she said and ran down the stairs without waiting for him.

Marsden hastened to follow her. He leaped down two steps at a time, moving at such a speed he feared he would trip and fall. When Marsden emerged onto the second floor's landing, a soft glow illuminated the west wing hallway. He could smell the smoke, and his heart leaped with panic when Alice screamed again, a desperate, pained cry.

By the time he reached Alice's bedroom, her screams had died down, but her whimpers were drowned out by Linton's shouts. He was whipping a blanket against the flames that had engulfed the canopy of Alice's bed. Marsden stared at the blaze, mesmerized. The fire crackled as it erupted from the fabric, spitting and spreading. In a corner beside the bed, Alice cowered against the wall, her eyes wide with fear. Her ashen face was strewn with tears.

Nancy shoved another blanket against his chest. "We must put it out!"

Marsden unfurled the blanket and dragged the burning canopy down from the bed, working with Nancy to beat at the flames. Linton ran into the adjoining dressing room and quickly reappeared with a water basin. He threw its contents over the remaining flames with a heavy splash of water. They stood over the smoldering ruins of the canopy, gasping for breath. Alice had curled into a ball and was crying into the linen of her nightgown. Marsden pulled off his dressing gown and draped it over her shoulders.

"You're all right now," he said. "The fire is out. The danger has passed."

Although she was now silent, she was shaking so violently he thought he could hear her teeth rattling against each other. At the sight of her distress, Marsden forgot the propriety of his position and huddled closer, wrapping one arm around her trembling shoulders.

Linton crumpled with exhaustion, slumping onto Alice's filthy, wet bed. The old butler was suddenly less foreboding, dressed in pajamas and a thick black robe, grey hair awry. Nancy was equally disheveled, her loose hair wild around her face when she crouched before Alice and Marsden. She, too, had lost her usual sour expression and was now genuinely concerned, her lower lip trembling as she stroked Alice's cheek.

"Are you hurt, my lady? Did the fire burn you?"

Alice gulped down air, the panic still not assuaged in the presence of her rescuers. She lifted one sleeve of Marsden's robe to cover her mouth and shook her head.

"Thank goodness you raised the alarm so quickly, Mr. Linton," said Nancy. "God only knows what could have happened."

"I had been downstairs," said Linton, his breath still ragged. "I was returning to bed when I heard Lady Alice screaming."

"What happened?" asked Nancy, gripping Alice's shoulders. "Did you leave a candle burning?"

"Beatrice," said Alice. "It was Beatrice."

Nancy's expression barely shifted, but her nostrils flared. "my lady—"

Lord Scarborough stormed into the room, striding toward the ruined bed with hands on hips. "What on earth is going on? What is this?" When no one answered him, he tightened his plush red robe sash with a savage tug. "What have you done, girl?"

"There was a small fire, sir," said Linton with a shake of his head, untamed hair flopping across his face.

Lady Scarborough appeared behind her husband a moment later, her silk robe open and hair draped neatly over her shoulders. She squinted into the room with a look of great suspicion.

"Is something burning?" she asked.

Marsden fought back the urge to laugh, a strangled cough gurgling at the base of his throat. The Falconers must have lain in their beds waiting for the screaming and shouting to cease before they bothered to climb out of bed, and the absurdity of the realization had Marsden shaking his head.

"Lady Alice accidentally left a candle burning," said Nancy and stood to face her employers. "She's not been harmed. We can take care of her."

Marsden watched Alice's face for a reaction, but Nancy's explanation did not move her. She turned her face back into the comfort of his robe's lapel and leaned more heavily into his arms.

"I think we should get Lady Alice out of this room," he said and lifted Alice to her feet, keeping one arm around her waist.

Lord Scarborough stepped over the ruins of the canopy to bar their way. "What were you thinking? You could have burned the whole house down!"

Alice set her teeth in a desperate snarl. "It wasn't me," she insisted, voice hoarse with crying. "It was Beatrice."

A bloom of anger flared red from the base of Lord Scarborough's neck, up and over his chin, into his cheeks.

In his arms, Alice sagged, and Marsden thought she might faint. He dragged her back onto her feet and side-stepped the earl before the confrontation could escalate.

"Perhaps some brandy?" said Lady Scarborough when they approached her, one limp hand reaching to stroke Alice's hair. Alice lurched away from her mother's touch as though Lady Scarborough's fingertips were as dangerous as the fire only just extinguished. The countess snatched back her hand and turned her face away when Alice and Marsden passed her.

The electric lamps were all glowing in the hallway. The earl and countess had lit their way when they finally left their rooms to investigate the source of so much commotion in their daughter's room. Nancy followed close on Marsden's heels and jostled him out of the way, taking over responsibility for Alice's limp frame.

"I'll take over from here," she said, urging Alice to lean against her. "Thank you for your assistance, Marsden."

Alice and Nancy shuffled down the hallway. Marsden was about to go back to his room when he noticed that a light was on in the room beside Alice's. A sliver of illumination shone out from beneath the door, and Marsden guessed it must be Beatrice's bedroom. He imagined her awake and listening to the chaos she had caused next door.

When he climbed the stairs back to the servants' quarters, Marsden found Mrs. Huston standing in her bedroom doorway. She tightened a shawl around her shoulders when Marsden approached.

"You heard the ruckus, then?" Marsden asked.

"I think the neighboring farms heard."

"Why didn't you come down?"

"I'm too old to go leaping out of bed every time Alice has one of her nightmares. I didn't realize there was trouble until I heard Linton shouting."

"Does it happen often?" Marsden asked. "Lady Alice's nightmares?"

In the narrow shard of light illuminating her face, her face fell. Just yesterday, she had denied the screams as belonging to Alice. "I shouldn't like to talk about it." She shuffled on her feet, the wool of her slippers scuffing together. "Do you think I'm needed downstairs?"

"I think Nancy and Linton have everything under control. I'm going back to bed."

Mrs. Huston nodded curtly and wished him a good night. Marsden returned to his room and propped the chair back under the door handle. He didn't exactly feel safe, but at least he was isolated. Now that he was reasonably sure of how the east wing had caught fire—and who was responsible—he wasn't entirely convinced that it was possible to ever feel safe at Maidenstone Hall.

Chapter Seventeen

None of the servants at Maidenstone Hall spoke of the fire at breakfast. The company kept steady eyes on their porridge, with almost no conversation shared. Even Badeley, usually so eager to chat, kept his mouth tightly shut but to consume his meal. Marsden was keen to enquire why Badeley had not scurried downstairs when the fire was burning in Alice's room but dared not be the one to break the silence. At the ring of a first bell, Nancy hurried upstairs with Lady Scarborough's breakfast tray. Linton and Mrs. Huston arranged a tray for Lord Scarborough in his study.

"Shall I wait for Lady Alice to ask for me, do you think?" Marsden asked.

Linton was hovering in the doorway, his brow furrowed. "I'm sure she will be ready for her lessons at the usual time, Mr. Fisher."

As soon as Linton departed, Badeley stood up from the table, gulping down the last of his tea. "I've got to get the car ready," he said. "I'm taking His Lordship to the station when he's finished breakfast."

"Will he be gone all day?" asked Marsden. His mood lifted at the idea of Lord Scarborough being absent. It would give him an opportunity to search his Lordship's study.

"Most likely, as he's going all the way down to London. Got to go." Badeley slid on his jacket and dashed onward to his duties. Marsden decided to follow his example, going upstairs to the conservatory.

Marsden waited for Alice for almost half an hour. He thumbed through a pile of books on the table and even read a few pages of *Footfalls on the Boundary of Another World*. Marsden rolled his eyes at Robert Dale Owen's examples of the "spiritual body" and put the book aside with a disgusted huff. He had seen enough brutal death in the last four years to reject the notion of a spirit choosing to "divorce" from the body.

Marsden checked his watch and decided that Alice was not coming down. This suited him perfectly well. When he left the conservatory, he passed the rear entry of the library and saw Lady Scarborough seated by the fireplace. On the opposite side of the hallway, the study door was closed, but a light shone from beneath the door, and Marsden could hear Lord Scarborough clear his throat. He had yet to leave for the station.

Marsden crept past the study and went up the main staircase to the second floor. The west wing was silent, the scent of a smothered fire strong in the air. The door to Alice's room was wide open, and Marsden poked his nose inside. The curtains had been tied back, and the window left ajar. The ruined bedding had been removed. Marsden stood over the bed, remembering the speed with which the fire had spread across the canopy. Alice was lucky to be alive.

In the morning light and safe from the early hours' emergency, Marsden could inspect Alice's bedroom without interruption. It was sparkling clean and feminine but not particularly indicative of her personality. The dresser top was almost without decoration but for a simple lace and linen cloth and plain ivory hair brush. Marsden had never seen her wear jewelry and was not surprised to find no sign of feminine trinkets among her belongings. The door to the dressing room was open, and Marsden let himself inside. He immediately guessed that Alice and Beatrice shared their dressing space. Two wardrobes lined opposite sides of the room. One wardrobe was lined with a series of simple, pastel dresses, skirts, and blouses. The pieces were dated and well-worn, and Marsden recognized them as belonging to Alice. Marsden opened the drawers but could not bring himself to rummage through her intimates.

The opposite wardrobe stored the apparel he had seen on Beatrice: bold colors in velvet and silk. Unlike her sister, Beatrice was attracted to the latest fashions. Her dresses were elaborate, beautifully tailored, and mostly brand new. Marsden leaned into the delicate silk sleeve of a blue evening dress and could detect no scent of soap or flesh. He wondered if Beatrice had even worn half of the outfits she owned, her side of the dressing room bulging with apparel while Alice's wardrobe shrank in comparison. The drawers attached to Beatrice's wardrobe, however, were empty. Marsden stood momentarily, staring down into the empty space and wondering where she kept her undergarments, if not in the dressing room as Alice did.

The door on the opposite side of the dressing room was shut. Marsden pressed his ear against the door and heard nothing. As a last precaution, he knocked against the wood. When he opened the door, Marsden was alone in Beatrice's bedroom. Unlike Alice's room, it was dark, the heavy curtains drawn tight. He couldn't resist the urge to spread them wide, drenching the gloomy room with light. Marsden looked down over the view, straight onto the dark water of the lake. At the sight of it, bathed in grey light, he immediately felt cold.

The decoration of Beatrice's bedroom was vivid: paintings littering the walls, luxurious bedding strewn in a haphazard mess, and a dresser covered in combs, ribbons, and costume jewelry. The dresser's mirror was divided by a thick crack, exploding from a shattered glass center. Something, or someone, had collided hard with the mirror; a heavy object or perhaps even a fist—Marsden's reflection split and multiplied in the remaining shards.

The scent of Lily of the Valley invaded the entire room: a bottle of the perfume stood on a side table by Beatrice's bed. Marsden lifted it to his nose and inhaled the strong fragrance he always associated with Beatrice.

"What are you doing?"

Marsden was sure his heart stopped. He almost dropped the bottle when his neck whipped at a painful speed. Dressed in pale pink, her hair tightly tied, Alice stood in the dressing room doorway, watching with keen, haunted eyes.

Chapter Eighteen

At the sight of Alice, Marsden gulped and quickly placed the bottle back on the table. "I was looking for you, my lady."

The thin press of Alice's lips was grim. "Yes, I know I'm late. I am terribly sorry, but I don't know why you thought you'd find me in my sister's bedroom."

"I didn't mean to snoop, but I'm afraid I got turned around up here. I wasn't entirely sure you would want to proceed with our lesson today."

"I admit I'm not really in the mood today." Alice strode to the window and closed the curtains. "But I don't want to be inside. Could we go for a walk, do you suppose?"

Lady Scarborough's grim face burst to the forefront of Marsden's mind. "I'm not certain your mother would approve."

"You won't get into trouble. I promise. Unlike Beatrice, I know where I'm not wanted."

"So she told you about our walk to the farm yesterday?"

Alice's eyes rolled high into her head. "Beatrice always gloats when she's been disobedient."

"Where is Beatrice today?" Marsden would have imagined her locked away in her bedroom for the cruel prank she played on Alice, but having found the room empty, he tried to imagine where she had escaped to—or perhaps where she had been imprisoned.

A muscle in Alice's cheek ticked, and she pushed herself away from the window with a savage shove of the frame. "You won't see her today."

"Is she being punished?"

"Beatrice is always being punished for something. Will we take our lessons outside today or not?"

"Very well, I'll fetch my coat."

Alice's eyes shuttered, and her thin smile was one of tired relief. "Meet me at the main entrance when you're ready."

Marsden hurried downstairs to retrieve his coat. Dreading that he would be seen by either Lord or Lady Scarborough, he darted quickly between the staircase and the door that led to the basement servants' hall. The opportunity to speak to Alice alone, freely away from the prying ears and eyes of the house, was too good to give up, but he knew he couldn't risk incurring the ire of Lord Scarborough and losing his position.

To his relief, he saw no one on the stairs and found the servants' hall empty. Retrieving his coat and scarf, he climbed the stairs to the salon to find Alice waiting by the large double doors of the entrance, wrapped in a navy blue coat. Her straight posture and reserved solemnity made her all the more striking. She held his attention just as Simon had. He opened the door for her, and they crept out of the house together.

Circling the Hall, they passed the rose garden and had begun their descent down the hill when Marsden saw a figure in the near distance, circling the lake. The vibrant auburn of her hair bounced across her shoulders as she walked. Even though he could not see her face, Marsden recognized the red coat. Beatrice had escaped the confines of the house after all. She moved with determination, head down against the wind as she strode around the water, keeping a wide birth between herself and the lake's edge when she approached a thick cluster of apple trees.

"Isn't that your sister?" Marsden asked. "I didn't think she'd be out today."

Alice faltered in her step, and Marsden could tell she, too, was surprised. Arms wrapped tightly around herself, the full line of her lower lip fell agape.

When she did not answer, Marsden said, "Where on earth is she going?"

"I think she's going to the orchard," said Alice.

There was something so peculiar about the listless tone of her voice that Marsden wondered if she had fallen ill. He craned his neck to examine her and could see her jaw tighten.

"Do you honestly believe she did it?" Marsden asked and nodded toward Beatrice's retreating back. "Set fire to your bed?"

"It wouldn't be the first time Beatrice has set fire to the house," Alice said with a sneer. She pointed toward the nearby forest and continued to walk. "Come along."

Marsden caught up with her, matching her pace as they moved further away from the house, in the opposite direction of the lake and the orchard. When he glanced over his shoulder to look for Beatrice, she was gone.

They walked silently toward the forest, just as he had with Beatrice the previous day. This time, instead of following the narrow path that passed Mr. Carlisle's farm, Alice led him slowly west, deeper into the thick grove of trees. Marsden was relieved to disappear into the forest, admitting to himself he had been afraid she too would lead him to the Carlisles' property. Grace Carlisle had worked a terrible magic on his imagination, and the question of her parentage still burned at the forefront of his mind.

"Alice, can I ask you a question?"

"Of course," she said.

"It's about Grace Carlisle."

Alice's pace slowed at a fork in the pathway. Above them, the sycamores swayed in the strong breeze, their leaves rustling wildly and casting an array of fast-moving shadows across her face.

"This way," she said, moving down the new path. "I'm sorry about yesterday. It wasn't kind of Beatrice to use you like that to gain entrance to the Carlisle's home."

"Is that why she took me with her?"

"Beatrice will do anything to see Grace. She probably thought they wouldn't turn her away if she brought an accomplice. The Carlisles won't refuse her, but I know my parents do their best to keep her away from the farm."

Marsden recalled the tender way Beatrice had played with Grace, the genuine affection and joy he had witnessed in her. He thought again of how much the little girl resembled Simon.

"Who is Grace?" he asked. "I know she's not kin to the Carlisles."

They had reached a narrow stream, the water passable over a small clam bridge. Alice was silent until she stopped at the bridge's center, leaning against the cool stone and peering down into the water below. Beneath them, the stream was running fast, energized by the recent rain.

"She's Beatrice's daughter," Alice said at last.

Marsden couldn't hide his surprise. He felt his jaw fall apart but did not care if she saw his astonishment. The tight knot of jealous anxiety that had begun eating away at Marsden's heart from the moment he saw Grace began to unravel. The blush rose in his cheeks as he realized his foolishness. It was so simple an explanation. The nausea that had swelled in his belly at the thought of Simon betraying him—of Simon fathering a child with an anonymous village girl—reared up again at the shame of having rushed to such a terrible conclusion.

"I've shocked you, I think," said Alice. "Perhaps I shouldn't have told you."

Marsden indeed wondered why she had revealed the secret, thinking perhaps Alice had hoped to damn Beatrice in his eyes. For the first time, he suspected that Alice was jealous of her sister.

"Who was the father?" he asked. "Do you know?"

Alice shook her head; her lips curled in anger. "Grace has no father."

"You mean he wouldn't marry Beatrice? So that's why she gave the child up to the Carlisles?"

"Of course, she didn't give Grace away. It was my father's idea. Did you never wonder why she hates him so much? He took away her baby, and she lost her mind for it."

"Is that why she set fire to the east wing? Because Grace was taken away? It was Beatrice, wasn't it, who set fire to the house?"

Alice lifted her chin to look him directly in the eye and raised one thin red eyebrow. "She set fire to the east wing because she hates everyone. Our father, our mother, Simon—me."

"What happened between you?" he asked. "Why do you live such separate lives?"

Laying her forearms across the stone wall of the bridge, Alice leaned dangerously toward the water. "We were inseparable once when we were little girls. We were completely interchangeable. Nobody could ever tell us apart. But then something terrible happened. It changed everything."

Marsden couldn't help himself. As always, his mind drove toward Simon. "Was it something to do with your brother? Is that why she hates him?"

When she faced him again, her expression was uncharacteristically severe. "Why are you here, Marsden?"

Alice looked more like Simon than ever in the face of her sudden anger. The elegant lines of her face elongated just as her brother's had done in a fury, just as it had when he and Marsden fought; when he had berated the men in his regiment; when he had turned the full brunt of his anger upon poor Private Thwaites.

Marsden found himself fumbling for words. "I beg your pardon?"

Alice stepped closer, crowding him. "What do you want from us?"

"I came to be your tutor, my lady. You know that."

"Really? You answered an advertisement for a female tutor to a young lady of high breeding in the Yorkshire countryside. On what, a whim? Because you were tired of being a soldier? If my sister hadn't frightened away every tutor before you, you'd never have stood a chance of getting this position."

Marsden offered up empty hands. His fingers trembled. "Why else would I be here? Your mother is the one who thought it was such a good idea to hire me."

"You ask so many questions, Marsden—question after question. Maybe you're here to spy on me. Maybe you're here to side with Beatrice."

Marsden scoffed, even as he backed away from Alice. "Side with her? Why on earth would I side with Beatrice?"

"Everyone else does. Our father is the only one who doesn't crumple at the sight of her. Women fear her, and men fall in love with her. Are you in love with her?"

Blind-sided by the turn in conversation, Marsden laughed in disbelief. "Of course not. What on earth makes you think that?"

"Ask Badeley."

Her face crumpled with hurt, and when she turned away from him, he was immediately sorry for his mirth. Without thinking, he placed a hand on her thin shoulder. She tensed but didn't push him away.

"I didn't mean to upset you, Alice. I'm sorry."

"Just promise me you're on my side," she whispered.

"Of course I am." Marsden let his hand slide down her arm. He hesitated briefly, afraid that she would not want to be touched, but the urge to calm her, to maintain her trust, encouraged him to grasp her fingers between his. "I promise you."

A cold gust barreled through the glade behind them, and a stray lock of hair took flight around Alice's face. She shivered, and Marsden turned her toward his body, protecting her from the wind. He was surprised when she released his hand, only to throw both arms around his waist and clutch at him with a strength he had not thought she possessed. Marsden's first instinct was to release her, to protect himself from the temptation to relish in the long-lost touch of another person. Still, his body immediately warmed to the contact, the tight muscles of his shoulders relaxing as he enclosed her thin frame within his arms. Unlike his uncomfortable confrontation with Beatrice in the servants' quarters, Marsden succumbed quickly to the closeness she afforded. It had been so long since he had held another soul so comfortably, with such ease. Not since Simon.

Marsden tilted his face downward, inhaling the enticing scent of her hair. Unlike her sister, she did not smell of floral perfume. Her fragrance was entirely individual; warm, clean flesh and old silk. When she rested the crown of her head against his collarbone, just below his chin, a spark of energy raced through his nerves, and Marsden looked back over his shoulder, checking to ensure they were not being watched. Alice vibrated against him as the icy wind swept again across the length of the bridge.

"Let's go back to the house," he suggested. "It's getting cold."

Alice nodded against his shoulder and allowed him to turn her back in the direction they'd come from. As they trudged back toward the house, she slid one arm into the crook of his elbow and peered up at him with a shy, adoring smile.

"Will you read to me?" she asked. Her eyes sparkled as the dappled light flickered between the branches swaying overhead.

Once more, the warmth of her voice reminded him keenly of Simon. The gentle way Simon had said his name. *Thomas.*

"Of course," he said as they returned along the forest path. "I'll do anything you want."

Chapter Nineteen

After supper, the terrible chill that had plagued Marsden all day still bit at his bones. All afternoon, he had read to Alice in the bitter cold of the conservatory, and come evening, he eagerly followed Badeley back to the garage, where the chauffeur promised he had a supply of Scotch to warm them both. Badeley gave Marsden the task of lighting the fire in the stove while the chauffeur fetched two cups and a bottle of Scotch from a box he kept hidden behind his tools.

Marsden whistled when he saw the bottle. "That looks expensive."

Badeley grinned proudly. "It is. I have to hide it down here. Linton disapproves of drinking in the servants' quarters." He poured a generous amount into the two scuffed cups and sat opposite Marsden on an old crate. "In the old days, the chauffeur didn't live in the house. It saves money to have me stay in the Hall, or so they say. The old chauffeur's cottage is let out now, and I have to sleep in that frozen attic with everyone else."

"I'm surprised you didn't hear Alice screaming this morning," said Marsden. "It woke the rest of us."

Badeley waggled his eyebrows. "Who says I was in my bed?"

Marsden scoffed but agreed to take the bait. "Where were you then?"

"A gentleman doesn't reveal all his secrets!"

"Were you with Lady Beatrice?" Marsden asked. He was instantly embarrassed at having been so blunt and averted his eyes to stare into his whiskey.

Badeley almost choked on a mouthful of the Scotch, doubling over as he forced himself to swallow. He coughed, pounding his chest as tears welled in his eyes.

"Lady Beatrice? Where on earth did that come from?"

"Alice seems to think you're in love with her."

Badeley's laugh, when he had recovered from his coughing fit, was forced in its confidence. "Bless her heart. Don't you listen to anything that girl has to say."

"Because she's ill? No one will even tell me what's wrong with her."

Badeley's ease dissipated immediately. He leaned back on the crate, running an oil-stained hand through the thick mane of his hair. "She's very fragile," he said. "Her brother's death took its toll on her. They tell us it's some kind of melancholy. You know, a sickness of the head."

"They?"

"The Lord and Lady up at the big house. The doctors. They say it's all in here." He tapped one finger at the side of his temple.

Marsden took a large sip from his cup. He didn't believe Alice was sick in the head. To him, she was simply a troubled teenage girl—timid for sure, but with Lord Scarborough as a father, Marsden could easily see the root of her nervousness, although the late-night screaming fits, he admitted, were not the behavior of a healthy young woman.

"You think her brother's death made her ill?" he pushed, lowering his voice. He felt a wave of sympathetic affection for Alice at the thought. "She took it very badly, then?"

"You might say that."

"Is that how she got the scar on her wrist? Did she try to hurt herself?"

Badeley's smile twisted. He leaned close, their faces inches apart. "You know, Lady S hoped things would go differently with you."

"Differently how?"

"She thought things would get better. But I reckon they've only got worse."

"What's worse? Lady Alice?" When Badeley only shrugged, Marsden thought he would burst with frustration. "Why is everything at this place a bloody mystery? What are they hiding?"

Badeley finished the last of his whiskey and stared into the bottom of the empty cup. "They're not trying to hide anything, my friend. Now, it's bloody freezing, so either we head back up and get warm by a real fire, or we have another and let the Scotch warm us."

Marsden held out his cup. "Another."

Chapter Twenty

Marsden woke on his bedroom floor with a dry mouth and still fully dressed. His skull throbbed with the movement when he tried to lift his head, and the pain only intensified when he racked his brain, searching for the day of the week, wondering if he was required to get up and work today. But he remembered he had seen Alice the day before, so she wouldn't be available for lessons today.

His relief was short-lived when a knock sounded on the door. Startled, he jerked up, wincing when his head again protested at the velocity at which he rose. He stared at the door, hoping it would remain silent, but the knocking returned, loud and hard. Marsden stumbled to his feet and reached for the door, running a shaking hand through his hair.

Linton stood on the opposite side of the door, immaculate as ever and scowling. Lord Scarborough stood behind him. The very sight of them together made Marsden nervous.

"Lord Scarborough," he said. "Is something the matter?"

The earl's hands were folded behind his back, elbows jutting out at sharp angles to expose the suede patches of his hunting jacket. His face was tight with restrained anger.

"I'm afraid," said Lord Scarborough, "there has been a theft in this household, and I must insist upon searching your room."

Marsden's stomach lurched, panic racing through his body. "Sir? I'm not sure I understand—"

"I can assure you that every room will be searched. This is a serious matter, but I am not pointing any fingers. Not yet, anyway."

Marsden risked a furtive glance at Linton. One corner of the old butler's mouth twitched, and Marsden's sense of alarm grew. He thought immediately of the violin case under his bed and willed himself not to look in its direction.

Knowing he had no other option, Marsden stepped aside and held the door open. Lord Scarborough stormed ahead of Linton but stood back as the butler rifled through Marsden's meager belongings. At least Linton was careful as he searched, opening and closing books in a precise manner, pushing aside the contents of the desk drawer, and sliding gloved hands gently into the pockets of Marsden's jackets and trouser pockets. A thin line of sweat beaded upon Marsden's brow when Linton eyed the length of the bed. The butler crouched to look under it, and Marsden feared he would be sick.

Linton drew the case from under the bed and opened it to remove the violin. He pinched at the velvet lining and lifted the inner case to reveal the hidden compartment. Marsden clutched at the door frame and closed his eyes. It was all over. Lord Scarborough would see the photographs, the letters, and the cigarette case. The earl would know that Marsden had been lying about his identity all along. Marsden would be forced to flee the house without finding the truth about Simon. That was, of course, if he wasn't arrested first for fraud and gross indecency. Marsden's heart squeezed at the idea of a lifetime in prison, forced into hard labor.

Marsden opened his eyes, prepared to see the fury in the earl's face. But Lord Scarborough was peering into an empty violin case. Marsden's throat tightened. His photos and letters—and the silver cigarette case—were gone.

Lord Scarborough relaxed. The pinched look of anger around his eyes and nose receded. His hands released their tight fists, and he turned to face Linton.

"I'm satisfied the case isn't here. Do you agree, Linton?"

The cigarette case. Lord Scarborough and Linton were searching for Simon's cigarette case. Marsden had to stop himself from patting anxiously at his pockets, frightened that he had hidden it on his person.

Linton replaced the inner lining of the case and faced his master with complete passivity, his face long and blank. "Yes, my Lord."

Lord Scarborough's chest puffed in a false air of righteous satisfaction. "I knew you weren't to blame, Marsden. No hard feelings, I hope?"

Marsden was acutely aware of having held his breath for the better part of the last minute. He could only stutter in response. Lord Scarborough swanned out of the room without another word. Linton returned the violin to its case. He kept one dark eye on Marsden the whole time, even as he knelt to slide the case back under the bed.

"You look unwell, Mr. Fisher," he said.

Marsden sat on the bed in a less-than-graceful manner. "I'm afraid I am, Mr. Linton." Linton placed a cold hand against Marsden's sweating forehead. "I do not believe you have a fever, but perhaps you should stay in bed this morning."

"Perhaps you're right. I think I shall."

When Linton left the room, Marsden collapsed onto his back, covering his face with trembling, damp hands. He was overwhelmed with fear. The loss of the cigarette case was one thing, but the letters and photographs were damning beyond salvation. Someone at Maidenstone now knew his secret, and the idea of what they could do with that evidence was terrifying. Marsden could not go to prison. He was sure he would die there.

Chapter Twenty-One

Marsden knew he had to leave immediately. If he stayed, he risked being present when his documents fell into the hands of Lord Scarborough. Marsden threw himself off the bed and reached up to drag a suitcase down from its place on top of the wardrobe. Tossing the case onto the bed, he filled it with his clothes. He had already roughly folded and shoved his shirts and woolen vests into the case when there was yet another knock on the door.

"Who is it?" Marsden asked.

"It's Badeley." He didn't wait to be admitted, opening the door to see Marsden leaning over the suitcase, hands on the bed to support his trembling weight. "What the hell are you doing?"

"I have to go," said Marsden, but his arms shaking became incessant, and he sank onto the bed beside the case.

"You look bloody awful. I don't think you should go anywhere."

The pounding in Marsden's aching skull intensified, a rush of pain circling his ears. He tipped forward to rest his head between his knees. "What the hell was in that Scotch?"

Badeley patted his back. "You did have quite a lot to drink, my friend."

Marsden kept his head down until the blood stopped rushing so vigorously behind his eyes. He could not recall just how much he had drunk. Nor could he remember making his way from the garage to the house.

"How did I get back? Did you help me?"

"No, you got here all by yourself."

"Did I say anything?" The idea that Marsden had given himself away, revealing the contents of the violin case and that Badeley had taken advantage of his drunken stupor to steal them was both plausible and horrifying. For all Marsden knew, his photographs and letters were now stashed away in the filthy confines of the garage.

"You said a lot of things," said Badeley, his smile wry. "Any secrets you're particularly worried about having shared?"

"Did I tell you about the case?" Marsden lifted his head to squint at Badeley but could see no glimmer of guilt in the other man's eyes.

"What case?" Badeley sat down beside him on the bed. "You're not honestly thinking of leaving, are you?"

"I can't stay. I have to leave."

"What, now?"

Marsden thought of the weaving journey by car to the station and said, "No, I need to get out. Get some fresh air. It's not raining, is it?"

"It's always raining—"

Marsden plucked a clean woolen jersey from his suitcase. Stumbling as he struggled to pull it over his head, he left Badeley behind in his room. He needed to get down to the garage before Badeley knew where he was going.

Halfway down to the servants' hall, Marsden had to pause to steady himself, willing every ounce of his being to push back the vomit swelling at the base of his throat. He rushed past the kitchen, hoping to avoid Mrs. Huston and any conversation she might start with him. Instead, he almost ran face-first into Holly as she stood on tiptoes to fetch her coat from the rack. Marsden stepped on her foot. She yelped but promptly laughed in response to her surprise and his disheveled appearance. He apologized for hurting her, but she dismissed his concern with a gentle pat on his shoulder.

"Don't worry about me," she said. "You just gave me a fright, is all. Are you going out?"

Marsden had no intention of revealing his plans to search the garage and simply said, "Yes, for some fresh air."

"Are you sure that's a good idea? The weather's bad, and you look frightful."

Marsden tried to smile but felt his lower lip shake with the effort. "I'm quite all right. Just a cold coming on, I think."

"Really? I thought maybe it was due to you staying up drinking all night in the garage."

Marsden didn't think he could feel any further deflated. "Hear about that, did you?"

"There are a lot of secrets in this place," Holly said and stooped to pick up two heavy iron pails. "But there are plenty of things the staff here still talk about. I don't suppose you'd give me a hand? If you're heading out anyway. I need to fetch more firewood for the library."

"I'm not sure I—"

"Excellent." Holly pushed one of the pails into Marsden's hand. "Her Ladyship's complaining of the cold in the library. I could use some help fetching the firewood."

Marsden did not want to help Holly. He couldn't very well sneak into the garage with her by his side—not to mention the problem of his throbbing head—but her suggestion of secrets, so casually offered, had caught his attention.

When he hesitated, pail wobbling in his shaking hands, she said, "You'll need your coat. It's bitter cold out."

Before Marsden could respond, she removed his coat from the rack and shoved it into his chest.

"Well, all right," he said, as though she'd truly given him a choice in the matter, and struggled into the coat as she led him out into a drizzle of grey rain. Following her away from the house and toward the garage, Marsden thought it was fortuitous that she should lead him back toward the place he wanted to go. All he had to do was help her fill a pail with wood and get on his way without raising any suspicion.

Walking just behind her, Marsden noticed how very small Holly was, wiry and thin. He said, "Do you usually collect the firewood? It's a heavy task."

"Aye," she said, almost yelling over the wind. "It's not usually a housemaid's duty, but then I'm not even a housemaid. I just come in before the house wakes to help Mrs. Huston with the breakfast for the family and see to the fireplaces. Not that they use very many of them these days."

"Can't they afford to have you working the whole day?" Marsden asked, thinking of the layers of dust and filth layering the lesser used rooms of the house, that Holly could be of much further use to the family.

"I couldn't say. I'd have thought there'd be no shortage of money since His Lordship sold off the estate, but they don't want a full staff again."

"Will they sell the house as well? Do you think?"

Holly wrinkled her freckled nose. "Can't say for sure. They live here most of the year now. The earl and countess sometimes go down to London, but they don't spend the season there anymore. Not since the war."

The small wooden building that stored coal and wood for the house was situated behind the garage. Holly fished a key from her apron skirt, although why she bothered to keep it locked, Marsden couldn't guess. The window pane above the door handle had been broken and was unlikely to keep out even the laziest thieves. Marsden followed Holly into the shed to discover that the window of the rear of the building, too, was shattered, a long branch from the birch tree outside having broken off and smashed through the glass. The firewood was piled on one side of the shed, and as Holly set to work loading already chopped pieces into one of the iron pails, Marsden swept away the cobwebs that hung in heavy strands from the ceiling and examined the damp room. A dwindling pile of coal rested opposite the wood, and at the far end, a vast collection of garden tools was gathering dust on a single workbench.

"Does His Lordship no longer employ a gardener?" Marsden asked Holly.

She paused in her work to wipe her hands on her apron. "Not since poor Mr. Locksley died. He'd been the gardener here for years."

Marsden's ears pricked. "He died? How?"

"The influenza. Poor man. Took him and his wife."

"And you? Have you worked for the Falconers long?" he asked.

"Since Christmas just passed. It's not a bad position. My sister worked here for half the money during the war. Then they dismissed most of the staff and didn't take them back against when it was all over—my sister included."

"I understand most of the staff was sent away when Lord Scarborough's

114

son went missing?"

"He didn't go missing," said Holly. "He died."

"Of course," he said and swallowed hard. "Did you ever meet the viscount? Master Simon?"

"No, I didn't know him, but I saw him in the village when I was a girl. He was ever so handsome, but my sister says he was a brute. Hand me that pail, will you?"

Marsden did not release the pail, clutching it against his chest. "She said what?"

Holly's shrug was far too casual. "Just that he didn't take no for an answer, if you know what I mean. Didn't fancy keeping his hands to himself. The pail, Marsden?"

Marsden passed the bucket into her reaching hands but did not offer to help fill it. Instead, he said, "Could she have been mistaken, do you think? Your sister? Perhaps she misunderstood his intentions?"

Holly snorted, a deep drag of air clogging her nose. "My sister isn't one to tell lies. She tried to convince me not to take the job here, but it was too good an opportunity to turn down." She crouched to fill the second pail. "I tell you what, though, she was sorely jealous about me being paid more money than her. I get paid three times what she did. A couple of years cleaning the earl's fireplaces and me and Jimmy will be set."

From the long sigh she released along with Jimmy's name, Marsden suspected love. "Is Jimmy your young man?"

Holly's cheeks beamed pink with a lover's grin. "Aye. When we've saved enough, we'll marry and move away."

"Why would you want to move away?"

Holly's lovesick smile quickly faded. "This place is cursed, Marsden. We'd be better off somewhere else."

"Is that what you meant when you said there were a lot of secrets here? Because you think the estate is cursed?"

Holly passed one of the full pails to Marsden, and he followed her out of the shed.

"The village used to rely on the estate," she explained, "but it's dying right in front of His Lordship, and there's no one to inherit the title. Master Simon died in the war, and then there was the fire. So, yes, I'd say this place is cursed."

"Won't his daughters inherit the estate?" Marsden asked. "That's possible, isn't it? I know they can't inherit the title, but surely there'll be money for them."

"Aye, there'll be money for Lady Alice, but who knows how much."

Holly locked the door again and turned back toward the house, Marsden hurrying to walk beside her.

"And Lady Beatrice?"

She came to such an abrupt halt that Marsden almost tripped over his feet as his head whipped around to face her, but his body continued forward. Darkness shadowed Holly's round face.

"You've not been to the orchard yet, then?" she asked. "Just follow the path from the east wing down to the lake, and you'll see it."

"I know where the orchard is," said Marsden. "I haven't walked through it, though."

A flicker of Holly's gentle smile crept back across her full lips. "You seem like a good man, Marsden. A clever man. I know you're probably here for the same reason as me, for the money, but I don't have to live in the house, and you do." She stepped closer, the mist of her breath fanning out against the lapels of his coat. "The Falconers are all liars. And their servants. Every single one of them. That's what I meant about secrets. I think you've been slow to catch on, but don't let them twist you all about."

A harsh gust whipped against them, making Marsden shiver, a sharp tingle of nervousness building in his chest. "Do you think I should leave? Am I not safe here?"

Holly's laugh was bitter. "Safe? With that witch in the house?"

"Do you mean Beatrice?"

"I mean," she said pointedly, "if I were you, I'd only stay as long as absolutely necessary."

"I was thinking of leaving," he admitted in a rush. "Today. Lord Scarborough searched my room this morning."

At his own mention of the search, Marsden thought of his lost belongings and couldn't believe he had allowed himself to have been so long distracted by Holly and her tales. He cast a hesitant glance back toward the garage, not wanting to return to the house in case he should run into Badeley. Holly sensed his reluctance and reached for the pail he carried.

"Here, give me that," she said. "I can manage. You don't look well at all."

Marsden let her take it out of his hand, the weight of the second pile of wood instantly dragging her shoulders closer to the ground.

As she shuffled away from him, Marsden called out: "What do you mean I've been slow to catch on? What have I missed?"

"Go to the orchard!" Holly answered over her shoulder. "But don't get too close to the lake."

"What's wrong with the lake?"

Holly stopped briefly to face him again, her face tightly earnest. "You can't say I told you. They'll wring my neck if they find out!"

She lumbered back toward the servants' entrance and did not look back at him again. Whatever secrets she was still hiding for the family, he guessed she would tell him no more. He thought of the orchard, standing decrepit and abandoned at the foot of the hill, beyond the lake, and could not imagine what she meant.

Marsden looked up at the house. Maidenstone Hall rose up into the dark sky, towering over the land around it. The dark windows stared down at him like black, hungry eyes, and he felt the tingling, creeping sensation along his spine of being watched.

Chapter Twenty-Two

Marsden's unease remained tight in his chest as he hurried back toward the garage. Whatever riddles Holly expected him to unravel, they could wait until he had retrieved his letters and photographs. He tried to imagine why Badeley would steal from him, and the terrible thought that perhaps the chauffeur wanted to blackmail him urged Marsden to run, almost tripping over his own feet in his haste to return to the garage. The wind was whipping him now, rushing him toward his destination as the clouds above grew darker and thicker.

At the doors, he knocked out of caution but was met with silence and let himself inside. The garage was musty and cold in the light of day, with no fire lit. The bottle he and Badeley had shared still sat on the table beside the stove, now empty. Marsden began a quick and cursory search, aware that Badeley may return at any moment. The shelves at the back of the garage were lined with tools and cans of oil. He searched around and beneath each item, hoping to find some sort of hiding place, but there were very few corners in which Badeley could have concealed anything.

A small cupboard under the workbench was mostly empty. When Marsden shut its door, the cupboard shook, unanchored to the wall or floor. Curious, he dragged it away to discover a hole carved into the wall; the bricks were removed, and the grouting tunneled away. A tin box was hidden within. Marsden scoffed, equally elated and amazed at finding the poorly concealed hiding place, his heart soaring with relief when he pulled the box free. But his relief was short-lived when he opened the box, shocked into stillness, finding not his belongings but thick stacks of money.

He removed the bundle of notes and flicked through them. Badeley had secreted away hundreds of pounds.

Afraid of being caught in the garage, Marsden didn't dare take time to count the notes, but he suspected there might even be well over a thousand pounds in the box. Marsden knew the staff was well paid, but the amount Badeley had stashed in his hiding place was well beyond the means of a chauffeur. He couldn't imagine how Badeley had accumulated so much money. Perhaps theft. Perhaps it had been Badeley, after all, who had stolen the cigarette case, not to blackmail Marsden but to sell. Even so, Marsden's letters and photographs were not in the garage, although he couldn't guess where else Badeley could have hidden them.

A crack of thunder made Marsden jump, jolting him with a reminder of the urgency with which he needed to move. He returned the box to its hiding place and replaced the cupboard in front of the hole, straightening it to be sure Badeley wouldn't suspect that it had been moved. He left the garage and closed the door behind him.

Marsden hurried back to the house, coat wrapped tightly around his chest against the barreling wind. He wondered how Badeley had known where to look, the mistake Marsden had made, the clue that had given him away. Badeley had judged him well and discovered his weak point. Again, Marsden thought of leaving immediately. If he stayed, it was true; he might recover his letters and even an answer to his questions, but the risk was greater now that his true identity was so close to being revealed. Another crack of thunder overhead heralded a sudden downpour of rain, and Marsden began to run, ducking his head against the cold sheet of water.

When he reached the house, Marsden wasn't sure where to go looking next, knowing full well the other servants' room had also been searched. Maidenstone Hall was a large house with many potential hiding places. He pushed on the heavy door of the servant's entrance and paused in the hallway when a loud crash emanated from the kitchen, followed by a cry from Mrs. Huston. Linton's voice, low and disapproving, echoed after her. Marsden closed the door quietly and removed his wet coat. He crept down the hallway to the kitchen and leaned beside the open doorway where he could more clearly hear their conversation without being seen.

"Leave it there, Mrs. H," said Badeley. "Nancy'll clean it up for you in a moment."

"Holly can do it when she comes back down," said Nancy on a growl.

"But you don't think he'll leave, do you, Badeley?" asked Mrs. Huston.

"Where on earth do you think he'll find a position as well paid? He'll stick around for the money, just like the rest of us."

"I don't like it," said Linton. "I know she's fond of him, but I don't trust him. I still think it's a terrible idea to encourage her in this way."

Marsden distinctly heard Nancy sigh in frustration. "I don't trust him either. He's a fraud."

"And she knows that," said Mrs. Huston. "But she's running out of time. His Lordship wants to send her away again, and he'll do it the moment he sells the house. If we could just convince Marsden—"

"Is that even likely?" said Badeley. "He's hardly a great seducer."

"I've seen how he looks at her," said Nancy. "Can't stop staring. He likes her, all right."

"Then he just needs to be persuaded to help her," Mrs. Huston persisted. "For all our sakes."

There was a long silence, and Marsden desperately wished he could peer around the wall to gauge their expressions. He imaged the four of them huddled around the table, glaring at each other in a flurry of anxiety. While he stood so close, their conservation about him made him want to burst into the room and confront them about how much they truly knew about him, about Simon's disappearance, and why they were so desperate for him to stay. Maybe, at last, they would stop playing with him and tell him the truth. Then, he could leave Maidenstone Hall and never look back.

"So what now?" Nancy asked. "Do we tell him about—"

"No," said Linton. "He's frightened enough already after this morning. We let him calm down and then make a plan. We need Marsden here for the time being."

Nancy snorted. "Do we even still call him Marsden?"

"Yes. For now."

A light touch landed upon his shoulder, and Marsden jumped out of his skin. A small hand slapped across his mouth to muffle his cry, and he twisted to find Beatrice pressed against him. She was dressed in her red coat. She raised her free hand to her mouth, placing the index finger across her lips.

Chapter Twenty-Three

Beatrice jolted her chin toward the stairs. She released the pressure on this mouth, but Marsden' didn't dare breathe. Numbly, mindlessly, he followed her to the staircase. As they ascended, the quiet murmuring of his colleagues faded beyond hearing.

On the ground level, Beatrice snatched at Marsden's hand, pulling hard and dragging him to the grand staircase and up toward the second floor. He hesitated, aware of the precarious position in which she was placing him, but she wouldn't release her tight grip.

"Where are we going?" He tried to keep his voice low, but Beatrice only scowled at him.

At the top of the stairs, she finally let go of his hand and turned toward the abandoned east wing. Beatrice pulled back the heavy canvas sheets covering the hallway. Dread reared up at the back of Marsden's brain at the thought of following her into the charred remains of the forbidden wing. If he were caught alone with her there, his missing letters and photographs would be the least of his worries.

He started to protest; "Lady Beatrice, if your mother sees us—"

"For heaven's sake, Fish," she said with a hiss, "be quiet. Mummy has no doubt already drunk herself into oblivion, but her room is on the other side of this landing, and you could wake her if you continue to talk at the top of your voice. If you're so afraid of being dismissed, bloody well act like it and keep quiet."

Marsden pressed his lips together. Beatrice offered the corner of the canvas for him to hold. In a surprising display of strength, she took hold of the door, propped at the hallway entrance, and pushed it out of the way. She brushed her hands together and crouched into the shadows to produce a small paraffin lamp and a box of matches. With the strike of a match, the light shone brightly. Beatrice beckoned Marsden beyond the door, and he let the canvas fall shut behind him. Shadows emerged in the lamplight, and Marsden's eyes gradually grew accustomed to the dark.

Inside the shuttered hallway, the stench of fire was devastating. Marsden dove into his jacket pocket to retrieve a handkerchief, pressing the cotton over his mouth and nose to protect his lungs from the foul air. Beatrice was unaffected by the smell, charging ahead with the lantern just above her face. From what Marsden could see, the hallway had been fully ablaze with a fierce fire, the remnants of art frames hanging empty on the crumbling black walls and the charred fibers of destroyed rugs crunching beneath their feet.

They walked only a short distance, passing two doorways before Beatrice stopped before the third on the left. The door handle creaked in her hand when she turned it. Marsden was not sure exactly what he had been expecting, but as the door opened to reveal the room beyond it, Marsden was shocked. Before him was a nursery, utterly untouched by the fire. He stepped inside, and the transition between the two worlds of ruin and finery was mesmerizing.

The room was a shrine to a long-lost childhood; dozens of toys, books, and dolls were arranged neatly on the shelves framing the windows. Two matching rocking horses stood in the middle of the room, their saddles coated in a thin layer of dust. The blue velvet drapes were wide open, but the room was eerily dark thanks to the storm now raging outside. Marsden shivered when Beatrice ushered him further into the room and shut the door.

A row of candles lined the shelves, and Beatrice lit a match, igniting the wicks and bringing a soft glow to the cold room.

"This was your nursery?" Marsden asked.

"It was." Beatrice blew out the match and gave one of the rocking horses a kick. "Now it's my sanctuary."

"So this is where you hide. I had wondered where you went." Marsden followed her into the center of the room, absorbing the bizarre contrast of the untouched nursery with the ashen destruction beyond its doorway. "It must be the same as when you were a child. It's like a room frozen in time. I can't believe it wasn't damaged by the fire."

"Time does tend to freeze here," said Beatrice. She wrapped her arms around her chest. "Just look at Alice and me. Frozen in time forever."

"Is that really how you feel?"

Beatrice snorted inelegantly and gestured to her long red coat. "Well, Daddy is hardly willing to spend the money to heat the whole house anymore, so, yes, literally frozen. Figuratively, we will all be stuck here until we die."

Marsden asked, "Why did you bring me here?"

Although indeed curious, Marsden had the distinct feeling of being toyed with. From the moment he had met her, Marsden had been wary of Beatrice—fearful she would intentionally have him dismissed or worse, set his bed to fire—but after the conversation he had just overheard downstairs, he was more on edge than ever and suspicious of the devious intentions the entire household had toward him.

Beatrice picked up an old teddy bear and plucked at its fur, her eyes averted when she said, "I thought you might want your letters and photographs back."

A clap of thunder crashed right above the house. Seconds later, a flash of lightning illuminated the nursery, slashing through the gaps in the wood panels covering the windows. Marsden's breath froze in his lungs. The crook of Beatrice's smile was chilling. He had been so sure Badeley was the culprit he had not paused to consider that Beatrice had been the one to steal from him. Now, he felt stupid for not having suspected her sooner. Immediately, he imagined a deep and sinister motive on her part: blackmail, extortion, or even simple entertainment.

"You stole them? But why?"

Her shrug was nonchalant. "Someone needed to save you from yourself,

124

and God knows I like you, Fish. If I hadn't done it, Daddy would have found them. I heard you guard your violin case as though it were made of gold. Bound to make people suspicious."

"And did you read my letters?" Marsden asked, his tongue heavy. His heart began to race, a deep panic swamping him.

Beatrice winked and danced across the room to one of the sets of shelving. She dropped the teddy bear and crouched to pull out one of the many books stacked alongside a collection of hand-crafted toys. She opened the leather-bound volume and held up the pages aloft for Marsden to see. A thick wad of paper had been carved out, revealing a deep cavity between the covers. It was packed with the collection of letters and photographs Beatrice had stolen. His fingers twitched by his sides, urging him to take them back from her immediately.

"They were certainly fascinating," she said, teasing. "Who knew my brother could be so eloquent? I certainly didn't. The photographs I found less enticing. Apart from this one." She lifted a photograph from her hiding place and examined it. "Who are these people, I wonder?"

Marsden recognized the picture's tattered edges immediately. She let him snatch it out of her fingertips, and he smoothed over the creased faces of his parents. His father stood tall and formidable in his best grey suit, with one hand on his wife's shoulder, who sat before him in a simple white dress gathered at the waist with a thick black belt. She cradled a baby in one arm, swaddled in a white blanket, while the other encircled a toddler. He flipped the picture and traced a finger over the faded scrawl of his father's handwriting. *Gerhard, Fredericka, Anton and Thomas. Hamburg. 1892.* Cholera had claimed his brother and mother only months later.

"It's my family," he said, clutching his photograph against his chest.

"And where are they now?" Beatrice asked. "Do they know about your extracurricular activities during the war?"

Marsden's first memory to hand was of his father's red face, bloated with rage and yelling. He felt the ghostly sting of his father's hand slapping his face and heard the thud of his belongings when they had been thrown on the doorstep. He recalled the numbness at receiving a telegram informing him of his father's death, just days after Marsden had returned from the war, and understanding at last that they would never reconcile.

"They're dead," was all he said.

Beatrice's expression flattened, her taunting mirth evaporating. "Oh dear," she said. "They did know, didn't they?"

Marsden wondered at his transparent vulnerability that Beatrice found it so easy to read him and know what he was thinking exactly. He wanted to read her in return. To gauge the danger in which he now found himself. But her short laugh was one of offhand dismissal.

"You must have been very shocked to read them," he said.

"Shocked? By what? That you have a proclivity for your own sex?" She blew the suggestion away with a soft pop of her lips. "I'm not that easy to shock. Besides, I was far more appalled to discover you were a Hun. I might have been worried if you hadn't been on our side during the war." She turned her attention back to the concealed letters and photographs. "I did think about burning them for you to get rid of the evidence, but then I thought that wouldn't particularly ingratiate myself toward you. Shall I keep them here? Or would you like to find a new hiding place in your room?"

Marsden gaped at her, mind torn. The idea that he would leave Beatrice in charge of his most personal belongings was laughable, yet the threat of Lord Scarborough or Linton searching his room again was just as frightening.

Impatient, Beatrice closed the pages of the book. "All right. I'll leave them be. They're right here inside *A Little Princess if you want them.*"

Beatrice put the book back on the shelf. Marsden urged himself into stillness, even as he longed to run across the room and tear at the bookcase. He burned with the restraint required to leave his belongings where they were—to stop himself from showing Beatrice just how desperate he was to retrieve them.

She stalked toward him, hands in the pockets of her coat. Marsden instinctively backed toward the door, but she followed him, forcing him to retreat until there was nowhere left for him to go, and they were face to face. Beatrice took one hand from her coat and withdrew the silver cigarette case, holding it so close to Marsden's face that he could see his reflection in the polished surface.

Beatrice's smirk was almost pitying when she said, "You know you've got the brand of kisses I'd die for. What is that from? A poem."

"A song," said Marsden, his voice strangled. "Lyrics from a favorite song."

She raised herself to stand on the balls of her feet. Beatrice was much smaller than him, but as Marsden recoiled from her, pressed against the nursery door, she almost became tall enough to meet him nose to nose.

"Did you truly expect to find him here?" she asked.

Marsden's stomach dropped. The plan he had so painstakingly constructed was crumbling before him in the hands of a nineteen-year-old girl. His cover was blown, and now she held all the cards in the game.

When he said nothing, he continued: "You know, had he lived, Simon would have married a pretty heiress to feed the family coffers. There would have been no place for you in his life."

While the jealousy that arose at the thought that Grace could have been Simon's daughter was a sour, simmering fury, the idea of Simon loving or committing himself to anyone else invoked a flaming resentment in Marsden. He placed a hand on Beatrice's shoulder to push her back.

"You don't know that," he spat. "You didn't know him the way I did."

"Oh, but I did," she said, resisting his hand and pressing closer. "He was careless in many things, my brother, but he was utilitarian to a fault."

"No—" he began, but Beatrice silenced him with the wave of a pointed figure in front of his mouth.

Holding the cigarette case before his eyes, she said, "I can't give this back to you. I think you know that. It must be returned to Simon's room so that Daddy will call off the search. You know what would have happened if he'd found it on you." She lifted her chin, staring him directly in the eye. "They hang people like you, don't they?"

Beatrice was wrong. He wouldn't be hanged, not anymore. But should Lord Scarborough have him arrested, Marsden had a life sentence to look forward to. It was almost as terrible an idea as hanging. He knew full well what happened to men like him in prison. Another inmate would kill him before the dark days of back-breaking labor did.

She must have seen the fear in his eyes, and for the first time since she had dragged him upstairs, Beatrice's smile softened into kindness. "Don't you worry, Fish. Your secret is safe with me."

Marsden almost choked on his strangled voice: "Safe? But you told the others. Badeley, Mrs. Huston—"

"Silly goose, they don't know about you and Simon, and I won't tell them. Badeley delivered the telegram to me when I made some inquiries in London about the marvelous Marsden Fisher, so obviously, he knows you're a fraud, but I haven't divulged anything else. As far as they're concerned, you simply lied about your identity to get the position as Alice's tutor."

"Why not tell?" he asked, disbelieving. "Why did you protect me from your father? If it's money you want—"

"I don't want money, Fish. I did it because I like you. Or maybe I just feel sorry for you." Beatrice pressed her chest against his, almost climbing him until her lips were against his ear as she spoke. "But you need to let him go. Simon's dead. He's gone, and he's not coming back."

A wave of courage swept up Marsden's throat, and he became determined to confront her. "How can you be sure? Simon is not buried in that churchyard and did not die at the Somme. He'd been AWOL for weeks by then. So where is he?"

Beatrice drew back enough to meet his gaze, bright eyes narrowed. "Don't tell me you've come to rock the boat, Fish."

"I came to find the truth. That's all."

She gave him a pitying look. "Then you've come to the wrong place, my dear. You won't find the truth readily available here."

Marsden thought again of the other staff talking about him behind his back, conspiring to manipulate him: Beatrice's theft, Alice's frequent disappearances, the falsified report of Simon's death, claiming he had died in battle when he had long been missing from the regiment. From the moment he had arrived at the house, everyone had been speaking to him through a veil of misinformation and half-truths.

"Why won't you just tell me?" he asked. "What do you want from me?"

Her shoulders drooped, and Beatrice appeared genuinely confused by his question. "What do you mean? Don't forget; you weaseled your way into this house all by your own volition. We didn't know you from Adam when you arrived."

"I heard the other staff talking downstairs. So did you. What is the great secret everyone is trying so hard to keep from me? Is it about Simon? Are you hiding him somewhere?"

Beatrice scoffed. "Now you are being totally ridiculous. I told you—"

"Is that where Alice goes every other day? Is she meeting Simon somewhere? Has he been in hiding all this time?"

Marsden shoved away from the door, dislodging Beatrice's hold. She did not retreat but took a single step back in the face of such desperate anguish dripping from his words.

"For heaven's sake, Fish," she said, "Alice is—"

"Don't tell me that she goes to York every other day. I don't believe it."

Marsden was suddenly and overwhelmingly incensed, his desperation dissolving into pure, stalking anger. The sweat of his fury slicked his brow, his shoulders heaving as he gasped for breath. He crowded over Beatrice now, rising to his full height once more, but from the straight set of her chin, the lengthening of her spine, it was clear she was not intimidated by his display of emotion.

"There are plenty of secrets in this house, Fish," she said, "but they do not all revolve solely around my brother. If you have any sense, you'll forget all about him."

"Then I should leave?" Marsden asked, insistent. His instinct that morning upon having his room searched had been to run, escape the claustrophobic mausoleum of Maidenstone Hall, and accept that Simon was not there, nor would he ever find him. But the thought of returning to London alone made him want to weep. He had virtually no money, no employment, and nowhere to live—he had nothing and no one. His father's death had left him stranded, and Simon's disappearance had paralyzed his soul.

An uncharacteristic softness enveloped Beatrice, her head tilting as she lifted one hand to his cheek, stroking the length of his beard just over the scar he hid beneath. Marsden didn't realize he was leaning his face into the warmth of her palm until he felt his eyes drooping with the movement, lashes fluttering with unexpected comfort.

"Oh dear God, no," she said, her smile beaming. "I do hope you will stay. I will be quite alone if you leave me here. You wouldn't do that to me, would you, Fish? Not when I have done so much to help you."

"Why is it so important to you that I stay?" he asked, raising a hand to clutch at her wrist. "What am I to you?"

"I need an ally," she said. "I need help getting what I want."

"Grace," said Marsden, guessing immediately. "You want to get Grace back."

Her nostrils flared, and Beatrice let her hand slip out of his grip.

"Know about that, do you? Of course, my sister told you?" When he only nodded, she said, "Yes. All right. I want Grace, and I can't do it alone."

"I don't know how I can help you."

"You underestimate yourself. You'd be surprised how helpful you could be to me."

"And if I do help you, you won't tell your parents about me, is that right?"

A tender expression of relief engulfed Beatrice's face, her smile returning. "I'm glad we understand each other. I'm sure you don't believe me, but I'm on your side, Fish. I need your help as much as you have needed mine."

"What about the rest of the staff?" he asked, thinking of their clandestine meeting in the staff dining room. "Why not ask them for help? Badeley already seems to be in your pocket."

"Because I can't trust them," she insisted. "They're on Alice's side."

"Must there be sides?"

"Yes, Marsden. And now you're on mine."

Signaling rather unceremoniously that the conversation was over, Beatrice swept past him to open the nursery door. Only then did he think to ask her:

"Beatrice, did you want to kill Alice? When you set fire to her bed?"

Beatrice grinned at him over her shoulder. "Is that what she thinks?"

"Yes. I can't say I blame her."

"I see. And did you enjoy swooping in to save her? Alice's knight in shining armor? I think you did."

Marsden's cheeks flamed red. "Not at all."

Her chuckle was pure, dark delight, and she said, "Oh, Fish, don't you worry. I have no intention of murdering my sister. It wouldn't be in my best interests, I can assure you. But I must admit, she is fun to play with. As are you."

She gave him a mischievous wink and closed the door.

Chapter Twenty-Four

The moment Beatrice was gone, Marsden rushed to the bookcase. He pulled on the spine of *A Little Princess* in such a scramble that two surrounding volumes also slipped free and fell open on the plush blue rug. His stolen papers fluttered out from between the pages, scattering before his feet. Marsden fell to his knees and clutched at the photographs, pressing the images against his chest in relief. When his hands finally stopped shaking, he tucked the pictures and letters into the breast pocket of his jacket. He would be damned if he was going to trust anything to the care of Beatrice.

Marsden collected up the two other books that had fallen open onto the floor in his hurry to find his letters. Only when he reached for the heavier of the two, he realized it was not a book at all. Unlike the other volumes of children's tales surrounding it, the thick leather-bound pages did not contain print or illustrations but elegant handwriting. The letters were small and perfect on the left page, the words almost running together in neat cursive. The writing on the right-hand page was no less legible but freer in style, looping wildly in larger lettering. Marsden flicked through a few more pages to find that every pair was the same, the handwriting alternating from left to right throughout the journal. Each entry was written as a letter, with a signature at the base of each page. Every single one was signed alternatively—Alice and then Beatrice.

Marsden closed the journal and slid it inside his jacket along with the letter and photographs he had only just retrieved. The hallway was still barely lit when he stepped out of the nursery, and he was relieved to see that Beatrice had left the lantern burning for him beside the wall of canvas separating the destroyed rooms from the rest of the house. Marsden hesitated in the hallway as he considered the other closed doors. If the nursery had survived the blaze, so too may have other rooms and hiding places tucked away in the dark.

He retrieved the lantern and attempted to open the other doors around the nursery. The first, closest to the landing, would not open. He kicked the door for good measure, but it would not budge. The next did open, but Marsden immediately regretted it as an ash cloud rained down upon him when the door shuddered, and the handle gave way in his hands. The room was dark, the windows boarded and filled only with the bare remains of charred furniture. Beyond the nursery, only two other equally damaged rooms were accessible before the ceiling collapse cut off the hallway. There were no other corners of the east wing where any human being could comfortably reside, even temporarily. The nursery had been the only room to survive the fire.

Marsden extinguished the lantern and returned it to its place by the entrance. He carefully escaped the east wing, replacing the door baring the hallway and ensuring no one else was on the landing before emerging from the sheets of canvas. Marsden ran back upstairs to the servants' quarters on light feet and slammed his bedroom door behind him. Once more, he slotted the chair under the door handle, then sank onto the bed, where he withdrew the contents of his jacket pocket, holding the letters and photographs against his sweating brow.

When he put them aside, Marsden turned his attention to the black leather journal, turning it over in his hands. He lifted it to his face and inhaled deeply. The scent of Beatrice's perfume lingered on the pages. The journal had been carefully maintained; no pages were dog-eared or ripped. The left-hand pages were perfect, without any ink smudges or messy corrections. Alice. The pages on the right were less impeccable, with several words scratched out and ink splashes often spilled across the paper. Beatrice.

The early pages were dated January 1919. Marsden glanced over the first short entries. As he leafed through the pages, the same names appeared repeatedly: Linton, Nancy, Badeley, Mummy, Daddy. Without reading every entry, he could perceive this was a journal of Alice and Beatrice's daily life at Maidenstone Hall. Largely, the notes were banal, with one reporting to the other about their sleepy lives; Alice frequently spoke about the staff, little slivers of gossip, and a longing for more interaction with the outside world, while Beatrice largely moaned about their parents. On the whole, the girls revealed little of themselves. It was as if they were sending postcards to an absent, distant relative of little importance.

Out of curiosity, Marsden skipped ahead to the date of his arrival at the Hall.

> *18th May 1919*
>
> *The new tutor arrived today. A man, can you believe it? And handsome. His name is Marsden Fisher. He plays the violin and speaks French. I always say this to you, every time, but please do not scare him away. Not this one. Let me have him for a short time, at least. Let me have someone else to talk to. I beg you.*
>
> *I told him I wouldn't be here tomorrow. Please do not tell him the truth.*
>
> *Alice*

Marsden flushed with pleasure at the basic compliments she had paid him. From the moment they met, Alice had wanted him to stay. She longed for his companionship. Her loneliness was etched into the fragile tilt of her writing.

On the next page, an entry for the following day began in Beatrice's less restricted hand.

> *19th May 1919*
>
> *I met him. I adore him already. He's a jumpy thing, isn't he? Did you see the gash on his cheek? Can you imagine what it looks like when he shaves? Perhaps I'll take a razor to his face while he's sleeping and*

find out.

You needn't worry about me frightening him away. I'm going to enjoy playing with him. We can share, can't we? I don't see why you should get to keep him all to yourself.

Poor old Fish, having to spend the whole day with you. Do try not to bore him to death, will you? At least until I can find out his story. There's something strange about him, I can tell. Badeley has promised to arrange for some digging in London. Another penny in his greedy pocket.

I like this new tutor, but I'm not sure yet that I trust him. If it turns out he's a spy, I will absolutely blame you.

Beatrice

20th May 1919

I saw what you did to Father's papers. Do you honestly think you can stop it from happening? It's because of you that he wants to sell. One more slip, and I swear he will do it. Taunting him will not get you what you want. Just because he agreed to hire another tutor does not mean that you and I are safe.

What on earth did you say to Marsden? He was so distant today. He kept such a close eye on his violin case. I think he didn't trust that it wouldn't be stolen. He guards it as his most valuable possession. I don't know how to make him trust me.

Please don't send Badeley on a fool's errand. I don't know how you can have any faith in him after all he's done. There is no need to be suspicious of Marsden; I'm sure of it.

Alice

Marsden cursed his own defenses. Alice had guessed how valuable the case was to him. It hadn't been difficult for Beatrice to find. He wondered who else had noticed his obsession with keeping the case so close, who told Linton exactly where to look for the cigarette case.

21st May 1919

I took Fish with me to see Grace this morning. I know you'll be upset, but I really don't care. I wanted him to meet her. That bitch Lucy hated us visiting, but there was nothing she could say in front of Fish.

I finally had a telegram from London. I knew Fish was too good to be true. You wouldn't hear a word against him, but I still asked Badeley to send a message to Caruthers asking him to look into the good Mr. Fisher. You might as well get the truth from me. I don't know his real name yet, but it is definitely not Marsden Fisher. I warned you. If I find out he's in league with Daddy, I will never let you hear the end of it. I've told you before that you bend too much to their desires. Do not forget, Daddy and Mummy are the enemy. They sided with Simon. If you do the same, I will never forgive you.

Beatrice did not sign her name this time. The word *never* was underlined repeatedly, the ink sinking deep onto the other side of the page. What had she meant? When she said, *They sided with Simon.* Hoping for further clues, Marsden kept reading.

22nd May 1919

Were you actually trying to kill me? Or did you just want to make a spectacle, as usual? I know you're upset about the horses, but there are easier ways to get attention. Marsden and Nancy could barely contain the fire. After it all, Marsden was so caring and attentive. I am sure that you have misjudged him. I trust him, even if you do not.

Father was furious. He blamed me, as he always does. I think perhaps he and Mother wish that I had died. God in heaven, I truly hate you sometimes. Just leave me alone.

Alice

The opposite page was almost entirely blank but for a single line in response from Beatrice.

Me, try to kill you? That's rich, don't you think, after what you did?

Marsden leafed through the earlier entries again and wondered if more journals in the nursery were reporting tit for tat between the sisters. He looked for further mention of Simon, but except for the accusation that Lord and Lady Scarborough had "sided" with Simon, his name made no other appearances in their conversation. The only pages that genuinely caught his notice were dated in early March when almost a week passed without a single entry from either sister. Finally, Beatrice recommenced the communication with a short, vitriolic note.

2nd March 1919
They're right about you. You are insane. How could you savage yourself like this? You'll be back in St. Jude's before you can even beg for forgiveness.

Marsden assumed the incident in question was Alice's self-harm. It had occurred so recently; no wonder the scar tissue looked so raw.

At the beginning of May, after months of brief and meaningless exchanges, a sentence or two on each page at most, Alice revealed the conversation that had brought Marsden to Maidenstone Hall.

5th May 1919
Mother has finally agreed to hire another tutor. I know what you think about it all, but you're better at entertaining yourself than I am. I promised her I wouldn't do anything rash or foolish again. As long as I behave myself and treat the tutor with respect, I can stay here at home. But you and I both know this is the last chance. You were right. I do not want to go back.

Marsden dropped the journal to rub at his aching eyes. His headache had returned with a vengeance in the wake of the sisters' bewildering back and forth. The suitcase, still open and half-packed, lay at the end of his bed. A desperate urge to flee had not waned. Now that his secrets were closely bound against him once more, he could run away and pretend that he was simply so offended by the accusation of theft that he was righteous in his resignation. But the journal had served to reawaken his curiosity. Even though Alice and Beatrice did not discuss Simon directly, they stirred up another nagging question, begging for an answer. Marsden was now keen to know what had turned the sisters against him. If he left now, whatever Alice and Beatrice were willing to share with him about Simon would be lost, and his disappearance would continue to torment Marsden's heart.

He shivered, his whole body aching with cold. Beatrice had not been unkind when she accused Lord Scarborough of refusing to heat the entire house. Marsden hid the journal under his mattress, a spiteful urge to avenge her theft. The letters and photographs he slid into his jacket pocket determined that he would never let them out of his sight again.

Chapter Twenty-Five

Marsden was well aware that he had missed luncheon, but his grumbling stomach urged him to leave the sanctuary of his room in search of sustenance. Confident that his belongings couldn't be searched twice in one day, he left Alice and Beatrice's journal tucked under his mattress. The letters and photographs remained in his jacket pocket when he went downstairs.

The rain was still battering at the windows when Marsden entered the kitchen to find Mrs. Huston busy slicing carrots. Her smile at the sight of him shone with relief.

"I do hope you're feeling better," she said. "There's bread left over from luncheon if you're hungry."

"I am feeling a little better," he said, slathering jam onto a piece of bread.

Mrs. Huston abandoned her work to sit across from him at the kitchen table. "You mustn't mind Lord Scarborough. He can be a bull in a china shop, but he's always been that way. I don't think he truly believed you were a thief."

Marsden was sure that Lord Scarborough had absolutely believed him to be a thief but kept his opinion to himself when he spotted an inconsistency in his known history of her. "You say he's always been that way," he said. "You were hired during the war, weren't you?"

Mrs. Huston's smile wearied. "Yes, to cook for the family during the war, but I had worked for them before."

"When?" Marsden asked, astonished. "For how long?"

"Almost twelve years. I was nursery maid to the young ladies."

Marsden could not imagine Mrs. Huston as a nursery maid. He could barely picture her as anything but a hunched old cook, dramatically protective of her soups and sauces. Surprised, he asked, "So you raised Simon and the girls?"

"Not Simon. Just Alice and Beatrice. I was with them from the time they were still in the cradle. They were such lovely little girls, so clever and affectionate."

"They don't seem very affectionate now. Were they friends as children?"

A shadow of pain spread across Mrs. Huston's face, dragging at the thick lines around her eyes and mouth. She turned from Marsden, pulling the board of carrots toward her.

"Yes," she said. "They were close as children."

"And Simon?"

Mrs. Huston kept her eyes on her work, but the movement of the knife in her hand slowed. "What about Simon?"

Marsden urged her on. "Did he and his sisters get on?"

"Simon wasn't really friends with anyone. He wasn't very..." She hesitated, as though choosing her words carefully. "He wasn't very loving toward his sisters."

"You didn't like him," he guessed.

Marsden couldn't reconcile the picture she painted of Simon with the man he had known during the war. From the moment they had met, Simon had been the center of Marsden's world; the young Viscount's charm, strength, and good looks had seduced him immediately. To hear so many unkind opinions about Simon had been hard to swallow, but none more so than from Mrs. Huston.

"It's not that I didn't like him. He was a very, very clever boy. But..." She let the sentence hang, face distorted by a hateful twist of her mouth.

Marsden edged closer to the edge of his seat, eager for any scrap he could get. "But what?"

The loathing disappeared, the memory that had encouraged the emotions fading as Mrs. Huston shook off the expression, only to say, "He was a boy, Marsden. Like most little boys, he could be very rough in his play."

"Is that all?" Marsden asked, holding back a scoff. "He was just a childhood bully?"

"Bully is not the right word."

"Then what is?"

Mrs. Huston threw the knife down upon the cutting board. "Why on earth are you so interested in hearing about Master Simon? He's long dead now."

Marsden willed every muscle in his shoulders and face to relax. Hoping to turn the attention away from himself, he redirected her focus to Alice. "I worry about Alice, that's all. I gather Simon was his parents' favorite. I'm concerned their grief has left her feeling neglected."

"He was the boy. Simon was the heir, so his father always paid more attention to him. Alice understands that. As for Lady Scarborough, I suppose she did love the boy." Mrs. Huston's shoulders heaved. "It's hard to tell what she truly feels if I'm being honest."

"Are you being honest?" Marsden hadn't meant to be so blunt, but from the sharp turn of Mrs. Huston's head, he understood that he had spoken more harshly than he had intended.

"What in heavens do you mean?" she asked.

Marsden couldn't stop himself. He was willing to take a risk. "What's in the orchard?"

The color drained rapidly from Mrs. Huston's face. She launched off her stool, the wooden chair tipping and banging on the floor as she exclaimed, "Who told you about the orchard?"

Marsden leaned back, intrigued to see the fear in her wide eyes. "Why does that matter? I just want to know what's there."

"There are a whole lot of very old apple trees in the orchard, Mr. Fisher," she said through clenched teeth. "Trees and nothing else. Mind your own business and leave it at that."

A loud crack of thunder echoed in the distance, causing Marsden and Mrs. Huston to startle. Mrs. Huston clutched at the little gold cross hanging upon her breast. The wind howled outside, making the glass panes rattle as the rain beating against the windows escalated from a patter to a constant deluge.

When she had recovered herself, Mrs. Huston asked, "Did you see Nancy on your way down? She hasn't been down to fetch tea for the ladies."

"I didn't," said Marsden, reluctantly accepting the segue in conversation.

"Perhaps you could fetch her for me. No doubt she'll be in the library with her Ladyship. Nancy often reads to her in the afternoon."

She turned her back on him and, subsequently, upon any further conversation. On a defeated sigh, he agreed, "Very well. If I find her, I'll send her down."

Chapter Twenty-Six

Marsden could barely contain his frustration with Mrs. Huston. Her apparent dislike of Simon and the blatant fear upon her face, when he had mentioned the orchard, had him clenching his fists as he climbed the stairs. He was lost in thought, desperately wishing the storm would dissipate so that he could investigate the apple trees just beyond the lake, when he opened the salon door to hear voices whispering.

Having already taken his first step out of the protection of the hallway, Marsden quickly fell back, sliding behind the doorway to hide himself. He peered around the corner to see Beatrice leaning against a marble column.

"Everything will work out," she said.

Beatrice gave her audience a confident smile and turned toward the staircase. She was on the second step when Badeley lunged into view and grabbed her wrist, forcing her to face him. He didn't follow her onto the stairs but stared up at her with an expression Marsden had never before seen on his face: panic.

"What if you're wrong?" Badeley asked. "If you're taken away, what am I supposed to do? Stay with your father forever? He won't pay me half so well when you're gone."

Beatrice extracted her wrist from his grasp and gently took up his hand. "Trust me, darling. Soon, Maidenstone will be behind us, and we will be free."

She leaned forward, releasing his hand to cup his cheeks and kiss him softly on the lips.

Badeley reached for her, evidently hoping for more, but Beatrice hastily backed away, retreating one step higher.

"Marsden's no fool," he said. "He could make trouble for us. What will you do if he finds…" Badeley's jaw worked as if he were mulling over the words he dare not speak aloud.

"Then I'll tell him the truth," said Beatrice without hesitation. "He's already on my side."

"I thought he was on Simon's side?"

At the mention of her brother's name, the plaster of Beatrice's perfect smile began to crumble. "I can see I shouldn't have told you about that. But he won't be long, not when I tell him what happened. Marsden won't refuse to help us then."

Beatrice was halfway up the stairs when she peered back down over the banister to face Badeley again, calling: "It's almost over, darling."

Badeley stood at the base of the staircase, staring after her. He was startled when Marsden cleared his throat and emerged from the shadows of the servants' staircase.

"Where the hell did you come from?" Badeley asked.

"From the kitchen," said Marsden. "Mrs. Huston sent me to look for Nancy. She has tea ready for the ladies."

Badeley's sigh devolved into a groan. "I wish I was having tea. But I have to take His Lordship to the station again. And in this ghastly weather, too."

"Where is Lord Scarborough going?"

"To London again. I'll pick him up later tonight. He says he'll catch the last train, but I don't know why he doesn't just stay there. He's down often enough to open up the house in Mayfair. He will have to do it anyway when the sale of this place goes through."

Marsden thought of Lord Scarborough's empty study and forced a smile. "Well, I'd better go and find Nancy."

"She's probably in the library with her Ladyship," said Badeley. "I'll be in the garage later if you want a drink. While the cat's away and all that."

When Badeley's footsteps had faded down the stairs, Marsden crossed the salon to the library. He peeled open the door and peered through the crack. Lady Scarborough was lounging by the fire; her head lolled to one side, and snoring. In a high-backed chair by her side, Nancy sat with ankles crossed, a book resting in her lap. Her chin pricked up at the creak of the door. She scowled and scuttled across the room.

"Tea is ready for the ladies," Marsden whispered to her.

Nancy gave him a curt nod and waved him aside. "Don't you go waking her."

Marsden placed a hand over his heart in a promise, and Nancy hurried away. When he was sure she was out of hearing, he snuck past the sleeping countess across the library to slip through the rear door. He closed it behind himself and immediately tried the opposite door handle. To his surprise, Lord Scarborough's study was unlocked.

The room was cold and dark, the curtains drawn and no sign of the fire having been lit that morning. The earl's mahogany desk was largely bare but for a tray of papers and a lamp. Marsden turned on the light and began his search. He pushed aside the chair to open the drawers on each side. The contents were disappointing: ink and pens, some loose sheets of paper, and a tin of hard candies.

One of the lower drawers was empty for a single book. Marsden opened it to discover it was a ledger—the Falconer family's accounts. Marsden traced the lines with a finger, recognizing immediately that the earl was in severe financial trouble. Lord Scarborough had already sold most of the estate, and still, the family was on the verge of financial ruin. The remaining money from the sale of the tenant lands could not sustain both the Hall and the London house, and the family would be bankrupt before the year's end if Lord Scarborough continued trying to maintain both properties. The family's extravagant spending was certainly of no help—the money spent by Beatrice alone on clothing and jewelry would force her father to take drastic measures.

Marsden was most intrigued, however, by the staff wages. He already knew his salary of £50 per year to be more than generous for a tutor. He was more surprised that the few remaining staff were amassing the wages of a much larger core of employees. Linton received £250 per year. Mrs.

Huston received £200, as did Nancy. Holly also received £50. The most shocking number, however, was Badeley's hefty salary of £350 per year. Marsden couldn't even begin to comprehend why a chauffeur would be paid so much. Lord Scarborough did not exude generosity.

Finally, scrawled beneath the staff wages in an untidy hand was a payment to St. Jude's Sanatorium, York. Only one entry, a substantial sum of £1,000, was made on the twenty-second of May—the same morning Alice's bed had caught fire.

Marsden replaced the ledger and tried to open another drawer, but it would not budge. Frustrated, he tugged at the handle, but it remained stuck. There was no hole for a key. He kicked at it, the thud of his boot against the wood louder than he would have liked. Marsden froze, frightened that Nancy or even Lady Scarborough might have heard the noise. However, after a minute of agonizing silence in which no one came to the door, he returned to the drawer, discovering that it would now crack open just an inch.

Something was jarring the drawer shut. Again, Marsden pulled hard and heard the rip of cloth tearing. The drawer gave way and opened, a large strip of white muslin coming with it, trapped in the mounting. The muslin had been wrapped around an object at the base of the drawer. Marsden drew it out and was surprised at its weight. Even before he unwrapped the cloth, peeling away the layers, he had already guessed it was a gun. The Webley service pistol was a military issue. He had seen so many of them during his service that it could not be mistaken for a gun belonging to a civilian in the wilds of Yorkshire. It was Simon's service weapon. Marsden was sure of it.

His hands trembled as he opened and inspected the chamber. Only one bullet was missing. Simon had fired the gun. A section of vertebrae in Marsden's spine faltered, and he sagged like a marionette into the earl's chair, the pistol slipping from his moist palm and clattering onto the floor. The bullets escaped the open barrel and spun across the hardwood boards. Marsden spilled onto his knees, grappling to catch them. They rattled against the cylinder as he forced them back inside the gun. Snapping the chamber shut, he sat back on his heels, panting, the gun clutched against his heaving chest. He knew Simon would never have returned to duty without his weapon. The cigarette case was one thing: it could so easily have been forgotten, carelessly left behind, but not the gun. Either Simon had departed Maidenstone with no intention of reporting back for duty, or he had never left at all.

Marsden was torn between taking the weapon as evidence or returning it to its hiding place. He had nowhere to conceal it among his belongings. The search of his room had made that abundantly clear. Marsden rewrapped the gun and placed it back in the drawer. When the time came to confront Lord Scarborough, he would return for it and have ample proof that Simon did not return to service.

Marsden carefully ensured that everything in the study was as it had been when he had crept into the room. He turned off the light and snuck back out into the hallway. The house's silence, usually welcome, was stifling. Marsden's ears were roaring. He didn't know where to turn. The thought of locking himself in his room instantly induced a feeling of claustrophobia. To roam the rest of the house, however, meant the possibility of encountering the family or the rest of the staff. Making polite conversation when he had just found Simon's gun hidden away in the earl's study was an unbearable option. He longed to escape. Rain be damned, he was willing to get wet if it meant a moment of peace outside of the confusion of Maidenstone Hall.

Chapter Twenty-Seven

Unable to face Mrs. Huston in the servants' hall, Marsden abandoned his coat and hurried to the entrance hall closet beside the main door. Inside, he found a collection of winter wear belonging to the family. He recognized Beatrice's bright red wool coat hanging at the forefront of the closet the moment he opened the door. Rifling through the hangers, Marsden found the remaining selection featured only varying shades of black and navy blue.

Marsden froze, arms splitting apart two heavy coats, when he glimpsed a flash of green. Right at the far end of the closet, pressed against the wall, was a long olive coat, standard issue in the British army. Marsden shoved the other garments out of the way and ripped the uniform coat from its hanger. It was too long to fit Lord Scarborough. Simon's lieutenant's regalia shone in the light of the hallway. The gun and the coat—Simon had left behind his two most essential uniform items. Marsden pressed one sleeve of the coat to his face. It smelled of mothballs. Without hesitation, he took it out of the closet and shrugged the coat up his arms. It wasn't a perfect fit, but immediately, Marsden felt warm and safe, as though he were draping Simon himself around his shoulders, the whisper of a long-gone embrace encompassing him. He pulled the lapels tight together and closed the closet door. The folly of taking and wearing the coat was apparent, even to Marsden's shocked mind, but upon finding it, he couldn't bear the thought of taking it off. Unlike the stuffy dinner jacket Marsden had borrowed from Simon's wardrobe, the coat was familiar and comforting and reminded him of his old life with Simon.

Marsden escaped through the main entrance door before he could be seen, his heart racing. The rain had barely abated, but he dragged the coat's collar around his ears and lowered his face against the wind. He ran down the drive and was already at the base of the hill before he gave any careful thought to where he was going. The afternoon was dwindling, and there couldn't be more than one or two hours of weak sunlight remaining. Marsden thought briefly about his mission to visit the orchard, of searching through the apple trees despite the downpour, but there was barely enough light, and after the surprise of finding Simon's gun and coat, he decided he wanted a drink—stiff and strong. He hurried toward the village to find one.

The journey was much quicker along the main road than the detour via the adjoining farmland he had taken with Beatrice. Within twenty minutes, he stood outside the Hunter's Arms, his hands and ears burning in the cold sleet and bitter wind.

It was quiet inside the tavern, the murmur of only a handful of voices echoing in the cavernous space. Beyond the foyer, the main room was cozy; thick green curtains lined the narrow windows, and a single fire burning in the far corner. Two men were seated at the bar, both dressed in light work clothes, and they turned to give Marsden only a cursory glance as he approached. The man behind the bar, tall and wiry with receding grey hair, pinched his mouth into a tight small when Marsden, wet and white, leaned against the bar.

"Just visiting these parts, soldier?" the bartender asked. Without asking Marsden for an order, he poured a pint of lager.

Marsden gazed down at himself, at Simon's coat. "Not a soldier anymore. I work at Maidenstone Hall now."

The bartender looked up from his work, eyes alight with interest. "The Hall? I thought I knew everyone up at Maidenstone." He placed the glass of beer in front of Marsden. "What do they call you?"

"My name is Marsden Fisher. I'm tutor to the Lady Alice."

The two gentlemen to his left swiftly gave up their conversation, and Marsden could feel their eyes fix on him as they swiveled on their stools.

"Lady Alice," said the bartender. "Now, there's a young woman we rarely see in the village."

"I've seen her," said one of the men, turning his back on his companion to face Marsden. "Down in the village this Sunday just past. She's a beauty, all right."

His companion snorted into his drink. "Pity she's not all there." He tapped a dirty finger against his forehead. "I heard they locked her away for being mad."

The bartender clicked his tongue. "You keep your opinions to yourself, Davey." He rested an elbow on the bar and stared Marsden down. "We don't see much of anyone from the Hall down here these days. Young Mr. Badeley comes in from time to time for a dram, but they mostly keep to themselves. That'll be a shilling, Mr. Fisher."

Marsden had reached into his pocket when a voice behind him piped up: "I'll pay for him, Lewis."

A lone patron seated in a small booth beside the fire was now waving. Marsden waved back and crossed the room to join Mr. Carlisle. When he approached, he could see the old farmer was not alone but accompanied by little Grace curled up by his side, a fabric doll in her lap.

"That's very kind of you, Mr. Carlisle," said Marsden. "Hello, Grace."

"You remember Mr. Fisher, do you, Gracie?" Carlisle asked the little girl. "I'd say he's come in to escape the rain, just like us."

Grace peered up from the quiet conversation she was enjoying with her doll and smiled briefly, shyly, before burying her face into Carlisle's shoulder. Carlisle gestured to the seat across from him. Marsden joined them and was again struck by the familiarity of Grace's petite face. When he saw her now, he felt no jealousy but sympathy for Beatrice. Grace was a beautiful child, and although he had never imagined being a parent, he could understand Beatrice's longing for the girl. Something about the roundness of Grace's cheeks, the soft curl of her blonde hair, made Marsden want to wrap her in his arms and hold her tight.

For a time, the two men drank in silence, enjoying the warmth of the tavern and ignoring the curious eyes of Lewis and the other patrons.

"Don't mind them," said Carlisle over the rim of his pint glass. "It's a small village, and the Hall is a favorite topic of gossip."

Marsden could understand the appeal. To a village whose Lord had sold his stake in their lives, the continuing presence of the Falconers must have caused quite the conundrum among the former tenants—particularly with Beatrice storming into their homes uninvited.

"I must apologize," said Marsden, "for my sudden intrusion into your home the other day. I couldn't help but feel we weren't welcome."

Carlisle's lips trembled when he smiled. "Not at all. My wife always enjoys having visitors who appreciate her baking."

"But I gather the ladies at the Hall have been asked not to visit. That's why you came to the house, was it not? To report our visit to Lady Scarborough? I can assure you if I had known—"

Carlisle raised a hand. "Please, Marsden, I wouldn't want you to think you weren't welcome. The truth is that my daughter is quite strict when it comes to the routine of Gracie's day." He patted Grace on the head, and she smiled up at him. "Lucy feels that surprise visits cause a disturbance. It was just that we didn't know Lady Alice was coming."

Marsden considered correcting Carlisle and telling him that it was, in fact, Beatrice who had visited. He suspected she allowed the Carlisle family to misidentify her to cause Alice trouble.

"She was very different as a little girl," said Carlisle, unbidden.

"Whom?" asked Marsden, drawn back into the conversation.

"Lady Alice. A very quiet, gentle little thing. Unlike her sister." Carlisle snorted with gentle laughter. "Quiet and gentle were not words you'd have associated with Beatrice Falconer."

"You knew them as children?" Marsden asked, somewhat taken aback. He couldn't imagine Lord Scarborough allowing his children to associate closely with his tenants.

"Oh aye, they often played on our farm. It's the closest to the big house, you see. It drove poor Ruth Huston to near madness, the way they would disappear into the woods and turn up unannounced in our pigsty, playing in the mud."

"They sound like they were positively wild."

151

Marsden had meant to joke, but a line dug deep between Carlisle's thick brows.

"Not Alice," the farmer said, quite insistent. "She would follow her sister anywhere, but she was a good girl. Beatrice, now, there was a wild thing, to be sure. Her obsession with fire was certainly not very ladylike. She was always setting things alight. One time, she took a handful of matches to a hay bale on my property. To this day, Malcolm Hughes swears it was Beatrice who set his barn burning."

Marsden leaned closer, lowering his voice: "And when did this happen?"

"Almost eight years ago now. Of course, nothing ever came of it, but old Mal still reckons it was her. He lost a stallion in that fire."

"Why did nothing ever come of it?" Marsden asked, although he imagined Lord Scarborough denying vehemently that his daughter would be involved. He knew the children of fine lords and ladies could sometimes escape their responsibilities and misdeeds when money was promised. It had been, after all, Marsden and Simon's hope that Lord Scarborough could use his influence to have them both sent home from the front.

Carlisle's face drooped. "It was just before the accident, you see. I remember it so well as the barn burned the summer she died."

Marsden stared at Carlisle. Something—he wasn't sure exactly what—had become stuck deep in his throat. He coughed to dislodge it. "The accident?"

"Aye. She drowned in the lake, poor lass. Did they not tell you how she died?"

"Who died?" Marsden spat the words. His fingers tightened around his glass.

"Lady Beatrice. Well, of course, they wouldn't talk of it. It was a terrible time. If you ask me, Lady Scarborough never really recovered. I rarely see her now, but she's a shell of the fine lady she used to be."

"She drowned," Marsden repeated. "Beatrice drowned in the lake?"

"The lake down by the Hall. I felt sorry for him then, the grand Lord up in his palace. A terrible way to lose a child."

"And Alice…" Marsden couldn't find the words. He found himself staring at Grace, mouth agape. She peered back at him with wide, owlish eyes.

152

"Is their last surviving child, aye." Carlisle paused to shake his head in sympathy, his eyes darting toward the little girl beside him. "When his son was killed in the war, I suppose Lord Scarborough didn't see sense in holding on to the legacy and started to sell off the estate. As far as I know, there are no male heirs left in the family, so the title will dissolve anyway."

Marsden pressed his palms over his face and rubbed his fingers against his eyes, trying to reset his thoughts. He had only just seen Beatrice that afternoon, back at the Hall. But it hadn't been Beatrice at all.

"When was this again? When she died?" His voice rasped, a terrible scratching all-consuming at the back of his throat. He took another long gulp of beer and swallowed hard.

"Eight years ago," said Carlisle. "She was just eleven years old, if I remember correctly."

"And everyone knows this? About Beatrice?"

Marsden could hear the fury in his voice, the anger directed at himself almost as much as the residents of Maidenstone Hall. He had accepted the fairytale of Beatrice being alive and well. He had believed the tricks and misdirection, some of his own creation; the photographs of Alice and Beatrice had convinced him of their existence, but he was a bumbling, gullible fool not to realize why there were no recent photographs of them together. Beatrice was long dead, and Marsden had conveniently ignored the clues.

Eyes narrowing in confusion, Carlisle said, "Of course, everyone knows. Most of the village lived here back then. Although I suppose nowadays it's part of the folklore of the place. Some say her ghost haunts the lake by the Hall."

The laughter welled up in Marsden's belly, bubbling and tickling at first in this throat and then bursting forth in uncontrollable heaving breaths. He choked on the sickness of the joke, coughing into his fist as he collapsed against the table, the hideous mirth boiling out of him. Across the table, Carlisle became alarmed and reached out to Marsden, ready to intervene. Red-faced and still chortling between coughs, Marsden shook off the older man with the wave of a hand. When he could breathe again, he took a series of long, deep gulps of his beer.

"I'm sorry, Mr. Carlisle," he said at last. "I don't mean to be inappropriate. I'm just a little shocked that no one would tell me these things."

"I suppose they have their reasons," said Carlisle cautiously, still eyeing Marsden with a clear suspicion the younger man might keel over at any moment. "Are you sure you're all right?"

"Absolutely, absolutely." Marsden waved down Lewis, signaling for two more pints. "It's just been one of those days."

The hysteria that had consumed Marsden began to subside as he and Carlisle sat in uncomfortable silence, waiting for their drinks to be refreshed. Clearly disturbed by Marsden's outburst, Grace huddled closer to Carlisle, and he draped his arm around her shoulder. Carlisle finally broke the startled hush, gesturing to Marsden's coat.

"So you were a lieutenant? In the war."

Tired of lying, Marsden sank further into his chair and said, "No. I was nobody."

Lewis brought the drinks to the table, delivering the fresh beer without a word. Marsden swallowed the last dregs of his first pint and set to work on the next.

"You look like you're setting my courage, my boy," said Carlisle.

Marsden put down his glass long enough to catch his breath. He tried to smile, but his lips would not cooperate. "I am, Mr. Carlisle. I certainly am."

Chapter Twenty-Eight

The sun had set when Marsden began his return journey to Maidenstone Hall, the dark clouds that hovered above him almost blocking out entirely the last of the daylight. The freezing rain had eased to an unpleasant drizzle, and he hunched his shoulders in Simon's heavy coat as he stumbled up the drive to the house. Marsden virtually fell through the front entrance of the Hall in his hurry to escape the cold. Shaking off the worst of the water, he had half removed the coat when Badeley appeared, seemingly out of nowhere. His heart leaped up into his throat when the chauffeur stepped before him.

"You scared the life out of me," said Marsden, breathlessly clutching his chest.

Badeley's expression was grim, his pale eyes narrow as he examined Marsden. "That's not yours, is it? Where did you find it?"

Realizing he meant the coat, Marsden removed it with hurried pulls at the sleeves. "I just borrowed it from the closet here. Don't tell His Lordship, will you?"

"Of course not. Best you put it back, though."

The depth of Badeley's tone conflicted with his tight smile, and Marsden heard the threat so thinly veiled behind it. He was reluctant to let go of the coat but returned it to its hiding place under Badeley's beady stare.

"Look at you," said Badeley. "You're a drowned rat. Come on downstairs and get warm."

Marsden did not want to go anywhere with Badeley. "Actually, I thought I'd go upstairs to change—"

155

"Don't be ridiculous. It's freezing upstairs. You come with me."

Badeley was upon him before Marsden could protest further, grasping his arm with tight fingers and guiding him across the salon. The forceful drag of Badeley's strength made Marsden's stomach lurch as he was hurried to the stairs and ushered down to the servants' hall with a speed that made his head spin. He may have drunk a little too much at the tavern, but Marsden was conscious enough of the situation to feel unnerved by Badeley's insistence they go together into the bowels of the house.

When Badeley steered Marsden into the servants' dining room, Mrs. Huston was pacing back and forth before the fire. She stopped and threw her hands in the air at the sight of him.

"And where have you been?" she cried. "We were so worried about you!"

"I just went down to the village, Mrs. Huston," said Marsden when Badeley brusquely pushed him down onto a chair by the fire. "I didn't mean to cause you any alarm."

"Why on earth would you want to go to the village? In this weather?"

"I fancied a pint at the tavern."

Mrs. Huston huffed, face red. "It's easy for some. I wish I could wander off to the tavern whenever the fancy took me."

A little drunk and amused by her frustration, Marsden was bursting to confront Mrs. Huston. And Badeley. He wondered what they would say in their defense if he asked them now why they pretended Beatrice was alive. Would they be ashamed, making him the butt of an ugly prank? Would they laugh at him for being so gullible? Simon, he thought with a shudder, would have been embarrassed by him, by his stupidity.

The accusation bit at the tip of his tongue, but he held it back when Nancy stormed into the dining room, head down. She was startled when she looked up to see Marsden.

"You're back!"

"So it would seem," said Marsden, aware he was swaying minutely in his chair. "Apparently, I was missed."

"We thought you'd run off," said Nancy, crossing her arms over her chest. "You could have told someone you were going out."

A sanguine smile crept across Marsden's face as he saw the chance to taunt her. "Why would I run off?"

"Well," said Nancy, refusing to take the bait, "you're back now. And her Ladyship is asleep in the library, Mrs. Huston. I'm not sure it will be worth your effort to make up a tray for her."

"And Beatrice?" Mrs. Huston asked.

"She'll have a tray in her room."

Marsden gawked at the two women, floundering before the ridiculous charade, apparently produced entirely for his benefit alone. The thought of Mrs. Huston making supper for a dead girl made him rigid with loathing. No, he reminded himself—not for a dead girl, but a young woman pretending to be one.

"Excellent," said Badeley and winked. "More food for us, isn't that right, Mrs. Huston?"

Mrs. Huston was not amused. "You'll get your supper at the usual time, you cheeky imp!"

"Get any supper at the tavern?" Badeley asked Marsden.

"No. I just had a couple of pints with Mr. Carlisle."

A thick silence melted over the dining room. Mrs. Huston sank onto the bench seating of the table, clutching at her apron. A rancorous cheer reverberated in Marsden's beer-addled mind at the sight of their nervousness.

Nancy leaned over him. "What did you talk about?"

Sensing her concern, Marsden delighted in a light shrug. "Oh, you know. Just this and that. We talked about the village and so forth."

"You mustn't put too much stock into anything old Mr. Carlisle says, Marsden," said Mrs. Huston, with a tone of urgency he had never heard from her.

"Why's that?"

"He's a bit of an old gossip. He'll repeat anything he hears, true or false."

"You needn't worry," Marsden assured her, "he didn't say a word about Grace."

For a brief moment, Marsden thought that Mrs. Huston would faint. She swayed in her seat when she cast a startled glance at Nancy, but the maid only stared back in silence, unreadable as ever. If her steely eyes could speak, Marsden was sure she was urging Mrs. Huston to be quiet. As usual, it was Badeley who couldn't keep his mouth shut.

"How do you know about Grace?" he asked, cocking his chin.

"I met her at the Carlisle's farm," said Marsden.

Mrs. Huston's spine sagged minutely. "Oh, yes. Of course. I thought you meant..."

"If you mean the child's parentage, Alice did tell me. To be fair, I had guessed something was going on when I met Grace."

Nancy's tight jaw dropped open. For once, her eyes, bright and water, betrayed her emotion. Fear. "She told you?"

Now that he knew that Grace was her daughter, Alice's insistence that her dead sister was the little girl's mother became all the more ghoulish. The very thought made him grimace. "Yes," he said. "Yesterday."

Mrs. Huston leaned in toward Marsden, one bony hand clutching at his wrist, her weight settling against his arm.

"You mustn't say anything; you understand that, don't you?" She stared at him with such intensity that Marsden instinctively leaned away from her.

Any thought Marsden had of confronting the group with his knowledge of Beatrice's death faded as he reveled in the new game he was playing with them. Their panicked reaction to the idea of Grace's true identity being revealed to the community allowed him to tie them into the same cluster of knots into which he had been bound. Let them fret, he thought. Let them see what it is to be led on a merry dance through nonsense.

"Of course," he said mildly, patting Mrs. Huston's hand where it grasped his arm. "Alice made that very clear to me. I can only imagine how people would gossip about Grace if they found out."

"She would be ruined," Nancy said with a vicious hiss.

"The family would be ruined, is what you mean," Badeley spoke so harshly that even Marsden was surprised. For the past week, it had been rare to see him without a smile, but now Badeley looked severe—even spiteful—his face white and taut.

"We would all be in trouble, Badeley," Nancy reminded him, chin dipped low, eyes now slits as she glared at him. "You, of all people, know that."

A service bell rang, and Mrs. Huston released her death grip on Marsden.

The shaking bell on the board above the dining table indicated the request was coming from the library.

"Her Ladyship is awake," said Nancy. She stood straight and faced Marsden. "There mustn't be any more talk of this."

She hurried out of the room toward her mistress, and Badeley, too, moved to leave.

"I'm going to do some work on the car," he said and stalked out of the room, slamming the servants' entrance door behind him.

Mrs. Huston rose slowly from her place at the table, wincing at the pressure on her joints as she stood. She paused to stare at him one last time, fearfully, longingly and then left Marsden alone in the dining room without another word.

Chapter Twenty-Nine

Keenly aware that he was still incredibly damp and cold, Marsden returned to his room. He planned to change into dry clothes and smile through supper as usual, waiting for the cover of night when he could attempt to retrieve Simon's gun and coat. With both pieces of evidence, he could finally consider confronting Lord Scarborough.

He was trudging up the servants' staircase when Nancy appeared at the top, blocking his way.

"She wants you," said Nancy.

"Who wants me?" Marsden asked, squinting up through the shadow she cast upon him.

"Lady Scarborough. She's awake, and she's asking for you."

Nancy jerked her chin over her shoulder, and he followed her up the stairs. After the conversation he had just had, Lady Scarborough's request struck Marsden as suspicious. He wondered if Nancy had tattled, revealing his visit to the tavern and his intimate knowledge of Grace's true identity, at least that she was Alice's daughter.

Marsden followed Nancy into the library, where Lady Scarborough lounged with eyes closed in her favorite armchair by the fire. The gramophone hummed quietly in the corner behind her, playing a song Marsden didn't recognize. Beside the countess, a decanter of brandy sat half empty on the table. She stirred as they approached.

"Mr. Fisher is here, my lady," said Nancy.

Lady Scarborough raised a limp wrist, eyes fluttering. "You can leave us now, Nancy."

Nancy gave Marsden a sharp, pointed look and stalked out of the room, closing the doors behind her with more force than necessary.

Lady Scarborough gestured for him to sit directly across from her. She placed one hand on the book in her lap. "I thought perhaps you could read to me, Marsden," she said. "Alice has told me you're so very good at it." She sighed and passed the book over into his hands. "Perhaps I should keep you as my personal reader when she goes away."

"Is Alice going away, my lady?" he asked even though her meaning was clear; he would soon be out of a job and forced to leave Maidenstone Hall. Alice was leaving. He was running out of time to act.

Lady Scarborough sank one cheek into her open palm and said, "I'm afraid it's become inevitable. Or at least my husband tells me so. Have you read this one before?"

Marsden inspected the book in his lap. *The Great Boer War.* "No, my lady. Do you enjoy the works of Sir Arthur?"

"He writes entertaining trifles, does he not? Simon was the one who loved his work. He was so enamored with—what was his name? Brigadier..."

"Gerard. I've always been a Holmes man, myself."

She sighed, eyes closed but moving behind her lashes as if picking at memories. "Brigadier Gerard. That's right. You remind me of him, you know? Simon, I mean."

Marsden thought this to be unlikely. He had never considered himself all that attractive, even before the bayonet slash had disfigured him. His hazel eyes were plain, his hair unruly and coarse. Simon had been tall, blonde, and beautiful. He had exuded an air of aristocracy that a man of lesser birth could not imitate, and his confidence had been particularly alluring. No one, including Marsden, could resist the beauty of Simon Falconer. Marsden had been transfixed the first time he had seen Simon storming across the parade ground to join the regiment, drowning in those unforgettable green eyes—the same eyes he and his sister had inherited from Lady Scarborough.

"He wasn't like the other boys," she continued, her voice listless, far away in another place and time. "Never interested in the girls in the village. Never keen to go to balls or parties. He just wanted to shoot and hunt on his own.

I think my daughter was right in what she said. He did complain about the war when he was home, but perhaps Simon was drawn to violence." She nodded toward the book in Marsden's hands. "My husband says this recent business in Europe was not much like the Boer War. That it was far worse."

"It was very awful, my lady," he said, "but you shouldn't think of such things."

Lady Scarborough let her head fall back against the chair and stared up at the ceiling. "I can't think of anything else. Sometimes, when I shut my eyes, I see only Simon. Dead. A bullet in his brain."

Marsden leaned closer. "Is that how he died, my lady? No one will tell me."

"So I'm told. I wasn't allowed to see—"

She raised a hand to cover her mouth as though she might be sick and fell forward in her chair, her thin frame crowding itself.

Marsden lurched, prepared to catch her if necessary. "Lady Scarborough, are you unwell? Shall I call for Nancy?"

Lady Scarborough sank back into the armchair, shaking her head, her hand still pressed against her mouth. A log of wood on the fire gave a loud pop, and in the echo of silence the sound made, Marsden realized that the music had ceased and the needle of the gramophone was scratched methodically against the inside of the record.

Eventually, Lady Scarborough dropped her hand into her lap and attempted a wavering smile. "My apologies, Marsden. I'm quite well. Could you change the record?" She waved toward the skipping gramophone, her hand flopping dramatically atop her thin wrist.

Marsden circled her chair to the gramophone and lifted the needle. Beside it, a heavy wooden box was bulging with records, and he began to flip through them.

"Uh... Handel?" When she shook her head, he continued to leaf through the titles. "Al Jolson?"

"Goodness, no," she said with a half moan. "Dreadful. He was one of Simon's favorites, you know."

Marsden did know and bit his lip. "How about John McCormack?"

"Fine. Fine."

Marsden placed the record and cranked the handle of the gramophone. As the quavering tones of an Irish ballad warmed the gloomy library, he rejoined Lady Scarborough by the fireplace, book in hand.

She said, "If you could begin from the first chapter, Marsden, I would be most grateful."

Her hands shaking, she reached across the armchair for the decanter and refilled her glass. Marsden noted Lady Scarborough's complexion was more ashen than usual, her bony wrists more pronounced, and her spine hunched. When she had settled back into the chair, the glass cradled in both hands, Marsden opened the book to the beginning of the first chapter;

"Take a community of Dutchmen of the type of those who defended themselves for fifty years against all the power of Spain at a time when Spain was the greatest power in the world..."

Marsden continued to read, and Lady Scarborough melted into her chair. He looked up sporadically from the pages to see her eyes fluttering, her grip loosening on the tumbler between her fingers. He watched the glass teeter against the arm of the chair but took a strange pleasure in hoping it would spill. Watching her nod off, Marsden, too, felt his exhaustion encroaching. The adrenaline rush of his day—retrieving his stolen belongings, his long walk to and from the tavern, the emotional turmoil of discovering the truth of Beatrice's death—weighed heavily at every bone and muscle in his body, already languid with cold and alcohol.

Arthur Conan Doyle's description of the Boer War was so tedious that the dull contents of the book made Marsden's eyes droop. Within the first chapter, Lady Scarborough had begun to snore lightly, and Marsden let the volume rest in his lap, allowing himself to rest his eyes.

Chapter Thirty

Marsden sunk deep into a trench, wading through knee-deep mud, searching for Simon. The earth walls were too short, and he ducked his head as bullets struck against the low ridges, throwing wet dirt into his eyes. With every step, he called for Simon, dragging the bodies of fallen soldiers onto their backs to better see their ruined faces. The trenches melded together, a never-ending maze of wet clay and blood until, at all at once, they faded into walls of wood, and Marsden stumbled through a doorway into a bedroom. The deafening whistle of mortar shells was immediately silenced, the winter rain ceasing and replaced with a room full of warm sunlight. At its center, Marsden found Simon at last, alive, well, and in the arms of another man. Sitting atop his new lover, Simon lifted his head from a leisurely kiss and grinned, an apathetic smirk that chilled Marsden to his bones.

Marsden was startled awake when a hand squeezed his shoulder. Blinking owlishly, he peered up at Linton, standing over him. When he looked toward the fire, Lady Scarborough was no longer in the chair across from him.

"Her Ladyship has just gone up to bed," said Linton. "You should do the same, I think. Mrs. Huston has put aside supper for you."

Marsden put down the book and went to the servants' stairway. The house was silent when he ascended to his room. He had no intention of returning to the servants' hall to fetch his supper. His stomach churned with the humiliations he had suffered that day. The insistence of the staff that Beatrice was alive and well only added to his bewilderment. Even Lady

Scarborough, in her drunken stupor, continued to play along.

Retrieving the package of letters and photographs from his breast jacket pocket, Marsden was pleased to discover that they were not wet from the rain. Another time, he might have leafed through the photographs and reread the letters to calm himself. Marsden could not bear confronting the person he used to be before the war scarred him so badly. Back then, he would never have been so easily fooled—at least not at the hands of a mentally unhinged nineteen-year-old girl. This family situation must have been the insanity that Simon had been so keen to hide from him—that Simon had not been ashamed of him or their relationship but of the lunatics residing at Maidenstone Hall. Simon obviously had no love for his own family, but they, in turn, had little affection to spare for his memory. If they could lie so easily about Beatrice, it stood to reason that they could lie about Simon's character, just as they had about his disappearance.

Marsden held the bundle of precious belongings against his lips and assured himself that every ugly portrait the family and staff painted of Simon was simply another one of their many lies.

Marsden waited long into the evening to creep out of his room. Confident that the house, at last, was at rest, he lit a candle and snuck down the servants' stairs to the ground floor of the house. His mission, to retrieve Simon's gun and coat, was simple, and he was confident that he could achieve both objectives in minutes, returning to his room quickly and quietly without fear of being caught.

At the door of Lord Scarborough's study, he pressed his ear against the wood and heard nothing from the other side. There was no light shining from beneath the door. He tried to turn the handle, but it would not budge. Marsden jiggled the handle with more force. It was locked. He cursed and retraced his steps along the hallway to the salon, where he strode across the checkered floor to the front entrance and tried the coat closet door. It, too, was locked. Marsden wanted to beat himself over the head for his inaction. He had ample opportunity that afternoon to steal both items. Badeley must have reported seeing Marsden in Simon's coat. Now, the coat and gun were no longer accessible.

He knew Linton was the only staff member with keys to every room in the house, and so Marsden ran down the stairs to the servant's hall to the butler's room. Seeing the door closed, he guessed it was locked but attempted to turn the handle all the same, only to confirm his suspicion. The throaty gurgle of someone clearing their throat behind him made Marsden jump. He spun around to see Linton himself standing in the shadows of the hallway. The old butler was still fully dressed and neat in his livery, as immaculate as ever despite the late hour. His beak-like nose appeared more elongated in the candlelight, his eyes wide and dark as the water in the lake, and Marsden shriveled at the sight of him.

"Is there something I can help you with, Mr. Fisher?" he asked.

A hot blush streaked along Marsden's neck at the embarrassment of being caught trying to sneak into Linton's office. He racked his exhausted brain and forced a tight smile.

"A light bulb," he said in a rush. "Mine is on the fritz. I assumed you kept them in here."

"No, I do not," said Linton, "but I would be happy to procure one for you in the morning. Good night, Mr. Fisher."

Marsden didn't dare contradict Linton and retreated up the stairs, sure he could feel the fire of the butler's hard stare against his back. As he returned to his room, he cursed himself for being so careless to be seen wearing Simon's coat. Determined as he was to get his hands once more on the coat and gun, Marsden would simply have to try again. He needed proof when the time came to challenge Lord Scarborough: evidence that confirmed Simon had never returned to the front. Come what may, Marsden would force Harrold Falconer to admit that his son had disappeared within the walls of Maidenstone Hall. After all, he had yet to search the orchard. Holly's needling and Mrs. Huston's fear gave him hope that there was still a dark corner of the estate yet to give up its secrets.

Buoyed by his self-assurance that all was not lost, Marsden began to prepare for bed. He had only just dressed in his pajamas when the light bulb above his head began to flicker and buzz. Now used to the strange electricity surges in the house, Marsden paid the static light no attention and simply switched it off at the wall. He climbed into bed just as Alice's screams cracked the night's silence from the floor below. Marsden pulled a pillow over his head and pressed it down tight, refusing to listen.

Chapter Thirty-One

Waking early, Marsden was motivated to start his day with a sense of purpose. He washed and dressed quickly, eager to leave the house before any of his colleagues could stop him.

However, any hope of slipping out of the servants' entrance unseen was ruined by Mrs. Huston poking her head out of the kitchen doorway when Marsden hurried past it to fetch his coat.

"You're up early," she said, forcing him to pause at the door and acknowledge her.

"I want to go for a quick walk before I start work this morning, Mrs. Huston," he said. He slipped on his coat, ready to escape her attention.

Mrs. Huston shook her head. "You and your walks, Marsden. Anyone would think you have an aversion to being inside, the amount of time you spend wandering around the outdoors. No matter the weather, too!"

"You should try it sometime," he said and opened the door, rushing outside before she could engage him in any further conversation.

The cloud of morning fog was thick when Marsden circled the west wing, and he could barely see more than a few feet in front of his face. He made his way down the hill, circling the lake. Its water was still, and Marsden slowed momentarily to stare down into its murky depths, its serene appearance so different to him now that he knew what had happened there eight years ago. Now that his imagination ran wild with the vision of Beatrice drowning in its black shadows. The water was clean with the recent rain, but the darkness of the lake was still unnerving. A gentle gust of wind rushed around his ears, and a soft whistle chimed in his ears, as delicate as a whisper, making him shiver.

A nagging part of his brain teased Marsden for the folly of plunging into the nest of trees for clues, but now that he had raised enough suspicion to ensure Simon's coat and gun were locked up, the apple orchard was Marsden's last option in searching for evidence of the Falconer's duplicity. Holly had spoken of it as if it were a haunted and terrifying place, and as he stepped into the dark shadows of the gnarled, neglected trees, Marsden immediately agreed with her summation. His hackles rose, skin prickling along his spine, and he began to believe he would find a terrible secret between the branches.

He stumbled through the expanse of apple trees for some time, tripping over their bulging roots and fallen branches as he paced up and down the rows of weathered trunks. The air was thick with stagnant moisture, giving Marsden the distinct sensation of wading through the mist as if it were muddy water. He was beginning to feel ridiculous, wandering through the orchard, searching for anything—the rubble of a building, a road, any sign of human presence. Just as he began to suspect that he had fallen prey to Holly's cruel joke, he caught sight of something dark rising between the trees at the center of the orchard. Among the trees, a slab of stone erupted out of the earth as a giant blemish, suddenly unmissable despite the fog. Blackened with age and dirt, a thin layer of moss crept up from the ground and clung to its slick surface. Marsden knelt on the damp earth to wipe away the worst of the dirt with his coat sleeve until he could read the inscription carved into the stone.

Beatrice Grace Falconer

1900-1911

Sitting back on his heels, Marsden stroked the gravestone, tracing the rough edges of the engraving with his gloved fingers. He thought of the large tombstone the Falconers had erected for their son over an empty grave in the village graveyard and was stung by the cruelty of hiding their daughter in a neglected orchard.

"Sad, isn't it?"

Marsden almost fell backward when he twisted abruptly to see Alice standing just a few yards away. The fog muted and dulled her figure, but he could make out her pale face and vivid hair. She was wrapped in an oversized black coat, her hands tucked inside the sleeves. Marsden didn't know what to say. He jolted to his feet, staggering back from the grave.

"My mother used to come here often," said Alice when she approached. "She would lay flowers, and the gardener would tend to the grave. Mother stopped visiting so often when Simon died. When we saw her walking the other day, I think it was the first time in months that she'd been down here."

"The red coat," said Marsden. "It belongs to your mother."

"It's her favorite color. Or it was. She doesn't wear that coat very often anymore. She barely leaves the house at all."

Marsden's fingers curled into fists by his sides. He said, "You let me think I had seen Beatrice. You let me convince myself that I had finally seen you two together at the same time, but it was your mother. You tricked me."

He fought the urge to kick the gravestone. Instead, he buried his face in his hands and tried to contain the fury welling inside him. Alice offered no recognition of his anger. She crouched to scrub at the inscription on her sister's grave, just as Marsden had done. When she stared back up at him, her pupils were overblown in the shadows of the fog.

Marsden wanted to scream into her silence. "Well? Don't you have anything to say to me?"

"Who told you she was here?" Alice asked. "Was it Mr. Carlisle?"

Marsden wondered which of the staff had told Alice he'd met with Carlisle. Probably Badeley, he thought.

"No, but he told me how she died. He assumed I knew all about the horrible tale of Lady Beatrice drowning in the lake."

"You must be very upset."

Marsden couldn't hold back the stifled laugh that erupted from his throat. "Upset? Dear God, you can't imagine how I feel right now. You must be so very pleased with yourself."

Alice's creamy brow creased. "I don't know what you mean."

"Is this how you entertain yourselves out here? With lies and fantasies—" He pointed to the headstone, his voice rising: "—about a dead girl? You must think I'm a damned fool!"

"You're not a fool," she countered, raising a placating hand.

In his anger, Marsden began to pace back and forth before the grave. "I certainly feel like one! I can't believe I fell for the joke for so long! How you all must have laughed at me."

"You mustn't blame the others, Marsden. It's my fault. Mrs. Huston, Nancy, Linton—they want to protect me."

"Protect you? From what? Surely I'm the only one in the whole county who didn't know that you parade around as your dead sister!"

Accosted by his barrage of humiliated anger, Alice's face crumpled into deep hurt, her eyes welling. "Is that what you think?" she asked, her voice trembling.

"What else am I supposed to think?" Marsden insisted.

"I'm not a bad person, Marsden. I'm just not very well."

He stalked toward her, stooping over her. "What is it that you want from me? Why did you bring me here?"

"But I didn't bring you here," said Alice. "You came to Maidenstone Hall on your own accord. You found the orchard all by yourself."

Distracted by his plots and plans and intent on his search for Simon, Marsden had quickly assumed he was being taken advantage of just because he was at hand and easy to manipulate. Now, he wondered if he had been invited to the Hall on false pretenses. Alice had not required a tutor at all. She had needed another victim to torment.

"What are you and the others planning for me?" he asked. "Why play this game?"

"No one is planning anything for you."

"I heard them! I heard them talking about me after your father searched my room. They want me to help you with something."

She said, "I don't know what you're talking about, Marsden. When was this?"

"Yesterday! You found me eavesdropping on them. Surely you remember."

Alice's head rattled from side to side as she stood to face him. "No—"

"You told me you wanted my help to get Grace back, but it's got to be more than that."

"That wasn't me."

Incensed, Marsden threw his hands in the air. "Come now, my lady, you can give up the charade."

"I mean it," she said, almost spitting. "That was Beatrice. I never remember anything that happens when she's around."

The howl threatening to erupt from Marsden's aching throat since she had arrived finally burst forth, the depth of his scream shattering the eerie silence of the orchard. A flock of squawking blackbirds exploded from inside the tree branches above them, sweeping into the air to escape Marsden's anger.

"Beatrice is dead!" he said at the top of his voice.

Alice visibly shook when she screamed back at him: "I know that! I was there. I saw her die."

She wiped at a tear, and Marsden instantly felt guilty for having yelled at her. His anger dulled at the thought of eleven-year-old Beatrice perishing in the lake's murky depths.

"What happened? he asked, softening, voice subsiding.

Alice sniffed and jerked her head back in the direction of the house. "Come with me."

Marsden didn't immediately follow her, watching her weave through the apple trees, black coat sweeping through the debris of leaves, rotting fruit, and branches, but when he began to lose sight of her through the mist, energy jolted into his legs, forcing him to hurry after her. Afraid she would disappear in the tendrils of white haze, he picked up his pace and even ran a few steps to catch her. She knew her way through the orchard by rote, and they emerged from the thick cluster of trees much quicker than he had anticipated. Beyond the orchard, the air cleared, and Marsden could see the shimmer of the lake.

Alice was silent, her tread quiet on the ground while Marsden clumped beside her in his heavy boots. Alice pointed to a small embankment at the lake's edge that cut into the water. By the water's edge, a handful of wooden poles emerged from the depths, skeleton remains of an abandoned jetty.

"This is where it happened," Alice explained.

"Did she fall?" he asked, staring into the still water.

"She was pushed. It wasn't an accident."

"Did you push her?"

Alice lifted her chin, defiant. "It was Simon."

"No," he said immediately. "Why would he do that?" In his disbelief, it was all he could think to ask.

"He enjoyed terrorizing us."

Marsden slammed the heel of one hand against his forehead, closing his eyes. It was one thing for siblings to bully and tease each other. It was another entirely for one of them to die when a prank went wrong.

"No," he said again. "He would have gone in after her. He could swim—"

He stopped short, so used to hiding his relationship with Simon. She already knew his darkest secrets, but Marsden's stomach still flipped at the confession.

Alice was nonchalant about the slip, stepping closer to stare at him with steely eyes. "You accuse me of lies and fantasy, but you have deceived us every day since you arrived here. Beatrice told me all about your letters. I know about the photographs of Simon and you."

Marsden would have felt chastised for his hypocrisy if it weren't for the sting of her insistence that Beatrice continued to play an active part in her charade. His fingers itched to shake her.

"Beatrice is dead—"

"And it was Simon who killed her," said Alice, "whether or not you are willing to accept it."

The burning desperation to defend Simon urged him on, pushing Marsden closer to the edge of the lake to persuade himself to cast aside the fear it evoked or to evade Alice's proximity.

"It must have been an accident," he said desperately. "Simon would never have—"

Alice, relentless in her sudden anger, wouldn't let him finish. "Drowned her? Held her down and drowned her. That's exactly what happened. And do you know why he did it? She stole his cigarettes. His precious, fancy, gold cigarettes."

An icy shiver shot up Marsden's spine as fast as the bile rose in his throat. "It's not true," he said, stammering.

"He chased her all the way down here, you know. She was clutching them when he dragged her into the lake."

Bile was rising in his throat. He said again, "It's not true. Nothing you say is true."

"Believe what you like," she said with an icy sneer. "I'm going back to the house."

Alice walked away from him, and Marsden felt no impulse to follow her. He stared back into the black water. Without willing the image into his mind, it appeared on its own—Simon and Beatrice in the lake. He couldn't help but imagine the scene as Alice had described it. The very idea of Simon, six years older than his sister, holding the tiny frame of Beatrice under the water made his stomach tumble and drop. Unbidden, the memory of a wet, dark morning at Verdun flooded over him—the memory of Gerry Thwaites, face down in a puddle, Simon above him.

The sun had not yet risen, and it had been raining when Simon discovered Gerry smoking in the trenches, an easy target for a German sniper. Gerry fell back upon the ground, scurrying to hide the still-smoking cigarette, when Simon had pushed the other man down in the mud. The trenches were laden with pools of filthy water, and Simon had held Gerry face down in a puddle for long moments. Gerry spluttered and struggled in Simon's arms, trying to lift himself out of the water, but Simon was larger and stronger. When Simon finally let Gerry go, the private fell onto his side, coughing and gagging on muddy water. *He deserved it,* Simon had said. In Marsden's mind, Gerry became Beatrice, small and helpless against the strength of her brother's larger frame.

His knees buckled, and Marsden fell onto the damp grass lining the lake's edge. His belly was empty, and he heaved up only foul air and saliva when the urge to vomit overtook him. Maidenstone Hall had been his last hope of discovering what had happened to Simon, but with every stone he turned, he wished he had never come to the damned place.

Sitting back on his heels, gasping for breath and shivering, Marsden was sure the cold would consume him. He staggered to his feet and hurried back to the house as quickly as possible, running up the hill to the servants' entrance. Marsden raced immediately to the stairs and travailed the entire way up to his room without removing his coat. He peeled it off along with his jacket and collapsed onto his bed, where he buried his head in his hands. A deep sigh expelled every ounce of oxygen in his lungs.

It was now, he decided. Now was the right time to leave. Nothing was worth the horrors he continued to unearth at Maidenstone Hall. The orchard had been Marsden's last hope of finding evidence of what had happened to Simon. Without the proof of Simon's gun and coat to suggest that Simon had never returned to duty, Marsden had no means to confront Lord Scarborough with any confidence, although he suspected the earl would never tell him the truth anyway.Marsden had failed in his quest, but right now, the terrible tale of Beatrice's death still ringing in his ears, he found that he didn't care.

Chapter Thirty-Two

It was still early, and Marsden hoped he could persuade Badeley to drive him to the station, even if the chauffeur needed to be convinced by exchanging a monetary bribe. The desperate urge to escape the ghosts of Maidenstone Hall drove Marsden to retrieve the packing he had begun the day before in a flurry of clumsy activity. He dragged out his half-packed suitcases from under the bed, slamming one against his shins with such force that he winced at the pain. He scrounged through his pockets and the lining of the cases, piecing together his money. Even without the salary he expected from Lord Scarborough, he hoped he would have enough funds to take the train to London and find a room for at least a few days. It may be time to sell the cufflinks. The thought buoyed him. With a little money, he would buy new clothes and find honest employment. He was done skulking around London, searching for Simon Falconer in every dark corner and alleyway.

Marsden set about packing the last of his belongings, throwing his books with little care into one open case. The remaining clothing in the wardrobe he shoved into the other case. He stomped upon the suitcase to secure the latches.

When a knock sounded on his door, Marsden was panting with exertion. "Who is it?"

"Nancy. I have a message from Lady Alice."

"Beg pardon?"

There was a long pause, and Marsden pictured Nancy scowling at the closed door.

"She sends her regrets as she thinks she's too ill for lessons today. She asked me to give you this."

A moment later, a small white envelope slid under the door. Nancy's thudding footsteps echoed away from his door, and Marsden scrambled to collect the note. His name was scrawled on the envelope in Alice's handwriting. He ripped it open, extracting a single piece of crisp paper. Alice's letter was scribbled, her nervousness bleeding through the ink.

> *Dearest Marsden,*
>
> *I know that you are very angry with me. I promise that I will explain everything if you give me a chance. At half past eleven tonight, please go to the kitchen, and I will be waiting for you. I swear that I will tell you the truth, but please do not be late. I cannot stay after midnight.*
> *Your friend,*
> *Alice*

Marsden crumpled the letter into a tight ball and threw it across the room. He had no intention of answering Alice's summons. He was tired of jumping to attention every time the Falconer family threw him a bone, salivating at every tiny piece of information about Simon could snatch. His position at Maidenstone had already become too dangerous. Alice and the staff knew too much about him. Marsden could not risk being blackmailed. There was, he reasoned, the possibility that Alice was ready to tell him the truth about Simon, but he thought it all the more likely she would only spout more evil about her brother.

In a spur of renewed energy, Marsden slid his jacket back on and patted the pocket where the bundle of photographs and letters was still safe against his chest. These items would not be packed. He had learned his lesson hard and refused to let them fall into the wrong hands again. With difficulty, Marsden managed to collect the handles of one suitcase and his violin case into one hand so that he could carry the bag of books in the other. Weighed down by all the possessions he owned, Marsden made his way downstairs.

He found the rest of the staff in the dining hall finishing their breakfast.

Mrs. Huston was the first to notice him, standing over Badeley's shoulder with the coffee pot. He thought she would spill the scalding liquid into Badeley's lap when she saw the packed suitcases in Marsden's hands.

"What's this about?" said Badeley upon Mrs. Huston's squeak of shock.

"I need you to take me to the station," said Marsden. "As soon as possible."

"You're not leaving?" said Mrs. Huston. Her voice cracked with fear.

"I'm afraid I must, Mrs. Huston. Can you take me now, Badeley?"

Nancy simply asked, "Have you told his Lordship?"

"I'll send him my apologies later. I really must go, I'm afraid."

Badeley pushed away from the table and stood to face Marsden. "Come on now, Marsden," he said. "You can't just run off like this. Lord Scarborough won't like it. And if I take you to the station, you know I'm the one who'll get an earful from him."

"Do as he asks," said Linton. Seated at the head of the table, he did not look up from his breakfast. "If Mr. Fisher wishes to leave, we cannot stop him. Although I'm sure he understands that he will not receive his full wages."

Badeley threw up his hands. "All right. I'll drive you. But I'm not carrying your bags."

"Marsden—" Mrs. Huston tried to protest again, but Marsden wouldn't be delayed.

"Goodbye," he said, following Badeley from the dining hall.

Marsden followed Badeley to the garage and loaded his bags into the car. Not wanting to be chauffeured, he climbed into the front beside Badeley.

The fog had mostly lifted when they drove toward the village, the lush green of the countryside racing past as Badeley sped along the road.

"Are you sure about this?" Badeley asked when they approached the station. "His Lordship—"

"Won't care about me leaving," said Marsden. "I'll be losing my position any day now anyway. Her Ladyship told me as much last night."

The car swerved as Badeley took his eye away from the road to gape at Marsden, his surprise evident as he corrected his steering and demanded, "What did she say? Has the Hall been sold?"

"I couldn't say. All I know is that Alice is to be sent away."

Badeley pursed his lips but said nothing more as he pulled the car up in front of the station. He remained in the driver's seat when Marsden climbed out of the vehicle and removed his bags. On a whim, he raised a hand to bid Badeley farewell. Badeley, in return, offered a grim nod.

Inside, the elderly station manager was seated behind a wooden desk, a tattered book in his hands. He shut the book when Marsden dumped his bags onto the floor before the desk.

"Can I help you?" the station master asked and dusted the front of his wrinkled blue jacket with one hand.

"I want to buy a one-way ticket to London via York," said Marsden. "How long will I have to wait for the next train?"

The older man shook his head, his thick white mustache vibrating. "No trains today, sir."

"No trains?" Marsden repeated, convinced he had misheard. "Not at all?"

"Tree across the track near Elvington. It took out the signal, so there are no trains to or from York today. I can still sell you a ticket if you want to try again tomorrow."

Marsden slumped, his heart sinking. "How much for the ticket?

"Three shillings, sir."

Marsden handed over the money. He tucked the ticket into his coat pocket and collected his bags. Struggling with their bulk, he staggered out of the station building and considered his options for the night's accommodation when he spotted Lord Scarborough's Rolls-Royce parked at the side of the road. Badeley was leaning against the bonnet, staring up at the grey sky with a cigarette in hand. He straightened when Marsden approached.

"Change your mind?" Badeley asked.

"No trains," said Marsden. "Did you know?"

"How would I know? This is my first trip to the station this morning."

"So, how did you know to wait for me?"

"I didn't. I just wanted a smoke. His Lordship won't let me have them in the car." As if to prove a point, Badeley took a long drag of his cigarette and flicked the remaining butt into the grass by the road.

"Do they have rooms at the tavern?" Marsden asked.

Badeley rounded the car to open the passenger door. "Not since the war. Old Lewis shut them up. I'll take you back to the Hall."

Marsden clutched at the handles of his cases. He didn't want to return to the Hall, but at least there, he could take advantage of a free bed and three warm meals. With any luck, the Falconers didn't even know he had left. He had no other option but to beg the station master to be allowed to sleep on the floor.

"Come on," said Badeley and took one of the cases of our Marsden's hand. "It won't be so bad. You can still run off tomorrow if you insist."

Marsden loaded the rest of his luggage into the car and joined Badeley in the front. He felt the embarrassment burning hot on his cheeks at being forced to return and sank deep into the passenger seat, hiding his face behind the raised lapel of his coat.

"Is this all because of what happened yesterday?" Badeley asked and started the car. "I don't know why His Lordship suspected you of stealing anything."

"I think Alice told him to search my room," said Marsden.

"Why would you say that?"

"It's just a suspicion. I should have asked her if it was true when I saw her in the orchard this morning."

Badeley jerked the car into gear a little too hard, and the whole vehicle shuddered. "What were you doing in the orchard?"

"We were visiting Beatrice."

From the corner of his eye, Marsden could see the grip of Badeley's gloved hands tighten on the steering wheel. Badeley was struck dumb with the single utterance of Beatrice's name and, for the first time in days, Marsden felt as though he was no longer grasping for the upper hand. He felt no closer to discovering what had happened to Simon, and he could not explain why the household allowed Alice to masquerade as Beatrice, but at least he was no longer a pawn in their game.

When they drove to the hall, an olive green Morris Oxford was parked at the front entrance. Badeley slowed as they passed it, leaning over the steering wheel to examine the car.

"Looks like we have a visitor," he said.

Badeley passed the mystery car and rounded the Hall to park directly in front of the servant's entrance. This time, he was far more willing to help Marsden with his bags. He carted both heavy suitcases down the hall toward the stairs when Marsden stopped him.

"Just leave them down here," said Marsden. "There's no point dragging them back up to my room only for me to drag them back down again tomorrow."

Badeley attempted an awkward smile. "Don't be silly. You'll want fresh clothes for your travels tomorrow. Unless you change your mind and decide to stay, of course."

Marsden wanted to say that he had no intention of changing his mind, but Badeley didn't wait for him to reply, trudging up the stairs with the cases without looking back.

Chapter Thirty-Three

With a whole day of nothing to do but entertain himself and hide as best he could, Marsden decided to go up to the library. If Lady Scarborough were there, he would borrow a book and wither away in his room the rest of the morning.

He was mere feet from the library when the doors opened. Marsden stopped short as Lord Scarborough caught sight of him, and a wolfish smile swallowed half of the earl's face. He waved a beckoning hand and said, "Marsden! Just the man I was hoping to see."

Marsden expected to have to explain his absence, sure that Linton or Nancy must have reported to Lord Scarborough that he had fled the house without so much as writing a resignation letter. The earl said nothing, however, of Marsden's morning escape and instead ushered him toward the library's fireplace. Lady Scarborough was perched in her usual armchair. Directly beside her sat a man Marsden did not know.

"This is Marsden Fisher," said Lord Scarborough. "Alice's tutor. Marsden, this is Doctor Alistair Webb."

Dr. Webb, a short, portly man with thin blonde eyebrows and a ruddy complexion, extended a hand to Marsden but did not stand. Marsden stooped to take the doctor's chubby palm in his own. Despite his diminutive stature, Webb had a firm grip, shaking Marsden's hand so hard that he felt the jolt in his elbow and shoulder.

"Please be seated, Mr. Fisher," said Webb. Before Marsden could obey, he quickly continued: "Tell me, how do you find Lady Alice?"

"Find her?" Marsden asked.

"Yes, tell me your impressions of the young lady."

"Just tell the truth," Lord Scarborough prompted.

"Lady Alice is a fine young lady," said Marsden. From the displeased huff that ruffled Lord Scarborough's mustache, Marsden guessed that such a diplomatic answer was not what his audience wanted to hear.

"Can you describe her demeanor?" Webb asked. "Her daily behavior?"

The way Webb accentuated *daily* caught Marsden's attention. He wasn't only asking about Marsden's interactions with Alice. Webb was already aware of Marsden's experience with Alice's act as Beatrice. The last thing he wanted was to look a fool and admit that he had accepted the character of Beatrice for so long.

"Lady Alice is a very clever girl," he said, weighing his words carefully. "She enjoys our lessons very much."

"Has she said as much?"

"Not exactly. But I can see that she's lonely, and I suppose I'm someone to talk to."

Webb, who had been scribbling on a notepad in an indecipherable scrawl, paused to glance at Lady Scarborough. The countess, leaning heavily on the armrest of her chair, shook her head with heavy regret.

"Of course, she's lonely," she said. "I keep saying as much."

"Would you say that she's stubborn?" asked Webb, returning his attention to Marsden. "Perhaps aggressive toward you?"

Marsden thought of the tutors who had come before him, frightened away by Alice's antics. Webb may well have asked him if he was afraid of waking to find his hair on fire.

"No, sir. She has never been aggressive toward me."

"How about the damage she did to Lord Scarborough's study? His documents?"

"I did not see Lady Alice damage Lord Scarborough's documents."

"And the fire in her room?" asked Lord Scarborough, interjecting not only into the conversation but thrusting himself physically closer. He stood behind the doctor, leaning on the chair to the point of crowding over Webb.

"I had thought the fire in Alice's room was an accident," said Marsden.

"A candle left burning. Lady Alice was certainly very distressed by the incident."

Lord Scarborough virtually snarled. "She's a talented actress."

Webb tapped his pen on the pad. "You say she affected distress?"

"No," said Marsden. "I said she was distressed."

"And how often do you speak to Lady Beatrice?"

Although he kept his eyes trained on Webb, Marsden was very much aware of Lord Scarborough staring at him. "I think you and I both know I cannot speak to Lady Beatrice."

Webb leaned closer, owl eyes blinking rapidly behind his thick spectacles. "You do not believe you are conversing with a distinct, separate personality?"

The sensation of his ribs crowding in on each other made Marsden's shoulders curl forward. He was being coached toward a certain conclusion but did not yet know what it was.

"I don't know what you mean, sir."

"Lady Alice blamed Beatrice for the recent fire, did she not? She claimed Beatrice was trying to kill her. Did you hear her say as much?"

"Yes," Marsden admitted.

"I would conclude," said Webb, his voice low, conspiratorial, "that Lady Alice and Lady Beatrice are at war. Wouldn't you, Mr. Fisher?"

As Webb inched closer, Marsden leaned back into his chair. "Sir, Beatrice is—"

"Dead? Yes, my boy, I know. But Lady Alice tried to convince you otherwise, didn't she?"

Marsden resisted the urge to insist that everyone in the house had wanted to convince him that Beatrice was alive. He held his breath. The penny dropped, clattering loudly in the well of his mind. Lord Scarborough had indeed wanted Alice to deceive him. While Marsden had been busy searching for the truth of Simon's disappearance, Lord Scarborough had been building a case against his daughter. He needed evidence—a solid witness to testify against her. As an outsider, unaware of Beatrice's death, he was the perfect candidate to offer assurance that Alice's performance of her dead sister was entirely convincing.

When Marsden did not speak, Lord Scarborough's chest puffed. A wave of triumph blossomed across the earl's face, and he smiled. "You see, Francis? I told you. I knew it would come to this."

Lady Scarborough closed her eyes, her expression taut and pinched tight with strain. "If only we could keep her safe at home, Harry—"

"But are *we* safe, Francis? With that girl in our home?" Lord Scarborough gestured to Webb. "Please, Doctor, continue."

"And the late Viscount?" Webb asked Marsden.

Marsden had enough sense to feign vague ignorance with a casual shrug. "Her brother, sir?"

"Yes. How often does Alice speak about him?"

"Rarely, sir."

"And what has she said?"

Plenty, Marsden thought. Alice had told him so much about Simon that he had not wanted to hear. Things that Marsden didn't dare repeat.

"She asked me once about the war," he said. "She said I wore the same expression her brother had when he was home on leave."

"And did she say anything else about when he was home on leave?"

The question hung in the air, and suddenly, all three sets of eyes were upon him in earnest; Lord Scarborough, Lady Scarborough, and Dr. Webb all staring at him in anticipation of his answer.

"No, sir," said Marsden. "Should she have?"

Marsden had expected the doctor to continue writing his notes, but instead, Webb replaced the cap on his fountain pen and slid it into the breast pocket of his jacket.

"Thank you, Mr. Fisher. That will be all."

Marsden hesitated to stand, hovering above his chair. Webb tilted his chin, expectant.

"Was there something else you wanted to add, Mr. Fisher?"

"I was wondering what will happen to Lady Alice?"

Marsden had a vision of Alice being dragged from the house, kicking and screaming by men in white coats, Webb hot on their heels. He suddenly feared what she would say in such a state, the promises she might make, and the secrets she might reveal to stay at Maidenstone. He feared she would take him down with her.

Webb smiled at Marsden, a grin so tight that his thin lips almost disappeared. "Don't you worry, Mr. Fisher," he said. "I can promise I will take good care of Lady Alice. She will be my most important patient. And so will Lady Beatrice. Whoever happens to be in control that day."

"Is she mad, sir?" Marsden asked. It was the only explanation he could fathom. Either Alice was unnaturally cruel or simply insane.

"We try not to use that word at St. Jude's," said Webb. "She is suffering from multiple personality disorder."

"And can she be cured?"

"That is certainly my intention, Mr. Fisher. Thank you again."

Lord Scarborough stepped in, guiding Marsden with a heavy hand to his shoulder toward the library doors.

"Well done," he said and ushered Marsden into the salon. "You've been very accommodating."

Marsden was certain his testimony was of little concern to Dr. Webb; the doctor's mind already made up about Alice's condition. He stood dumb, too bewildered to respond as Lord Scarborough turned away, but then the earl paused abruptly in the doorway to face Marsden again.

"I meant to tell you," he said. "You'll never guess who I met in London yesterday."

"Who, sir?"

"Major Caldwell. George Randall Caldwell," Lord Scarborough said to clarify when greeted with Marsden's blank expression. "Your battalion leader. You did say you were with the eighteenth?"

"Oh yes!" Marsden tried to keep his voice level. "Goodness. Was he well, sir?"

"Tolerably so. I dare say he's missing his left arm, but I suppose one adjusts to these trials."

"His left arm, sir?"

"He lost it to a mortar shell. Surely you remember?"

Marsden rubbed a trembling thumb across one eyebrow, struggling to think fast. "I had heard it was his right arm, sir."

"No matter," said Lord Scarborough. "I told him one of his boys from the eighteenth was working for us, and he was very pleased to hear that you were alive and safe."

Marsden thought his jaw would crack from the pressure of forcing a pleased smile. "Thank you for telling me, sir."

Lord Scarborough's matching grin was almost vicious, every one of his aging teeth exposed and visibly sharp to Marsden's eye. With a flourish, he closed both library doors. The silence of the salon's lofting ceilings bore down on Marsden, and he pressed his hands against his ears, a wave of nausea driving him on, forcing his legs to move. He ran across the salon and up the main staircase, two steps at a time where he could. On the second floor's landing, he stopped to catch his breath and gather his thoughts. The idea that Lord Scarborough had already discovered that Marsden wasn't who he said he was made him collapse against one of the stone columns that framed the entrance to the family wings, his legs wobbling. If Major Caldwell had recognized the name, his new identity was no longer safe—particularly if Caldwell knew that the real Marsden Fisher was dead.

He was wiping at the sweat newly gathered on his brow when he heard muffled voices emerging from the west wing. Hoping to avoid further confrontation, Marsden hurried to the servants' staircase and hid just behind the door, leaving it ajar so that he could see out onto the landing. He was glad of his hiding place when he saw Alice round the corner, checking to see if the coast was clear. She beckoned to someone in the hallway behind her, and moments later, Nancy appeared. The maid was clutching a bundle of black cloth. Alice handed her a small bag and whispered something Marsden could not hear. Nancy nodded and left her young mistress, heading toward the servants' stairwell.

Marsden flattened himself against the wall and held his breath as Nancy opened the door and ran right past him and up the stairs without noticing he was there. When she was gone, he peered back onto the landing to see that Alice had disappeared. He couldn't guess what she had given Nancy, but the covert transaction had piqued Marsden's interest. Everyone in the house, it seemed, including straight-laced Nancy, had a secret.

Chapter Thirty-Four

M arsden was haunted by his conversation with Dr. Webb for the rest of the day. In particular, the doctor's questions regarding Simon. *And did she say anything else about when he was home on leave?* What, Marsden wondered, had Webb thought she might have said? Or rather, what was Webb afraid she might have said? It was clear now that Lord Scarborough had allowed Alice to continue with her costume play of living as Beatrice for the sake of building evidence against her—Marsden himself was now a witness for the doctor's report—but the turn in questioning toward Simon was something else. Something more sinister that Marsden could not yet decipher.

Although he had eaten supper with the rest of the staff—all gloomy with the appearance of Dr. Webb and the certainty of Alice being committed—Marsden returned quickly to his room and paced the short length of the space, agonizing over his conversation with Webb, Lord Scarborough's delight in mentioning Major Caldwell, and his upcoming appointment with Alice. He had not yet decided whether or not he would meet her, as she had requested, just before midnight. Whenever he decided to do as she asked, he became nervous about her intentions. She was a pathological liar and, as her father had claimed, an excellent actress. Marsden couldn't believe a single word she said. If it weren't for the nagging doubt raised by Webb's questions, he would have denied her.

When Marsden stopped pacing to check his watch, it was half-past eleven. Alice would already be downstairs waiting for him. His decision made, Marsden smoothed back his hair and tightened his tie. Before he left the room, he reached under the mattress and retrieved the journal he had taken from the nursery. He lit a candle and made his way downstairs.

Alice was still there, as promised, when Marsden entered the kitchen. The room was lit by a single bulb hanging over the table. Bundled in a thick dressing gown, Alice was perched on a stool at the far end of the table, her arms wrapped around her knees.

"I thought you weren't going to come," she said.

Marsden felt no need to apologize. He placed the journal on the table. "I wasn't entirely sure I would. But I thought you might like to have this back."

Alice's astonishment at the sight of the journal was unmistakable. Her eyes widened, and she reached to snatch for it, but Marsden quickly put his hand on the black leather cover before she could touch it, dragging it away.

"How did you get that?" she asked.

"You showed me your hiding place in the nursery, remember?"

"Did you read it?"

"I think you wanted me to read it."

Alice sank back. "You still don't believe me. You're still angry."

Marsden drew up a stool and sat down beside her. He left his candle burning and placed it on the table between them. He thought of the many times he had felt sympathy for her, the ease with which the lies had rolled off her tongue, and imagined how she must have laughed at him behind his back.

Interlacing his fingers on the tabletop, he kept his eyes fixed on his cufflinks when he spoke. "You're right. I am angry. Everyone has been lying to me from the moment I entered this house. Would you expect me to be anything but angry after being played the fool?"

"I told you, I'm not lying." Alice planted her feet on the floor and pulled the dressing gown more tightly across her chest. "Everything I told you down by the lake was true."

"And I don't believe you. I refuse to believe that Simon hurt Beatrice on purpose. He wasn't—"

"What?" she said. "A violent bully?"

Again, a vision of Gerry Thwaites spluttering in the mud flashed across

Marsden's mind, but he pushed it away. "You were a child. Have you not considered that you were mistaken?"

Alice leaned forward, her face bright in the candlelight. "What hold did he have over you exactly? You seem to think Simon was perfect, but if you really knew him, you wouldn't think so."

"He was…"

Marsden held his tongue. *Everything,* he wanted to say. Simon had been everything to him. He couldn't hope to make her understand why he loved Simon. Every touch of Simon's hand, every secret kiss had fueled Marsden— driven him on through his first days of the war—and urged him to overlook every fit of temper, insult, and time Simon flirted with someone else. Every sin, on Simon's part, had been forgivable. Alice had been right. Simon had cast a spell over him. Marsden hadn't seen him in three years, and still, Simon consumed every moment of his day and night.

"He wasn't perfect," Marsden acknowledged. "I know that. But what happened with Beatrice must have been an accident."

Even to his own ears, he knew he sounded desperate, and Alice scoffed openly at him.

"Of course, Father told everybody it was an accident," she said. "Simon was about to go Cambridge, and the scandal would have ruined him. So Beatrice was buried in a dark corner where she would be forgotten, and everyone continued on as though the whole thing had been a terrible accident. Mrs. Huston was the only one who objected to the lie. They soon got rid of her."

Marsden remembered Mrs. Huston, seated where Alice now perched, with sadness in her eyes when he had asked her why she had left the Hall. He imagined Lord Scarborough asking Mrs. Huston to go, perhaps even threatening her. The pain in the old woman's eyes had been genuine. As for Alice, he still couldn't be sure.

"Even if I believed you," he said, "none of this explains the act you've been performing. Is it just revenge against your father? For refusing to see Simon punished? Or are you just insane?"

Alice drew his candle closer, her fingers twitching as she picked at the drying wax pooling in the porcelain holder. "It first happened when Simon died. She just came back."

"What do you mean? Who came back?"

"I mean, I just woke up one morning to discover I had missed a whole day. At first, I thought I'd had a terrible nightmare. I woke up sweating and screaming. When the day broke, I discovered I had not been myself the day before. Rather, I had been Beatrice."

Marsden hung his head, immediately made weary by her story. "Alice, please don't—"

"I remembered nothing of it," she insisted. "I had to rely on the staff and my parents to inform me. Can you imagine what that was like for me? Being told that I had been hysterical and raving and insisting, over and over, that I was Beatrice. It was terrifying, Marsden, to lose all control of myself. A doctor was called to sedate me. When I woke up again, I was myself once more. That was almost three years ago."

"Three years ago," he repeated. "Are you claiming that you've been doing this every day for three years? Switching back and forth? Why?"

"I don't know! I have no control over it. All I know is that the change happens at midnight. One moment, I'm myself, fully in control; the next, I'm gone; Beatrice returns, and I remember nothing of it."

Marsden gaped at the lunacy of her story. It was pure madness, but not once did she stumble in the tale. Either Alice truly believed everything she was saying, or she was a better actress than even he had thought.

"You still think I'm a liar," she said when he did not speak.

"It sounds like something out of a novel." It sounded like a tale from the collection of ghost stories and spiritualist texts in her collection of books in the conservatory. They were an easy source of inspiration.

"But it's true, Marsden. It is real. She came back. Beatrice came back and is living inside me. I have to share my body with her."

"It's just a ghost story, Alice. How could you possibly expect me to believe it?"

She leaned across the table, half on her feet. In the dim light, she appeared otherworldly, pupils wide and black as she clawed toward him. "You will. I know you will. You're the only one who can help me."

Marsden shook his head, adamantly refusing to be lured into her madness. He said, "I can't help you. You need a doctor."

"I've seen them. They thought I was schizophrenic at first. They wanted to keep me locked up forever, but my mother brought me home when they realized I was pregnant."

Having almost forgotten entirely about Grace, she was again at the forefront of Marsden's mind. "What about Grace's father? Is he truly dead? Couldn't his family help you?"

Alice kicked the stool out from under her so suddenly and violently that Marsden jumped with shock when it crashed against the wall behind her.

"All of this started because of him," she said. "It's because of him that Grace was sent away. Since then, the only requests that my father has granted me were to have Mrs. Huston return and allow me to have a tutor. I'm not permitted to have friends. I can't leave the grounds."

Marsden understood this was the real reason for panic when she wandered away from the estate; Alice had been forbidden to leave the grounds or interact with the populous beyond them. But she had been offered many a chance to interact with her tutors and shunned every one of them before him.

He asked, "If you wanted a tutor so badly, why did you frighten them away?"

"That was Beatrice," she sneered. "She's a menace. She's bored, and she loves to taunt our parents. Whenever they deny her or antagonize her, she acts out. My father decides to sell the house; she destroys his documents. He sells her horse; she sets my bed on fire. I can give you a hundred examples."

Marsden bit back his frustration. Again, it was Beatrice's fault. Always, Beatrice was to blame. "I don't know what you expect me to say, Alice."

"Say that you'll help me," she said, begging. "Say that you'll get me out of here."

"Why me?" he asked, genuinely bewildered. When Alice had confessed her hope that he would help her get Grace back, he had not expected that she wanted to abscond with him. "Why not one of the others? Linton? Mrs. Huston?"

"They're all in the pockets of my father. They don't dare be seen publicly siding with me. He would destroy them. You're not even who you say you are. He would never be able to find you once we're free of this place."

Above them, the light buzzed and flickered. There was a soft pop, and Marsden looked up at the sound, but Alice was not distracted.

"I need to leave Maidenstone," she said again. "Soon enough, the Hall will sell, and my parents will move to London for good. They will not be taking me with them."

"Because you're going to be institutionalized again."

"Exactly. My father wants to lock me away. That's why Dr. Webb was here today. He thinks I have a personality disorder. I'll never get out again if he takes me to Saint Jude's." She leaned over him, hands clawing the table, fingernails gripping the soft wood. "You know what they specialize in, don't you?" When Marsden shook his head, she set her lips in a grim line. "Lobotomy."

Marsden believed this, at least. He had seen the line in Lord Scarborough's ledger dedicated to Saint Jude's. The money had been a down payment for the return of the Falconer's unhinged daughter into the locked depths of an insane asylum. Marsden could barely believe a single word that came out of Alice's mouth, but having met the doctor himself, he could well accept her fear of Saint Jude's was genuine.

"What do I have to do, Marsden?" she asked. "How can I—"

Again, the light above them flickered, more violently this time, casting erratic shadows around the kitchen. The bulb's filament sizzled and crackled at an almost deafening volume, and when Marsden could see Alice again in the light, she was frozen completely, rigid in an expression of fear. Her fingernails dug into the well-worn wood of the table. He winced as the nail on her right index finger broke under the pressure. She was silent for long, painful moments, unnervingly still, her eyes wide.

Marsden reached a tentative hand toward her. "Alice…"

The scream that ripped from her throat was so visceral that Marsden thought the vocal cords would tear in her throat. Above them, the light bulb burst and shattered, glass raining across the table as Alice lurched backward.

Marsden lunged for her but was not in time to catch her when she fell onto the floor. Her skull landed with a sickening crack against the slate tiles, her arms and legs flailing. He dropped beside her, vainly attempting to hold still her thrashing arms.

"Alice!" he cried. "Alice, what's the matter?"

Alice's spine bowed. Her whole body twisted and jerked in his arms. Her mouth stretched open, her lips fixing into a long, gasping expression of horror. In the candle's flickering light, she had taken on the visage of a demon, and Marsden's body tightened with fear. He almost dropped her, but the fit ceased as abruptly as it had begun. One moment, she was thrashing and choking in his arms; the next, Alice became utterly still, hanging almost mid-air between Marsden and the floor for just a fraction of a second before collapsing. He shook her with trembling hands. He placed his ear against her mouth. She wasn't breathing. When Alice didn't move or breathe, Marsden released her, collapsing onto his side in desperation to separate himself from her frozen body. He was sure she was dead.

Chapter Thirty-Five

Marsden clutched at his chest, sure his thundering heart would burst out from beneath his ribs as he stared down at Alice, lifeless on the kitchen floor. Panic overwhelmed every one of his senses.

"Jesus," he gasped. "Jesus Christ."

The scuff of a footstep sounded in the hallway, and Marsden scuttled behind the kitchen table, staring at the doorway, his eyes watering. Sure that someone must have heard Alice's screams, he imagined the scene—one of the staff bursting into the kitchen to find him beside Alice's dead body. But no one came through the door. The silence continued but for the pounding of blood in his ears. There were no footsteps on the stairs.

Alice suddenly gave a heaving intake of breath, her whole body pitching off the floor. Marsden swallowed a yell of surprise, choking on the sound instead. Alice rolled onto her side and coughed repeatedly, shoulders heaving. Then she slumped and lay inert, simply breathing. Marsden crawled back toward her, taking her shoulders in his hands and squeezing.

"Alice? Are you all right?" He was embarrassed to hear the tremor in his voice but even more afraid she might yet expire in front of him, the reprieve only temporary.

She opened her eyes, gazing up at Marsden with eyelashes fluttering, and groaned, relaxing her neck, resting her head onto the cold slate.

"Oh," she said with a sigh. "It's you."

"What on earth happened? I thought you were dying, Alice."

A pained grimace spread across his lips. "God, no. Surely you can tell us apart by now, you fool." She reached for him. "Help me up, will you? It's bloody uncomfortable down here."

Marsden's tongue was numb when he took her hand, unable to speak as he guided her back to her feet. She tilted her chin toward him and raised a cold hand to his cheek. Her lazy smile winked at him in the flickering light of the candle.

"My hero," she said. "What would I do without you, Fish?"

Marsden stood frozen as she rose onto the tips of her toes to kiss him, lips pressing hard against his own. His head snapped back, neck working at speed to extract himself from her touch. Her name emerged as a stammer: "Beatrice."

There was no mistaking the glint in her eyes, the mischievous curve of her grin, and the flirtatious tone of her voice. It was unbelievable, inconceivable—but undeniable. At that moment, Marsden recognized a completely different personality.

Beatrice cast a wary eye around the room, absorbing her surroundings. "Why on earth are we in the kitchen? Did you steal me down here, naughty boy?"

Marsden's shock faded, replaced by disbelief. "You asked me to meet you here, remember?"

"Did I?" She paused to examine him, a deep frown folding her brow. "Are you quite well? I must say, Fish, you look quite shell-shocked."

"Shocked?" Marsden wanted to rip at his hair. "You just had a screaming fit loud enough to wake the whole house and then collapsed. I was afraid you were dead."

Beatrice shrugged off his concern. "It happens sometimes, but I can assure you I'm quite all right. As you can see, no one else came running. Alice does tend to be a little over-dramatic."

Whatever had lodged in Marsden's throat the evening, he found out about Beatrice's death returned suddenly, dropping into the base of his esophagus, catching there and stinging. He snagged a finger into the space between his neck and shirt collar, pulling, trying to breathe.

"Who?" he asked.

Beatrice's smile faded. "Alice, dummy. She did tell you the truth about me, didn't she? I assume that's why you two had this little rendezvous?" When Marsden only gaped at her, she released a heaving groan. "I must say, I'm a little disappointed. I was hoping you'd figure it out on your own a little quicker. I almost told you myself."

"Of course, I figured it out," he said in a rush. "It was obvious something was going on."

Her eyebrows danced. "Truly? You certainly never said anything." She noticed the journal still lying on the kitchen table. "I say, is that mine? Naughty Fish, didn't anyone ever tell you it's rude to read someone else's diary?"

Marsden did not stop her from snatching it up from the table but said, "Clearly, you wanted someone to read it? Why else write it all down?"

Beatrice slid the journal into the pocket of her dressing gown. "That's how Alice and I talk to each other. Surely that's obvious." She leaned against the kitchen table, crossing her arms. "Now, tell me all about this conversation you just had with my sister. Why did she decide to tell you now, I wonder?"

"Because I found the grave."

She gave his arm a gentle pat. "I suppose that was a little startling. But at least you know now what happened to me. Did she tell you everything?"

Marsden spoke through gritted teeth: "Yes."

"That must have been difficult for you, learning something so heinous about your precious Simon."

A singing blush burned across Marsden's cheeks. He turned away from her, self-conscious in the path of her enquiring gaze. "I hardly think you're in a position to judge me."

Beatrice's laugh was brief and fragile. "Good heavens, Fish, I question your taste in men, but I can assure you that I don't judge you. I feel a little sorry for you, to be honest."

"Why would you feel sorry for me?" he spat.

"Because you loved him, and now he's dead."

It was a low blow. Marsden's heart squeezed as the old doubt resurfaced. "Is he?"

"Dead? Quite. Thank God."

Beatrice collected the candle and walked to the door without looking back at Marsden. He followed her, trailing after the light of the candle when she left him in the darkness of the kitchen. She opened the butler's office door, and Marsden was surprised it was unlocked. Beatrice turned on the light and helped herself to a decanter of sherry and two glasses Linton kept in a dresser behind his desk. She poured generous servings for them both. When she handed over the glass, Marsden stared into the rosy liquid, steeling himself.

"I know you want to ask me," Beatrice said, settling herself into Linton's high-backed chair.

"Do you know for a fact he's dead?" Marsden asked. "Or do you simply believe what your father tells you? Because I know that Simon didn't die at the Somme."

"And how do you know that?"

"Simon had already been absent without leave for months by the time he was officially reported dead. I told you that."

Beatrice hummed in denial. "No, you must have told Alice."

Marsden slammed his glass on the desk, the sherry sloshing over the rim. "You are Alice."

"You don't believe that, do you?" Relaxing back into the chair, one hand resting behind her head, Beatrice sipped from her glass. "I truly don't remember anything that happens when Alice is in control. You'll have to remind me what you know about Simon's disappearance."

Marsden wanted to wipe the coy smile off her face. Dr. Webb thought she had a personality disorder, but Marsden suspected she might be evil. She was, however, cooperating, and for a time at least, he would let her play on in the interest of interrogating her.

"Your father used his influence at the war office to cover it up, I imagine?"

Beatrice's grimace was foul. "Daddy can be quite persuasive when he wants to be. I imagine some money may also have been exchanged, knowing him."

"I know he was here," said Marsden. "He left behind his uniform coat and service weapon. Not to mention the cigarette case I gave him."

"Oh yes, the case. I put it back in Simon's room, by the way. You know, we had wondered who the illusive "T" was. I think we all imagined a Teresa or a Tabitha. Not a Thomas."

Marsden sank into the chair opposite Beatrice and threw back the sherry, gulping hard and cringing at the burn against his throat. When he looked back at her across the top of her glass, Beatrice's smile was sympathetic.

"Poor dear," she said. "Shall I call you Thomas? Or do you prefer to keep going by Marsden? I prefer to keep calling you Marsden, personally."

"I suppose I wasn't very careful about covering my tracks," he admitted.

"Well, darling, it certainly wasn't very difficult to discover that Marsden Fisher had died by his own hand while on service, so you were clearly not him. Very naughty of you, I must say, stealing a dead man's identity. Then, when I saw your photographs, it was only reasonable to guess that you were in the same regiment as Simon. My man in London placed you with the description I gave him." With one finger, she stroked at her cheek, imitating his scar. "Your injury was very carefully detailed in your war office record."

Marsden was flabbergasted. "How can you possibly know all this?"

"Badeley can be useful at times, believe it or not. I use the telephone when my parents aren't looking, but he sends the odd telegram for me when I can't get to it."

He remembered the secret conversation she had shared with Badeley outside the cemetery the day she had dragged him to the Carlisles' farm. The paper Badeley had given her could have been a telegram from London and featured details about the real Marsden Fisher. He hated the idea of someone investigating him—and what they might do with that information.

"Who is this man of yours in London? Who else has he told about me?"

Beatrice tapped one finger against her nose. "Company secrets, darling. But I will admit, one of Daddy's lawyers thinks I'm quite pretty and thinks doing the odd favor for me will earn him favors of his own in the future. He wouldn't dare tell anyone." She gave him a salacious wink. "So, now you know the truth about me, and I know the truth about you. Whatever will we have to talk about now?"

"I didn't come here to learn the truth about you," said Marsden.

"Oh please," she said, groaning in exasperation, "must we continue talking about Simon?"

"He went on leave, and he never returned to duty. He came here, to Maidenstone. Where did he go next?"

Beatrice picked up a lock of her hair and began twirling it between her fingers. Staring down at the tip of the red curls, she said, "What on earth makes you think he ever left?"

The sherry was suddenly biting at the lining of his stomach. "He never left?"

"My darling Fish, we've been telling you all this time that he's dead. Did you honestly not believe us?"

Marsden felt the blood drain from his face. He tried to swallow but found that his throat was closing in upon itself. "He died here?"

"You honestly never considered the possibility?"

"How?"

"You'll need to ask Alice about that. I wasn't here when it happened."

"Tell me!" he insisted.

She waved a hand, hushing him. "For heaven's sake, keep your voice down. I told you, Alice is the one who should explain. It happened before I came back."

Marsden collapsed against the chair and dropped his head into his free hand. "I don't understand."

Beatrice stood and walked around the desk to stand beside him. The touch of her hand on the top of his head was gentle.

"I know you're sad, darling. But it's for the best you know that Simon is gone, and he's not coming back."

"How did he die? Please."

"I told you, you'll need to ask Alice. You could try interrogating my parents, but they won't tell you just because you inquire politely."

This Marsden believed. He had once foolishly hoped that Lord Scarborough would confess everything if confronted with the evidence of Simon's failure to return to duty, but why should he? Marsden was no danger to the Falconer family. No one would ever believe his word against Lord Scarborough's.

Marsden's jaw ached. He thought he might weep. "Will you at least tell me where he is?"

Beatrice lifted his chin, her touch soft as she forced him to look up at her. "Tell me you believe it, Fish. That I'm here, even though my body is gone? Alice and I have shared this one for almost three years. I can't say why, but I promise you, she is not insane. No matter what our father or Dr. Webb says. Tell me you believe me."

Marsden knew he would say anything—truth or lie—if only she would tell him what he wanted to know. He sniffed, blinking away his tears. "I believe you."

Beatrice leaned back against the desk, releasing him. Marsden sat up and leaned closer as though she would whisper the secret to him. Her smiles and smirks were entirely gone now.

"He's with me," she said at last.

"With you?"

"Yes, darling." She swallowed the last of her sherry and left the glass one of Linton's copy books. "Now, if you don't mind, it's very late, and I think I will go up to my bed." She rubbed at the back of her head. "I have a smacking headache. Did I hit my head when Alice left?"

Marsden stood and hurried to block the doorway of the office. "What do you mean, he's with you?"

Beatrice lifted her chin. He thought she might argue or even push him out of the way, but instead, she reached for the lapels of his jacket, pulling each edge together to button it tightly. The act of tidying him was unnervingly intimate, and Marsden felt his bravado recede at her touch.

"I know about you, Fish," she said. "The real you, that is. I know you were born in Hamburg and are the son of an Oxford professor, now deceased. I know you were educated at King's College for a time, so you are no fool. But when it comes to my brother, you have allowed yourself to be blinded by my parents, by Alice, and by every other member of the staff here. In this one thing, I beg you, use your brain."

"Is that why you won't tell me? You want me to figure it all out on my own?"

"Don't you get it, Fish? If I just tell you everything you want to know, you will give up your folly and leave. You'll leave me here with Alice."

She leaned forward on the tips of her toes and stroked the length of his beard. When she kissed him again, Marsden allowed it. He did not close his eyes but gazed down his nose at the delicate freckles scattered across her cheekbones. Marsden was sure he had never been kissed so gently—not by Simon or anyone else. A sharp tingle raced down his spine, and he was shocked to recognize the sensation as desire. The feeling wasn't entirely unwelcome but quickly replaced with guilt.

When he grasped her fingers and drew them away from his face, he stared at the exposed length of her wrists. "What happened here?" he asked and nodded toward her scar.

The softness she had released into her kiss disappeared. Beatrice tugged her wrists free of his grasp and tucked her hands into the sleeves of her dressing gown. "Again, you'll have to speak to Alice. Goodnight, Fish."

Beatrice spun in a perfect half-circle and disappeared into the dark hallway. When he could no longer hear the soft tread of her retreating bare feet, Marsden reached for Linton's decanter of sherry. He considered returning to his room but was too exhausted to move. The ordeal of Alice's transformation into Beatrice and the ensuing conversation had drained him. He poured himself another drink and returned the decanter to its place. He swallowed the sherry quickly, this time enjoying the burn. He took up both glasses and the candle and returned to the kitchen to wash up.

As he stood at the sink, rinsing out the glasses, Marsden thought of everything that Alice had told him and that Beatrice had told him. He had been so sure that Alice was lying about her lack of control over her double life, but having seen her fit and scream before him, he began to consider the reality of Beatrice. The very idea of two young women living inside Alice's body at the same time was preposterous. Yet, Marsden couldn't deny he accepted something of what they had said: that Alice at least truly believed her sister's ghost possessed her. Marsden didn't know much about insanity, but he certainly didn't believe in ghosts. Whatever was happening to Alice, he was beginning to suspect she did need Dr. Webb's treatment after all.

He wondered if Alice would ever have confessed the truth to him if she had not found him kneeling beside her sister's grave. Marsden's hands froze in their task, water dripping from a wet glass down his wrists as they hung mid-air, and he envisioned Beatrice's sad, dark burial site between the apple trees. A laugh born of both realization and horror escaped his mouth in a soft bark.

Marsden decided then and there that he wouldn't wait for Alice—or Beatrice— to tell him what had happened to Simon. Not when he was now sure he knew exactly where Simon was buried.

Chapter Thirty-Six

The rest of the staff were thankfully absent when Marsden descended to the servants' hall, breakfast having long ago been served. He was barely a few feet from the servants' entrance when Mrs. Huston's shrill voice rang out behind him.

"Marsden! You slept late. You're not sneaking out, are you?"

She appeared even more flustered than usual, standing in the hallway and weighed down by a coal bucket, her apron covered in soot. A hint of anger was folded into the crease of her pinched eyes.

"I wasn't sneaking anywhere, Mrs. Huston," he said.

"Good." She dumped the bucket in the doorway of the kitchen. "I would hate it if you left without saying goodbye. I assume you're looking for Badeley to take you to the station."

"Actually, I admit that I thought long and hard about what Mr. Linton said last night. I thought it would be best I resign formally and be sure of my pay before leaving."

"I'm glad, but I'll be sad to see you go. With Holly dismissed, it feels like we're being picked off one by one."

"Holly was dismissed?" Marsden asked. "When?"

"Yesterday." Mrs. Huston pointed to the filthy state of her apron. "Why else would I be left to light the fires? Mr. Linton went down to the village to tell her, but he said she didn't seem very upset."

A sharp stab of guilt pierced Marsden's gut. He suspected it was his fault Holly had been fired. She had asked him not to reveal that she had told him to go to the orchard, but then he had gone and blabbed to Badeley. No doubt, Badeley had told Lord Scarborough, just as he had surely reported seeing Marsden wearing Simon's coat.

"You know, Marsden," Mrs. Huston went on, "sometimes I feel as though the whole household is being dismantled around us. Very soon, there won't be anything left." She removed her apron and threw it down onto the coal bucket. "Now, get on with you. I'm sure you'll want to speak to Lord Scarborough. I believe he's in his study."

Marsden thanked her, but when Mrs. Huston stepped into the kitchen, he returned to the servants' entrance rather than retreat up the stairs.

As he walked toward the garage, Marsden looked over his shoulder to ensure no one was watching him. He did not see any sign of Badeley when he hurried past the garage entrance and made his way back to the wooden shed that hid behind it. It was easy for him to reach through the broken window and turn the latch.

Once inside, Marsden went directly to the rear corner of the room where the old gardening tools lay rusting. He was delighted to have some luck at last, immediately finding a large shovel propped up in one corner next to the bench. A thin layer of soil encrusted the cutter edge of the blade. Marsden picked it up and tested its weight. It was certainly sturdy enough for his intended purpose.

There was no one in sight, but Marsden did his best to tuck as much of the shovel beneath his coat as possible when he left the shed. The cold steel banged against his right shin as he walked down to the orchard, trying to behave as naturally as possible in case he was spotted from the house.

Once inside the relative protection of the apple trees, Marsden felt safer—hidden. Although it was the second time he had been in the orchard, he did not find Beatrice's grave immediately. He wandered through the trees for some time, convinced that the headstone had been directly in the center of the orchard, but then he began to doubt himself and wondered how far he had strayed in circles the last time he had found the grave.

When he finally stumbled upon the headstone, it emerged suddenly as if by magic when he was looking in the opposite direction. He stood over the grave, staring down at the overgrown earth, in a trance. He thought that no one would know where to find Beatrice's body if they took away the headstone. She would simply disappear beneath the wild grass and encroaching tree roots, forgotten. It was the ideal hiding place for one unwanted grave. Perhaps it was the hiding place for a second, unnamed resting place.

He's with me, Beatrice had said. Or was it Alice? Marsden couldn't be sure anymore, and the thought of the confusion she had caused him made his head ache. Even if there were two different personalities crammed inside Alice's pretty head, she was still only one girl. Beatrice lay beneath his feet and had done so for years. Marsden knelt beside the grave and lay the shovel down in the tall grass. He smoothed his fingers through the long green blades, damp with the night's rain, and placed his hands firmly on the ground. Marsden had never been a religious man, but he had seen enough death in his short life to comprehend the vile nature of what he intended to do. It was the only path forward he could see, digging until he found what he was looking for, the truth he'd come to Maidenstone to unearth. Everything Marsden had worked for lay resting beneath his hands. All he had to do was pick up the shovel and dig.

When he closed his eyes, Marsden could picture Simon with astounding clarity: the breadth of his shoulders, the scent of his cologne, the way the wave of his blonde hair fell across his left eye when he laughed. He pictured Simon's body beneath the soil, rotting and corrupted by earth and worms; he saw Simon pressing the ashen face of Gerry Thwaites into a muddy puddle in a trench at Verdun; he saw Simon holding Beatrice, small and helpless, under the black water of the lake. Marsden fell back, snatching his hands away as though burned by the ground. No matter what he chose to do at this moment, he knew he was damned.

Marsden clambered back to his feet, too fast and staggering as a wave of dizziness hit him. He placed both hands on the headstone, folding at the waist while he centered himself and waited for the ringing in his ears to pass. When he felt strong enough to stand again, Marsden shrugged off his coat and threw it over the headstone. His jacket followed, his skin prickling with the cold when he rolled his shirt sleeves, preparing himself for the toil ahead. He crouched to pick up the shovel, gripping the handle so tightly that his knuckles cracked. With a deep breath, he drove the dull steel into the hard earth and began to dig.

Chapter Thirty-Seven

Marsden had no idea how long he worked in the soil above the grave. The hard ground was merciless, thick with roots, and heavy with rain. With every scoop he shoveled away, the neighboring dirt would collapse into the hole he was trying to create. He had barely cleared three feet of the hard ground, and the soil piled beside him was rank with mold and rot, occasionally causing him to gag. It was slow, tiring work that made his blood boil.

His exertions made him so hot that he paused to remove his waistcoat and wipe the sweat out of his eyes with a handkerchief. Marsden looked for the sun, but the dark sky was thick with rain clouds. He was hungry and thirsty but didn't dare pause his work to return to the house. Explaining his filthy appearance to Mrs. Huston when he went to the kitchen to find sustenance would be impossible.

He struggled on, aware that the light was fading with the approaching storm that loomed overhead. Marsden knew he was running out of time and doubled his efforts.

The longer he dug, the deeper the doubt sank into the pit of his stomach. At first, he dismissed the sensation as hunger, but with every inch, he worked farther into the earth, Marsden could not deny the suspicion creeping upon him. All of his hard work could be pure folly, yet he could not stop. He had come this far, and even if he kept digging only to discover that Beatrice was alone in this grave, Marsden had to keep going until he was sure. If he did not, Beatrice, too, would haunt him all of his days, along with Simon.

Marsden was digging with the last of his energy, the daylight swallowed up by the building mist and looming storm clouds, when a light bobbing between the trees caught his attention. He dropped the shovel and crouched down in the hole he had created, peering over the top to see who was moving among the gnarled trunks of the apple trees. At first, the figure was obscured by the beam of a flashlight. Marsden ducked his head again, hiding from the searching reach of the light. Above his heavy breath, he could hear the crunch of detritus under bootheels as they approached the grave. The light bounced off the headstone, just inches above Marsden's head.

"For heaven's sake, Fish. I thought for sure you'd be done by now."

Marsden let out the breath he had been holding and hauled his tired body up to the lip of the grave, only to receive a head-on barrel of light shining directly into his face. He raised one forearm to cover his eyes. "Beatrice?"

"Who else would it be? Silly boy."

"I'm not always sure whom I'm speaking to anymore," he admitted. "Could you point that somewhere else, please?"

Beatrice relented and shone the light instead into the open hole where he stood. She whistled and said, "Goodness, I take it back. You have been busy."

Climbing out of the hole was a challenging process. Patches of darkness swam before Marsden's eyes, his retinas burned by the flashlight's beam. When he faced her, his stomach clenched at her smug grin.

"Have you come here to laugh at me?" he asked.

Beatrice's smile did not fade. "Why on earth would I laugh at you?"

Marsden gestured at the hole. "Is this where you tell me this was all a game to you? That all I will find down here is the remains of an eleven-year-old girl?" He lunged at her, tearing the flashlight from her hand. He shone the beam of light down into the dark pit. "I have been digging for hours, and now I can only assume that you're here to tell me you've been toying with me all along."

Beatrice remained calm in the face of his anger. She moved slowly, reaching for Marsden's wrist and directing the light back toward her own face. She didn't flinch away from the brightness, her pupils expanding.

"You asked me where Simon was. I told you. Do you still want to find him?"

Marsden did not hesitate. "Yes. I do."

"Well then, you'd better be quick. You've been out here forever, and soon enough, I won't be the only one to come looking for you."

"I swear," he said, pointing a trembling finger in her face, "if you're lying—"

"I swear." Beatrice placed a hand over her heart. "If you keep digging, you'll find what you're looking for."

"How do I know I can trust you? Really? What's in it for you to lead me here?"

"I told you, Fish. We're allies. I help you, and you help me."

"I thought you were hoping I would help you with Grace, and in turn, you wouldn't tell your father the truth about me. Wasn't that our deal?"

Beatrice gestured to the grave. "Clearly, I needed to offer you a little more incentive."

Marsden followed her gaze down into the open earth and knew he had no choice but to trust her. Not when he'd already come so far. Every muscle in Marsden's arms and back ached in protest as he climbed back into the hole. He picked up the shovel, and as Beatrice pointed the light onto the area of his toil, he continued to dig. She knelt beside the grave and sat back on her heels.

"Are you ready?" she asked. "For what you find down there?"

The shovel hung mid-air, and Marsden said, "I don't know."

"So why put yourself through all this misery? Why can't you accept it when I promise he is dead?"

He rammed the shovel hard into the ground. "Because I have to see him myself. I won't believe it otherwise."

"Did you love him that much?"

Years of holding his tongue had ingrained in Marsden a habit he could not abandon. Even now, he could still not say the words aloud. Instead, he continued to dig.

"Why?" she asked. "I don't understand how anyone could be so enamored with him."

"Simon was my family," said Marsden. "He was all the family I had in the world."

"He truly was my blood," Beatrice said with an angry snort, "and I can assure you Simon was the worst kind of family you can imagine."

"He was different with me. He loved me."

"Did he tell you that?"

Marsden wondered how she knew the truth. No matter how many times Marsden had sworn his undying love when they were safe and alone, Simon had never said as much. He wanted to know how Beatrice had guessed.

"Simon was not a suitable replacement for them, you know," she said, pressing. "Your own family. You know that, don't you? He would never have introduced you to us. He would never have acknowledged you as someone important to him. Have you never wanted a real family of your own? A wife and children?"

"Of course," he admitted.

Beatrice's pale cheeks lifted in surprise. "Really? That does surprise—"

"Do you honestly think I like being abnormal? Being a social pariah? It cost me my place at Oxford, my relationship with my father. Do you honestly think I don't wish some days that I could simply be happy to marry and father children and be like everyone else?"

"Then why don't you?"

"Because Simon..."

Because marriage and children had never been a possibility, when he had looked into his future with Simon, time had arrested him in a bauble in which only he and Simon had existed. He had been hurt beyond belief when he was not invited to join Simon at Maidenstone. Beatrice was right. Simon had been ashamed of him. Even if he had lived, Marsden would have had no future to look forward to.

The thought made him furious, and Marsden struck the shovel into the soil with renewed force. The blade struck something much softer than the unforgiving earth. Noticing something had changed, Beatrice leaned forward to shine the light directly where the shovel had landed. He pulled the shovel back to reveal not a further layer of dirt but a thick fold of canvas. Marsden crouched to wipe away the earth.

"Go on," said Beatrice. "You're nearly there."

He stared up at her to discover that her face had become taught, her smiles long gone. A strange numbness engulfed his hands, but Marsden continued, dragging the flat edge of the shovel across the canvas, every jerking movement of the blade exposing more fabric. Beatrice climbed into the hole with him, took the tool out of his hands, and lifted it next to the gravestone. Then she kneeled beside him and, with the torch on the ground by their knees, they began clearing the dirt with cupped fingers. The process was slow, but as they scraped and dug with their hands, the shape of the canvas was revealed to them. Marsden sat back and stared down at the narrow roll of fabric, one end turned back toward him, inviting him to touch. He reached for it, but Beatrice caught his hand.

"Don't," she said.

For the first time since he had met Beatrice, Marsden saw genuine fear in her eyes. Despite the growing darkness around them, broken only in places by the flashlight's beam, her eyes fixated on the canvas, and he could now see what she feared most.

"You're scared of seeing him," he said, amazed. Despite all of her encouragement, she was just as nervous as he was at the idea of seeing what was beneath the canvas.

Beatrice rested one trembling hand on the fabric. "I have the same nightmare all the time," she whispered. "I dream that Simon isn't dead at all. That he'll come back and kill me in my sleep."

Marsden's heart lurched at the child-like fear he heard in her voice. For once, he believed her. Simon also haunted his dreams, but not with such violence.

"You said yourself, again and again, that he's dead. Wouldn't you rather see? Believe it for sure?"

Marsden reached for the top end of the layer of canvas and pulled it back a few inches to expose a glimpse of the contents within. Beatrice turned her face away when he held the flashlight above his head. In the bright light, the dirty blonde hair now visible at the top of the folded canvas seemed to glitter. Marsden held his breath when he pulled back the rest of the cloth.

He had seen dead bodies before, but he was not prepared for the sight of Simon Falconer's remains.

The emaciated waste of Simon's face, the last remnants of blackened skin, and grave wax around the cheekbones left no impression of the young man in life. The jaw hung loose, far from the top row of teeth, frozen in skeletal terror. There was an unmistakable bullet hole toward the top of his skull, just above Simon's eyes. Marsden's fingers trembled when he brushed back what remained of Simon's hair. Tears burned in his eyes, and his jaw ached as the muscles clenched in his face. Any ounce of hope he had brought with him to Maidenstone died inside him, burning a hole in his stomach.

His voice shook when he spoke: "Who shot him?"

Beatrice had pressed herself against the grave wall, fists clenched in her lap. "You know who."

Grief welled at the back of his throat, burning. "Just tell me. No more riddles."

"Alice was there, not me. She tried to blame it on me, but I only came back after she was dead."

"Alice?" he said, incredulous. "You're telling me Alice did this? You did this?"

"Not me!" She was snarling now, the veins in her throat bursting to press against her skin. "It was Alice."

"But why? Why did she kill him?"

Beatrice threw herself across the grave, clutching at his shoulders. He caught her, holding her by the waist when she fell against him.

"He would have killed her first if he'd had the chance," she said. "After what he did to her, he deserved it." Her breath stuck in her throat, a horrible, rasping, choking sound.

"What?" he demanded. "What did he do? Do you mean the accident in the lake?"

She was hysterical now, beating her fists against his chest. "Why do you care? You won't believe it!"

Marsden held her more tightly, but she fought him, digging her slender finger into the creases of his shirt. He shook her, fighting her off. "Just tell me, Beatrice."

Beatrice took a gulping breath and seized in his arms, fists raised towards her chin, her entire body stiff. She said in a rush, "He forced himself on her."

Marsden couldn't prevent the gurgling wheeze of disbelief that erupted from his throat. "No," he said. "I don't believe you."

"That was the night I came back," she persisted relentlessly. "The night it all started."

Marsden opened his mouth to argue, but the words got stuck behind his teeth, his chin jutting forward as the speech arrested. A vile thought bubbled up from the depth of his gut and forced its way through the thin line of his lips. "Grace. How old did you say she is?"

Beatrice's white face became hollow and slack. "Two years old."

The words died on his tongue. He tried to swallow, but a sickly thrum pulsed along his throat, almost gagging him. Grace. She was not yet three years old. Alice had said that Grace had no father. Had she meant no living father? He had immediately recognized Simon's looks in Grace but quickly dismissed the idea because Alice told him that Beatrice was the girl's mother. He had dismissed it too quickly because the truth had hurt too much.

Acid raced into Marsden's mouth, and he began to weep again. Hot, angry tears flooded his eyes and burned his cheeks. It all made terrible sense. To hide their shame, Lord Scarborough had hidden Grace with the Carlisles and locked his daughter away from the prying eyes of society. It had been an effective, if not callous, plan—until the consequences of Alice's madness could no longer be denied.

Marsden's body surrendered, collapsing back against the grave as his tears slowed, releasing the bitterness and mortifying disappointment of the moment. After almost three years of searching for Simon, the horror of the truth was unbearable. Beatrice let go, releasing her hold on him.

"Why didn't you tell me what had happened?" he asked.

Beatrice scoffed around her own tears. "What would you have said if I told you what he had done to Alice? Our parents didn't even believe us. They were going to leave us to rot in the asylum until the pregnancy could no longer be hidden, and they had no choice but to bring us home before the family was ruined."

Marsden drew a dirty hand over his face, wiping away tears and mucus. "Tell me now."

"Why? You won't like it."

He shook his tread, trying to piece together how he could explain himself to her—his time at Maidenstone Hall had been a series of humiliations, each day confronting him with the reality of Simon's true nature. He had sloughed them off repeatedly, explaining away the stories as resentment and jealousy, but the accusation of Simon molesting his sister was too odious to ignore.

"I'm very sure I won't," he agreed. "Ever since I came here, no one except for your father has had a single good thing to say about Simon. I'm beginning to wonder if I knew him at all. If you tell me, I'll know for sure."

Lightning flashed above their heads, and in the crack of light, Beatrice's eyes were glassy, her jaw set. When she spoke, the mist of her breath was visible like tendrils of smoke.

She said, "The first thing I remember is lying on the library floor. Simon was lying beside me. He was dead. The gun was still in my hand, but I couldn't have told you how it got there."

"You don't remember anything at all?" Marsden asked.

"I told you, Alice was in the room when he died."

"So what does she say happened?" He held up his hands as though he could physically stop her from dodging the question. "And don't tell me I have to ask her."

Beatrice bared her teeth, steeling herself as she began: "The way Alice tells it, he was drunk. His leave was almost over, and he didn't want to return to the front. He'd been drinking almost constantly and arguing with our parents since his arrival. Then, on the last night, he became violent." She paused to lick her lips. "He found Alice in the library. He'd had a terrible fight with Daddy. He wanted the old bastard to get him out of the war, but Daddy called him a coward, and Simon flew into a rage. He was so angry he took it out on Alice."

"But why?" Marsden asked. "Why Alice?"

Beatrice's expression was scathing. "Are you suggesting that she did something to deserve it?"

"No, of course not. Had it happened before? Had he attacked Alice like that before?"

"Not like… that. But he had beaten her many times."

"How did she get the gun?"

"I don't know. I just woke up, God knows how long later, my whole body in agony, and Simon lying dead beside me. His eyes were wide open, just staring up at the ceiling."

"You must have been terrified," he said, head shaking sadly.

Her laugh was strangled, almost animalistic. "You're telling me. I was perfectly happy being dead, thank you very much."

Marsden was keenly reminded that Simon was not the only Falconer buried beneath them. Just beneath Simon's body, Beatrice's coffin remained undisturbed. "Is that really how you remember it?" he asked. "One moment you were dead, and then…you were here?"

"I know it sounds ridiculous," she said, "but I promise it's true. Do you believe in ghosts, Fish?"

He stared back at her, his head aching with the heaviness of all he had learned. A sad, broken part of his soul wanted to believe it. At the very least, Marsden could accept that she truly believed it.

"I didn't think so. But I do believe in you, Beatrice."

This affirmation made her smile. Not her usual, cunning grin of mischief, but a gentle curve of her lips suggesting relief. "I didn't ask for this, you know. Neither did Alice."

"Before that night," he asked, "what do you remember?"

Her gaze moved past him, falling upon some dark corner beyond his shoulder. "The water. I remember the water. Simon, as well. Funny, isn't it? He was there when I died. Then, I was there when he died."

Marsden didn't think it was funny at all. He gazed down at the little that remained of Simon and decided that if it all were some kind of cosmic joke, it was a cruel one. His journey to find Simon had been bitter and the conclusion had broken his heart. He felt he had wasted the last three years of his life.

When he did not speak for some time, Beatrice asked, "Now what?"

He did not know how life would go on now that he had finally found Simon dead, but Marsden knew he could not leave his lover to rot in an unmarked grave. Lord Scarborough would never let him expose the truth of Simon's death, but when Marsden thought of Simon's smile, the touch of his hand, the warmth of his kiss, he could not bear the thought of leaving the body where it lay.

"I want to take him back to the house," he said. "We need to bury him properly. In the churchyard."

Beatrice sniffed. "Whatever for?"

"You said you feel frozen here. Everyone is frozen here, stuck, because of what happened. You'll never be free of Simon if he stays here. Neither will I."

He expected Beatrice to react badly, to protest, and argue with him—she was young and full of loathing, and she had never loved as he had— but she stared down at the grave below her knees and lay a hesitant hand on the earth, still covering her brother's remains, surprising him when she said, "You're probably right. Besides, Daddy will hate it."

Marsden heard the budding smile in her voice. If Lord Scarborough was likely to be upset by their plan, Beatrice could be relied upon as a willing participant. The thought of acting against her father and exposing the truth of Simon's death was enough to convince her.

As he exhaled a long sigh of exhausted relief, Marsden saw the expression on Beatrice's face change, panic drawing her fine features taught. She lifted one hand rapidly, reaching out into the space behind him.

"No!" she cried, just before something hard connected with the back of Marsden's skull.

Chapter Thirty-Eight

M arsden's first thought was that a grenade must have gone off. He was in a muddy trench, and an explosive had detonated beside him, leaving his ears ringing. He expected to open his eyes and find Simon beside him. The very thought almost made him smile. The memory was so close: a mortar landing in the trench by his feet, Simon launching at him, picking him up off his feet, and throwing him into a neighboring ditch. Marsden hoped that he would wake and see Simon lying beside him, but the pain at the back of his head when he tried to open his eyes was so sharp that a wave of nausea rose in his throat, and he immediately squeezed them shut.

He rolled to one side and vomited. When the bile had passed and his stomach ceased cramping, Marsden flopped onto his back and knew he was not in a trench in the French countryside. The war was over, and he was lying on a hard bed, a thin pillow beneath his throbbing skull, a determined reminder that he was back in England. He was at Maidenstone Hall.

Marsden reached for the back of his head, lifting it just enough to probe at the matted, wet mass of his hair. The smell of blood in the air was thick and metallic. He attempted once more to open his eyes. In the dull light of his bedroom, he held up his hand to examine with blurred vision a thick slick of red gore across his palm. He laid his damaged head back onto the pillow and winced at the pressure against the wound.

Marsden racked his throbbing brain for a memory but could not place how he had returned to the house. The last thing he remembered was crouching inside Simon's makeshift grave with Beatrice. He rolled onto his side again, hoping to dull the ache in his head, when the door lock clicked.

Nancy let herself in and took the key from the lock. She closed the door behind her and slid the key into her skirt pocket. From her grim expression, Marsden expected little sympathy. In fact, her flaring nostrils suggested she was particularly displeased with him.

"How are you feeling?" She almost stepped in the evidence of Marsden's nausea and crinkled her nose in disgust. "Not good, I see."

"I feel like I was hit by a train," said Marsden, covering his face to shield his eyes from the light. Every movement hurt, and he hissed at the pain when he tried to press himself up to sit.

"It was a shovel, actually," said Nancy. She stepped to the side of the bed, avoiding the pool of vomit, and tilted his head down so that she could examine the back of his skull. She sucked the air through her teeth. "He didn't have to hit you so hard."

"Who?"

"Badeley," she said with an angry click of her tongue.

"Did he have to hit me at all?" Marsden asked, attempting to be wry.

"I'm going to have to stitch this."

He didn't like that sound of that. "I think I'd rather see a doctor."

"Don't be silly. I trained to be a nurse, you know. During the war."

"I didn't know that. Did you serve?"

Nancy released his head and stood back. He couldn't be entirely sure, but he thought she looked sad through the thick porcelain mask of her everyday service face.

"I didn't. I handed in my notice here at the Hall but had to stay."

"Alice," he guessed. "You stayed to help with Alice."

Nancy clasped her hands and squeezed. "Something like that. Just rest. I'll be back with the things I need for your head."

Marsden wanted to ask her what she meant, but she bustled out of the room as quickly as she had entered it. He heard a click and knew she had locked the door again.

While Marsden waited for Nancy to return, he scanned the rest of his body and was relieved to discover that he wasn't suffering any other injuries.

He tried to sit up taller, wincing at the pain behind his eyes as he leaned forward to see that his shoes had been removed. He wore only his trousers and shirt. Marsden lifted a hand to his thudding heart. His letters and photographs had still been in his jacket pocket. He had removed it in the orchard. Marsden moaned, not in pain, but in misery.

Nancy reappeared, carrying a tray. Mrs. Huston was just behind her, a large metal bucket in hand. Nancy placed the tray on Marsden's desk and crossed the room again to lock the door.

He asked, "Is that necessary?"

In silence, Nancy fetched a bowl of water and a cloth from the tray. Mrs. Huston knelt by the bed, avoiding Marsden's gaze as she mopped up his vomit.

Nancy tilted his head with a gentle grasp at the back of his neck to clean his wound. Marsden hissed when she dabbed at the congealing blood. The pain was excruciating. His vision swam, and he closed his eyes to calm the swell in his stomach.

"Try to be still," said Nancy.

A needle pricked at the top of his skull. Marsden bit at his lip. The needle stabbed again and again around the gash, and Marsden fought the urge to cry. When she had finished, Nancy wrapped a bandage around his head and fastened it. She and Mrs. Huston worked together to help him lie down again, padding his aching head with two pillows and pulling a blanket over his body.

"How long will I have to stay here?" His vision was still blurred, but Marsden could see the ladies cast each other a grim, nervous look.

"Until you're feeling better," Mrs. Huston suggested.

"And how long will that be?"

"Until His Lordship has a chance to speak to you," said Nancy.

Marsden asked, "And Beatrice? Is she all right?"

"You needn't worry about Beatrice," said Mrs. Huston. "She's safe in her room."

"Is she being kept locked up, too?"

Nancy and Mrs. Huston were quiet, and Marsden accepted their silence as confirmation. Both he and Beatrice were prisoners now.

"What time is it?" he asked.

"It's late," said Nancy. "You've been unconscious for most of the evening."

"So it's not yet midnight? Beatrice is still in control?"

Mrs. Huston sank onto the corner of the bed. "So you know?" When Marsden attempted a feeble nod, she insisted, "It's not her fault."

"Who else knows the truth about Beatrice? Apart from the staff here at the hall."

"Just Dr. Webb," said Nancy. "And the other tutors knew, of course."

"Why did you say nothing? Why keep it from me?"

Nancy's shrug lacked any sense of apology. "For Alice's sake. To keep her calm. To keep her out of the institution."

"We can't let Dr. Webb take her back," said Mrs. Huston. "Alice is terrified of that place."

"And with good reason. You should have seen her when the countess brought her home the last time. Alice was broken. That's why Beatrice comes back."

"What do you mean?" Marsden asked.

"The more unhappy Alice is," said Nancy, "the more stressed she is, the stronger Beatrice becomes. All this talk of selling the house has only made Beatrice act out more than usual. Alice's fear feeds Beatrice."

"So all this time, Alice has thought she was Beatrice, as what? A coping mechanism?"

Nancy's brow furrowed, perplexed. "Thought she was Beatrice? No, Marsden she is Beatrice. Alice is possessed. The ghost of her sister lives within her."

Marsden pinched at the bridge of his nose. He had expected such an explanation from Mrs. Huston but not from serious, practical Nancy.

"You don't believe it," she guessed.

"I believe that Alice is a traumatized young lady—"

"You too!" said Mrs. Huston. Her expression was so earnest that she looked like she would burst into tears at any moment. "You think she's lost her mind, just like Dr. Webb. It truly is Beatrice, Marsden. You didn't know her when she was alive. If you had—if you'd loved that little girl the way I did—you'd know her anywhere. When she takes over, there is no doubt Beatrice is in control."

"So why is she here for a day at a time?" Marsden asked. "Why does Beatrice come and go at midnight?"

Nancy gave a weary sigh. "It's not for us to guess. She claims she doesn't know. She says she doesn't know why she's here—"

"But she does," said Mrs. Huston, emphatic. "She knows. She came back to punish us all."

"To punish you?" he said. "For what?"

"For our part in what happened. When Beatrice died, you know what happened, don't you?" When Marsden nodded, she clasped her hands together at her chest. "Simon was never punished for what he did to her. Then, when he was killed, Lord Scarborough refused to tell anyone about what Simon did to Alice. Simon became a war hero, and Alice was locked away. None of us said a word."

"But you said something, didn't you, Mrs. Huston?" he asked. "At least when Beatrice died."

"And she was dismissed," said Nancy.

"I couldn't bear it," said Mrs. Huston, her eyes swimming in unshed tears. "I couldn't look at Simon after what he did. But I promised I'd stay quiet without a fuss when Lord Scarborough asked me to come back. For Alice's sake."

"Be honest," Nancy said to her. "You stayed quiet because you needed the job."

"That's all that stopped you from going to the police? Fear of being dismissed?" Marsden couldn't hide the disgust in his voice. At their guilty expressions, both women cast their eyes away from his accusing glare; he wanted to kick himself for being so slow. He had seen the figures in the earl's ledger but failed to see the connection. "That's why you're paid so well. To keep your mouths shut. Lord Scarborough has been bribing you into silence."

"We didn't ask for the money," Nancy said quickly. "Well, Badeley did, of course, but not me. Not Linton."

Marsden would have laughed were he not in so much pain. "Of course, Badeley asked for the money. Is that why he hit me? He was afraid I would interrupt his blackmail scheme?"

"He's sorry now," said Mrs. Huston. Something in her low tone suggested that perhaps Badeley wasn't genuinely sorry at all.

"Am I a prisoner now that I know the truth?" he asked. "Or does His Lordship plan to offer me money too?"

"You're not a prisoner," said Nancy. "You just need to stay until you feel better."

"Until His Lordship deigns to see me, is that right? Do you think he'll offer me a very substantial bribe?"

Nancy began to clean up the items she had used to clean and stitch his wound, her movements an awkward flurry. "Quite honestly, that's the last thing you should worry about when it comes to His Lordship. Not now that he knows who you really are."

Marsden saw the embarrassed flush cross Mrs. Huston's pale cheeks. His stomach plummeted. "He has my things. My letters and photographs."

"Yes," Mrs. Huston confirmed. "When Badeley and Beatrice brought you in, she had wrapped your jacket around your head. It was covered in blood. The letters fell out—"

"I want them back."

Nancy shook her head as though he were a lost cause. "If I were you, I would let them go. Walk out of here and never come back."

"Will I even be allowed to leave?"

"Of course, you will. Once His Lordship—"

"Has seen me. Yes, I know. Do you think," he said, covering his eyes with one hand, "that you could turn off the light when you go? It's only making the pain worse."

Marsden did not want to continue this discussion with either woman. He knew he would face enough judgment from Lord Scarborough soon enough. Mrs. Huston gave his ankle a gentle pat. Their tread was light as they swept out of the room. The light was switched off, and Marsden was swallowed by the darkness. Despite the intense agony roaring at the back of his skull, he heard the key turn in the lock.

Chapter Thirty-Nine

Marsden had hoped that he would succumb once more to unconsciousness, but instead, he lay in the dark of his room, kept awake by the throbbing pain in his head. The nausea had passed, but his discomfort could not be relieved with rest. He could not be sure how long it had been since Nancy and Mrs. Huston had tended to him, but in what seemed like no time, he heard the snick of a key turning in the lock, and the door opened again. He squinted into the pale light of the hallway when a sliver of illumination fell across the floor. A figure hesitated in the doorway before entering and quickly shutting the door. The floral scent of her perfume followed her into the room.

"Fish? Are you awake?"

"I'm afraid so," he mumbled.

"I'm going to turn on the light. Cover your eyes."

Marsden did as he was told and listened for the flick of the switch. He separated his fingers and allowed himself to adjust gradually to the light.

Beatrice, dressed entirely in black, stood before him grim-faced. Her crepe dress was funereal, high around the neck, and raised at the shoulders into puffed sleeves. It was old-fashioned and nothing like her usual attire.

"Ghastly, isn't it?" she asked, gesturing at the dress. "It was made for Simon's funeral at the churchyard. I wasn't there, but Alice told me it was a solemn affair. Nancy picked it out for me to wear. She has a peculiar sense of humor, don't you think?"

"I thought they'd locked you away, too. How did you get in here?" Marsden asked.

Beatrice raised one hand to reveal a key between her fingers. Although she did not smile exactly, she did look entirely pleased with herself, her eyes sparkling with mischief. "Magic, as you can see."

Marsden groaned in relief at the idea of freedom. "Thank God. How did you manage to get your hands on that?"

"I still have some allies left, Fish. You're not the only one."

"Not Badeley, I assume."

"That slimy fool," she said, her nose crinkling. "I thought we had an understanding. Clearly not."

"I saw you kiss him," said Marsden. "I thought maybe he was your lover."

"What kind of young lady do you think I am, Fish?"

"Then what were you two planning? I heard you, you know."

Beatrice sat down on the edge of the bed and folded her hands across her lap. She held the key between her thumb and forefingers, sliding the cold metal in circles between them.

"You never cease to amaze me," she said. "Here we all were, thinking that you were boring old Marsden Fisher, war veteran and teacher, haplessly tending to my silly sister. Not only are you a master of deception and disguise, but you're a spy, too."

"You weren't exactly being discreet. Were you planning on running away with Badeley?"

Beatrice smirked. "Why do you want to know? You're not jealous, are you, Fish?"

"He seemed to think I would get in the way of your scheme," he said

She looked upon him the way one might gaze upon a puppy, all at once adoring and sympathetic. "I would never have intentionally let any harm come to you, darling. You know that, don't you?"

He didn't know. He couldn't be sure of anything with her. "Did you tell Badeley I was in the orchard?"

"Of course not. I told you, Badeley and I had an understanding. He was supposed to help me, not hinder me. Smacking you over the back of the head with a shovel and handing you over to Daddy most certainly hindered me, I can assure you. I should never have trusted him. He's been in Daddy's pocket since the night Simon died."

"Badeley was there? The night Simon died?"

"Who do you think buried the body?" Beatrice asked with a sneer. "It certainly wasn't my father."

Marsden's eyes rolled back as he understood Badeley's exorbitant salary. "What else has he done for your father?"

"He was the one who delivered me and Alice to the asylum. Then he brought us home when they realized we were going to have a baby." She paused and looked down at her hands. For a moment, she looked as though she might cry. "He was the one who took Grace to the Carlisle farm. And to think I considered marrying him."

For a moment, Marsden thought he had misheard. "Marry whom? You don't mean Badeley?"

Beatrice sniffed, warding off any tears. "Don't look so surprised, Fish. A husband has far more authority than a father when it comes to the welfare of a woman. I may still need a husband to rescue me, you know. In that, at least, Alice and I agreed."

"Why? To get Grace back?"

She nodded. "On my part, yes. And to keep Alice out of the lunatic asylum. The likes of Dr. Webb can't touch us if we're beyond Daddy's control."

Her argument made some chaotic sense to Marsden, but the thought of her marrying Badeley made him scoff. "But why Badeley? Of all people?"

"Don't judge me too harshly, Fish. Until you arrived, he was the only option. I had to think quickly. There was a time when I was sure my parents would never send us back to the asylum, not while they were afraid of what I would say, but I underestimated Daddy, it seems. I'm afraid I might have pushed them a little too far." She paused to consult the small watch pinned to the bodice of her dress. "Never mind about all that now. It's almost midnight. I will need you to fill Alice in on everything that's happened tonight. I don't trust the others to get it right."

"And then what?" he asked. "Help you escape?"

"I would have thought you'd rather want to get out of here." She pointed to his bandaged head. "Do you think you could muster it?"

Marsden threw his feet over the side of the bed. When he tried to stand up, the room immediately spun around him, and he stumbled. Beatrice rushed to catch him and help him back onto the bed, where he folded over his knees, grasping at his shins as the bile rose in his throat once more.

"I might need some time to recover," he said, winded by his exertion.

She brandished the key once more with a delightful grin. "Well, when the time is right, I'll be able to break you out."

"How did you really get that? Did you steal it?"

"I told you, I'm not entirely friendless. Linton gave it to me."

Marsden couldn't have been more disbelieving if she'd told him the key had been delivered to her by the Arch Angel Gabriel himself. "Linton?"

"He's known Alice and me since the day we were born, Fish. He may have a thick crust, but I can assure you that underneath it all, he wants what's best for us. He likes you too, you know." When he gave her a look of contemptuous doubt, she held up her right hand. "I swear. Goodness knows he doesn't trust you as far as he can throw you, but I think he was quite hoping that you would fall in love with one of us. I mean my sister and I, of course. But then that was not taking into account your desire for your own sex."

She meant to joke, he knew, but a hot blush raced along the length of Marsden's neck and blossomed in his pale cheeks, exposing his embarrassment at the memory of the physical reaction Alice and Beatrice herself had instilled in him. He couldn't be sure if it was their familial similarity in appearance to Simon or simply the comfort of being touched by another human being for the first time in so long, but he couldn't deny that no woman had ever elicited such a response in him the way the sisters had. Or rather, Alice and her alter-ego had.

"You know nothing of what I desire," he said.

"So you like women as well? That is a relief." She shuffled closer, leaning against his shoulder. "In that case, which of us do you like best? Between Alice and I?"

Marsden recognized the bait and refused to take it. He tried to look away, but she wouldn't let him escape, taking his chin between delicate fingers.

"It's me, isn't it?"

He was in no condition to evade her, but even if he had been at his best, Marsden wondered if he would have tried to escape the press of her lips against his. He closed his eyes and let her cradle his head, her fingers sliding through the hair at the top of his neck and skimming along the edge of the bloody bandage. He shuddered when Beatrice's tongue skimmed along the sensitive curve of his upper lip. She was nothing like Simon. He had been hard, unyielding—always the stronger of them both. Beatrice was soft and warm, compliant even in her insistence. When she lifted one of his limp arms, guiding it around her narrow waist, Marsden embraced the stark contrast, willing himself to relax and take some comfort in the heat of her body. In her arms, Simon's ghost retreated a little further.

Beatrice pressed harder against him, her fingers tightening in his hair. Unbidden, his head wound throbbed when she stroked too forcefully against the base of his skull. Marsden hissed in discomfort, and she pulled away.

"I'm sorry," she said, brushing her fingers along his cheekbone. "Does it hurt terribly?"

Marsden gaped at her and nodded. Beatrice guided him gently back onto the bed, holding his head with one careful hand. She arranged another pillow, and he allowed her to position him against it. She was so close that he could smell the perfume on her wrists.

"Your perfume," he said, "it's always so strong."

Beatrice brushed his hair away from his eyes, allowing him to inhale the sweet scent on her skin again. "It's always been my favorite. Alice can't stand it."

He caught her left hand, drawing it back toward his face so he could smell the perfume up close. She did not protest, even when his fingers slid down her wrist, drawing back the cuff of her sleeve. The scar there, long and thick, appeared less red in the dim light of Marsden's bedroom.

He traced the scar with his thumb. "Why did you do it?"

"We've been very lonely," she said, allowing the intimate touch. "Alice and me. I was angry when I found out what she had tried to do to us, but I suppose in the end I should thank her. It's why Mummy brought you here.

She thought your presence would stop Alice from trying again."

When Beatrice freed her wrist from his grasp and reclined beside him, Marsden could feel his heart softening toward her. For all of her bravado and mischief, he believed that Beatrice, too, had been lonely and suffering, locked away in the dark, dusty halls of Maidenstone. Even if she wasn't real, just a figment of Alice's tortured mind, her pain still resonated with him. He knew what it was to suffer a great loss, to be isolated and lonely. He had not grown up with a family, as she had; his mother and brother died from cholera when he was still a baby; his father was barely present in his childhood, always diligently working for the university. Even the little he saw of his father was snatched away when Marsden had been caught in a moment of intimacy with another student at Oxford. The army had offered some brief camaraderie, but the war was over now, and Marsden was left alone again.

Beatrice slumped onto her left elbow and dragged her right knee across his waist. Her dress hitched up around her knee, and Marsden gave in to the temptation to stroke the skin of her lower thigh. He had attempted intimacy with so few women in such a limited capacity, and he was sure Alice would never let him touch her this way. His fingers traced along the hemline of the dress. Marsden knew nothing about women's clothing, but he was sure he felt something small and hard inside the hem, as though lined with pebbles. Marsden thought to ask her, but at the same moment, she sighed into his neck and tapped at his shoulder with a sharp fingernail.

"I've been meaning to ask you," she said, "Who was Marsden Fisher? I mean, the real Marsden Fisher?"

"No one. Just a soldier I met during the war."

"But why him? Why take his name? Did you like him?"

"I barely knew him. He shot himself in the middle of the night on the bank of the Meuse. But I remembered he was a schoolteacher in Cornwall. Maybe that's why his name came into my head when I applied for this position."

"Didn't you feel guilty? Stealing his name?"

Yes, he thought, but said, "No. It's not as though he's using it. And honestly,

I didn't think to steal it for so long."

Beatrice pursed her lips. If she had any further opinions on the matter, she held her tongue as she checked her pinafore clock once more. "I'm afraid it's time for me to go. I hope I'll see you soon."

Marsden only nodded, not willing to make any promises to her. Instead, he took her hand, rubbing the delicate bones of her knuckles between his fingers. Beatrice endowed him with a bright smile when she leaned close again to kiss him, her lips hot. When she pressed herself against his side, he wrapped his arm around her shoulders and welcomed the comforting weight of her head against his chest. It had been so long since Marsden had held anyone this way, in bed, so comfortably, and the sensation reawakened within him a deep longing for a sense of belonging, for unconditional love.

Beatrice murmured into the collar of his shirt: "Look after Alice for me?"

Marsden pressed his chin against the top of her head. "I will."

Above them, the bulb buzzed and flickered. Marsden squinted into the flare of light, the bright flash painful amidst his concussion. In his arms, Beatrice became entirely still, and he wondered if she had fallen asleep. A moment later, she shuddered. The light sparked and cracked. She gasped and lurched upward, rocketing out of his arms. Her eyes widened, her mouth gaped, and Marsden immediately knew she was about to scream. He captured her again, restraining her with one arm around her back, and slapped a hand across her mouth.

"It's just me," he said, hissing. "You have to be quiet."

She did not relax in his arms, but she ceased her struggles, the rush of the exhale from her nose hot against his fingers. She blinked rapidly, and when Marsden took his hand away from her mouth, she pulled herself out of his arms. Her eyes darted around the room as though she had never before seen it.

"What am I doing here?" she asked, clearly distressed. She climbed over Marsden, slipping off the bed to stand beside him.

Marsden, head pounding, could not follow her. "Alice? It is you, isn't it?"

"Of course," Alice snapped. "Why was she here?"

"A lot has happened since you were—" He hesitated, unsure what to say.

232

"While you've been gone, I suppose."

Alice pointed at the bandage on his head. "So I can see. What happened?"

"Badeley happened."

"He attacked you?" She hugged her arms around her chest and shoulders and sat on the chair at Marsden's desk. "Tell me everything."

"Do you remember anything at all? The orchard?"

"I was with you in the kitchen. That's the last thing I remember. You'll have to tell me what happened once Beatrice was awake."

Awake. It was a strange concept, the idea of Beatrice being awake and Alice sleeping—hibernating—but it was the aptest description she had offered since he had learned of Beatrice's death. They couldn't exist at the same time. Marsden thought of their shared journal; the notes volleyed back and forth, ensuring both were aware of everything that had happened while the other was absent.

And so Marsden told her everything: searching for Simon in Beatrice's grave, digging up his body, being attacked by Badeley, and Beatrice escaping her prison to creep into his. Alice listened, silent and passive. He was sure he could find no emotion in her expression at all.

"You found Simon," she said when he had finished his tale. "Why would you do that? Why dig him up?"

"I had to know for sure," he said. "I couldn't believe he was dead until I could see the proof with my own eyes."

"And do you feel better for it? Knowing that he truly is dead?"

"No," he admitted. "Not now that I know what happened."

She clasped at her left wrist, wringing at the thin circle of bone under the scar. "Beatrice told you. What exactly did she say?"

"I'd rather hear your version of what happened. You owe me that much."

The wringing ceased. "Why do I owe you?"

Marsden managed a tired, pained lift of his shoulders, not so much a shrug as a resignation. He thought of Simon dead on the library floor, a single bullet hole in his forehead. "You killed him."

Alice stared directly into his eyes, jaw firm set. "He would have killed me. He was in a rage and took it out on me, as he always did."

"But he—the way he hurt you—Beatrice said he'd never done that before."

"No, Marsden, he had never raped me before." She was unrelenting in the wake of his wince. "I'd barely seen him for the better part of five years. After Beatrice died, our father kept him busy at Cambridge and then with the war. When Simon left home, I was a little girl. It was as though he came back and realized for the first time that I had become a woman. The way he sneered at me—it changed."

Marsden couldn't help but imagine the scene and was bewildered that no one had helped Alice—that no one had come running. "Did you scream? Surely someone heard?"

"He broke my jaw." She rubbed at her chin with one hand, remembering the injury. "I couldn't have called for help, even if I'd wanted to. I couldn't speak. He just kept hitting me and hitting me. With his gun, if you can believe it. His fists alone weren't enough; he had to…" Alice paused to swallow so loudly Marsden could hear it. "He called me a tart. A whore. He said I was a good-for-nothing flirt, just like Beatrice had been."

Marsden gazed up at the ceiling. The flaking paint was swirling above him. His stomach churned, but he couldn't tell if the nausea rising in his throat resulted from his head wound or a response to the horror of her story.

"Is that when you shot him?"

"When he was finished, he went over to the fireplace to find a cigarette. He just stood there, smoking and sneering at me. He said that I had deserved it. The gun was lying on the floor beside me. He'd needed both hands to hold me down, you see. So, I picked it up, and I pointed it at him. He laughed at me and…"

Marsden closed his eyes. "You pulled the trigger."

Her eyes glazed over as she lost herself in the memory. "It was very loud. It made my ears ring."

Marsden remembered what it was like, the deafening ring of a shot going off by your ear. The pain that followed was excruciating.

"How could they possibly hide what had happened?" he asked. "Surely you were seen by a doctor?"

"My father has become very adept at paying people to be silent. Once I had recovered—once they understand that Beatrice had come back—I was not so easy to keep quiet, so he shipped me off to St. Jude's."

"And your mother just went along with it? Why?"

"My mother does not have the strongest fortitude," Alice said dryly. "I'm sure you've noticed."

"You mean the drinking?"

She nodded. "It started after Beatrice died. A few too many brandies after dinner. A few too many glasses of champagne at parties. After what happened with Simon, she began drinking to excess every day. I doubt she's been truly sober since Grace was born."

They sat together in an awkward silence, avoiding each other's gaze. Marsden felt a tear burn at the corner of his left eye.

"I think she must have known," said Alice.

"Who?"

"Beatrice. She must have known that I needed her. I couldn't face what I had done, so she came back to protect me. When we were children, she always took the blame."

"I thought you hated her."

Alice's grimace was sad. "I do, sometimes. But she always seems to take the brunt of it all. I don't recall anything of the moment after I pulled the trigger. Nor do I remember Grace's birth or Badeley taking her away. Beatrice withstood it all. For that, at least, I suppose I should be grateful to her." She trailed off, staring into space as if conjuring up an image of Beatrice, this time as an angel rather than a burden.

Marsden pointed to Alice's left wrist. "Then why did you try to kill yourself? If you felt as though Beatrice was here to help you?"

She stared solemnly down at her scar. "It was a mistake. I was just so lonely. Beatrice may have returned, but I can't pass the time of day with her. Before you came here, I had no one to talk to. The other tutors ran away from Beatrice, and the staff here are too afraid to be seen talking to me."

Marsden said nothing, instead absorbing the sensation of his fingers and toes tingling with pins and needles. His eyes were heavy. He was in pain and desperate to rest.

"Now what?" Alice asked when the silence between them dragged on.

"Beatrice seems to think that you and I should escape together," he said.

When she spoke again, her voice sounded closer. Marsden couldn't be sure. He couldn't keep his eyes open.

She whispered right next to his ear: "Would that be such a terrible idea?"

Marsden tried to speak, but the weight of his tongue made it impossible. He felt Alice's hand on his own. Before he passed out, he thought perhaps it wasn't such a terrible idea after all.

Chapter Forty

When Marsden woke again, it was to the unnerving sight of Linton's frown hovering above his face.

"How do you feel, Mr. Fisher?"

Marsden's feet were completely numb, and there was a sharp ache wringing the nerves at the base of his neck.

"I've been better," he said. "I don't suppose there's any chance of me seeing a doctor now."

"That all depends on you," a second voice said.

Marsden twisted his head on the pillow to see Lord Scarborough seated at the desk. He avoided Marsden's gaze, taking an exaggerated interest in a groove in the wooden surface. Marsden struggled to sit up, pushing himself up on trembling arms until Linton stepped in to help him with a hand at his back.

"Sir—"

"You may leave us, Linton." Lord Scarborough shooed Linton with a savage flick of one hand. Linton, in turn, gave a terse bob of his head and hastily left the room.

"What exactly are we going to do with you, young man?" Lord Scarborough asked when the door closed behind Linton.

Marsden wanted to laugh at the absurdity of the question. "Are you suggesting that's up to me, sir?"

"It can be if we can come to a suitable gentleman's agreement, Mr. Bäuerle."

His name—the name he'd used all his life until applying for the position at

Maidenstone Hall—distracted Marsden, but he recovered quickly enough to draw his spine straight and return Lord Scarborough's loathing glare.

"How long have you known?" he asked.

Lord Scarborough, pleased with himself, smirked at having disconcerted Marsden so thoroughly. "My suspicions were raised when I spoke to Major Caldwell. I mentioned your name, and he was quite surprised, having heard that Corporal Fisher had committed suicide. It was after Caldwell lost his arm, but he was a conscientious leader and kept an ear out for word of his men. I did consider confronting you with it after you'd spoken with Dr. Webb."

"And yet you waited."

Lord Scarborough's thin smile became menacing. "Yes. I waited."

Marsden wanted to swipe the smirk off Lord Scarborough's face with a vicious punch. Instead, he took a deep breath and exhaled through his nose, struggling to maintain his composure. "In that case, sir, I would like to see a doctor, and then I would like to leave."

"I'm sure you would. But I will only agree to that if I'm assured that you can be relied upon to keep what has happened here to yourself."

Marsden resisted the urge to scoff. Chest puffed, mouth pursed with authority, Lord Scarborough appeared precisely as the parody of the English gentry that Marsden had always assumed him to be: a snobbish, lazy man whose pride and sense of entitlement had destroyed his family. He could not, however, resist the desire to taunt Lord Scarborough.

"Do you mean, sir, that you wish me to refrain from sharing that your son murdered one of your daughters and raped the other?" At the sour expression on Lord Scarborough's face, Marsden was buoyed and pressed on; "Or are you referring to the killing of your son by your surviving daughter in self-defense."

"Self-defense!" Red-cheeked and sputtering, the earl could barely contain his rage. "It was murder. That little devil murdered my son. Her insanity was the only reason she didn't go to the noose."

"But Alice was never arrested, sir," Marsden reminded him. "You took justice into your own hands and sent her away to assure her silence."

"I decided as a jury would have done. My daughter suffers from a psychosis. This dual personality Alice developed, impersonating her dead sister—what else would you call her but insane?"

"So you will send her back to the asylum, and your secret remains safe." The terrible realization settled upon Marsden so suddenly that he felt the blood drain from his face. "Where does that leave me? In a hidden grave with Beatrice and Simon?"

Lord Scarborough waved a tired, dismissive hand. "I am not a murderer, Mr. Bäuerle. Besides, why would I need to hurt you when I already have in my possession the ultimate guarantee that you will not speak a word of what has happened here."

There was the rub. Marsden knew full well that Lord Scarborough had the upper hand. "You mean my letters from Simon. The photographs."

"You know that the truth of Simon's death would be detrimental to us both," said Lord Scarborough. "I want my son's dignity to remain intact, and you do not want to be reported to the police. They may have done away with capital punishment for degenerates like you, but I'm sure hard labor in a London prison is no more desirable. Would you truly risk prison to see me and my family ruined?"

"So, I keep your secrets, and you let me go without further repercussion? You want to blackmail me."

Lord Scarborough dared to appear offended. "I am a gentleman, young man, and a gentleman does not stoop to such means. I will, however, ensure that your word is worthless should you choose to break your promise."

"You mean no one would believe the testimony of a sodomite like me. No against the word of a pompous rich earl."

"Of course, they won't!" Lord Scarborough launched out of his seat, glaring down at Marsden. "What proof will you have?"

Marsden counted on outstretched fingers as he made his list: "Simon's uniform coat, his service weapon—his body, for heaven's sake. They all prove he died here."

The color in Lord Scarborough's cheeks faded, his temper receding. He said, "Of what weapon are you speaking? What coat?" The irritating smirk returned. "There is certainly no body. At least not one that will ever be found."

Marsden hung his head in resignation. "You've already moved him."

"Moved whom, Mr. Bäuerle?" Lord Scarborough cleared his throat. "Now, I suggest you be ready to leave as soon as you feel well enough. If I hear of you again from this moment—if I hear any mention of your name in relation to my family—I can ensure that you will end your days in prison."

Marsden rose slowly to his feet. He wavered, dizzy, but insisted on matching Lord Scarborough's steely gaze. "Will you tell me just one thing?"

With a harsh tug on the lapels of his jacket, the earl nodded once. "Well, what is it?"

"When Simon was here, I gather he asked you for help. He wanted to return home from the front, permanently."

Scarlet crept up the earl's neck. "It was a brief moment of weakness on my son's part. He knew his duty. He would have returned to the front as ordered."

"I'm sure you're right, but I was wondering—" Marsden picked at the words in his mind as he stared down at his shoes. "Did he mention me at all?"

"You?" Lord Scarborough examined Marsden, eyeing the younger man from head to toe with a look of blatant disgust, his upper lip curling. "You were hoping I would have you both withdrawn from your battalion?" He shook his head, and his smile, when it finally emerged, was wicked. "No, boy. Simon never spoke of you. In fact, I'm sure he didn't think of you at all. Nor will I when you have left this house."

For all the bravado with which he had blackmailed Marsden, Lord Scarborough was now keen to exit, storming across the room. He slammed the door behind him, the bang rattling Marsden's fragile nerves. The key turned in the lock, and Marsden was imprisoned alone once more.

Chapter Forty-One

Marsden clutched at his forehead and swayed in the center of the room. His head was pounding, and he worried that he would vomit again at any moment. However, he was determined to take the opportunity afforded by Lord Scarborough and leave without further repercussions while he still could. When his offer of freedom was presented, he would be ready. Glancing down at his bloody shirt, Marsden determined his first step at least would be to change.

His suitcases were stacked beside the wardrobe. Marsden attempted to crouch before them, but his knees gave out beneath him, and he almost fell. Grasping at the corner of the cupboard, he righted himself and waited for the room to stop spinning. When he was sure again of his balance, he retrieved a clean shirt and pair of trousers from one of his bags and pressed himself back onto numb feet.

As he dressed, Marsden considered the problem of his letters and photographs. He could barely stand the thought of looking at the pictures or reading the letters now that he had been so brutally forced to face Simon's true nature, but Marsden didn't know how he could leave them behind. He had kept the letters close to his heart every day for almost three years and felt naked without them. Nor could he shake the fear that they could later be used against him by Lord Scarborough—or worse, fall into someone else's hands. Marsden did not enjoy the idea of his future being held at the mercy of any man. If he did not retrieve his documents, he knew he would spend all his days looking over his shoulder for the lingering shadow of his relationship with Simon Falconer.

Marsden could barely contain his boredom. His head wound demanded that he rest, the back of his skull pounding every time he stood and forcing him to while away the hours sleeping and waiting for any sign of his imminent release. None of the staff came to release him, nor did Alice, even though she had a key.

In the afternoon, Mrs. Huston arrived with a bowl of soup and tea. Marsden noticed her nervousness, fumbling with the key and almost dropping her tray. She diverted her eyes when she placed his meal on the desk beside him. He was practically amused when she lifted the soup bowl to reveal an envelope concealed beneath it; his name scrawled across the cream paper. Mrs. Huston briefly caught his eye and just as quickly looked away, brushing her hands upon her apron. Without another word, she hurried from the room, dutifully locking the door behind her, just as every one of Marsden's visitors had done since his incarceration. He couldn't help but laugh when he lifted the soup bowl to retrieve the envelope. Mrs. Huston, sweating and shaking with fear, was not cut out for a life of spy-making and espionage.

Marsden recognized Alice's handwriting on the envelope and withdrew the letter to see that the missive had been written in a hurry; the ink smudged in numerous places, her letters slanting dramatically down toward the right-hand corner of the page.

Marsden—Thomas—whoever you are—

We have to leave now. I ask you for nothing more than to help me leave this place. Dr. Webb intends to return for us tomorrow morning, and I am not so proud that I am unwilling to admit that Beatrice and I need your help to get clear of Yorkshire. Traveling alone, our father will easily find us, but if you can help us get to London, then she and I can disappear from his reach forever.

I know you've been promised clemency, but you must not trust my father.

Be ready. I cannot tell you when we will come for you, but it will be after dark.

Love, Alice.

Marsden imagined Alice's circling wrist as she wrote frantically across the page. In answer, he twisted the gold cufflink at his wrist with shaking fingers. Sympathy for her wriggled inside Marsden's belly. He could not ignore the guilt he would feel if he left Alice in the surgical hands of Dr. Webb. And it wasn't an entirely ridiculous plan. They could easily disappear if he and Alice could creep out of the house unseen and make their first way to York and then London. But Marsden wasn't entirely sure he wanted to run away with Alice. He felt something for her—something akin to affection—but to run away with her was certain to be tied to her for longer than the duration of their escape. He would not be able to abandon her once they were free. By escaping with her, he would be taking on an enormous responsibility. A responsibility he never imagined would ever be his.

Despite the appeal and subsequent fear of absconding with Alice, the problem of his photographs and letters again reared its ugly head. He wasn't ready to let them go. Not yet. He would have to retrieve them before fleeing the house. There was no way he was leaving any trace of himself behind at Maidenstone Hall.

Marsden did not know how he would get his personal items back, but he suspected that Alice was his best chance. If she wanted his help, she would have to help him in return.

Chapter Forty-Two

Marsden prepared himself for flight by dressing warmly and securing the little money he had left in his pockets. He considered taking his bags, reluctant to leave his few possessions behind, but was sure they would be a burden. Content with his preparation, as little as he was allowed in the situation, Marsden lay back on his bed and winced in pain when he placed his injured head upon the pillow. The worst symptoms of his concussion, terrible nausea and debilitating dizziness, had ceased, but he promised himself that he would still see a doctor when they were safely away from the Hall.

He had barely made himself comfortable when the door opened, and Marsden was startled to see Linton standing in the doorway, one index finger pressed against his lips.

"We must be quiet, Mr. Fisher," he said, pulling the door behind him. "Did you read the note from Lady Alice? Will you come?"

Marsden rose to his feet, pointed to his bags, and said, "I suppose I'll have to leave these here?"

"You will. Are you ready otherwise?"

"No. I cannot leave without the letters and photographs Badeley took from me."

Linton gave a snort of harried frustration. "Mr. Fisher, there is no time."

"We must make the time," Marsden insisted. "I will never be free of this place if I have to leave them behind."

"I understand Lord Scarborough agreed—"

"To keep them hidden unless I broke my promise and revealed the truth

244

about how Simon died. He did. But if I'm going to help Alice run away, I need to disappear completely. There can be no evidence that I was here." When Linton continued to hesitate, Marsden lost his patience. "Come now, just tell me, do you know where they are? I'm assuming Lord Scarborough has hidden them?"

Linton gave a reluctant nod. "I believe he has stored them in his study, but I would definitely not suggest attempting—"

"Good," said Marsden. "Just a quick jaunt to the study, and we can be on our way."

Marsden barged past him, forcing Linton to follow him into the hallway. The two men crept down the servant's staircase, and Linton paused as he opened the doorway, listening for anyone else on the landing. Believing the coast to be clear, Linton beckoned Marsden forward, and they emerged onto the second floor.

A ghostly face appeared before them as they rounded the corner of the west wing and passed into the dark hallway. Both Linton and Marsden froze in surprise. Alice raised both hands to calm them and stepped into the light. She was still wearing the mourning dress, the black crepe blending almost entirely with the shadows of the dark hall.

"I'm sorry," she said in a whisper. "I couldn't wait any longer. You were gone too long, Linton." She turned to Marsden, nervous, longing naked across her face. "You got my letter?"

"Yes."

"And you will come with me?" When he nodded, she lunged at him, slotting herself neatly into his embrace by wrapping her arms around his waist and pressing her cheek against his chest. "Thank you," she said into his shirt.

Marsden ignored Linton's pointed look of discomfort and wrapped his arms around her. Immediately, he felt anchored, as though the warmth of her body was a physical assurance that together they could achieve safety.

"We have to hurry," said Linton. "Mrs. Huston has been tasked with distracting Mr. Badeley and His Lordship, but I do not know how long she can keep them occupied." He extracted Alice from Marsden's embrace and forced her down the hallway. "It's time to go."

Marsden would not let Linton derail his first imperative and refused to move. "I told you, I can't go without my letters. We have to retrieve them."

Linton huffed with exasperated fury. "There is no time! If you don't leave now, you may be unable to leave at all."

"Why do you want them?" Alice asked.

"If we don't retrieve the letters and the photographs of me with Simon, your father will always have a hold over me. He's a powerful man. He has enough evidence to have me arrested for fraud and gross indecency. Do you honestly think he can't make me disappear before I can say a word about Simon or what happened to Beatrice?"

Alice turned to face Linton. "He's right. My father will be furious when he realizes Marsden helped me escape. He'll come looking for us." She laid a hand against his shoulder and reminded him, "You trusted him enough to ask him to help me. You must trust that he's right in this."

"I have no choice but to trust him!" Linton took Alice's hand in his own, a shockingly familiar gesture for the stiff butler. "If you do not leave now, child, you will be returned to the hands of that odious doctor. I could not bear it."

Marsden had never seen such a display of emotion from Linton. He was stunned that the old butler even had the capacity to become teary as he had now. Alice placed her other hand over Linton's, a gentle grasp of conciliation.

"I promise you," she said. "Everything will be all right. But we must act now."

Alice hitched up the hem of her dress and took off across the landing, not looking back. Marsden and Linton followed in her wake. When they caught up with her, Alice peered through the banister to see if anyone was visible at the base of the stairs.

"The coast is clear," she said. "Quietly now."

"Aren't you afraid of being seen?" Marsden asked. "Shouldn't we take the servants' stairs?"

"With any luck," said Linton, "Mrs. Huston already has Mr. Badeley and

246

his lordship occupied, and her ladyship—"

"Is most likely passed out somewhere," said Alice. "I don't think we have to worry about her."

At the base of the stairs, momentarily exposed in the lights of the salon, Marsden paused to ask, "What is Mrs. Huston doing to distract his Lordship?"

Linton scratched at the stiff line of his shirt collar. "To be honest, Mr. Fisher, I hate to think. But we must get to the study before he returns. Hurry now."

They hurried into the hallway leading to the study. At the door, Alice rattled the knob. Lord Scarborough had locked it. Linton fished into his pocket to retrieve his keys, hands shaking as he shuffled through the ring, searching for the right one. At last, he found it and had just placed the key in the lock when the sound of shouting reverberated from another part of the house. Linton paused. Badeley was yelling from the servants' stairway. He was calling for Linton.

"We have to move," said Marsden.

Linton twisted the key in the lock, and the door opened. Marsden pushed him into the study, and Alice followed closely behind.

"Lock the door!" she said and ran to the desk. "If my father has your letters anywhere, they'll be here."

She began tearing open the drawers, shuffling their sparse contents. Marsden joined her, filing through the papers on Lord Scarborough's desk. Linton stood at the door, ear pressed up against the wood, listening for footsteps.

When Alice opened the desk's bottom drawer, she paused. "What is this?"

The gun was partially unwrapped, a sliver of dark metal visible when she lifted it from the drawer. Marsden snatched it from her and removed the muslin.

"That's Simon's gun," said Alice. "That's the gun I…" She lifted a trembling hand to her mouth.

Marsden was not unsympathetic to her distress, but he did not have time to comfort her. He rotated the chamber and checked the safety catch before sliding the gun into the waistband of his trousers.

"Why do you need that?" Linton asked.

The cold metal was comforting against the skin of Marsden's back. The sensation spoke to him, urging him to believe it was right for him to take the gun.

"Just in case," he said. "Keep looking, Alice."

She obeyed, dragging out every piece of paper, checking between them. "What if they're not here?"

"Then you leave without them," said Linton. "You should have left already."

Marsden had already abandoned the desk and was checking every other nook and cranny in the study he could find. He lifted cushions, opened boxes, and upended vases, but it was all to no avail.

"What about the library?" he asked, breathless. "Or Simon's room?"

Linton threw up his hands and hissed, "Enough! You must leave now!"

Even as Linton opened the study door just a crack, Nancy's yells echoed from the salon. Marsden dropped a cigarette box, its contents spilling across the floor.

Linton gestured with wild arms for Alice and Marsden to follow him as he opened the door. "Quickly now. We may have to go out through the front door."

When they emerged into the hallway, Nancy raced past its mouth, running toward the front door. "Did you make the call?"

Unseen, Mrs. Huston's answering cry was equally frantic. "I don't know how to use the bloody thing! You'll have to do it."

Marsden risked peaking around the corner to see Nancy rushing to the telephone at its place in the entrance hallway. Mrs. Huston had the earpiece in hand.

"Heaven only knows what you were thinking," said Nancy and took over control of the telephone. "Hello? Operator? I'm calling from Maidenstone Hall. It's an emergency. There's a fire."

Marsden gave a low whistle, and Mrs. Huston turned immediately, shocked by the sound. Seeing him lurking in the shadows of the hallway, she gaped in horror.

"What are you still doing here?" she rasped, trying to whisper but failing. "Where's Alice?"

"I'm here, Mrs. Huston." Alice appeared from her hiding place behind Marsden. "What's happening?"

"I set fire to the garage."

Chapter Forty-Three

A bewildered laugh escaped Marsden, punching out of his throat before he could stop it. "You did what?"

"It was just supposed to be a distraction!" Mrs. Huston cried. "Something to divert Badeley and his Lordship while you got away. I didn't know it would take so quickly."

Marsden thought her choice of distraction entirely appropriate. He imagined it was what Beatrice would have done for attention. "Where is Lord Scarborough now?"

"Outside with Badeley. Nancy's calling the fire crew now." She glanced over her shoulder at Nancy, who was scowling back in return. "I'm afraid it all got a little out of hand."

Marsden took her shaking hands in his. "Never mind that. Will we be seen if we take the servants' entrance?"

"I wouldn't risk it; they'll see you. If I could draw them away—"

"No, Mrs. Huston. I think you've done enough distracting for one night. We can't have them know you helped us. What if we leave by the front door? Where is her Ladyship?"

"She's upstairs, I think. The main entrance might be your best option, but you'll have to leave now."

Marsden took one step toward the light, but just as he entered the salon, Badeley's voice again emerged from the servants' hall, calling for Nancy. His footsteps echoed on the stairs. Mrs. Huston blanched and ushered Marsden back into the hallway. He pulled Alice back into the darkness.

"Quick," said Linton, "the library."

They shuffled back along the hallway, Linton opening the rear entrance to the library and herding Marsden and Alice inside. He urged them to stay quiet and shut the door when he left them alone. Marsden pressed his ear against the heavy door. Linton's heavy footsteps echoed away from the room as he ran to meet Badeley.

Alice clutched at Marsden's jacket sleeve. "Now, what do we do?"

Marsden surveyed the room. The fire was alight, and a solitary lamp shone beside one of the large armchairs. "We need to hide. Behind the curtains."

He pushed her toward the windows. They were halfway across the room when a flash of movement in the corner of his eye caught Marsden's attention, making him halt and swing toward the fire.

"You know," said Lady Scarborough from her seat by the fireplace, "my son had the most atrocious handwriting."

She stumbled particularly over the word *atrocious,* her tongue tripping. She was curled in her armchair, bare feet tucked under the hem of her cream silk dress. Just as it had the day he and Alice saw her walking to the orchard, her vibrant hair fell loose over her shoulders. Marsden had never before seen Lady Scarborough so casually presented. She cradled a full tumbler in one hand, the firelight glinting off the cut crystal and the whiskey within. In the other, she held a letter. One of Marsden's letters. The others, along with his photographs, were spread across her lap. Lady Scarborough waved the paper back and forth in a jerking motion.

"Simon wrote this to you, didn't he? My husband says so." She squinted to examine the writing once more in the poor light of the fire. "But he writes to Thomas. Is that what my son called you?"

Marsden dared sneak a glance at Alice. She had abandoned her search for a hiding place and inched toward him, seeking the protection of his shadow. He shook his head, urging her with one raised hand to stay back.

"Yes, my lady," he said. "That's what Simon called me."

"They're not very loving, are they? His desire is clear, but—well—when my husband told me who you were to Simon, I thought these letters might have been more romantic, but they're quite cold. I suppose that's not particularly surprising, Simon being the way he was, but still. Did you love him?" Lady Scarborough released a melancholy sigh and glanced up at Marsden over the letter. When Marsden did not answer, she smirked. "Come now, my boy, I knew full well what my son was. Any living, breathing human being was prey to him. I suppose you were hoping he would be here?"

"I didn't know what I would find here," said Marsden. "I just had to know the truth for myself. I had to know what happened to him."

"Well, we never lied about him being dead. And thank goodness he is. The better for us all." Lady Scarborough lifted the glass to her lips and took a deep gulp. Hauling herself up and out of the armchair, the letters fell from her lap onto the floor. She grabbed at the chair's back when she swayed. "I'm sure you wish you'd never come. You probably didn't know what a little bastard he was."

She groped for the whiskey decanter on the table beside her and almost fell, tripping on her feet. Alice sailed across the room before Marsden could react, swooping in to catch her mother. Lady Scarborough gawked at Alice, wavering in her daughter's arms.

"Which one are you?"

Alice straightened Lady Scarborough with gentle hands. "It's me, Mother. Alice."

"I get so confused." Lady Scarborough tried to drink from her glass and pouted when she found it empty. "I never could tell you and your sister apart. Where do you suppose she goes?"

"Do you mean Beatrice?"

Lady Scarborough sagged, her spine crumpling. "You know, when she came back to us, I thought perhaps she'd been sent to punish me. I've told so many lies. I need a drink."

Alice put herself between Lady Scarborough and the whiskey decanter on the table beside the fire. "I think you've had enough tonight, Mother."

The countess did not appreciate being diverted and protested, struggling with Alice, who stood between her mother and the trolley of liquor bottles. As they squabbled, Marsden eyed the collection of letters and photographs now spread across the floor. This was his opportunity. He could scoop them up, and Lady Scarborough would be too drunk to stop him. He was ready to lunge for them when Lady Scarborough, incensed by Alice's interference, let out a tight cry. She pushed Alice, shoving her daughter backward. Before Marsden could reach for her, Alice stumbled and lost her footing. She tried to right herself, but one shoe caught in the long hem of her dress, and Alice fell onto her right side, her forehead cracking against the table beside her mother's armchair. The sound was sickening.

"Jesus!" Marsden forgot the letters and lunged for Alice. She lay on her side, stunned and blinking. A thin trickle of blood streamed from her, a cut along her hairline. He crouched to help her sit up, grasping both shoulders while she swayed and blinked, exaggerated sweeps of her eyelashes.

"I didn't mean it!" Lady Scarborough bent over Alice, trying to fuss but unable to maintain her balance at the precarious angle. "Are you hurt, my darling?"

Alice opened her eyes wide and stared up at Lady Scarborough. For a moment, she gazed upon her mother with such a peculiar expression, her brow furrowed, lips curled, that Marsden worried the blow had affected her vision. She swayed in Marsden's arms as she glanced around the room. When Lady Scarborough tried again to touch her, a clumsy hand patting at her hair, Alice snarled and batted the countess away.

"I'm just fine, Mummy. Help me up, will you?" She clutched at Marsden, and he hauled her back onto her feet.

"I'm so sorry." Lady Scarborough was crying, trying to stroke Alice's hair. "I would never hurt you, you know that, don't you, darling?"

Again, Alice shooed her mother's hands away. "You're drunk." She stooped to collect up the decanter of whiskey beside Lady Scarborough's chair. "You're a drunk." Without warning, she upended the decanter and poured its contents on top of the papers on the floor.

"No!" Marsden jolted toward her, but Alice put up one hand, pressing it against his chest and pushing him back. She dropped the decanter and snatched the letter still crumpled in her mother's hand. In a smooth turn, Alice spun and bent to hold the paper over the flames. When it caught fire, she held the burning letter in the air between them.

"Let him go," she said to Marsden. "Then we can leave."

Realizing her intent, Marsden held up both hands toward her. "Don't—"

She opened her hand and dropped the letter onto the alcohol-soaked pile at her feet. The liquor sizzled as it caught fire, and Marsden jumped back when the papers exploded into flames. He watched in horror as the last of his connection to Simon burned to ash.

Chapter Forty-Four

Marsden looked around the room in panic, searching for something to douse the fire. There was no water, not even a vase of flowers—just the carefully arranged rows of decanters on the liquor trolley, the brandy, whiskey, and port inside them shimmering bright amber and burgundy in the light of the fire. Marsden ran to the windows and began to tug at the velvet curtains. He dragged them off their rungs, the length of fabric jerking onto the floor in thick folds. He knew he must make a ridiculous figure, dragging the heavy fabric panel across the room, but Marsden was determined. With one end of the curtain, he beat at the burning pile of paper and the satellite fire it had caused, now burning along the fringe of the rug and singeing the nearby furniture. As he flung the velvet over the charring letters, the rush of air flung a small mass of the burning paper and ash onto the chair where Lady Scarborough had been sitting.

Alice stopped him, arresting his arms mid-air. "Let it burn! What does it matter? We need to go."

Lady Scarborough had retreated into the corner of the room and was leaning against the liquor trolley. The fire reflected in her eyes, but she showed no sign of fear. Instead, she began to laugh. A gentle giggle at first, a light shake in her shoulders, but then she opened her mouth wide and laughed out loud.

"She's right," Lady Scarborough said and turned to the collection of decanters behind her. "Let it all burn."

She picked up one of the half-full bottles and threw it with both hands.

Despite her inebriated state, her aim was surprisingly accurate, and the glass bottle came very close to hitting Marsden in the head. It sailed past him and smashed against the mantle of the fireplace.

Lady Scarborough cackled with delight when it broke, liquor and glass bursting across the floor and feeding the fire. She picked up another. Marsden rushed toward her, hoping to stop her before she drew attention from someone outside the library. A second decanter landed inches before his feet, and he leaped back as the liquor splashed over his trousers.

"You must forget this place, Marsden," she said. "You must forget all about him. He was a monster."

Alice was suddenly beside him, grasping his hand. "Leave her. Let's go."

Her grip tightened when the heavy double doors at the library's main entrance swung open. Hands still on the door handles, Badeley was openly surprised to find Marsden standing before him, jaw gaping. His interest in Marsden, however, was only fleeting when he saw the fire spreading across the library floor.

"What the hell happened?" said Badeley when he rushed into the room. He glared at Marsden. "Did you do this? Did you set fire to the garage as well?"

"Don't worry, Badeley," said Lady Scarborough, almost singing to him with a joviality that denied the seriousness of the situation. "Everything is under control."

Badeley paid no heed to his inebriated mistress. He leaned back through the doorway, yelling into the empty salon: "Nancy! Linton! Fire!" He cast an angry glance back at Marsden. "How did you even get down here? How did either of you get down here?"

"We're leaving, Badeley," said Alice, tucking herself tightly behind Marsden. "You can't stop us."

"The hell I can't," said Badeley and stalked toward them both.

With a speed and athleticism that surprised everyone but herself, Lady Scarborough collected up another decanter and lobbed it at Badeley. He ducked as the glass bottle flew over his head and then popped up again with a look of pure astonishment.

"You can't take her, Badeley," said Lady Scarborough, staggering on the spot. "Not this time. I won't let you."

"What on earth is going on here!" Lord Scarborough stood in the doorway, his tie torn loose, his usually immaculate hair and face ravaged with heat and sweat. He examined Marsden and Alice, free of their prisons, and his drunk wife. "For heaven's sake, why has no one put out this fire? Francis, get out of there!"

Nancy and Linton appeared behind him almost directly, both panting for breath.

When Linton saw the fire, his knees buckled. "Nancy, get blankets! I'll fetch the water!"

Lord Scarborough turned on his wife. "Francis! Come here now! Badeley, get my daughter out of here."

Lady Scarborough only laughed at him, a bitter snicker. Furious, Lord Scarborough stalked toward his wife. At his side, Badeley skirted the fire and approached Alice. Neither woman backed away. Lady Scarborough picked up a glass tumbler. Lady Scarborough hurled the tumbler at her husband. The glass connected with the corner of his eye. It did not break, but the impact threw Lord Scarborough's head backward. The earl howled and covered his face.

Still standing behind Marsden, Alice lifted his jacket and grabbed the pistol. Alice pointed the gun at Badeley.

"I'm not going anywhere with you," she said. The gun did not waver in her hand.

Badeley halted and instinctively raised his hands. Marsden stepped back from Alice.

"Alice," said Marsden, "put the gun down."

Lord Scarborough had drawn his hands away from his face to reveal a nasty gash above his right eyebrow. Seeing the gun in Alice's possession, he blanched. "How did you get that?"

"We're leaving," said Alice and backed toward the rear door of the library.

Badeley's hands floated down to his sides. He snickered at Alice, his face twisting in a cruel grin. "You won't do it," he said and sprang into action once more, dashing toward her.

Alice squealed and belatedly pulled the trigger. Badeley reached her in time, shoving one palm under her wrist and jerking the gun toward the ceiling. The bullet shot above their heads, and the pistol slipped from Alice's fingers, clattering beside her feet and sliding toward the piano. Marsden lunged at Badeley, arms around his waist and knocking the other man onto the floor. Badeley gave a shout of surprise when they landed with a bone-crunching thud. They struggled, Marsden wrapping one arm around Badeley's neck. Badeley twisted and bit Marsden's hand, where it clutched at his shoulder.

Marsden shouted in pain, and Badeley wriggled free enough to throw an elbow into Marsden's stomach. Badeley lunged for the gun, but Marsden grabbed his ankle, holding him back. Badeley kicked wildly and pulled his foot free, scrambling to stand and reaching for the gun. Marsden followed, hauling himself up and throwing a knee into the back of Badeley's thigh. As he and Badeley struggled, Marsden was vaguely aware of Lady Scarborough's laughter and Alice's cry of distress. He saw the crepe of her dress swish as she started toward them. The blood was thundering in his ears.

"Stop it at once!" Lord Scarborough yelled, still clutching his bleeding brow, but the two young men were intent on overpowering each other. He staggered around the growing fire to where they wrestled on the floor and stooped to collect the gun.

When the shot rang out, Marsden jumped, his whole body lurching with the sound. Badeley also jolted—in awe or pain, Marsden could not yet tell. The gunshot made his ears ring. Shaking off Badeley's weight, all Marsden could be sure of was that the bullet had not struck his body. Before him, Lord Scarborough stood with the gun still smoking in his hand, a drawn look of horror on his damp face. Badeley was patting himself down, checking for injury. Behind them, Lady Scarborough moaned, staring at where Alice stood before her.

Alice's head was bowed toward her chest, staring down at the bloody hole in her abdomen. She placed one shaking hand over the wound. The blood had drained from her face, and she buckled at the knees. Marsden hurried to her, failing to catch her but clutching at her as best he could when she collapsed. She sagged into his arms. Alice was speaking, but Marsden could not hear her. The resonating gunshot still burned his ears, and the growing fire's crackle drowned out everything else. Lady Scarborough, in a belated reaction, suddenly screamed.

In the chaos, the fire spread, following the trail of brandy and whiskey that Lady Scarborough had showered across the oak floorboards and oriental rugs. The curtain Marsden had dragged across the room was now fully ablaze, as were the armchairs and sofa beside the fireplace.

"It's all right," said Marsden to Alice, breathless as the smoke plumed around them. He coughed and yelled at Badeley across the approaching flames. "Help me, won't you?"

Lord Scarborough dropped the gun, the weapon hitting the floor with a metallic crash. "I didn't mean to," he said, in shock.

"Dead God," said Badeley, clutching at his own chest and stomach.

Marsden yelled again, "Help me. We need to get her out of here. Now! Badeley!"

Badeley finally moved, helping Marsden to haul Alice up off the floor. Looking anxiously at the blood pouring from the wound in his daughter's belly, Lord Scarborough backed away from them. Lady Scarborough pointed an accusatory finger at her husband.

"What have you done?" she said, her voice high-pitched and cracking. "What have you done, Harry?"

Within the space of a moment, her inebriation evaporated, and her eyes cleared, darting away from Alice and across the floor. She crossed the short distance between herself and her husband and crouched to pick up the gun. Lord Scarborough did not flinch when she pointed the pistol directly at him.

He raised his hands in calm surrender. "Francis put it—"

"You did this!" She shook the gun in front of his face. "One by one, you have killed my children."

The earl was not afraid. Although his breath heaved and his eyes darted toward the approaching fire, he showed no sign of belief that his wife would actually hurt him. He reached his hands toward her. "Francis, give me the gun."

"I hate you," said Lady Scarborough, the tendons of her throat straining with anguish.

As if on cue, Linton and Nancy arrived again at the doorway, clutching blankets to smother the fire, a large bucket of water weighing each of them down. Nancy, startled to see the gun in Lady Scarborough's hand, gave a small cry and dropped her bucket, water sloshing on the floor around her feet. Lord Scarborough turned his head to see his servants behind him.

"Don't worry—" He began to reassure them, but Lady Scarborough would not be ignored.

"Harry!"

He turned to face her. She pulled the trigger.

Chapter Forty-Five

The shot reverberated around the room. Nancy screamed. Marsden and Badeley ducked on instinct. Lord Scarborough whipped both hands to his throat. As the shot's echo faded, Lord Scarborough's gurgling choke was barely audible above the rising roar of the fire. At first, he appeared to be unharmed, but for his hands cradling his throat and the hissing gurgle escaping his mouth. But then the blood began to seep out from between his fingers.

Linton was the first to act, dashing into the room toward Lord Scarborough, who collapsed into his arms. The earl slumped onto the floor, Linton unable to support his dead weight. Lord Scarborough released the hold on his throat, and blood rushed from the wound. He choked one last time, trying to gasp for breath. Then, his breath stopped altogether. Linton, covered in his master's blood, stared down at Lord Scarborough's lifeless body in wide-eyed dismay.

Hearing Lord Scarborough's last gurgling breath, Marsden himself stopped breathing. He looked fearfully at the gun, still in Lady Scarborough's hand. Marsden would be powerless to stop her if she chose to turn it upon himself or Alice. He gathered Alice closer, taking her weight from Badeley. But Lady Scarborough dropped the gun. She stood over her husband's body with no remorse or any other sign of emotion at all, her face entirely blank. She simply turned and returned to the trolley to select one of the last remaining bottles of whiskey.

The air in the room had become so thick with smoke that Marsden and Badeley began to wheeze.

"We have to go," said Marsden. "Now."

Badeley nodded, and they both put all their effort into dragging Alice out of the room, circling Linton, who was still crouching over Lord Scarborough's body. The butler stood slowly, straightening in jerking movements, and reached out a trembling, bloody hand toward Lady Scarborough.

"Come away now, my lady," he said. "Please."

Lady Scarborough's smile was peaceful—beatific. Without a word, she lifted the decanter and upended the bottle over her head. The liquor streamed down over her hair and soaked her dress. She dropped the decanter and reached for another, the last. It was almost full. She repeated the motion, tipping the alcohol over herself. Understanding her intention, Linton stepped over Lord Scarborough's body, hastening to stop her. But she moved too quickly in her focused intent, side-stepping him before he could reach her. Linton cried out, a pained and mournful groan of denial as Lady Scarborough took three long strides and ran into the fire. The alcohol in her hair and clothes caught fire immediately.

Francis Falconer went up in flames so fast that Marsden could only watch in abject horror from his place in the doorway where he and Badeley had paused and turned just in time to see her catch alight. Nancy ran toward Lady Scarborough, still clutching a blanket. She unfurled it as she darted around the growing fire, pushing Linton out of the way. Nancy tried to throw the blanket over her mistress, but Lady Scarborough was wild in her demise, flinging her arms, staggering across the room, and bringing the flames with her. Nancy screeched and jumped back, the blanket collecting the fire and burning her hands. Linton threw his arms around her shoulders and pulled her out of the room.

Lady Scarborough did not scream in pain. She was barely human as she burned with the library. Her jolting, angular steps came to a staggering halt in the center of the room, where she crumpled and dissolved into the fire.

"It's too late," Marsden called to Linton and Nancy. "Get out of there."

Marsden dragged Alice out of Badeley's hold, scooping her into his arms. Badeley ran ahead of him, opening the main doors. Linton followed close behind, dragging Nancy with him while she cried from the pain in her hands and the terror of seeing Lady Scarborough perish in the fire.

When Marsden staggered outside with Alice in his arms, Mrs. Huston came scurrying toward him, a lamp in one hand. She had run from the burning wreckage of the garage, and Marsden could see the light and smoke of the fire billowing from around the corner of the west wing. Mrs. Huston halted when she saw Marsden carrying Alice into the night air. She howled with despair as she saw the blood on Marsden's hands and rushed to Alice's aid. Exhausted and barely able to breathe, Marsden sank to the ground and allowed Mrs. Huston to take charge of Alice's care. Nancy dashed past them and vomited onto the gravel of the drive. Badeley followed close behind, sprinting into the darkness of the grass just beyond the house, where the others could still see him, but he felt safely removed from danger. Linton was the last to emerge from the house, coughing violently. He collapsed onto the steps and buried his face in his hands.

"The earl?" Mrs. Huston asked, peering around Linton. "Our Lady?"

"Gone," said Marsden, matter-of-fact in his shock. "They're both gone."

Mrs. Huston, although momentarily started into stillness, was not vastly moved by this news. Instead, she returned her attention to Alice with the efficiency of a well-worn governess. "We have to get her to a doctor," she said, removing her apron to press it against Alice's wound.

Marsden looked for Nancy, still on her knees and gasping as she spat the last traces of bile from between her chattering teeth.

"Nancy, a little help here?"

Wiping at her mouth with her sleeve, Nancy joined them. When she pressed her shaking fingers against Alice's pulse, Marsden could see the blisters on her hands from where she had tried to starve the flames engulfing Lady Scarborough with a blanket.

"Don't you worry, my love," said Mrs. Huston, stroking back the strands of hair plastered to Alice's sweating forehead. "Help will be here soon. Nancy already called."

"I called for the firemen," said Nancy, snapping, "not an ambulance."

"Then they'll turn around the moment they get here," said Marsden, "and take her straight to a hospital."

He had tried to speak with authority, but Marsden could hear the nervous waver of his own voice. Stretched out on the drive, pale and shivering, Alice's condition was dire. Mrs. Huston's apron, pressed against the bullet wound, was now soaked with Alice's blood. Marsden's heart sank. He had seen gunshot wounds like this before—seen more than one soldier die from the damage caused by a single bullet.

Alice waved a weak hand, searching for Marsden. He grasped it, winding his fingers through hers.

"Just hang on," he said, lifting her shoulders so her head rested in his lap.

She stared past Mrs. Huston, watching the fire illuminate the library's windows. Flames completely engulfed the whole room. In the open doorway of the house, the fire was growing, encroaching into the wooden frames of the salon and the adjoining hallways. The orange light reflected in Alice's glassy eyes.

She whispered: "Look, Fish, isn't it beautiful?"

Marsden, unsure that he had heard correctly, pulled her closer and crowded over her face. "Alice?"

When she did not respond, he leaned back to see she was no longer conscious. Panicked, Marsden shook her shoulders. She was still and an unnatural shade of white. In the distance, the bell of the fire truck echoed in the dark. Marsden knew he could not wait. Heart racing, he slid his arms under Alice and lifted her off the ground with a heaving groan. Staggering as he found his feet, Marsden juggled her light weight until he found his balance. Mrs. Huston tried to stop him, but he was already moving, running as quickly as his tired feet and smoke-filled lungs could carry him toward the fire crew, even as they came hurtling up the drive. Mrs. Huston and Nancy, unsure of what else to do, followed him. Linton and Badeley remained, standing back to watch the house burn.

Chapter Forty-Six

Alice was still in the care of a surgeon when the detective from Pocklington arrived to interview the staff of Maidenstone Hall. They huddled together in the hospital's waiting room at Harswell, awaiting news of Alice's condition. Linton, Nancy, and Mrs. Huston, at least, were anxious to hear from her surgeon: Marsden suspected that Badeley had joined them at the hospital only because he had nowhere else to go.

Linton, coughing heavily and frequently, refused to sit down, pacing the hallway. Mrs. Huston had not stopped weeping since their arrival. Badeley and Nancy sat apart, attempting to avoid each other's gaze. Nancy, her hands now bandaged, kept her burned fingers close to her chest, wincing every time she moved them.

Upon seeing the detective and a policeman in uniform speaking with a nurse, Marsden wondered if it was too late to escape without being seen. But the thought of leaving Alice alone in the hospital made his stomach churn with guilt.

Nancy poked at his shoulder. Her eyes were imploring when he met her gaze, but her lips barely moved as she spoke: "What are we going to tell them?"

Marsden shook her off. "Just stay calm and tell them the truth."

Nancy blanched. "You can't be serious."

Mrs. Huston's tears dissolved into an expression of wide-eyed panic. "But what about the fire? Will I be in trouble? What about Alice?"

"No one needs to know you set the fire in the garage," said Marsden. "In that, at least, we'll lie. We'll say it was an accident."

265

"You can't possibly think they'll believe that," said Badeley. He was scowling at Mrs. Huston. "There just happened to be a fire in the garage and the house at the same time?"

"You will not tell them that Alice started the fire in the house. It was Lady Scarborough."

Badeley scoffed. "Why should we lie? This is all Alice's fault. We've lost everything because of her."

Marsden leaned in close so that Badeley could not escape his gaze. "You and I know I could tell them everything about your part in the night Simon died. Just feign ignorance. Tell them you didn't see anything."

The detective and his uniformed henchman were now within hearing distance, and the group fell silent. Detective Roche was an average man with average height, average build, and average mustache. Nothing was particularly memorable about the stiffness of his stance or the dull brown tweed of his suit. His piercing eyes did, however, have a dark, intimidating shine when he examined each of the staff in turn as they named themselves.

When it was Marsden's turn, he hesitated. He almost considered offering up his real name but coughed to cover his indecision. "Marsden Fisher," he said at last. "I'm tutor to Lady Alice."

"It looks to me," said Roche, "like you took a nasty blow to the head, Mr. Fisher. Did that happen this evening just past?

Before Marsden could answer, Badeley leaped in: "The night before last. He had a bad fall."

"Goodness. You must be a clumsy fellow, Mr. Fisher."

Marsden's smile was thin. "So it would seem, sir."

"I'm sure you're all eager for news of Lady Alice," Roche continued, "but I must take statements from each of you as soon as possible. Now, ideally."

"Is the fire out?" Linton asked.

"Yes, although I'm afraid there's not much left of Maidenstone Hall. The fire was fierce, but the bodies of Lord and Lady Scarborough have already been retrieved."

The group met the news with sickened silence. Badeley buried his head in his hands. Nancy twisted her chair so that she faced the wall.

"Perhaps I should go first," said Marsden before anyone else could speak. "The sooner we get this over and done with, the better."

"The matron has kindly offered us the use of her office," said Roche. "Would you follow me, Mr. Fisher?"

Marsden walked between Roche and the silent policeman to a small office down the hall. It was dingy, the windows small and dirty, but the room itself was immaculate, as you would expect from a hospital matron. Marsden sat across from Roche, who had already seated himself behind the matron's desk. The detective took his time finding comfort, shifting in the small wooden chair to adjust his coat before retrieving his notebook. Marsden wondered if this leisurely show was designed to make him nervous. Eventually, Roche sat back and opened his hands to ask Marsden to proceed.

"Where shall I start?" Marsden asked.

"Let's start with the fire in the house, shall we? How did it start?"

"There was an argument between Lord and Lady Scarborough."

With a smooth tongue, Marsden explained in sparse detail Lady Scarborough's inebriation, her sudden fit of violence during which she began to smash decanters of brandy and whiskey around the room, the gun Lord Scarborough kept in the study, which his wife took up against him during their argument; Lady Scarborough's suicidal dance into the fire.

Roche allowed Marsden to talk, writing the occasional note and sucking on the end of his pencil. "So she shot her husband? And then set fire to herself?" Roche sounded dubious, his voice low as he summarized Marsden's account. "And why exactly were you in the room, Mr. Fisher?"

"Lady Alice and I had agreed to meet in the library."

Roche did not attempt to hide his smirk. "A little hanky-panky between the tutor and his student, eh? That hardly explains why Lady Scarborough was so angry with her husband."

"She blamed him for the death of their son. I gather Simon Falconer had wanted to return home from the war, and Lord Scarborough refused to arrange it."

"And Lady Alice? Was it your liaison that upset her mother so much?"

"I'm afraid Lady Scarborough was very inebriated. And I admit she was displeased when she saw Alice and I together. Lord Scarborough attempted to take the gun away from his wife. They struggled, and the gun went off accidentally. The bullet hit Alice."

Marsden found it relatively easy to keep a straight face through the few lies he told when so much of what he said was true. From the pinched crease at the corner of Roche's mouth, Marsden couldn't be sure if the detective believed his story, but Roche shrugged and snapped his notebook shut.

"Very well, Mr. Fisher. I'm sure we'll speak again, but you can go for now. Oh—" he said, staring off across Marsden's left shoulder as though pretending to remember something that had struck him earlier and had remained forgotten until now. "Your colleague said you slipped and hit your head. Was that what happened?"

Marsden silently cursed Badeley but said, "Yes, I slipped. I was coming down the stairs, and the floor was wet. I fell and banged my head on a step."

Roche gave a curt nod, and Marsden stood to leave. As he turned for the door, the same nagging doubt that had bothered him since he caught sight of Roche forced him to address the detective again.

"There's one more thing," he said, one hand on the door handle. "I'm sure you might check up on me, and I think it's probably best you hear it from my own mouth—my name isn't Marsden Fisher."

For the first time since Marsden had sat before him, Roche appeared genuinely interested in his testimony. He leaned forward in his seat. "Oh yes?"

"It's Bäuerle. Thomas Bäuerle."

"And why did you lie about your name?"

"Quite simply, when I returned from the war, no one would give me any work. A German name is not exactly an asset these days. Marsden Fisher served alongside me in France. I suppose his name came into my head when I applied at the employment agency."

Roche pursed his lips. "Very well. Fortunately, I have more important things to worry about than you using a false name. Off you go. If you wouldn't mind sending him in, I'll want to speak to young Mr. Badeley next."

When Marsden returned to the others, Badeley looked panicked at his presence being requested.

"I told him that Lady Scarborough blamed his Lordship for Simon's death at the front," Marsden told Badeley, voice low, aware that the policeman had followed him part way down the hallway. "That's why they were fighting. But you didn't see any of it."

"But I didn't see any of it," Badeley recited. "Fine with me." He disappeared out of sight into the matron's office, and Marsden joined Linton, Nancy, and Mrs. Huston. They wanted to know immediately what he had told Roche. His only concern, he admitted, was Roche's repeated interest in his head wound.

"He asked you about it again?" Linton inquired.

"He wanted to know the details. I said I had slipped and hit my head on the stairs. Perhaps he thought I'd got into an argument with the earl or countess before they died." A horrible thought occurred to him. "What if Roche goes into the orchard? Did Lord Scarborough move Simon's body?"

Linton had the decency to look ashamed as he admitted, "No, but Badeley and I filled in the grave. Roche will never know of Alice's involvement in Simon's death unless we admit it."

"Forget Simon," said Mrs. Huston. "None of us will say anything. If only Alice hadn't set the house on fire, none of this would have happened. She could have got away right under his Lordship's nose. Why did she do it?"

To force Marsden's hand, he told himself—to force him to leave—but he wouldn't admit it to the others. Nancy was right. If he'd only run when she had asked him to, Lord and Lady

may still be alive, Alice would not have taken a bullet in the gut.

"Our only priority," said Marsden, "is making Alice blameless. Roche cannot know she set the fire. No one can admit that she killed Simon."

"I thought that's what you wanted," said Nancy, "to expose the truth of Simon's death."

"Not if it means Alice going to the gallows. I understand now why you've lied all these years."

"You want to protect her," said Mrs. Huston. "I knew you would."

Marsden fought back the rising blush in his neck and cheeks. "I promised I would help her. I haven't forgotten that promise."

"I'm worried about Badeley," said Nancy, nodding toward the matron's office where Badeley was being interrogated. "He's so angry. He might give everything away just to spite her."

"He'll keep his mouth shut," said Marsden. "He doesn't want to be implicated in covering up the circumstances of Simon's death. Believe me; he won't say a word."

Chapter Forty-Seven

For the next hour, the staff was summoned into the matron's office one by one to speak with Roche. Each returned to the waiting area pale but relieved to be free of the detective's beady stare. Linton was the last to emerge, as stoic as ever but severely exhausted. He slumped into a chair and covered his face with one trembling hand.

Roche assured the group that he was finished with them for now, but they should be prepared to answer any further questions as he saw fit.

"I'm assuming you'll be staying locally for now?" Roche asked before he left.

"Indeed," said Linton. "We will be staying close to Lady Alice."

"I'm out of here," said Badeley the moment Roche was gone.

"Where are you going?" Nancy asked.

"Back to the Hall. If the fire's out, I want to see if I can salvage anything from the garage." He delivered a pointed stare in Mrs. Huston's direction. "I don't care what you lot do."

If his whole jaw had not been burning with the strain of exhaustion, Marsden might have laughed at Badeley. He knew full well why Badeley was so desperate to return to the Hall, hoping against hope that the fire might not have destroyed some of the small fortune he had amassed, hidden away in the garage.

"But how will you get there?" Marsden asked Badeley.

"I'll figure it out," Badeley said and stalked away from them, almost colliding head-first with a young doctor as he rounded the corner. When Badeley did not stop to apologize, the doctor brushed himself off and approached the remaining staff. He wore thick spectacles, and his pale hair was thinning, but this did nothing to disguise his youth.

"I'm Doctor Dobson," he said. "I believe you're waiting for news of Lady Alice."

"Well?" said Mrs. Huston, rushing to her feet. "How is she?"

"The surgery took longer than I would have liked. There was a moment where I wasn't sure she would pull through, but I'm fairly confident of success now. I was able to remove the bullet and staunch the internal bleeding. As long as we stave off any infection, Lady Alice has a good chance of recovery."

Mrs. Huston sank back into her chair and began again to weep. Between sobs, she asked, "Is she awake? When can we see her?"

"She's not woken yet, but we'll keep her under close observation until she does. I'm afraid we'll need to limit her visitors for the time being, but I can't see the harm in letting you wait outside the ward. You'll need to speak to the matron." Dobson eyed Marsden's blood-stained shirt. "And you'll certainly need to wash up and change your clothes before seeing Lady Alice."

"We can't exactly just go back to the Hall and dress in new clothes," said Nancy. "God only knows what is left."

"I'm sure we can find something for you here at the hospital," said Dobson. "Do you have any friends you could stay with nearby?"

"No," said Linton. "I can't say that we have any friends."

Dobson almost smiled, his lips beginning to curl until he understood that Linton was not speaking in jest. "I see. Well, I'll speak to the matron and see if we can't come to an arrangement."

Before Dobson could leave, Linton stopped him. "Speaking of clothing, where is the dress Lady Alice was wearing when she arrived?"

Dobson was bewildered by the question, his small brown eyes repeatedly blinking behind his spectacles. "The dress? I'm afraid I don't know. One of the nurses most likely disposed of it."

"She'll be needing it back. You must find it."

"Needing it back? My dear fellow, it must be quite ruined."

Linton would not be refused. "I still need you to find it. It must not be destroyed."

Dobson agreed that he would have the dress found and returned if possible. Marsden could not resist questioning Linton when the young doctor disappeared down the hallway.

"Why do you want her dress?"

Linton drew himself taller. "my lady will want the dress. That is all."

True to his word, Dobson ensured that fresh clothes were found for Marsden and the rest of the staff. Freshly washed, Marsden slipped on a shirt and briefly wondered where it had come from. It had occurred to him that the clothes may very well belong to a patient who had entered the hospital alive and left in a coffin, but he chose not to dwell on the morbid thought.

Nancy, Linton, and Mrs. Huston also emerged, washed, brushed, and dressed in donated clothes. Out of uniform, Linton and Nancy both appeared smaller to Marsden.

"I want to stay," said Mrs. Huston. "I want to sit with her. Do you think we can see her now?"

Marsden promised that he would arrange it and made short work of finding the matron, who did not seem overly pleased about so many visitors hoping to storm the room in which Alice was recovering. In the face of Marsden's pleading and Mrs. Huston's tears, she finally agreed to lead them to the ward on the provision that only two visitors enter the room at one time until Alice was awake.

"You go in," said Linton to Mrs. Huston. "Take Marsden. Nancy and I have something to attend to."

Marsden had no idea what Linton referred to but had no time to query the choice when the nurse ushered him and Mrs. Huston into the ward. She led them to the end of the long white room where Alice lay hidden behind a partition of grey linen; Marsden held his breath.

Alice looked dead; her frail body was tiny in the hospital bed, and her naturally pale complexion was now a shade of white closer to grey.

"She's a miracle," said the nurse, whispering as she made a show of tucking the tight corners of the hospital bed. "We didn't think she would survive."

Mrs. Huston sank to her knees beside the bed and clasped Alice's hand. "Beatrice is a survivor."

When the nurse frowned in confusion, Marsden quickly intercepted: "Alice. You mean Alice, don't you, Mrs. Huston? It's been a very long night," he told the nurse. "We're all exhausted."

"Of course," said the nurse. "I'll leave you alone with her, but please let her sleep."

Marsden promised that they would and was relieved when she departed.

"It's Beatrice's turn today," said Mrs. Huston. "When she wakes up today, Beatrice will be here."

Marsden imagined her waking and didn't know how he would explain to Beatrice the events leading to her parent's death and Maidenstone Hall's destruction. As Mrs. Huston took up the younger woman's limp hand in a tight grasp, Marsden wondered if Beatrice already knew.

Chapter Forty-Eight

Marsden was dozing, slumped in an uncomfortable chair when he was startled awake by a movement beneath his hand. He sat upright to find Mrs. Huston snoring on the opposite side of the hospital bed, her head resting on the edge of the mattress.

"Marsden?"

The voice summoning him was thin and cracked, tight with the damage of smoke and pain. Marsden squeezed the tiny fingers within his own. "Beatrice?"

Her brow pinched, and she gazed up toward the ceiling. "No."

Marsden exhaled the breath he had been holding. "Alice."

"Where am I?"

"You're in the hospital. Do you remember? You were shot."

Alice shifted and winced as the movement flared the pain of her injury. "My parents?"

Marsden squeezed her hands again. "I'm sorry. They're both dead."

Alice closed her eyes. Marsden couldn't tell if she was upset by the news, but certainly, no tears fell.

"When was this? How long have I been asleep?"

"It was last night. You've been asleep all morning." Sunlight filtered through the curtained windows. "It's still day."

Her lower lip trembled. "Why isn't Beatrice here?"

"I don't know."

"And the others?"

Marsden nodded toward Mrs. Huston. "She hasn't left your side. Linton and Nancy are here, somewhere. Badeley went back to the Hall to see what he could salvage from the garage. I don't know why he bothered. I gather there's not much left."

At the mention of Badeley's name, Alice's nostrils flared. "I don't want to see Badeley."

"It's all right," said Marsden. "You don't have to see him. I should warn you, though, there's a police detective who will be eager to speak to you about what happened last night. His name is Roche."

"What did you tell him?" she asked.

Marsden repeated the contents of his interview with Roche once more. She listened in silence, concentrating on his every word.

"Did the detective ask about Simon?" she asked when he had finished.

"No. No one has said anything about Simon, except that your parents fought about him. The detective doesn't know you started the fire in the library either, so don't tell him."

"I set the fire? I don't remember much of anything."

Marsden recalled her dark, intent look as she poured the whiskey decanter over his precious letters and photographs. He knew now; he couldn't have stopped her if he had tried.

"You burned my letters. The ones from Simon."

Alice's eyes widened, her head craning off the pillow. "You must be furious."

He shook his head. "No. You were right. I needed to let them go."

"Is the entire house gone?"

"Roche said the Hall was almost completely destroyed."

"I should be arrested," she said, voice shaking. "This is all my fault."

Marsden squeezed the white knuckles of her hand. "No, Alice. You won't be arrested. All of this will be over soon enough. And when you're well enough to travel, you can leave this place."

Alice's clammy fingers tightened in his own. "Will you stay with me?"

"I have no intention of leaving this hospital. I'll stay right here with you."

"No, I mean..." She hesitated, casting her eyes down her nose, embarrassed. "Will you stay with me when I leave the hospital?"

Lying prostrate in the hospital bed, pale and shaken, Alice made a sad, vulnerable figure. Marsden saw the tears well in her eyes as he hesitated, and when he wiped at her wet cheek with a warm thumb, he knew he couldn't possibly abandon her. He knew he would protect her as Simon had failed to do.

"Yes," he said. "I promise."

Chapter Forty-Nine

Alice slept for much of the afternoon. Although Mrs. Huston refused to leave her side, Marsden knew they would need substantial food and a strong cup of tea. He left the ward searching for both and rounded a corner to see Nancy and Linton standing together in the hallway. Marsden had not seen either of them in hours and was surprised to see them now, whispering to each other. Nancy clutched a bundle of black fabric against her chest, and Linton appeared to be giving her stern instruction, a finger raised and wagging at her. Marsden approached, hoping to overhear them.

"How is she?" Nancy asked when she saw Marsden. She pressed the bundle of cloth more tightly against her chest, but Marsden recognized it immediately as Alice's ruined dress.

"Alice is sleeping now, but she was awake for a short while," he said. "She's in pain, of course, but she hasn't complained once."

"And is she..." As if Marsden could decipher a secret code from the movement, Nancy circled her chin once.

"Beatrice didn't come back today if that's what you mean." Marsden couldn't be sure whether Linton and Nancy were surprised or relieved to hear the news, as neither made any visible reaction. "Are you going to come in and see her?"

"No." Nancy nodded at the dress in her arms. "I need to find some clothes for Alice."

"She's hardly concerned with such things just now, Nancy."

"She'll want to be comfortable. She'll need—" She fumbled for a moment.

"She'll need a dressing gown."

Marsden fought back a snort of laughter. "A dressing gown?"

"Yes. If you'll excuse me, I need to be getting on."

Nancy whirled on the spot, ready to hurry away, but as she turned, something fell from within the folds of the dress and landed beside his feet. She quickly crouched to retrieve the object, but Marsden was faster, stooping to collect a small piece of glass the size of a grain of wheat. When he stood, holding it to the light, he recognized it was not glass at all. Nancy snatched the diamond out of his hand before he could react.

"Where did you find that?" he asked.

Without her answer, Marsden remembered the small, hard objects he had felt in the hem of her dress as Beatrice lay in his arms the night Badeley had struck him with the shovel. He grabbed the dress in Nancy's arms, searching out the hemline and the pebble-like lumps within.

Nancy saw the comprehension lift on his face and gestured to hush him before he could say more. "Don't say anything."

"It was sewn into the hem," he said. "Alice's dress is full of them, I assume?"

"It's not what you think," said Linton. "Nancy has stolen nothing."

"Then who did?" When neither responded, Marsden knew he had been foolish not to guess what was in the bag he had seen Beatrice pass to Nancy two days before. "Beatrice. She stole them from her mother, didn't she? Did you encourage this?"

"She took the jewelry and then told me what she'd done," said Nancy. "All I did was remove the gems from their settings and stitch them into the dress."

"That's all you did?" said Marsden, his rebuke clear.

"She was going to need money when she ran away. I had to help her."

"You need to get those out of here now. Before the police return. How do you think it will look if Roche discovers she was stealing from Lady Scarborough just before the fire?"

Nancy looked to Linton, who nodded. She stuffed the loose diamond back into the dress folds and hurried away. Linton turned back to Marsden.

"Dr. Webb is here," he said.

"Webb?" Marsden's heart sank. "What the hell does he want?"

"He wants Alice when she's well enough to travel."

"You can't be serious."

"He told me so himself. He's with the surgeon now. I wasn't allowed to participate in the meeting, but Dr. Webb is here with a purpose."

"To take Alice to the sanatorium," Marsden guessed. "What can we do?"

"We prevent him from taking her. He cannot remove her now, but we must intervene when the time comes."

"How?"

Linton raised one eyebrow as though it were obvious what should be done. "I'm sure you'll think of something, Mr. Fisher."

Marsden felt a weight settle upon his shoulders. He had already agreed to help Alice escape from Maidenstone Hall, but now the stakes were higher, and their options were limited. He could hardly spirit her out of a window with a hole in her stomach. Not with the police and Dr. Webb hot on their heels.

"Fine," he said. "Let me think. I promised Mrs. Huston a cup of tea. If you could find her one, I will speak to Dr. Dobson."

The hospital was not large, only two floors in total and hardly a maze, but Marsden found himself quickly lost as he tried to find Dr. Dobson's office on the ground floor. As if he'd been waiting in the shadows, Marsden turned a corner and almost ran directly into Dr. Webb. The psychiatrist was in the company of Dr. Dobson, and from the sour look on Webb's face, Marsden guessed that he was disappointed with the result of their meeting. In stark contrast, Dobson was openly relieved to see Marsden, rushing to bring him into the conversation with arms outstretched.

"Mr. Fisher!" he said. "I was just showing Dr. Webb to the door."

Webb disregarded Marsden, sneering at his contemporary with visible contempt. "I shall return, Doctor." Casting a foul look in Marsden's direction, he stalked toward the hospital's entrance.

"What was that about?" Marsden asked as he and Dobson watched Dr. Webb storm out the door.

"I do believe," said Dobson, "that Dr. Webb didn't like bowing to my authority. I told him he could not see Lady Alice, and he did not respond well."

Marsden was glad to recognize Dobson as an ally against Webb. "I'm glad you turned him away."

Dobson gave him a grim smile. "I know all about Dr. Webb. I know about his preferred methods of treatment. But I'm afraid I can only keep him away for so long. He will have the right to take her eventually."

"Pardon?" Marsden asked, startled.

"He claims that she had been declared insane and that her late father granted him custody of Alice. I understand they had arranged for her to receive treatment at St. Jude's before Lord Scarborough's death. If he has the appropriate paperwork—"

"Then he can take her." Marsden placed his hands on his hips, staring down at his feet as his mind began to race. "Is there nothing we can do? She's hardly a child."

"No, but she's not considered an adult either. She could apply to be an independent ward of the state and have the declaration disputed, but that may take time."

Marsden offered his thanks and was about to return to Alice's bedside when Dobson stopped him again.

"The matron tells me she spoke to a Detective Roche not so long ago," he said. "He telephoned to ask after Lady Alice and said he would visit her tonight."

Marsden's shoulders slumped. "I see."

"I can turn away Webb for now, but I can't keep an officer of the law from her, I'm afraid."

"I understand. Thank you for the warning."

Marsden walked back to Alice's ward, his shoulders sagging. He was troubled enough by the intrusion of Dr. Webb, but now he also had to worry about Roche interrogating Alice in her weakened state. The detective did not present himself as the sharpest of police officers, but Marsden knew underestimating him would be a mistake, especially if Beatrice decided to show herself.

Chapter Fifty

Marsden was pacing the hallway when Roche returned to the hospital that evening. The detective's insistence that he be allowed to speak with Alice alone had been firmly rejected by Mrs. Huston. Withering before her red-faced determination, Roche had agreed that she could sit in on the interview if she remained quiet. Linton and Marsden remained in the hall outside the ward, unable to relax.

While he waited, Marsden weighed in his mind the options available to him and to Alice. Every time he considered leaving her and returning to his shell of life as Thomas Bäuerle, he returned to his promise to help her, and he became breathless with guilt. But there were few possibilities available to them. She could run, and he could help her. Still, he doubted she understood the enormity of abandoning her entire life—her identity, her privilege, even with a handful of diamonds in her pocket. Alice could also contest Webb's declaration of insanity, but she was still just a child in the eyes of the law. Who knew how long it would take her to become free of him?

Suddenly, Beatrice's ridiculous plan to marry Badeley didn't seem so foolish. At least Alice would now be free of Webb's reach had she been a married woman—at least for as long as Badeley had not agreed that she should be institutionalized. The thought gave Marsden pause, and he halted his pacing. If Alice was a married woman, she could be free of Webb, gain her inheritance, and she could—if she wanted to—be a mother to Grace. If there was a way to protect Alice and Grace, Marsden knew he could rest easy, as if he had undone at least some of the damage wrought by Simon.

He could protect her. He could protect Grace. He would not have to return poverty-stricken to a cheap boarding house and scrounge for work. They would all be safe and comfortable. Maidenstone Hall, Harrold and Frances Falconer, and even Simon, would be behind them. Perhaps it was the only way to escape Simon's ghost, even in the presence of the sweet little girl who shared his piercing eyes.

Marsden's reverie was interrupted by the arrival of Roche in the ward. The detective spotted him immediately and approached him with such speed, arms swinging wildly by his sides, that Marsden feared for a moment that Roche intended to arrest him. But Roche had lost all interest in Alice's side of the story and did not hesitate to reassure Marsden and Linton, who had been hovering by the doorway to the ward.

"Lady Alice had little to add to your accounts of the events that took place leading to the death of her parents," he said, in a tone just a little too cheerful for the situation. "She won't make much of a witness. There will still need to be an inquest, but I'm confident the verdict will be murder-suicide."

"Will we be asked to give evidence at the inquest?" Linton asked.

"Most likely, but it should be straightforward. You may be required to testify to Lady Scarborough's state of mind and her alcoholism." Roche paused to suck his teeth. "Poor woman. She really did lose her mind, eh?"

"So you won't need to speak to Alice again?" Marsden asked. He could barely believe that it could be over so quickly. So simply.

"I doubt it. The poor girl has been through enough. And I'm afraid I must hurry on to other matters. There's been a suspicious death in Market Weighton, and their senior detective is in Edinburgh. I've been asked to attend."

Marsden quickly offered support, shaking the detective's hand, eager to see him go. As Roche strode away, Marsden and Linton huddled together in the hallway.

"We should warn Lady Alice about Dr. Webb's visit," said Linton.

Marsden agreed. Although Dr. Webb had been refused access to Alice for now, he knew the psychiatrist would be back. He didn't want to frighten her, but Marsden knew Alice should be prepared for Webb's return. With her fate held in Webb's hands, she had important decisions to make.

When Alice received the news of Webb's arrival, however, she did not look as fearful as Marsden imagined she might.

"I don't have to see him now, do I?" she asked.

"No," said Marsden, "Dr. Dobson has sent him away for now. But he will be back. He claims to have legal responsibility for you."

"If he wants her, he'll have to come through me," said Mrs. Huston, her hands balled. Then to Alice directly, "You don't have to go with him. You have the means to disappear, my lady. Don't forget. We'll help you."

"And forfeit her claim to her inheritance?" said Linton. "It's not right."

"I think," said Marsden, "that Alice and I should speak alone for a moment. Do you mind?"

Alice nodded at Mrs. Huston's worried expression. Linton helped Mr. Huston out of her chair and guided her out of the ward.

"Did you know," he asked when they were alone, "about Beatrice's agreement with Badeley?" When Alice shook her head, he continued, "They had agreed, should anything happen that may land her—both of you—in the sanatorium again, he planned to marry her."

"He planned to marry Beatrice?" she repeated, appalled.

"I mean you—he meant to marry you when Beatrice was in control."

"But why now?"

"So that he could swoop in and rescue you. As your husband, he would have been in control of you, legally, so to speak. Your father could no longer have you committed without Badeley's permission."

"And with Simon gone, Badeley would marry an heiress." She spat the words. "Finally. Some twisted sense of chivalry."

"I doubt he truly understood your father's financial situation," Marsden reasoned, "but he knew the Hall would be sold and that he may lose his position. I'm sure he was looking for a backup plan."

It amused Marsden now to consider the bind into which Badeley had tied himself. For the better part of three years, he had been demanding an exorbitant salary from his employer and yet showed surprised disdain when Lord Scarborough had decided to sell the Hall, so dire was the Falconer family's need for additional funds.

"Of course," said Alice. "He's such a rat. I don't know why she would trust him."

Marsden offered a consolatory smile. "I think she was desperate. She wanted a way to get Grace back. It wasn't an entirely ridiculous suggestion, after all."

"Really? How can you say that?"

Marsden held his breath. The plan had occurred to him so recently when Linton had laid the burden of Alice's rescue entirely on Marsden's conscience, but now it became the only feasible response to an urgent situation.

"If you agree," he said, "I think you and I should marry. Immediately."

Alice stared back at him, lips parted in surprise. "You want to marry me?"

"Think about it for a moment. Webb can't take you away without my permission if you're my wife. You would legally be my charge, and there would be no risk of him finding a way to commit you against your will."

"Can he still do that?"

Marsden realized that Alice had believed herself freed by the death of her parents. Still only nineteen, she had not reached the age of maturity, and Lord Scarborough had paid Dr. Webb a substantial amount to take Alice off his hands, an agreement the doctor was keen to uphold. Marsden imagined her shackled in the asylum, the pawn of Webb's experimental treatments, and the idea made him want to gag. But he also knew the suggestion was sudden and evidently shocking to Alice. Knowing all she did about his history, he understood why she would think he'd never propose the idea himself.

He said, "We can wait to discover his plan if you wish. I seriously doubt Webb can have you transferred before you're well enough to travel. That gives us time."

Alice chewed on her lip. Marsden was sure he could see the thoughts racing through her brain reflected in her darting eyes.

"But why would you marry me?" she asked. "I know you don't like—you don't prefer women." She lowered her voice, her whole body sinking as if

285

hiding in her bed. "You loved Simon."

"Yes, I did."

"Is that why you would do this? Out of loyalty to him? Because I can assure you, Marsden, you don't owe him anything."

Marsden's shrug was slow, calculated. "Maybe it's out of loyalty to you. Perhaps I can right the wrongs he committed against you. And against Grace."

Alice reached for his hand, working her little fingers between his own. "We could take her back? She would be mine?"

Marsden was not sure how easy it would be to retrieve Grace from the Carlisles, but he was willing to give Simon's daughter the life she deserved.

"We can make it happen," he said. "If that's what you want. I know it's what Beatrice wants."

"The Carlisles would never let me have her if they knew about Beatrice— about my condition," said Alice. "You didn't tell them, did you?"

"No. Of court not." Marsden did not want to admit again that he had believed for so long that Alice and Beatrice were two separate girls. He would not have divulged his mistake to Mr. Carlisle even given the opportunity.

Marsden saw a moment of bright hope in her eyes, only to see the light quickly fading, a sharp, dark focus returning. She squinted at him, examining him as if for the first time.

"And you're not like Badeley? Wanting to marry an heiress."

Marsden hung his head. "Alice, I can't pretend I'm not poor. I literally have nothing to offer you financially. And I certainly won't pretend there it isn't an attractive idea, having a home again, a family— "

Alice held up a hand, her arm flinging up off the bed in a flurry to stop his speech. "That's what I wanted to know. That we would be a family."

"Yes," he said, realizing that this was what she had always wanted. She had hated her own family for so long, but he dared not suggest she would be trapped with him forever. "If it doesn't work out—if you change your mind later or meet someone else, we could— "

"We should make arrangements," she said sharply. "As soon as possible. If you're sure."

He had not expected to agree so readily. Marsden knew she had every reason to doubt him as an acceptable husband. His love affair with her brother alone was problematic, but Alice smiled at him, and he could find nothing disingenuous in the curl of her lips.

"I really do care about you," he said.

Tears welled in her eyes. "Are you sure?"

"Yes. More than any person alive." He was only a little surprised to discover that he honestly meant it. He felt the weight of responsibility, the burden of her rescue, lifted from his shoulders, knowing he was doing the right thing.

"But what about Simon?"

Marsden couldn't deny the shine on his memories of Simon had been severely tarnished. The ache he had felt at Simon's absence now dwindled to a dim flame in the farthest corner of his conscious, but it was still there, still burning. Despite everything, Marsden could not quash the memory of his love for Simon. Alice, however, did not need to know this.

"He's gone," said Marsden. "He can never hurt you again."

Alice nodded, lower lip trembling—from sadness or joy, he couldn't be sure. She lifted and kissed the back of his hand.

"But Alice," he said, "you do know that you won't be Mrs. Fisher?"

She giggled, an abrupt burst of breath and delight, and Marsden thought it was the most beautiful sound he had ever heard.

"Yes," she said. "I know. But I can still call you Marsden, can't I? I do prefer it."

Something in her returning grin, weak as it was, reminded him of one obstacle he hadn't considered. "And what about Beatrice? Do you think she'll agree to this?"

Alice visibly deflated, her face falling. "I think it's best she hears it from me, don't you?" When Marsden nodded in agreement, she asked, "Can you see about fetching me a pen and some paper? I'll write to her."

That evening, while Alice slept, a cream envelope sat propped beside a glass of water on her bedside table. Marsden had fetched it for her along with paper and ink, provided generously by the matron. Now, the letter had been written and sealed inside the envelope; a single name scrawled across its pristine surface—*Beatrice.*

Marsden's fingers itched to open the envelope and read the letter inside: to know Alice's thoughts about her impending marriage. He resisted, turning away from the temptation and placing a soft kiss on Alice's forehead. She stirred slightly but did not wake. When Marsden left the ward, he uttered a quiet prayer that he would not regret his decision come morning.

Chapter Fifty-One

The earliest the vicar would agree to perform the marriage was Sunday afternoon, four days hence. The Father wondered if Alice may be well enough to travel to the church by that time, but Marsden immediately quashed the suggestion, insisting that he and Alice be married before she was discharged from the hospital. During their brief meeting in the chapel, the nervous vicar had been sweating heavily, and Marsden wondered if the old man's trembling was natural or due to the substantial bribe bestowed upon him, a rather large diamond placed in his palm by Linton. No matter his unspoken objections, the vicar agreed that the banns would be considered read come Sunday. The announcement of their marriage would be dated in the parish ledger at least three weeks earlier.

Privately, Marsden was grateful for the suggested delay, even if it was only for a few short days. He might need that time to convince Beatrice that marriage was the only way to be free of Webb and for Alice to obtain their inheritance. In the morning after his proposal, he arrived at the ward, prepared to argue for the case of regaining custody of Grace—likely the outcome most appealing to Beatrice—only to discover the envelope addressed to Beatrice still sitting beside the bed, unopened. Alice lay in the bed, one hand resting over her wound, staring at the ceiling. When she saw him step around the linen partition, she shook her head, knowing immediately the question on his mind.

"Beatrice isn't here."

Marsden sat down beside her. "I see. Should I get rid of this?"

Alice stopped him when he reached for the envelope. "No. Leave it. Just in case."

Raised voices in the hallway distracted them from their conversation, and Marsden stood from his chair. He squeezed her hand. "I'll go and see what that's about."

Marsden stepped out of the ward to see Dr. Webb, red-faced and eyes bulging, staring down Dr. Dobson and a plump nurse. Marsden wasn't surprised to see Webb, but his hackles rose the moment the psychiatrist turned and laid eyes upon him. Webb's angry grimace faded, replaced with a sharp-toothed, condescending smile.

"Mr. Fisher!" said Webb when Marsden approached. "I've been waiting to see Lady Alice. Dr. Dobson informs me I may only see her upon your arrival." He waved his hands before Marsden's person as if performing a magic act. "And here you are."

"Dr. Dobson was right to make you wait for me," said Marsden.

"Because you and Lady Alice are engaged to be married?" The accusation in Webb's question was explicit.

"Yes," Marsden replied. "You can forget about having her transferred to your sanatorium."

"We'll see, Mr. Fisher."

Webb's smirk turned Marsden's heart cold. He faced Dr. Dobson and the nurse, standing by in case they were needed. "I'll take care of this."

Dobson did not hide his concern but ushered the nurse away from the doorway to the ward. When they were out of earshot, Marsden returned his attention to Webb.

"What exactly, sir, is your obsession with this young lady? Why are you so determined to take her? I know her father paid you a great deal of money, but you will receive no more."

"Money? I do not care about money." Webb stepped closer, removing his glasses. Leaning toward Marsden, he said, "Do you not find her fascinating, Mr. Fisher? She is the most interesting example of multiple personality disorder I have ever encountered. At St. Jude's, she would be the jewel of my collection. Just imagine the work I could do with her. And Beatrice.

Think of the studies I could publish."

Marsden found the whole notion abhorrent. "You think she can bring you acclaim. She's just a science experiment to you."

"I think I can cure her, Mr. Fisher. If my findings can help others, all the better."

"Well, Doctor, I hate to disappoint you, but there has been no sign of Beatrice these past two days. Alice has been entirely herself since she arrived at the hospital."

Webb's confidence faltered only a little, his smile wavering. "I don't believe you. I want to see her myself." He stormed past Marsden, barging into the ward and passing each bed in active inquiry, too proud to ask where he could find Alice. He found her at last in the last bed of the ward.

Alice's expression teetered between revulsion and fear upon seeing Webb. She reached for Marsden, holding her hand to him when he hurried to her bedside.

"What is he doing here?" she asked Marsden.

"I'm here as your doctor," said Webb, "to inquire after your health."

"You are not my physician."

Webb, refusing to be rejected, pulled up the chair in which Marsden had so recently been sitting and planted himself beside her. "I was devastated to hear about your parents, my dear. I thought I might assist you in this terrible time."

Alice glanced up at Marsden. "I have all the assistance I need."

"And Beatrice?" Webb asked, probing. "Perhaps I could also speak to her about the fire."

Marsden stepped in front of Alice's bedside table, hoping Webb would not see the letter addressed to Beatrice before he could hide it from view.

"My sister is dead," said Alice. "And my mother set fire to the house if that is what you were wondering."

Marsden was relieved when Dr. Dobson joined them, hovering just behind Webb.

"Dr. Webb," he said, "I know we agreed that you could speak to Lady Alice in Mr. Fisher's presence, but I do hope you are not pestering my patient."

"I don't feel well enough to speak to this man right now," said Alice.

"This man thinks it's appropriate to interrogate Alice about her dead sister at such a time," Marsden informed Dr. Dobson. "I hope you agree that this is not the time for such questions."

Webb scoffed at Marsden, but his grin quickly faded when faced with the displeasure of the surgeon.

"I think Mr. Fisher is right, Dr. Webb," said Dobson. "It is perhaps time for you to leave. I don't think Lady Alice will be up for any more visits until next week, at least."

"Do you mean to say," said Webb, "that I will not have a chance to speak to Lady Beatrice? I was so hoping to meet with her."

"That's enough, sir," said Marsden. He rounded the bed to take Webb by the elbow and haul him out of the chair. Steering the doctor away from the bed, Marsden was unrelenting, directing the other man down the length of the ward and out into the hallway.

"You have no right," Webb said when he extracted himself from Marsden's grasp. "No right at all to handle me so."

"You," said Marsden, "have no right to be here, Doctor. Alice is not under your care, nor will she be in the future."

"I almost had her," said Webb, fists clenched against his chest. "If Lady Scarborough hadn't hesitated for so long—if she hadn't denied the need for further treatment—Alice would already be at St. Jude's. You know Lord Scarborough had permitted me to collect Alice? I would have done so already if it weren't for his death."

"And now your opportunity has passed. Lord Scarborough is dead, and Alice will be my responsibility."

Marsden had meant to leave Webb in the hallway and return to Alice, but the doctor could not resist a parting jab:

"And what will you do, Mr. Fisher, if Beatrice returns? Who will you turn to when your wife tries to burn you alive in your bed?"

Marsden refused to be baited. "Beatrice is dead. Alice is alive and most certainly in no need of your services. Good day to you, sir."

Marsden hurried back down the length of the ward, past the other hospital beds where the patients lay unaware of his troubles. He returned to Alice's bedside to find her crying into a pillow.

"He's gone," said Marsden, sitting beside her and clutching her hand. "He won't be back, I promise."

Alice sniffed loudly and wiped at her tears. "He was trying to bait her. He was trying to get Beatrice to come out, but she's gone. She's gone for good."

As this was a sharp deviation from her opinion just a short time ago when she had asked him to leave the letter for Beatrice, just in case, he asked, "Are you sure?"

Alice laid one hand over her heart, fingers massaging her ribs as though she was searching her very soul for any remanence of Beatrice's ghost.

"Yes," she said without hesitation as if she had only just considered the new possibility of having all her days to herself, her brow lifted in surprised realization. "Dr. Dobson says it was a miracle that I survived. I shouldn't have survived. Perhaps Beatrice died for me."

"Perhaps," said Marsden and sat down on the edge of the bed. "How does that make you feel?"

"I suppose it's for the best," said Alice with a sniff. "For you. For Grace. But I'm alone now."

Marsden squeezed her hand. "No. Not alone."

Her face shone with a joy he had never before seen in her. "No," she repeated. "Not alone."

Alice was married in her hospital bed, propped up amongst a mountain of cushions and pillows. Nancy had procured a white silk dressing gown for the bride, from where Marsden could only guess, although he suspected that one of Lady Scarborough's missing jewels had paid for it. The matron had delighted at the news of a wedding in her ward and had arranged a bouquet of white lilies for Alice to hold on her lap as she and Marsden said their vows. The vicar pronounced them man and wife with sweat beading on his forehead.

Before the wedding, Marsden had briefly feared that he might be unable to go through with the marriage. It had seemed like such a good idea at the time, marrying Alice to save her, but he did have a moment of doubt as he dressed in a suit procured for him by Linton. Staring at his reflection in the mirror, Marsden was shocked to see himself preparing to be married: an eventuality he had never imagined in the past. But when he sat down on the side of Alice's bed to kiss her, her familiar green eyes gazing on him adoringly, his heart was light—assured that he was doing the right thing.

Linton, Mrs. Huston, and Nancy watched from the end of the bed. Linton's usual stern countenance had softened ever so slightly, but still, he kept his hands clasped behind tightly behind his back. Nancy did not offer her approval nor any objection, her expression entirely blank. Mrs. Huston wept through the entire ceremony, dabbing at her eyes with a handkerchief.

Badeley did not attend the make-shift wedding, nor was he missed.

Chapter Fifty-Two

Marsden and Alice did not return to Yorkshire until summer's end. When the train pulled into Everingham station, it was not Badeley's handsome face that met Marsden. This time, it was Mr. Carlisle. He had brought his battered truck and apologized profusely to Alice when he helped her into the vehicle's cab. But Alice was not concerned about dirtying her wardrobe, apparently ambivalent to the fate of her pristine white linen dress, assuring Mr. Carlisle that she was perfectly happy to ride in the filthy truck. Instead, it was Marsden who fussed over the dusty seat, placing a wide handkerchief across the cracked leather to protect her dress and his new grey suit, purchased on Saville Row only days before. Alice sat between the two men, clutching at her black velvet purse, smiling through the bumps of the uneven road.

When they arrived at the Carlisle farm, Alice could barely contain her nerves. She removed her yellow silk gloves and wrung the fabric between her straining fingers as Mrs. Carlisle ushered them inside. Marsden stopped the movement with one hand, offering her a reassuring smile. The tortured wringing ceased, but he sensed that Alice was still anxious. She clasped her mouth shut when Mrs. Carlisle brought Grace into the room.

Although it was not the first time Marsden had met Grace, her resemblance to Simon was still startling. Some months older now, he was sure she would continue to grow into a constant reminder of her father—a part of Simon that Marsden would always be able to keep close—a child to raise as his own.

"Here she is," said Mrs. Carlisle. She was trying to be jovial, but the pain in her voice was unmistakable. "Do you remember Lady Alice, dear?"

The little girl stared at Alice without fear and offered up her hands in silent permission to be held. Alice passed her gloves to Marsden and lifted Grace into her arms. He could see the tears in her eyes as she cuddled Grace close, awkwardly at first but gradually becoming accustomed to cradling a child.

Looking over Grace's blonde curls, Alice faced Mrs. Carlisle. "Thank you."

"Well, a child should be with…" The older woman hesitated, unsure if she should speak the secret.

Alice did not share her hesitation. "Her mother," she said, rocking her weight from one foot to the other, swaying gently with Grace in her arms. "A child should be with her mother."

"I'm sorry Lucy wasn't here to say goodbye," said Mr. Carlisle.

"Was she very upset?" Marsden asked.

"She came to see reason. Little Grace is better off with her parents."

Marsden knew Carlisle hadn't meant to suggest that he was Grace's real father, but something in using the word *parents* made his heart swell. He had never imagined that he would be a father. For the first time since the fire, Marsden thought of the lost photograph of his family, destroyed along with his portraits of Simon. At last, he could replace it with a family portrait of his own.

"We have something for you, Mr. Carlisle," he said and opened his palm to Alice. She juggled Grace in her arms and reached into her purse to extract a thick envelope. Alice lowered her eyes when Marsden took it from her and offered the small package to Mr. Carlisle.

The old man immediately raised his hands in refusal and said, "We didn't agree because—"

"I know," Marsden assured him. "I also know that Lord Scarborough paid you a small allowance for Grace's care, but we both know it wasn't near enough. There isn't enough money in the world to repay you for all you've done."

There had been, Marsden knew, a great deal of negotiation and wrangling involved in the attempt to have Grace returned to her birth mother. The Falconer's lawyers, still in disarray at the unnatural death of their client and the inheritance of an estate by a single daughter so abruptly married, had scrambled to fulfill Alice's requests—Marsden at once complicated and simplified matters. The Falconer family's London home had been rapidly prepared for the newlyweds while the cinders of the country estate still metaphorically smoldered. Fortunately, the sudden desire to bring a young child into the home wasn't entirely unexpected by Lord Scarborough's most trusted attorney, William Caruthers. Standing before them in the Mayfair house's parlor, the lawyer blushed and blustered in front of Alice, and Marsden realized that the poor man had been Beatrice's secret man in London. Fortunately, Caruthers had enough sense to be discreet as he began inquiring with the Carlisles regarding Grace. Marsden didn't know what he had offered the Carlisle family or if some sort of bullying had been employed, but they had eventually agreed to return Grace to Alice.

Attempting to appeal to Carlisle's love of his farm, Marsden gestured toward the front of the house. "I noticed you could do with a new fence along the road. Perhaps this can help."

Still, Carlisle hesitated. It was his wife who eventually stepped forward to take the money from Marsden.

"You'll come visit us, won't you?" said Mrs. Carlisle. She was trying not to cry, and Marsden hoped he and Alice could leave before she did.

"Of course we will," said Alice.

Placing one hand on the small of her back, Marsden wondered if they would. Somehow, he doubted it.

"I'll bring the truck around," said Carlisle, sensing it was time for the young family to leave. However, Alice resisted, insisting they walk back to the village.

"It's not far," she said, "and it's a glorious day. Grace and I have some things to pick up in the village before we go to the station anyway."

With the Carlisles watching from the door, Marsden, Alice, and Grace set off for the village, back along the dusty country road along which they had so recently arrived. Grace quickly became tired, and Alice insisted on carrying her, although she must have been heavy by the first half-mile. Alice made no complaint and whispered to the child as they walked. Marsden couldn't always hear what she was saying, but the smile on his wife's face was comforting.

Before their journey north, Alice had announced that she'd ordered clothes from the local seamstress in Everingham for Grace to wear on the trip home. The child was to shed all remnants of her life in Yorkshire. Marsden was surprised only momentarily, having recognized already Alice's peculiar and quiet way of planning ahead when he least expected it. He himself had spent many hours at the hands of a tailor, visiting him unannounced at the Mayfair house and fitting him for a new wardrobe to Alice's liking. Marsden admitted her liked the experience of creating a new wardrobe for himself. Even so, as they approached the storefront belonging to Mrs. Croft, the seamstress, Marsden wondered if the task of shopping for Grace was one from which he could be excused.

"Do you mind if I stop in at the tavern?" he asked. The idea of standing around while Grace was fitted into her new clothes sounded tedious, and he was hot from the walk.

Alice smiled as she extracted a few coins from her purse and pushed them into Marsden's hand. She stood on her toes to kiss his cheek and promised, "I'll be no more than half an hour. Meet me back here?"

Marsden agreed and waited outside until mother and daughter had disappeared into the small store where Mrs. Croft worked her magic on last season's cloth from London. He walked the short distance to the tavern and was delighted to enter the shade of the front door.

He went straight to the bar and was stopped short almost instantly by the man who stood beside him, leaning on the countertop.

"Marsden?"

Eyes still adjusting to the darkness of the tavern after the brightness of the midday sun, Marsden almost didn't recognize the face before him. "Badeley. My God."

Chapter Fifty-Three

Badeley's blonde hair was cut close to his skull, accentuating the weight he had lost around his cheeks and jaw. His eyes were bloodshot, and Marsden guessed he was more than a little drunk. The handsome, smartly presented chauffeur Marsden had once admired was long gone. He couldn't help but wonder if Badeley, too, had struggled to recognize him, the way the other man stared at Marsden in astonishment. While Badeley had shrunk and aged, Marsden knew he had changed for the better since his marriage to Alice; well-fed, immaculately dressed, and groomed, he was no longer the wasting, messy shell of a man he had been upon his arrival at Maidenstone.

"Do you still go by Marsden? Or do I call you Thomas now?" Badeley asked and reached for the half-empty pint of beer on the counter before him. When Marsden hesitated, Badeley delivered a playful punch to his shoulder. "Never mind. I didn't expect to see you around here again."

"We've come for Grace. Alice and I."

Badeley snorted into his glass. "I should have known. That girl always had her eye on the prize."

Marsden let the jibe slide, signaling the barman to order a pint before sitting on the stool directly beside Badeley. "I didn't expect to see you either," he said. "What have you been doing with yourself?"

"Ambulance driver. Doesn't pay quite as well as my last position, but at least now I don't have to put up with bloody Nancy nagging me or Mrs. Huston's awful cooking. Don't get me started," he took a long breath, ready to launch, "on how much I don't miss Linton, constantly appearing from around a corner, always watching. You know, just once, he caught me helping myself to a bottle of wine from the cellar, and next thing you know, he started skulking around the servants' hall at all hours, pretending to tinker with the electrics. We were always having problems with the lights, but I think he only made it worse."

"What did he know about the electrics?" Marsden asked, surprised by the idea of Linton assuming to know anything about electricity.

Badeley shrugged. "Nothing. I think it was just a cover for his spying. Don't know why he worried about me stealing. I could still afford my own back then."

The bitterness danced on the top of Badeley's tongue, his tone dark. Marsden tried to muster sympathy for the other man, but the feeling was dampened by the memory of a shovel meeting the back of his skull. His pint of lager arrived, and Marsden was instantly soothed by the bitterness of the bubbles.

"I have wondered about you," said Marsden. "Since that night. We didn't see you again after you left the hospital."

"I doubt Lady Alice has thought about me." Badeley dug into the pocket of his shirt and extracted a cigarette. As he struck the end of a match upon the bar top, Marsden could clearly see the shadows under Badeley's eyes.

Badeley breathed in deeply, and as he exhaled a wave of smoke, he asked, "How is married life treating you, then?"

"You heard." Marsden wasn't sure at first why he was displeased that the news had reached Badeley and decided that he didn't like the idea of Badeley knowing his business.

"Of course. It was the talk of the village. Lady Alice Falconer married the lowly tutor. You played the game well, my friend."

"I wasn't playing any game, Badeley. Not like you, at least."

"Is that what you think I was doing? Playing?"

"I think you were on the team of whoever offered you the most money."

Badeley chuckled darkly. "Well, I didn't get anything in the end, did I? Fool that I am, I didn't keep my money in a bank. I bet Mrs. Huston didn't think about that when she set the garage on fire. I wasn't as lucky as you and Lady Alice. I imagine you two will be rich enough when the land the Hall was on sells."

Marsden didn't feel the need to confirm the imminent sale of the property on which Maidenstone Hall, now mostly rubble, had stood. A wealthy American oil heir had taken a fancy to the notion of English country life. He'd made inquiries when upon hearing about the possibility of a large property in Yorkshire going relatively cheap. But money was not why he married Alice, no matter what anyone else thought. Unlike Badeley, he thought only of protecting her and Grace and reverting Simon's legacy from one of pain and anguish to a future of promise.

"I do care for her," he told Badeley.

Surprisingly, Badeley didn't laugh, snort, or counter this statement. "Whatever you say, Marsden. Do you still go by Marsden?"

"I do. Alice insists. She says she can't think of me as Thomas now, after all that we've been through."

"How is Lady Alice? Is she still enjoying her miraculous recovery?"

"She is very well, thank you."

"No visits to the lunatic asylum, then?"

"There has been no sign of Beatrice, if that's what you mean. She's gone for good, it seems."

Badeley reached again for his glass. "Funny about that. Didn't you ever wonder?"

"Wonder what?" Marsden asked.

"Admit it. You didn't always believe her. About Beatrice."

Marsden did not like having words forced into his mouth. He said, "I didn't know what to believe. I'll admit, I stopped believing in ghost stories when I was a child, but you couldn't see her—see what happened to her every night—and not believe in something. But whatever was going on inside Alice, it's over now."

Badeley gave a careless shrug. "Well, I suppose it doesn't matter. She got what she wanted in the end, didn't she?"

"Would you have married Beatrice?" Marsden asked, thinking of her foolhardy plan to escape the clutches of Lord Scarborough and Doctor

Webb.

"I don't know. I admit I thought about it when the baby came along. She begged me then, you know…" Something in Badeley's shoulders gave way to an invisible weight, and he sagged against the bar. He looked utterly defeated.

"The baby?" Marsden asked, brows pinching. "Do you mean Grace?"

Whatever dark shadow had settled upon Barlow suddenly lifted as he shook his head and reached again for his glass. "I'll admit I thought there might be money in it, but I couldn't be sure of Lord Scarborough, what he'd do. And the truth is I didn't want to be married; I just wanted her to pay attention to me. She was like the sun when she was Beatrice. The others were afraid of her, but I always wanted to be in her light. Didn't you feel the same?"

In the wake of Badeley's drunken melancholy, Marsden remembered Beatrice, always spirited and playful, attracting every ounce of energy when she entered a room. She had been so alive, and now Marsden had to admit he sometimes lay awake at night, his calm, timid wife by his side, and wondered how his life would have been different if she had been the one to remain in control. It would undoubtedly have been a more noisy, exciting, and unpredictable life. In one thing, however, Dr. Webb had been right—Marsden would most certainly have kept the household supply of matches hidden.

"Beatrice has been dead for a long time, Badeley," said Marsden at last. "Whatever she was to Alice—ghost or madness—she's long gone."

Badeley's smile was thin and sad. "At least you get to look at her every day. I'd say you were the victor there."

In this, Marsden could agree. In the days since her escape from Maidenstone Hall, Alice had become all the more beautiful, darkness lifted from her in their new life. She shared her brother's striking beauty and looking upon her every day; he was reminded of the best of Simon.

Marsden took a last sip of his beer and checked his watch. Alice would be finished in Mrs. Croft's store by now. "I wish you well, Badeley," he said when he stood. "Despite everything, I do wish you that much."

302

Badeley stared down into his glass. "And the best of luck to you, my friend. The best of luck."

It was, Marsden thought as he left the tavern, a strange farewell. *The best of luck.* For the first time in his life, financially secure, married, and a father, Marsden was reasonably certain that he wasn't in need of any luck.

303

Chapter Fifty-Four

Marsden met Alice in the street just as she exited Mrs. Croft's with a bundle of boxes dangling from one hand. In the other hand, she clutched at Grace's tiny fingers. He had already meditated on the wisdom of telling Alice about his conversation with Badeley, but the sight of his wife and daughter, smiling and together again at last, was too pleasant a distraction. Alice's white dress gleamed in the sunlight, the wide black belt cinching her waist, accentuating the illumination of her gown. Her red curls, bound in a thick braid resting over one shoulder, also seemed to sparkle. She looked, he thought, more beautiful than ever. Badeley, he assured himself, was only jealous.

He gestured to the boxes. "I thought you were buying just one outfit for the journey."

Alice smiled, pleased with herself and knowing he was only jesting. The money, of course, came from her coffers after all. "I thought a few dresses were in order until we can shop in London. Doesn't she look wonderful?"

Grace did indeed look charming. Alice had dressed the child in a lightweight pink coat of fine wool. Her blonde curls were framed by a red beret. Grace beamed with pleasure in the light of his adoring smile, her pink cheeks lifting high with a broad grin. She looked, Marsden thought, most like Simon when she smiled.

Marsden crouched before her, adjusting her beret although it was already perfectly positioned. "You are the most beautiful girl in the country," he told her. To Alice, he said, "We should hurry if we want to catch the next train."

They walked quickly to the train station, their speed aided by Marsden carrying Grace while Alice carted the collection of boxes from Mrs. Croft's store. They only had to wait a short time for the next train, and the moment they stepped into a first-class carriage, Marsden felt relieved of a heavy burden, as though the miseries of their life in Yorkshire would soon be behind them.

The journey, although long, passed in tranquility as Grace slept with her head on her mother's lap. Marsden wasn't sure how Alice would explain to the child that she was truly Grace's mother. They had already agreed they would tell Grace that Marsden was her father. Perhaps, when she was older, Grace would examine her rough, dark-eyed father and doubt the truth of the claim, but Marsden couldn't bring himself to refuse the opportunity to have the little girl call him Daddy. Just the thought of the word on her lips made his heart soar.

After changing trains at York, they sat in silence, watching the green countryside pass by. For much of the journey, Marsden debated the benefit of informing Alice about his meeting Badeley. He didn't want to upset her, but considering everything that went wrong at Maidenstone Hall, and Badeley's part in it, Marsden assumed she would like to hear about the conversation at the tavern. At least it could be some comfort to her to hear of Badeley being brought so low, as if he had finally been punished for his misdeeds.

Finally, he admitted, "I saw Badeley."

Alice was startled by the confession, spine jolting straight. "Where?"

"In the village while I was at the tavern."

"What did he say? Did he approach you?"

"He just happened to be sitting at the bar. He wished me luck if you can believe it."

"Luck? What a strange thing to say." Alice scoffed and shook her head as if ridding herself of the worry the conversation had caused. "But we never need to see him again. Good riddance, I say."

Marsden decided that this was an excellent opportunity to change the topic of conversation and brought up instead the matter of a nursery maid for Grace.

"Why, we've got Mrs. Huston, of course," Alice replied, as though there was never another possible consideration.

Marsden had expected this since Mrs. Huston had joined them in their London home. Nancy, too, along with Linton, had also been offered continuing employment with the family.

"Are you sure?" he asked. "Mrs. Huston is not a young woman anymore. Grace could be a handful for her. Besides, who will cook for us?"

"We'll get another cook," said Alice. "Mrs. Huston raised me, and I want her to help me with Grace. I wouldn't think of hiring anyone else."

The train rattled closer toward London, the grime and smoke of the city visible beyond the rolling green pastures. Tired from the journey, Alice yawned, and Marsden crossed the carriage to sit directly beside her, wrapping behind her to rest around her waist. She leaned her head on his shoulder.

"Looks at us," she said against the crisp new linen of his jacket sleeve, "a married couple talking about maids and cooks and such. Things are so different now. Can you believe it?" She reached down to twist the round gold cufflink threaded through his shirt. It was new, a wedding gift from Alice, his father's old cufflinks now packed away amongst the many expensive trinkets she had bought him since they had moved into the Mayfair house.

"I didn't believe I'd ever have a family of my own," he said. "I couldn't have imagined this becoming my life."

She lifted her head to stare up at him, her green eyes wide. "But you are happy, aren't you? With me?"

Marsden pulled her closer to his side and stroked Grace's hair with his other hand. His new, comfortable life was a far cry from the miserable existence he abandoned when he had traveled to Maidenstone Hall in the spring. Marsden found he liked waking up warm and fed, and he very much liked having his own home and never having to scrounge for money.

"Yes," he said. "I am happy."

Alice's smile was dazzling. "I knew. From the moment we met, I knew we would love each other. My lovely, darling Fish."

She lifted her chin to kiss him on the mouth. As he returned the kiss, a firm press of his lips against hers, he was surprised to inhale the subtle scent of Lily of the Valley. Not once since their marriage had Alice worn perfume. Marsden breathed deeply, and the scent flooded his senses, freezing him in place.

The train's whistle blew as it pulled into the station, and Marsden jolted away from her. Alice extracted herself from his arms and shook Grace awake. The little girl rubbed at her eyes and sat up beside her mother. Alice stood and gathered Grace into her arms while Marsden remained in his seat, staring up at his wife, mouth slightly ajar. As she stepped out of the carriage and onto the platform, Marsden hesitated behind her in the doorway. He raised a hand to lips, brushing at the place where she had just kissed him.

He had to raise his voice to be heard over the din of the platform when he asked, "What did you call me?"

Alice's expression when she turned to face him was unreadable. "What? When?"

"Just now. I think you called me Fish."

A nerve at the corner of her mouth twitched, but her eyes did not shift, staring right back into his own. "Did I?" When Marsden nodded dumbly, she stifled a low laugh. "Goodness. How strange. I'm sure it won't happen again."

She reached for him, offering one gloved hand. Alice's smile was pure sunshine on the dingy station platform, and Marsden was reminded of something Badeley had said to him about Beatrice just that afternoon. *The others were afraid of her, but I always wanted to be in her light.*

He had hesitated too long. Alice's slender wrist began to shake as it hung before him, waiting for him to accept her. A minute tremble quaked at the corner of her perfect smile. On her hip, Grace wriggled and reached for Marsden. He stepped down from the carriage and took her readily into his embrace. She stared at him with solemn eyes, her little hands framing his face and stroking the short length of his beard. In the sunlight, he noticed for the first time a soft tint of red, a strawberry shade of blonde in her soft curls, and he thought that perhaps she didn't look very much like Simon after all. At last, Marsden took Alice's hand.

Grace's face exploded into a joyful grin, eyes squinting with pleasure, a chiming giggle escaping her rosebud lips. Marsden couldn't help but return a reflexive grin, muttering: "Eye on the prize."

Alice slid one arm into the crook of his free elbow. "What did you say?"

Marsden kept his eyes on Grace as he shook his head, perhaps a little too sharply. "I was thinking," said Marsden, raising his voice so that Alice could hear him over the din of the busy platform, "that we should look into having the fireplaces replaced in the house. Install gas heaters instead before winter arrives. Then we won't have to worry about Grace and the open fires."

Alice's pretty eyes sparkled. "If you wish, darling."

She tugged him into movement, and they walked arm in arm; Grace clutched to Marsden's chest while a porter rushed behind them with their boxes. They made their way across the crowded gloom of the station, and Marsden noticed the people around them stopping to stare, parting to watch him swan along the platform with his perfect family: his beautiful young wife and pretty daughter. He imagined they envied him—the poor, lowly German, the social pariah. He, once disgusting and unnatural, now possessing what other men desired. His past, fears, and loneliness all evaporated in his wake as he succumbed to becoming the man society always wanted him to be. His father would have been proud.

They emerged into the brilliant late summer sunshine, and Marsden allowed himself the nervous satisfaction of believing that anyone would be right to envy him and all that he now possessed. He clutched Grace closer and felt Alice's grip on his arm tighten. Her fingertips felt like firelight through the sleeve of his jacket.

Marsden allowed himself to simply let go and be grateful.

Acknowledgements

The lyrics from "You Made Me Love You," as quoted in this novel, were written by Joseph McCarthy. A small excerpt from *The Great Boer War* by Sir Arthur Conan Doyle is also included.

I wish to express my many thanks to my early readers; Chloe Jory, Nina Batt, Rick Moody, Shanna McNair, Scott Wolven and Pip Drysdale. Very special thanks also to Elizabeth McKenzie for her editing expertise and warm encouragement.

About the Author

Alison Clare was born in Western Australia to a pair of extreme bibliophiles. She pursued many different lives in the UK, Canada, and the United States before completing a Masters of English at Loyola Marymount University in Los Angeles. She shares her writing and reading time with a wine-maker husband, exuberant daughter, and a neurotic Border Collie.

SOCIAL MEDIA HANDLES:
　Instagram @aliclarewrites
　X @aliclareauthor
　Tiktok @aliclareauthor

AUTHOR WEBSITE:
　www.aliclare.com

Milton Keynes UK
Ingram Content Group UK Ltd.
UKHW041405080224
437497UK00003B/531